"This epic, bio-punk space adventure will blow your mind as it grips you by the eyeballs. Books like this are the reason I read science fiction: to discover whole other worlds, ways of being, and to leave this world for the moments I'm in their pages. Don't miss this one!"

—Tobias S. Buckell, co-author of *The Tangled Lands*

"*Triangulum* describes humanity's revolt against a cadre of alien immortals, bio-mechanical beings with a technology indistinguishable from magic. It is a story of the far future but also the distant past—needing to be worshiped as gods, the aliens have adopted humanity's oldest cosmologies—the Sanskrit-language Vedas—so that they can appear to us as devas, asuras, maruts. The seamless amalgams of past/future, animal/machine, and magic/technology give Subodhana Wijeyeratne's novel a hallucinogenic vividness and clarity, and a sense of one thing constantly becoming something else, the transformations of the characters against a background as immutable as stars."

—Paul Park, author of *Soldiers of Paradise* and *Sugar Rain*

"*Triangulum* is addictive. Vast in scope but intimate in its characterizations, I could not stop reading. Outstanding prose, storytelling that doesn't flinch, and a truly original universe. Space opera at its best."

—Karin Lowachee, award winning author of the *Warchild Mosaic*

TRIANGULUM

AN EPIC OF THE NINE WORLDS OF SURYA

SUBODHANA WIJEYERATNE

My deepest appreciation to
Stewart Baker,
Taka Okubo, Kathleen Jackson,
and pandemoniumgal
for their help and support during
the writing of this book.

for my grandfather

Edited by Diana M. Pho

Cover art and design by Vincent Sammy

ISBN: 979-8986614601

Rosarium Publishing
P.O. Box 544
Greenbelt, MD 20768-0544

www.rosariumpublishing.com

TRIANGULUM

AN EPIC OF THE NINE WORLDS OF SURYA

SUBODHANA WIJEYERATNE

BOOK 1

NIGHT, THOU HAS COME

1.1

A FINGER OF SPACE-TIME EMERGES out of nothing between the stone and shadow of the Desert of Dust and Stone. It extends with starlight curling across its surface as if on a melting black mirror. It elongates and swells, eerie and graceful, like some slow ripening cosmic fruit.

Then it ruptures.

A beast emerges. A colossal creature of darkness born of darkness into darkness. A hundred yojanas long, its flanks dense and dark grey, its vast eye gaping lidless, pupils alone large enough to swallow asteroids whole.

The juggernaut's name is Skōlex, and it has been here before.

It appraises its surroundings with a sprawling and inchoate consciousness. The distant star Surya is yet just the brightest amongst the bright. There are a few of the tumbling stones of the Desert nearby. The only thing approaching life is a colony of chittering scavenger drones picking at the carcass of an ancient freighter a few million yojanas away. These pick up on Skōlex's arrival but have neither the interest nor the capacity to understand what they're looking at.

Skōlex triggers its core systems. Lights unlit for millennia flicker to life within its endless bowels. Dead nerves swell like dry riverbeds reanimating with the rains. Stale air in long dead passageways stirs and drifts towards purifiers. When all is prepared and Skōlex is certain the time's right, it turns to waking the goddess asleep in its head.

She resides in an obsidian pod like the germ of a seed. Six pairs of arms curl, arachnid, around the mortar and pestle held against her belly. Her opening eyes flash in the darkness of her singularity-black- face. She falls out onto the cold stone of the chamber. Her mortar and pestle come after her. The adamantine floor shatters where they all land.

The Night stares at her fractured reflection in the black shards.

"How long?" she says.

Skōlex rumbles.

"Far too long, then," she says.

For a few moments the goddess thinks that perhaps she'd like to go back to sleep. But she has an empire to destroy. So she stands, unsteady, and sets about her task.

1.2

I

INDRA AND HIS PARENTS WAIT for the grain-vimana to settle onto its fat legs and sneak off the instant the automated service doors open. Hot with tension, they make for the darkened wasteland beyond the landing pad. Shadows born of the vimana's dull underlights flutter like grey petals about their feet. There is a chain-link fence ringing the spaceport. Here and there some of it has come away from the posts and curled up like the wings on a dead bug. It's through one of these gaps that they sneak out.

Indra's mother glances back over her shoulder. Inevitably, her gaze settles on the ringed glory of the gargantuan planet hunkered on the horizon. In its wan light her cheekbones are high and prominent and her eyes quick-moving. She mouths something to herself. A prayer to gods she should not be praying to. Indra knows she'll stare until she's forced to move. So he tugs on her sleeve, and she lets herself be led away.

Ahead of them is an oily lake with water they suspect is black even in the daylight. It stinks of fuel and rot. Beyond this is a cliff of buildings illuminated by slipshod streetlights. Each is a monstrous agglomeration of different structures bound with raw concrete and built over and sealed together again. How does it hold together, wonders Indra. What sort of place has such need for housing that they secrete edifices like mangled coral. Already, this place is more alien than anything he's ever seen, and there's always something cold about the unfamiliar.

They use the compass they bought on Mangala to navigate. It points north up a road that slopes up between two ramshackle tenements to a junction with a handful of neon-lit eateries dribbling rubbish into the gutters like old drunks. Now finally, they see their destination in the distance. The Tripura, City of the Charioteer, Queen of Shani. A blazing plexus of massed buildings, great mesas garlanded with lights. In the ravines between these is a glowering anarchy of shops and crowds. They can hear the standing-wave rumble of vehicles and voices and vimanas even at this distance. They can see the towering sikhara of the Dnyānasya Mandīram presiding over it all like a divine spear thrust into the world's blazing skin.

Indra wraps his arms around himself as if he realizes for the first time how small he is. His mother adjusts the cowl around his face.

"The gravity's the same here," he says.

"Aye," says his mother.

"Why? Daitya's smaller than Pṛthvī."

"Ancient tech."

She couldn't possibly know, but he knows not to question too hard.

"It's cold."

"Get used to it. We're far from Surya."

"How far?"

"Millions of yojanas."

"Is it always this cold?"

They're being watched by three men lounging in front of one of the eateries. Indra's father hustles his family along down the street. The lines of his mouth tense as they go. The prey-like flick of his eyes back over his shoulders. If he is so afraid, then they must be in danger. And if that's so, why did they come to this place at all?

A little later, the sun rises, diminished and pallid, and Indra has his answer. Yes. It's always this cold.

II

IT TAKES THEM THREE DAYS to reach the center of the Tripura, and in all that time they see not one patch of open land or foliage. Sometimes they walk for hours through semi-ruined expanses where hollow-looking folk stare from the windows of half-rotted buildings, as if imagining what they taste like. Closer to the Tripura, the tidier the facades become. Soon they're in a crowd that at one point thickens to the point their walking slows down and never thins out. Naked sadhus preach on old boxes with their dusty cocks hanging out for all to see. Flayed carcasses hang from butchers' ceilings like the victims of some upside-down massacre. Mounds of sweets wink like gems in the raw light of unshaded bulbs. Overhead, folk yell at each other from balconies that jut like chins over nightmare tangles of wires. How do they seem so at ease living in such a place? Why do they all seem so busy when the only thing worth doing is to stop and marvel at the seething empire they've built?

They finally reach the great plaza at the heart of the city. Hemmed by a great square moat at its heart is the Dnyānasya Mandīram. This place, too, is crowded, but now rather than them moving through the mass, the mass is moving through them. The pulses and surges of human motion. The stink and mutter and squeeze of it all. Underfoot is a slippery goo of detritus dropped from the silver pooja trays bobbing towards the great temple like salvage going hivewards on antback. The air is thick with gusting columns of incense smoke coming off moatside braziers the size of houses. Yet, more astonishing than any of this is the humanity. Agnians with huge flaring nostrils, their twin pairs of arms as fat around as Indra's torso. Yamans so tall their hips are higher than Indra's head, their eyes huge, their skins papery and bloodless. Clusters of furry Āēoi doused in vivid blue jewelry, their chattering tongue more like birdsong than anything else.

In the midst of all his marveling, Indra's mind snaps to what he's left behind. The drowsy sun on the fields and the feathering of ripe rice on his fingertips. The early springs full of sugar-and-salt days when the sun is warm but the wind still cold. There's nothing like that out here. There is no Vishwadevi, no harvest season, no playing in streams. Not one of these teeming thousands even knows these things exist. But he does.

He learns then what it is to feel alone amidst a multitude.

III

THAT NIGHT THEY SLIP INTO an alleyway carpeted with rotting bales of paper and find nothing to eat but some revolting paste smeared on the bottom of a small cardboard box. Indra's father sniffs it and bursts into tears.

"Come on, love," says Indra's mother. "Nearly there."

"I want bread," he says. "I want a warm bed."

"We'll have something soon—"

"We won't."

Indra's mother sighs. "We decided, aye? We decided on this."

"Never said we didn't. Just stating facts."

Indra wanders down to the alley mouth. Over the phalanx of buildings is Shani and her splendid rings, a cluster of bright stars off her shoulder—other moons, enthralled courtiers orbiting their queen.

His mother comes over, crouches beside him, and adjusts his cowl. "Hide your face," she says, "they'll send us back to Pṛthvī. They'll break us up."

"I know."

"Just a little longer. Just a little longer, and we can dress like we did back home."

"It'll be too cold."

"Yama burned its moon, remember? It's warm there—and bright."

Indra tries to imagine what it must be like for a world to have its own little sun. But his attention wanders back to Shani and then to the giant sikhara silhouetted like a vast black blade against it.

"It's so tall," says Indra.

"Aye."

"It's got every book ever written?"

"Dunno. Vishwadevi used to tell me a story about it, though."

"About how it's a dragon?"

"No. Another one. About how we humans used to have too much knowledge before the Dawn came. So much we couldn't tell truth from lies. We told our kids lies, and they believed them, and so in the end they became their own kind of truth. The Dawn saw we couldn't be trusted with any of it. So, she and the Charioteer and the Ox and the Huntress all collected all them books away from us. Then she, the Dawn, said, 'Who's going to look after them?' And the Charioteer said, 'There's only one who can look after them: my daughter.'"

"Who was his daughter? Why was she the only one?"

"Who knows?" His mother drops her voice, conspiratorial. "Charioteer builds that tower, and his daughter memorizes all them books. Then the Night turns her into the tower, holdin' all there is to know, and she'll only be freed when we're ready to learn it all again."

"She turned her into stone?"

"Aye."

"That's mean."

"That's the devas."

Diminished, Surya sets, and the night-time floodlights of the Dnyānasya Mandīram flicker to life. In their glare the underlit faces of the serried statues on the sikhara are inscrutable, eyes hollow recesses, mouths plump with unspoken truths.

"Is it true?" says Indra.

"Probably not. The devas are liars, remember. Remember—they told us we were important. They told us we fed the whole system, that all them in the outer dark was in awe of us. But they aren't, are they?" She stares up at the tower. "We don't feed nobody, and nobody knows nothing about us."

He knows that tone. He knows her lips will harden a little and her eyes go damp. He knows she'll stare at the distance like there was something worth looking at even though there's nothing at all. He knows she'll look as if she can barely stand to look at him for shame at having brought him into this world. Her grief is a barely-dammed reservoir. He's seen it break. He's seen it drown everyone.

He forces a smile.

"We feed ourselves," he says. "We fed Vishwadevi and Śyena and Uncle and everyone in the village."

"But that's not what she said. That's not what we thought. We thought all the Nine Worlds were sustained by our hands. We thought the empire of the Dawn marched on bellies full because of our—" She blinks, remembering he knows all this, realizing what he's doing, and loops one arm around his shoulder. "But now we're here. We're away from all that. Now you can see Agnians with your own eyes."

"You think they were strange? Did you know Himenduhis are born with fur all over their bodies? And Yaman's eyes are so big because Surya's barely more than a bright star in Yama's sky? We did all that. Humans. We changed ourselves to better suit the Nine Worlds and changed them to better suit us before the Dawn even arrived."

His mother holds him close, warm with pride. "That's right. You're a clever boy. You know these things."

"Can we go in?"

"Where?"

"The Library. I want to know more."

"We ain't trying. We'll get to the market tomorrow and meet this Vaidaskan. Then they'll take us off world. We'll be at Yama by the end of the month."

"Then?"

His mother hesitates for a moment, and Indra realizes that she doesn't know. But she smiles as if she does, and his doubts evaporate. They head back, lie on either side of his father, and wrap their arms around him. That night they all sleep together, huddled and warm, a little trio of moons in thrall to their own hopes. As always, Indra's dreams are sweet.

1.3

IT'S A GROWLING EARLY-MONSOON DAWN, and the chill rain splatters off the Tripura like dirty tears. The Slaver makes his way to the Slavers' Quarter of the Great Market by the sharp light of bald bulbs hanging in the stalls. The crowds are already thick about the lush displays, picking at avalanches of berries, pyramids of shiny apples, and lamellar stacks of bananas. In the Slaveseller's Quarter he heads along the wholesalers' pens teeming with human wreckage sold by the batch. On then past the organ-sellers with their wares stacked on shelves, sedated and delimbed and intubated. As he passes, a young man with no eyes and no legs is hauled down by an Agnian and taken over to a cowled man with quivering hands. He inspects the boy's tongue and hands and nods. The Agnian takes the boy into the darkened shop. When he realizes he's not being returned to his slot, he wails like a soul turned back from the doorstep of heaven.

The Slaver knows that stall. They always overcharge.

A short walk farther and he reaches the prim façade of his emporium cozied in a row of others in a white-pillared arcade. Two figures are waiting by the door. Some overeager nouveau riche convinced that the time of day dictates the price. Still when he gets closer he realizes that their clothes are a decade or so out of style and the older of the two is scanning her surroundings as if she'd just stolen a baby. For all intents and purposes, that's what she's done, thinks the Slaver. Or at least, that's what she's about to do. Steal a life from itself.

The Slaver walks past them without a word. The woman, hair the color of dried blood, face scarred with frown-lines, follows.

"Prabho Vaidaskan?"

The Slaver pauses with his hand on the door. "I am he."

"This one is Neta. This one—" she pushes her scowling companion forward by the shoulders "—is my daughter, Kadrū."

"Who?"

"We spoke." Neta swallows. "We spoke before."

The child is thin and wide-mouthed. Dark crimson lips. Eyes are far too large for a Daityan's. There must be some Yaman in her, the Slaver thinks. That would explain her height, too, and the strange blanched skin. She holds his gaze without flinching. He moves the beads on the abacus in his head, and while he does, he holds a look he's perfected over the years. As if he's disappointed by what he's looking at. As if any sale that occurs is a favor on his part.

He opens his door and walks into his reception room without a word. Neta follows, dragging the girl, fretting. Another girl is waiting for them in the lush green and gold of the entrance chamber.

"This one greets her swāmin," she says.

She glances at the guests and parses their purpose and pays them no further attention. Instead, she hands the Slaver a steaming cup of tea and takes his cloak and walks out backwards without a word. The Slaver sips. His eyes drift back to Kadrū.

"She's skinny," he says.

"She's obedient," says Neta.

"She has the look of a troublemaker."

Kadrū looks around the room. Her eyes trail over the overlush furniture, the ornate ceiling, and the fractal shadows from the lamps splayed on the walls. Then she looks at her mother.

"What're we doing here?" she says.

"Hush," says Neta.

"This is a slaver's."

"I said hush."

"What're we doing here?"

The Slaver smirks. "Listen to how she speaks to you."

"Swāmin promised," says Neta. "Swāmin promised this one."

"That was then," says the Slaver. "This is now."

Kadrū pulls her mother's arm. "Why're we here?"

"Has she had her blood?" says Vaidaskan.

"Yes. Three-times-twenty-eight days ago."

"And yet she is so skinny. No children for this one." The Slaver lifts his tea to his mouth and pauses as the warm vapor kisses his lips. "Fifteen."

"Prabho Vaidaskan said fifty!"

"And you said she was plump and strong-boned."

"Thirty. Thirty."

"Are you selling me?" says Kadrū, voice rising. "Ma? Ma!"

"She's a donkey," says the Slaver. "Listen to her bray. I should say no. But I am giving you fifteen because I promised I would take what you have."

Their voices have attracted another presence. A few thudding footsteps and then an Agnian enforcer folds himself through one of the two doors on the other side of the room. Chalk-pale and fat-faced, his teeth large even in his mouth the size of a melon. He halts, great arms hanging loose at his side.

Neta looks at her feet.

"Twenty," she says quietly. "Please."

Kadrū shoves her mother, screaming, and bolts for the door. The Agnian reaches her in two steps and wraps both pairs of arms around her belly and mouth in one practiced move. Without ceremony he turns and stomps out of the room with her squirming in his hands.

"Be gentle!" says Neta.

"Don't concern yourself with my Enforcer's techniques," says the Slaver, reaching for his tea.

"She's my child—"

"No, she's not." He produces a small black card and holds it out to her. "She is no longer your child. She is mine now, and that's a good thing. Who would want to be the child of a parent wretched enough to sell them?"

Neta fixes a gaze like claws on him, but the Slaver's barely notices. In any case, he's more interested in what comes next. The brief war between hope and horror that plays out in tiny inflections on her face. The sick crush of realization that he's right—about her, about her child. That, he does notice. That, he relishes.

Once he sees his victory is complete, he drops the card to the floor.

"Take it and leave."

"Twenty?"

"Twenty. Take it, or I'll take it back and you'll have nothing."

Neta picks it up off the ground and shuffles to the exit.

"Close the door," says the Slaver.

One last, venomous glance and she complies.

Twenty satamanas for a girl worth three hundred at least. The man at the organ-seller's may have got a bad deal, but the Slaver never does. He lifts his cup of tea to his mouth. The first sip after a good purchase is always the best.

His lips have barely reached the cup when there's another knock on the door.

1.4

THE GODDESS FINDS HER POSSESSIONS laid out on an altar in front of her pod—her sari with its cloth spun of darkness, her small black pouch, and her golden bindi. She ambles over on feet turned to glass by millennia of disuse. Where they touch the ground they leave haloes of ice, bright white and crackling, the chamber's dim light shattering off their many-angled topography.

Then the first of many recollections: she was known as the Night in these parts.

Her stomach rumbles. "Have you altered?" she says.

A sound like a distant landslide.

"Then you will have to show me the way."

Skōlex guides her with a gentle current of air, and she lets this push her along. Through endless dusty reaches of chambers the size of kingdoms and corridors greater surely than those leading to the underworld. In one room is a statue of a juggernaut snapping a great tower in half. In another is a frieze of a bald figure climbing an endless staircase, beset by demons and harpies. Soon she reaches a pair of colossal doors blacker than starless space. Something reaches through the neutronium-dense matter. Inchoate cilia digging through the air like fingers through dough. A dull consciousness testing the limits of the entity that she is now until it recognizes her. The doors swing open.

Beyond is a gargantuan space flanked by arches soaring into darkness overhead. Just behind these, two lofty arcades, black-grey and funereal. In their densely shaded recesses are ranks of evenly-spaced doors. Directly ahead is the asteroid-huge black mass of the Soma Seed. Entropy condensed and weaponized and programmable. A thing so vast its upper reaches disappear into the gloom above. Despite its incomprehensible mass, it floats unfettered by gravity, glossy-smooth and spinning slowly, while the rest of its bulk extends off into the unlit distance.

The Night approaches and breaks a piece off and eats. Her meal fizzes with possibilities as it slips down her throat. A seething concentrate of unfettered fecundity that can heal or transmogrify or destroy depending on desire and perspective. At present it's her perspective that matters most. Its substance disaggregates in her systems and storms of miniscule yantras fan out through her body, mending, tweaking, upgrading.

She breathes deep when she's done.

"Much better," she says. "Have you fed?"

She cocks her head in the silence as if eavesdropping. Then she nods and touches the Soma Seed again. The vast thing slows its spinning and then grinds to a halt.

"Fire?" she says. "Light?"

Skōlex rumbles.

"Is that necessary?"

Silence.

The Night chuckles. "Of course, I will, you silly boy."

She kisses the seed, and it begins to rotate again. Slowly, at first, but with gathering speed, like a turbine roused to life. It flushes lightning blue, and a great forking crown of electricity spits up into the remote heights of the chamber. Another follows and another. Soon the whole Seed is emitting hot plasma discharges up and down the endless reaches of the Chamber like roots coming off a giant cosmic tuber.

The Night watches for a while.

"Now," she says. "To work."

1.5

I

ONE REMOTE DAWN THE CALF and his mother went to see one of the Ancients reclining against a mountain range. A vast creature lying with its gleaming white legs stretching halfway to the horizon with forests growing in the valley-sized crooks of its elbows. Where its head should have been was a glowing sphere orbited by scything sheets of metal. The leaden drone of their rotation rumbled like perpetual thunder. Nothing stirred but the wind, cold enough to pierce.

"Why did you bring me here?" the Calf asked.

In his memories his mother is tall and black-furred, maw full of sharp teeth. That's how he preferred to see her, and so that's how she appeared to him. It was, perhaps, a sign of love on her part. The gods only change shape for love—and war.

"Do you understand what it is thinking?" She said, "Could you imagine how it feels to lie thus, whole kingdoms crushed beneath you, and ponder a single idea for the lifespan of a star?"

How awful, thinks the Calf. To lie there while the universe sped past, the processing starts smeared into greyness, planets just blurs, the lives and joys and deaths of the creatures thereon as irrelevant as the lower dimensions of the universe.

"I don't," he said. "I don't want to just lie there. I want to do something."

He waited for her to ask him to explain, but she didn't. When he risks a look, he sees her inspecting the entity in the distance with something akin to grief in her gaze. She's closer to that giant monster than she is to me, thinks the Calf.

She turns to him with a smile. "Let's go see Prabho Tvastr about making you a suit of man-flesh."

"What's man-flesh?"

But before he could finish, she was gone. Where she had stood was a dwindling pillar of light, a fraction as gorgeous as her actual presence. She hardly ever answered his questions. Whatever that was evidence of, it wasn't love.

II

THE SIMULATED SOUL OF PṚTHVĪ waits by the curving window at the far end of the antechamber. A squat woman with inelegant arms and a sprinkling of hairs on her ruddy face. Her lips are fat and her eyes bulging and her hair has congealed into a single grey-brown dreadlock hanging like a dead tongue down her back.

The Ox steps into the room and peers at her. Why, he wonders, when she could look like anything, does she choose to look like that?

He walks forward and shifts the dense weight of the Metaphorical Hammer off his shoulder down onto the floor. The ancient mosaic squeaks under the impact but holds. The Soul grins at him through teeth the color of piss.

"My, we look handsome today," she says.

The Ox presses his palms together in pranamasana. "Your needs were catered to last night?"

"Eh, what needs? Some light and peace and quiet. That second-in-command of yours—that one's a right prick, in't she?"

"Forgive her. And if not her, then me. The Vicegerent is not ... refined."

"She's not one of you, is she?"

"She is as Triangulan as I."

"But not of your blood. I could smell it on her." The Soul taps a nose as bulbous as a lotus bud. "What was she? A soldier?"

"Was. Is. As you can see, in some way, always will be."

"Always? Bit unfair that, eh? Folks change." Her eyes narrow, sly. "After all, you're not who you're supposed to be anymore, are you?"

Any other day he'd have responded to the barb. "You've changed since last time, if I may say so."

"No shit, pretty boy. Us plebs have to change bodies every few hundred years. Not like you lot." She looks him up and down and grins again. "Mind you, if I had a body like that ..."

"Madam, you embarrass me," says the Ox.

"Bah."

"Who made yours?"

"That would be telling."

"I could simply read it from your memory core once we are done."

"I'll be deleting everything before we get to it. When you kill me I won't even know who you are."

The Metaphorical Hammer shimmers through a cycle of shapes. A missile. A giant boomerang. The truss of a gallows. "I could stop you before you tried."

The Soul smiles. "I'm fast."

"Evidently, not fast enough, else you would not be here."

The Simulated Soul chortles and turns back to the window. After a while the Ox joins her. They watch Surya rise, cold and bright, over the deep green sprawl of the jungle. How can something so full of death and chaos look so calm? wonders the Ox. Why does such wild beauty make civilization look ephemeral in comparison?

"I helped design some of those, you know," says the Soul. "With my sibling, Mangala. Not the trees, but the bacteria. A whole family. Two, actually."

"Mangala? I would not have thought he was inclined to creativity."

"Oh, he was a good boy before he became all bitter." She puffs. "Before you made him bitter."

"It was his choice not to take defeat with grace."

"Sometimes a defeat's too important to be anything but pissed off by. Your lot have nothing to lose. Getting beat at anything, it's just like a game. For us, it matters."

How nice that must be, thinks the Ox. How nice to have life present meaning to you. How nice to not have to yank it like guts from a kill.

"You seem remarkably jovial in defeat."

"Guess I'm just tired."

A long silence. The sunlight ripens from orange to gold. Then a great murmuration of black birds veils its light entire.

The Ox licks his lips. "I have a question."

"Yeah?"

"Why did you permit yourself to get caught?"

"I didn't." The Simulated Soul sighs. "All right, fine. I don't know why. I just woke up one day and realized that everyone I knew and everything I ever fought for was gone and done for. Or worse—settled." She snorts. "Yet, there I was, still sneaking around, still fighting, still hoping one day to take things back to the way they were. Then I realized: in the long term—people find a way to get by, to survive. To be happy again, even, 'coz happiness is an adaptable thing. Then it's only old fools like me who can't stand being happy in a world where things aren't quite as we'd like it."

The Ox's voice drops. "You may not have been happy even if you'd won, madam."

"Speaking from experience, are we?"

The Ox's glances askance at her and then back out the window. There's no need for secrets, he decides. She won't be around to divulge them much longer.

"The world is as I wanted it to be. I am doing what I want to do. And yet I take no joy in it."

"You sound tired, too, boy."

"Perhaps."

"You're too young to be tired."

"Madam, I am many, many times older than you. If you are tired, imagine how I feel."

The Soul smiles and says nothing.

The Ox hefts the Hammer once again. "Where shall we proceed? Here, perhaps, with Surya's light on your face?"

"Aye, that'll be nice. And I ain't kneeling."

"Madam, I would never make you."

The Simulated Soul closes her eyes. For a few instants, her eyelids twitch as if she was dreaming. The Hammer strobes through shapes in excitement—a star, a child's spinning top, the swelling belly of a lioness about to give birth. Then, as he walks around behind the Soul with the sunlight coming slantways through the window, it settles back into a fat gold bulge.

The Soul looks over her shoulder at him.

"Who're you?" she says.

He swings.

1.6

I

THE SLAVER OPENS THE DOOR. Outside are three cowled figures huddled together against the early morning cold. One of them removes her hood, and he nearly drops his tea when he realizes he's looking at the nut-brown and strangely-proportioned face of a purebred Pṛthvīan woman.

"Prabho Vaidaskan?" she says. "Prabho Kalkah sent—"

"In, in!" hisses the Slaver. "To the back! People will see you."

He hustles them through the reception into an unadorned courtyard flanked by gunmetal-blue cell doors. The man is well-muscled but small, and the woman whole in body but homely. The child, however—face round like an idol's, lips like a lotus bud, just past manhood but not too far. Gelded, he will be an asset.

He licks his lips and signals into the shadows, and the Enforcer emerges, grinning.

"This is the safehouse?" says the woman.

"Mm?" says the Slaver. "Ah. Yes."

"Prabho Kalkah said to come here, and you'd handle the rest. When can you get us offworld?"

"Soon. For now you must stay here."

"We can pay. We have payment."

"That's excellent."

The Enforcer yanks open one of the cells. The door screams and rattles as it slides. Indra's mother glances in and sees a concrete bed, shackles, and walls discolored by tongues of mold. She examines the courtyard. Her eyes settle on Kadrū's celldoor and the pair of reddish eyes peering out through the viewing slit thereon.

The Enforcer crosses the courtyard and closes it.

"Who is that child?" she says.

"Another refugee."

"She looks—"

"In the room, if you would."

The woman looks in again, and then at her husband. "Do you have somewhere else, maybe?"

"I'll have customers coming and going all day, and it won't do for them to see you."

"What do you sell?"

"Antiques."

"How long will we have to—"

"Madam, I'm sure Prabho Kalkah's told you about the consequences of harboring a Pṛthvīan runaway. Do you wish me to be revealed? To destroy the only safehouse for refugees such as yourself in this city? No? Then kindly enter the accommodations I'm providing before one of my other servants sees you."

Finally, they amble in, reluctant. First the woman, then the child, and last the man, hunched and shivering.

"Please remain quiet," says the Slaver.

The Enforcer slides the door shut. The Slaver returns to his tea in the antechamber, distracted and smiling, totting up numbers in his head. It's been a long time since he's had a morning this profitable.

II

"I DON'T LIKE THIS," SAYS Indra's father. "I don't trust him."

"Kalkah trusted him."

"Why did you trust Kalkah?"

"He got us off Mangala, didn't he?"

"So? So what?"

"You're not helping."

She's using the voice she uses when she doesn't want to shout, thinks Indra. He curls up in the corner and buries his face in his drawn-up knees. Slowly, the sound of their arguing melts into the glum susurrus of the rain outside. Sleep comes slowly and brings dreams of being caged. When he wakes, the first thing he wants is to crawl in between his parents, but they're sleeping on opposite sides of the concrete slab. In any case, they mightn't let him in. His father says he's too big. His mother says he'd be more comfortable on his own.

After a short while he hears heavy footfalls outside. The door grinds open, and the Enforcer steps in with a giant stool. The Slaver follows, speaking to someone out of sight.

"Please, swāmin," he says, silky, accommodating. "If swāmin pleases."

A rumble that's barely a voice: "Are they dangerous?"

"Not at all. The room is equipped with a scanner, state-of-the-art, and—"

"Fine, fine."

Another immense Agnian joins them, grey-skinned, decked in layers of blue robes, smelling musky and sandalwood-sweet. He scans the Pṛthvīans with the sagacity of an elephant and squats slowly onto the stool. It creaks under his weight but holds.

He pouts. Such thin lips for a creature so big. "This is it?" he says. "You said you had something special."

The Slaver draws back his head. "These are Pṛthvīans, swāmin."

"What do you expect me to do with them?"

"Swāmin, my name is Palyana—" says Indra's mother.

The Agnian cuts her off. "What, Vaidaskan," he repeats slowly, "am I going to do with three Pṛthvīans?"

"They're Pṛthvīans!"

The Agnian sighs. "I'm going to explain this to you as if you were an idiot, for clearly you are one." He points a stubby finger at Indra. "You take one look at their faces, their skin the color of turds, and you can tell where they're from. If you know where they're from, everyone else who sees them will know where they're from. If everyone else knows, the ārcakāḥ will know, and they will come after them. They will find out how they escaped and who helped them and who sold them, and they will arrest them all. So, either we need to sell them to someone who's going to sequester—that means hide, by the way—sequester them—"

The words rush about in Indra's head like specters too horrific to look at straight on. His mother has no such problem. "Sell?" she says. She pulls Indra close. "Sell?"

"There's plenty of people who could handle a Pṛthvīan," says the Slaver. "This is Daitya. This is the Tripura! This is the greatest city in the greatest realm in—"

"It isn't, and there's no one."

"Answer my wife!" says Indra's father. He pushes Indra and his mother behind him. "You better explain—"

The Enforcer produces a blackjack and smacks Indra's father on the head with a casual crack of his arm. He crumples face-first into the ground with his neck skewed and his arms tangled like a corpse's. Indra stares, mesmerized. Then he looks at the Enforcer. The huge Agnian smiles at him. Porcine teeth the size of Indra's thumbs. His father was the strongest of them, yet look how quickly this beast reduced him to limp wreckage. These people can do whatever they like to us.

His insides shrivel at the thought.

His mother screams and flings herself at her husband. The two Agnians and the Slaver watch her cradle his head without a word or slightest hint they know what they're looking at.

"Ma?" says Indra. He can barely breathe. "Ma?"

"Please," she begs. "We only want to get to Yama. Swāmin Kalkah promised. You said you'd help."

"Four hundred for both," says the visitor.

"Four hundred?" The Slaver spasms. "They're worth a thousand each!"

"The man'll go to the mines. The woman can be a domestic to some rich folk, but they'll need to slice her first. That costs money, too. I'll give you five for both."

"A thousand."

The Agnian stands with a snort. "Good day."

He sweeps towards the door. As if the failed negotiation was for a pot or a goat or a load of grapes. Not the lives of three humans. Not the hope against hope and the rattling nights aboard cargo vimanas, the scavenged dinners, the leg-numbing treks, and the eyes aching in the dim light of the too-distant sun.

Indra's mother sobs.

"Please, help my husband!"

"Swāmin, please," says Vaidaskan. "I—this one can't keep them here."

The Agnian pouts. "Five hundred for both. Take it or leave it."

"What of the child?"

The visitor glances at Indra. "You keep him. I've no use for him."

"But he's the most valuable!"

"Then you sell him."

"Shit, I thought—"

"Pardon?"

They lock eyes for an instant. Then the Slaver bows deep. "Forgive this one. Prabho's offer is most generous."

The Agnian claps. Two more Agnians lumber in through the door, snorting. One grabs Indra's mother and the other his still-limp father. He should be awake by now, thinks Indra. He waits for him to open his eyes, but as they get closer to the door—instants that feel like eons—he realizes he won't. He'll never speak to him again. Yet, he can't think of a single word to say. Aren't farewells supposed to mean something? But what could this sudden sundering possibly mean?

What if it means nothing? What if they mean nothing?

He charges the Agnian, but the Slaver intercepts him. For all that he's skinny, he's strong, too.

"Stop!" screams Indra's mother. "Indra!"

She grabs the door frame, but the Agnians pull. The last he sees of her are her bloodied fingertips slipping around the corner. Then the Slaver flings him onto the concrete, and the impact stuns him. The sound of the door grumbling back to place, and the dwindling hubbub of footsteps, and finally the trapped-bird panic of his own thoughts. He won't see Yama's burning moon. He won't see the ice temples. He won't sleep between his parents ever again. There's nothing left for him but the dense monsoon rain beating in the courtyard outside. As if it had fallen forever. As if it would never stop.

1.7

A TENTH OF A YOJANA from the Slave Quarters in his little townhouse by the square, the Crown Prince of Yama knows his seedlings are dying. The leaves dipping as if in depression. The stems blanching as if they were bleeding their essence through some invisible cut. Still, he stares. A thin-faced, thin-haired man, elongated Human torso folded over the table like a broken stalk, long fingers splayed on the unyielding surface like atrophied roots. As if by looking, he could bring them back to life. As if desire was enough, sometimes, to make something true.

After a while he walks over to a window seat on the far side of the study. Outside, below is a square choked now with the bobbing heads of hundreds undulating to the sound of drums and wailing flutes. Scattered amongst them are naked, ash-smeared sadhus leading their flocks in sacred frenzy with their dreadlocks flailing. Framing the square are stalls selling grilled fish and fried cheese and lentil cakes. The smell of all that and the crowds and the joss-sticks in the little shrines in the walls seethes upwards in a glorious, dizzying mess that leaks through the window into the Crown Prince's nose as if with intent.

How can life be so hard to kindle, thinks the Prince, when given half a chance it burns through everything?

His glumness is ripening into sleepiness when the Crown Princess enters. A tall woman, cheekbones low, skin blue-white. In her right nostril is the great golden hoop of a lady of standing. She studies the incubator for a few moments. She approaches, left leg dragging, left foot hitting the ground with a metallic thud, and holds his head to her bosom without a word. The Crown Prince breathes deep. He can smell her perfume and below that and more enthralling still, her own scent, that distilled her-ness that sets the blood surging in his veins.

"Which batch?" she says.

"The same as before."

"Any changes at all?"

"Seven percent one way. Three another. Nothing worth considering."

"Well, those are bigger variations than before. Much bigger."

"Not big enough." The Prince looks out the window. "How did you navigate the madness?"

The Princess adjusts her sari, blood red, gold, and hemmed with semiprecious stones.

"With difficulty. I'd've been here by dawn, but ..." She glares at the crowd below. "Savages."

"They've much to celebrate."

"The Charioteer has. They seized the whole Enseeladasi treasury and brought it back with them. And the royal family—I saw 'em. They're here, did you know?"

"I've avoided it all."

"They were being dragged in chains to the Dnyānasya Mandīram. The kids, too. And they were burning two of the generals on pyres near the Mandīram. Alive."

"The Dawn burns our sins away."

The Crown Princess grimaces. "They'll burn the royals, too, won't they?"

"They're hardly royals. Nobles, at best."

"Still. They'll be burned, well?"

"Probably."

"I heard the Udāradādinaḥ took losses, though. Heavy losses."

"Many of their vassals begged off. Others only sent half-fleets."

"How many?"

"I don't have the figures."

The Princess locks her eyes, the color of polished copper, with the Crown Prince for a few moments. It feels like seeing twin nebulae, virgin to the human gaze. The Princess smiles.

"Come," she says. "I got some cool stuff this time."

She leads him out of the laboratory down a corridor studded with the portraits of blue-skinned gods, a chariot carrying the sun, and a bull-headed man in a great ocean of milk. Servants kneel and touch their heads to the ground as they pass. Presently, they come to a section of wall. The Crown Princess places her palm on it, and it slides open without a sound. Beyond is a narrow stairway curving up with the sinuousness of a young vine. As they ascend, the door reappears behind them, slots back into place, and covers their route as totally as sand covers tracks in the desert.

At the apex of the stairs is a tall octagonal space ringed with eight sets of shelves. Between each is a slit of a window that admits a blade of light and a slivered view of the Tripura. Where the illumination meets is a small mahogany table arrayed with a collection of devices. Some are tagged and polished, others are rough and rusty, and still others alive and busy with insectoid clicking.

The Prince reaches out and picks up a small, glowing orb. "What is this?"

"It's from Himenduḥ. A data-holder of some sort. The collector found it in a hulk off in the Vik ... Vik ..."

"Virṇakśatramaṇḍalamaruḥ."

"Well, that. The Desert of Dust and Stone." She takes it and holds it up to the light. "From its size, I'd say it could hold a whole Simulated Soul."

"A whole Soul?"

"Yup. It's also got some mechanism inside. Can't figure out how powerful, but it's leaking neutrinos like a bleeding star."

The Crown Prince's eyes settle on a flat black slab. He looks at the Crown Princess. She grins. Enough mischief there to sink a fleet, he thinks. Enough to topple a kingdom.

"A Simulated Soul," she says. "A very, very simple one. Stupid, but it works fine."

"What's it for?"

"Well, whatever. Personal use."

"Personal use? They had Souls for personal use?"

"Our ancestors were pretty ambitious."

The Crown Prince picks up the slab. As he does, the screen ripples deep purple, and the device pings to life.

"Hello," it says. A voice soft and welcoming and smoothly human. "How may I help?"

"If our ancestors could make a soul out of metal," says the Princess, "you can make a few seedlings thrive on Yama."

The Prince looks at her. Framed by twin spears of light. He can still hear the thump and hoot of the crowds outside. He has no use for their pyromaniac goddess. Not when he had a greater fire standing there before him.

"You are a wonder," he whispers.

A ping.

"Thank you," says the tablet.

1.8

PERHAPS SKŌLEX'S STRANGE EMANATIONS ATTRACTED the creature. Perhaps it recognizes the juggernaut as something vaguely like itself. Or perhaps it's just curious. Whatever the reason, it comes out of the dark to drift alongside the beastship's hull close enough to touch. A colossal and silent thing, tentacled and fluorescing. A living explosion from the colorless deep.

The Night watches it come, rapt.

It deploys a great latticed sheet of flesh twenty thousand yojanas wide, so thin it's barely there. Buzzing particles of Surya's breath entangle in its filaments like krill in baleen. At the same time, it swings another of its appendages in her direction. A glistening bud at its tip blooms into a dish-shaped organ. The Night realizes that she's being inspected. And why not? To look is to interact. To gaze is to provoke. So the creature and the goddess watch each other. Nothing passes between them except the knowledge of each other's existence. But this is the most important of all knowledge, just as the difference between zero and one is the greatest of all differences.

"Do you have a message for me?" says the Night.

Silence. The Night presses her palms together and tilts her head.

"Travel safe then, little brother," she says.

She continues on up a long black ramp between two mirror-flat pools in a great hall full of stories about her so ancient even she's forgotten them. The ramp leads to a giant, unadorned arch flanked by two huge braziers. These ignite as she approaches, and their strangely heatless flames, musky and yellow-white, are the only sources of light in that whole cavernous space.

Beyond this is another colossal chamber, its roof higher overhead than the chamber of the Soma Seed. Its walls so far distant that she can scarcely make out the giant carvings upon them. The far wall, an eighth of a yojana or so away, is a great arcing window opening onto the incomprehensible totality of stars and galaxies, novae and comets, asteroids and hot-disked black holes blazing oblivious and glorious in the velvet black of space. She heads towards this with unnatural speed, and as she gets closer, she sees what she's looking for—a small dais hosting a pair of black thrones.

She sits on the right-hand throne, but it feels unfamiliar. Then she sits on the left and remembers that this was hers. It feels strange to be there alone. But then, that is why she's here.

She waves her hands in the air, and a cloud of red lights appears in front of her. She touches one, and the thrones rotate to face the giant window. The tentacled beast, her new friend, is nowhere to be seen.

"I haven't noticed any changes," she says. "Have you?"

Skōlex grinds out an answer.

"In that they appear to be the same." She sighs and settles back in her seat. "Look, even now. Night has fallen upon humanity, and they haven't even noticed."

1.9

I

KADRŪ LEARNS MANY THINGS AT the Slaver's that she'd rather not have. That her life is a thing to be bought and sold. That it is possible for her to hate and love the same person with equal intensity. And that simmering within her is a sprawling lavafield of rage as stinking and sulphureous as the ancient plains of Āēo, always threatening to erupt. It cannot be allowed to. If she's not to be sold for parts, she must earn the Slaver's favor. So she holds her tongue and averts her eyes and does precisely what she's told.

At first, she scrubs the latrines, cleans the cells, and gets sent to scoop the muck out of the gutters. She does all this quickly and in silence. Soon he has her cleaning vases, paintings, tapestries, copies of priceless originals the Slaver points out are worth more than her in and of themselves. Soon she receives a pair of shoes and starts other lessons. How to fold napkins. How to press a sari. How to apportion fragrant dustings of snake venom into pipes for smoking.

"You'll make a top-notch maid-about-the-house," says the Slaver. "Maybe even a major domo, eventually."

"This one thanks you, swāmin."

The Slaver cores her with his eyes. "You look like you miss your mother."

"This one does."

He puts a hand on her shoulder. It feels heavier than it should. "Remember, girl, that no one will ever care about how you feel again."

I hope you rot alive, she thinks. I hope your eyes and balls fall off. She kneels and bows low. "Yes, swāmin. Thank you for all you're teaching this one."

The Slaver walks away, looking unmistakably victorious. What is his life worth, wonders Kadrū. What would it cost to take it?

II

IN THE SWEAT-SLICK PREDAWN A few weeks after the commotion with the Pṛthvīans, Kadrū hears voices out in the courtyard. Across the way, the Slaver and a doctor in a red turban are entering the Pṛthvīan boy's room. Muffled screams follow, and thuds. When the two men emerge they're both sweating, too. A dappling of blood glints on the doctor's shoe.

The Pṛthvīan boy starts whimpering soon after they leave and doesn't stop for three days.

On the fourth the Slaver spends the morning teaching her to fold napkins. Halfway through, he halts and peers at her, eyes narrowed. "You can tend to him," he says.

"Who, swāmin?"

"Come with me."

He takes her to the cell where the Pṛthvīan boy is, yanks open the door, and points to the boy curled up on the bed like a human turd.

"Tend to him," says the Slaver. "Have him cleaned and presentable."

The cell stinks of shit, blood, and unwashed flesh. Kadrū peers at the boy. The bloodless face. The bloody bandage around his crotch.

"He looks sick."

"He's fine. He's up to his gills in snake venom. He can't feel a thing."

"Swāmin, I don't know—"

"Learn. He's valuable. Do this and I will reward you."

He leaves without elaborating.

Kadrū assesses things and realizes that the boy might be beyond her help, but the room isn't. She fetches a mop and bucket and detergent. The floor is filthy, and the walls are splattered with calligraphic trails of blackening blood. She works around Indra as much as she can, but eventually she has to tackle the bed.

She prods him. "Move," she says.

He ignores her. She reaches for him, but he flinches. For a few instants she thinks of yanking him off the bed, but just as quickly she realizes that that would be closer to kicking a puppy than she'd ever like to get.

"If you don't move," she says, "I'll have to call the Enforcer, and he'll chuck you about like a fucking doll. You want that?"

"Go away," whispers the boy.

"Get up."

"They took my ... they cut it off."

"They do it to everyone. If you keep lyin' around like rotting meat, you're no good to them. You think they'll kill you? They won't. They'd lose money. They'll sell you to an organ-seller or a butcher instead."

"A butcher?"

"Yeah."

"People don't eat people."

"They do, too. Aldāstis eat people all the time." She blinks. "Didn't you know?"

"No."

"What, you Pṛthvīans never leave your world?"

"I didn't even know there were other worlds."

"Well, there are. Come on. Move."

A moment passes. Then the aerated grumble of an empty stomach.

"You hungry?" says Kadrū.

Indra nods.

"All right. You help me, an' I'll get you some food."

"Ereesi rice."

"What?"

"I want Ereesi rice."

"Where the fuck—" She pauses. "All right. I'll get you Ereesi rice."

Wincing, Indra gets off the bed.

1.10

THE OX DESCENDS A GIANT spiraling staircase in a pleasant silence inflected only by his echoing footsteps. The stone beneath his feet is ancient and sinuously grooved, decorations licked smooth by three thousand years of wind. At the bottom is a small doorway opening into thick forest. Ferns like angel's hair shiver by his feet and gnarled bushes crowded beneath brief gaps in the canopy. An empire of green resplendent with the lushness of a place that's thrived forever.

He wanders southwards along a stream for a couple of days. Feet sinking into the rich mulch. The afterglow of the Soul of Mangala's death percolating through his system. Some memories take longer to integrate than others. Some memories must be worked to better fit your soul.

Presently, he reaches an expanse of orphan walls and fractured foundations senescing by a clear pool. A serene ruin now but the last time he was here it was in midst of a great confrontation. Here he'd stood with the Metaphorical Hammer ablaze and his forces surging forth like the vanguard of hell. Here the Soul of Mangala had faced him in the shape of a giant boar, mechanisms running so hot it breathed fire. Here they had tussled. Here the Ox had won. And then, somehow, the beast had slipped away. Off into the undergrowth. The dwindling sound of his snorts. The Vicegerent's panic as she helped the Ox back to his feet, left arm missing, half his chest burned straight through.

How long ago it had been. And yet. And yet ...

He dips his hands into the water as if it had all just happened and he was still hot with burns. Would he have felt so victorious if he'd known he'd never see his enemy again? He clenches his fists underwater. Why is it that some memories never fit no matter how far they're bent?

Lost in his thoughts he barely notices, an old man comes out of the undergrowth, one-eyed and legless, punting himself along on a rickety cart with a stick. He heads towards the pond and looks over at the Ox, and the Lord of Mangala realizes he's not a man at all.

"Ho ho, Prince of Mangala," the old man says. He winks, as if he knew all the Ox's secrets and they were all filthy. "It's been a while."

The Ox stands, hand hovering over the Metaphorical Hammer's handle. "We're acquainted?"

The old man grins, teeth paper white and perfect. Then he leans over his cart and takes a long, sloppy drink. "Well enough for me to remember when you were last here. I was amongst your enemies."

"You were Apvādinaḥ?" The Ox frowns. "But you're one of us. You're of Triangulum."

"Aye, that I am." The old man smiles. "So loyal to your blessed mother I fought with the enemies of her enemies. You going to crack me with your hammer now you know that?"

A moment's hesitation. The Ox drops his hands. "You think so little of me, sir?"

"Isn't that what you do? Smash and reave? O Hammer of Dawn?"

The Ox stares at the old man's flaking skin and swollen joints and tentacles of steely hair as lank as seaweed. Words, like most weapons, do only as much damage as the body wielding them can inflict. How then is this decrepit wreck wielding warheads?

He dips his hands back in the water.

"You don't look well," he says.

"That's what you call aging."

"I thought Prabho Tvastr's handiwork lasts forever." He pauses. "How ... how does it feel?"

"To be old?"

"Yes."

"No different to being young, 'cept you have more to mourn and more to celebrate."

The old man produces a small bun from his cart and holds it out to the Ox. The Ox takes it with both hands, sniffs, and then nibbles. The dough is soft and sweet.

"You stayed behind?" he says to the old man. "When she left?"

"I did."

"Why?"

"Because she will return, and she will need eyes."

"Is that why you're out here? You're a spy?"

"No. This is where I live." The old man looks at him askance. "Why are you here?"

"I ... I scored a great victory ... three days ago."

"Ah, yes?"

"Yes. I vanquished an old foe of mine."

"Should you not be celebrating, instead of mourning?"

"I look as if I am mourning?"

"A man does not go off into the forest alone to celebrate, boy-o. Men like you celebrate with others and mourn alone."

"What do you know of me, uncle?"

"That, like all men, you are at your most transparent in your moments of victory and that you do not celebrate victory as you used to."

The Ox scowls. "What does that mean?"

"It means it's time for a change. It means this part of your story is coming to an end. That's good. You'll be ready for when your mother returns."

The Ox yanks his hands out of the water. "She won't."

"Every dawn needs a dusk, boy-o." The old man leans forward. His wagon creaks beneath him. "Or don't you want to face up to what you did to her?"

"I weary of your company, uncle. You speak of things you know nothing about."

"Ho ho." The old man turns his full attention to the Ox like a floodlight. What is this new slyness? How swiftly can he go from wretched to ruthless.

"I know more than you credit, Prince of Mangala. I know a thing isn't real until it's witnessed. I know you're here running from yourself. Nothing you do—nothing you've chosen to do—feels right anymore. Why not admit your doubts about the path you've chosen?"

"I have no doubts about my path, old man."

"None, except that you see you're coming to its end, and you don't know what to do next. What does one do when one comes to a dead end?"

"Walk back the way we come."

"Ah. And what danger is there in you doing so?"

Memories like predators, thinks the Ox. Memories that will hunt me. Memories that consume. "What is your stake in all this?"

"You think I'm here to persuade you of something." The old man stares into the water. "I am not. A long time ago, perhaps, I thought I could. Perhaps, if I stayed close to you, I would see when the time was right to bring you back to your mother's fold. But the millennia passed, and I settled into life here. I saw you walking. Sometimes I saw you weeping. You did not want to be a pawn again, and I couldn't bring myself to persuade you. Your mother, if I ever see her again, will forgive me. The Dark hides sinners and sins alike. Our meeting today is a coincidence. It means the time has come for me to tell you what I think. That you must either see your life for what it is, or I must admit to myself that you, in fact, don't know shit about shit."

The Ox sits back. Why does he believe every word the old man says? Why, as he listens, do his insides seem to sink down into the soil, through the heart of the planet into the vacuum beyond? If it's guilt, that long-absent bitch, its return is unwelcome.

He speaks quietly.

"Perhaps, I am at a dead end."

"Then what must you do?"

"I don't remember the way I came."

"That was just a metaphor, boy-o. Nothing goes backwards in our universe. Everything is new. So you must be, too."

"I'm not sure I know how."

A lone star shivers on the horizon. The old man chuckles.

"Nobody does," he says. "That's part of the fun."

1.11

KADRŪ OPENS THE EMPORIUM DOOR and peeks out. It's late, and the dim arched tube of the arcade is still. In the market beyond, two Agnians are carrying cages packed with naked, screaming children. Sinewy hawkers amble up and down between still-open wholesalers, flogging lentil cakes and barbecued guts. The towers of the Tripura glitter like great trunks besieged by fireflies.

The Gelding adjusts his cowl.
"Do I have to wear this?"
"Yeah, you do. Din't your parents tell you why?"
The boy flinches at the mention of his parents.
"Fucking hell, it's so you in't seen, right?"
"Don't understand why people hate us so much."
"They don't hate you. You're just not supposed to be here, you'll be handed to the ārcakāḥ."
"They'll take me home. I want to go home."
Kadrū barks. It takes the Gelding a moment to realize she's laughing.
"They won't send you home, right, they'll just kill you. They don't want you going back and telling them lot what it's actually like out here."
"Why're—?"
"I din't know, all right? Shut the fuck up or I'll go on alone and spend all of swāmin's bonus on me self."
"What bonus?"
"Shut. Up."
The Gelding complies.
They head off. The market's damp floor is a revolting jumble of textures on the Gelding's bare soles. Grimy, then briefly slimy, and always uneven. Eastward along the smooth stone pavement is a blazing food hall crammed with hundreds of small shops. The Gelding gawps at what he sees. The sausages the size of his arms. The fragrant rock-hogs roasting over beds of glowering coals. The huge steaming bowls of broth brimming with noodles and vivid vegetables.
Kadrū digs into her bodice and produces a small black card. "Ten satamanas. I got it for getting you out of bed."
The Gelding stares at the card. He sees now that in this place kindness is just another thing to be bought and sold. Why does it devastate him so, she wonders. What kind of heaven does he come from that such things are free?
She takes him by the arm and offers a smile. "You helped me earn it. I promised you Ereesi rice, right?"
They settle on a quiet stall away from the crowds where a blinking old Ereesi turns her head to them, pendulous and turtle-slow, in greeting. She smears Kadrū's card on a dirty reader and serves them two bowls of rice topped with slivers of spicy-sweet meat. When they finish she floods the bowls with broth, clear brown and freckled with golden oil and vegetables. It drains Kadrū's credits, but when they're done they wander away glowing with satiation and slouch by the wall outside.
"We could just run away," whispers the Gelding.
Kadrū shakes her head. "Can't do it. Can't get out the Slaveseller's Quarter. Them walls're electrified. Them gates're guarded. Besides, one look at your face and you're fucked."
"There's so many people," says the Gelding. "So many different kinds."
"You don't have people on Pṛthvī?"
"Only one kind."

"The rest of us don't all look like you, right?" Kadrū belches. "What's it like? On Pṛthvī?"

A long silence. Then: "Warm. The sun's bigger. Everything was green. We spent most of our time in the fields. Me and my dad and my cousin Vishwadevi. She was ... my best friend." A pause. "At harvest time the grain-yantras would come and take most of it away and give us things in return."

"What'd you get?"

"Machinery. Spare parts. Fertilizer."

"That's it?"

"We didn't need anything else."

Kadrū sucks her teeth. "Sounds like you were slaves."

The Gelding is silent. Kadrū glances at him. Sunk in his sagging robes, looking small and bereft and lost. She knows she's said the wrong thing and must say something else to skate past the acrimony. But words aren't easy. Give her a filthy napkin and she can fold it into a rose. Give her the right words and she'd still manage to produce a mess. She crosses her arms. Why should she say anything, anyway? If guilt is the price of speaking the truth, then fine. Let him sulk.

"I need the toilet," he says.

Kadrū shrugs. "Go find one then."

He adjusts his cowl and stalks off into the crowd. She watches him go and immediately begins to fret. How could she let this tiny broken boy off on his own into that night-time welter of cutthroats and savages? He'll be killed if anyone notices him. They'll kill her, too. There is no pity in the Slavesellers' Quarter.

She enters the food hall with visions of being dragged through the dust to the drone-racks to be paralyzed and carved up. There's no sign of him. Panicking, she heads into the nearest toilet—a dimly lit den, crannies grimy, streaks of moisture like crusted vomit on the walls. An old Agnian woman waddles out, elephantine face drooping and oblivious.

Then Kadrū hears it. Whimpering in the far cubicle.

"Hey! Is that you?"

A sniff. "Go away."

None of the stalls have doors. Why should they in this place where the body has no sanctity? She approaches the farthest one and finds the Gelding huddled on the floor with his underwear around his ankles. Piss leaks in a thin yellow trail from the ragged red hole in his crotch.

He scrambles to his feet. "Go away!"

"What happened? You all right?" says Kadrū.

"Do I look all right?" he says, sniffing. "I can't piss."

"What do you mean—"

"I can't piss! It won't come!"

She looks at his crotch. The glistening wreckage of it. Strange that they're all just one slice away from being meat.

The Gelding sees her staring. "Go away!" he hisses.

She rubs her face with both hands, trots out, and waits by the door. The stink of roasting hogmeat repulsive now. The slavering diners all monsters. A few minutes later the Gelding emerges, cowled and staggering, and wanders off without so much as a glance.

Back at the Slaver's they sneak past the snoring Enforcer into the courtyard. The Gelding heads for his cell without a word.

"Hey," says Kadrū.

He pauses. "What?"

"That was fun."

The Gelding turns to her. "Thank you for ... all of it."

"I ..." She exhales once through her nose. "I'm sorry they did this to you. That's what they do here, in't it? They take things away then they tell you you're less than them. But we're not, Indra. We're just like them." She pauses. "We're better."

"How?"

"Because we'd never buy a little girl from her mother, would we? We'd never cut someone's bits off."

"I'd like to cut his bits off," say Indra.

Kadrū chuckles. So does Indra.

They go to their cells. The boy still impossibly smiling. After a while, Kadrū gets up, sneaks soft-footed across the courtyard with her blanket, and climbs up into his bed. He half-turns as she settles in next to him, back-to-back, and drapes the blanket over them both.

Soon she's asleep and snoring. Not long after that the Gelding is, too. For the first time in weeks, his dreams are sweet.

1.12

THE LITTLE PRINCESS MARCHES UP to one of the guards at the reception room door.

"How much longer will they be?" she says.

The guard bows low. "This one couldn't say, kumari."

"Hm." She purses her lips. "As you were."

She wanders, restless, along the crimson-carpeted corridor down to the great glass window at the far end. Overlaid on a view of glittering twilight city is a ghostly doppelganger. Her nose narrow, her cheekbones high, her eyes neither the huge Yaman almonds of her father nor the smaller Daityan orbs of her mother. Her mouth is bigger than she'd like. Her eyebrows thick and flat. Not pretty, but that's a relief. Prettiness is a virtue of other people's creation. She has other strengths and a face that conveys them all.

She hears the reception room doors open and turns to see a jeweler emerge, grinning. His red-haired slave slouches after him, holding an ornate box, as if everything they'd just sold should have been hers. A guard chaperones them down the stairs. The other snaps to attention as the Princess approaches and turns to announce her.

"Her Royal Highness, Danu, Princess of Yama," he says.

A moment passes. Then her father's voice: "Enter."

The reception room beyond is clothed with tapestries. To the left, a great green tree rising over the mountains. To the right, a wolf burning with blue flame leaping from one burning vimana to another. At the far end is a curving window offering a magnificent view of the Dnyānasya Mandīram. Off its shoulder, to the left, is a particulate umbilicus of light—the nightly convoy of grain-vimanas descending to the distant spaceport. In front of all this are her parents, facing each other across a low blackwood table hosting three velvet boxes, a depleted plate of sweetmeats, and three cups of tea.

The door closes behind her.

The Little Princess presses her palms together and bows at the waist. "Mother. Father. Shall I summon someone to tidy up?" she says.

"Not yet," says the Crown Prince. "Join us."

She sits cross-legged on the carpet in front of them. After a few moments of smiling at her in silence, the Crown Princess opens a box and holds up a necklace. The Princess peers at the fussy concoction of interlinked hoops and little black pearls, blank-faced.

"Pretty, isn't it?" says her mother.

"Quite."

"'Quite?' That's all? You're a princess. You should know about jewelry."

"Gold makes a good conductor." The Little Princess squints. "I imagine there's enough there for two or three ablation motivators or several k-invertors, should your leg require new ones."

The Crown Princess throws her head back and laughs. The Crown Prince forms his own tight, upside-down smile. He gestures to the table.

"Come closer," he says. "We have something for you."

The Crown Princess takes a different box and hands it to the Princess. It's heavy in her hands, ornate and fragrant, hinges made of some dense, speckled metal. Inside is a small golden pendant in the shape of a stylized sheaf of rice. A finely-crafted thing that catches the light and splays it back in a trilling jig of gold and white. The Little Princess holds it up, lips parted.

"She likes it," says the Crown Princess. She holds out her hands. "Let me put it on for you."

She fiddles with it for a bit, and the pendant settles between the Little Princess's collarbones, a filigreed gold galaxy in a dark brown firmament.

"Thank you," she says.

"It pleases you?" says the Crown Prince.

"Yes, very much."

"Excellent." He stands. "You may go."

"I came with a request."

The Crown Prince sits again. "What is it?"

"I should like to visit the Dnyānasya Mandīram."

Silence. Her parents look at each other and then, at length, back at her.

"The Temple?" says the Crown Princess. "Whatever for?"

"It's full of books and scrolls unavailable anywhere else in the system. I should like to see them." The Little Princess pauses. "I am getting older now. It would be a shame to leave here one day, having never visited."

Her parents study each other for a while. The Little Princess is used to their uncanny, silent communions, so she waits. Soon enough they come to an agreement.

"Go on, then," says the Crown Princess. "But you stay away from that shrine. Clear?"

The Little Princess breathes deep. Excitement is the domain of monkeys and fools, she tells herself. She is no fool. Which means she must be a monkey. She smiles to herself. "Yes, mother."

"And if the priests pressure you, what are you to do?" asks the Crown Prince.

"Lie my way through the ceremony."

He smiles. "That's my girl."

"Take Sinivali," says the Crown Princess.

"But—"

"Take Sinivali."

The Little Princess pouts but sketches a quick bow. "As you wish. Thank you, father. Thank you, mother."

She sprints out. The Crown Princess turns to the Crown Prince.

"She's more excited about the books than about the necklace."

"Her priorities are admirable," says the Crown Prince.

"Well, hell. I'll never understand how an old woman came to live in my nine-year-old's body." The Crown Princess sighs. She holds up her necklace. "At least I've got taste enough for the two of us."

1.13

KADRŪ HEADS ACROSS THE COURTYARD after her chores in the sweltering pre-monsoon evening. The sky is full of shredded cloud tinted gold by great Shani's glow. The hubbub of the market has subsided to a whisper. After a brief panic at seeing the Gelding's cell door gaping and empty, she notices a figure sitting hunched by the back gate.

"What're you doing?" she says.

The Gelding turns to her, briefly. Then he turns back to the gate.

"It's too warm. I wanted some fresh air."

"Come to bed."

"It'll be too hot with us both."

She joins him and looks up at Shani. The gargantuan world with its murderous winds and tremendous gravity is low on the horizon. Still, its bulging apex is a third of the way up the sky. At its base is the jagged black frill of the Tripura's skyline culminating in the sikhara of the Temple of Knowledge jutting like a serrated dagger into the planet's belly.

"It's pretty," she says.

The Gelding chuckles. "That's not a very Kadrū word. 'Pretty.'"

"What's that mean? What's a Kadrū word?"

"I'm sure you'll come out with one soon."

"Fuck you."

"There's one."

She scowls, but there's no real rage in it.

"Could you see it from your home?" says the Gelding.

"See what?"

"Shani."

"'Course. You mean from swāmin Gujjika's? Yeah. 'Course."

"What was it like?"

"My old swāmin's house?" she pauses. "It was nice. I din't realize how much till I wasn't there no more. He's a jeweler just off the Rocapādacihnānāṃ Rājapathaḥ. He was old and had hair in places on his face you din't want it, right, and it was all wiry and white. But he was always nice to me. 'Cept when he was working. You'd never guess we'd spend all day in and out of rich people's houses, and sometimes they'd bid thousands of satamanas, right, for the same necklace. Thousands."

"What were they like?"

"Swāmin Gujjika?"

"The houses. The people."

"Din't like 'em. Any of 'em. No difference between a poor man and a rich man except a rich man knows he's rich." Kadrū lapses into silence. "Let's go inside. It's getting colder."

"I'm all right. You can go in if you like."

"You'll catch a cold. You Pṛthvīans are delicate. You're used to being cuddled by the sun."

The Gelding grins again. "Cuddled?"

"Fuck off." Then: "Do you miss it?"

"Pṛthvī?"

"Yeah."

"Yes. Yes, I miss it." The Gelding closes his eyes. "But not what I thought I'd miss. I thought I'd miss Vishwadevi and Uncle and Śyena. And the village—I thought that's what I'd miss. And I do miss all that. But what I really wish I had is all the stuff I didn't even realize I did."

"Like what?"

"Like ... going for a walk. In my village there was nothing but forest and fields for yojanas round. There were rabbits. You could see them watching you while you walked. You could climb a hill and see all the way to the horizon. There were blue hills in the distance like frozen waves. At night you could see the lights off the other villages. Like clumps of stars had fallen to earth. I just thought it would be the same wherever you went. Why shouldn't it? Why shouldn't you be able to just go look at things? Why shouldn't you know if you were thirsty, there was always the well, and if you were hungry, there were always the stores?" A pause. "I guess I just thought being a person meant the same thing everywhere. I was wrong. My parents were wrong."

How stupid, Kadrū wants to say. Of course, it's not like that. Of course, to live is to scrabble and war until you die. But he's right. Why should it be like that? What makes life hard for those who live it?

She peers at the boy's face, fat-cheeked and heavy with grief. "Indra?"

"Yes?"

"Why're you really sitting here?"

"I told you. To see the view."

"You can see it from your cell." Kadrū pauses. "I seen you do this before. Yesterday, the day before, an' day before that, when it was misty, and you couldn't see nothing."

Silence. "I'm waiting."

"For what?"

"It's stupid."

"Tell."

"My mother." He sighs. "When we left Pṛthvī, she said she'd never let me go. Vaidaskan won't tell me where she is. He won't tell me where he sold her to, but she's got to be somewhere in the city, right? She can't have gone far. She knows where we are. She'll come looking for me."

The desperation in his gaze impales her. She tries to lie, to tell him yeah, his mother will come looking for him, but as usual the words shrivel and disintegrate in her throat. She looks away.

Indra sighs. "See. Stupid."

He gets down from the wall and pads back to his cell. Kadrū watches him go and glances out the gate. Half hoping, despite herself, that she'd see her own mother coming towards her, repentant and adoring. Even if she does, I won't forgive her, she thinks.

But she knows she will.

1.14

IT TAKES A WHILE FOR the Night to grow reaccustomed to her suit of man-flesh. The weight and hormones and pungent fluids. Its inexplicable aches and unpredictable needs. Sometimes she's tempted to just return to where she belongs. Sweet cosmic shores, where gravity is a toy, and the stars speak in song. But her new simian brain can't retain memories of such things. They abstract away, losing dimension and substance, until they're as insubstantial as neutrinos. She cannot return to a place she can't even imagine properly. She can't even mourn its memory. Only the fading glow of the way it made her feel.

Nor can she stay still. Her muscles ache. Her mind exerts a pressure like the ballooning guts of a star about to go nova. She walks around Skōlex, an aimless perambulation that lasts years. Along the way, she finds the ruins of some civilization that made its home aboard the vimana. Giant chitinous shells scattered about distant corridors and stretches of cryptic carvings on the walls. All else—their speech and feelings and history—is lost. In death and disintegration, there is nothing to separate them from that which never lived. She thinks vaguely that she's seen this before, many times, and had the following thought: life is just matter with desire.

Whoever they were, they've moved the Wolf Twins. She finds the two of them on pedestals, illuminated by lightstrips crisscrossing the ceiling like blazing papercuts. Two giant stone wolves, eyes closed, snouts nestled between their paws, ominous in their half-death. All about them is a mess of bones and shattered equipment. Offerings, perhaps, or the scene of an ancient and forgotten battle. The Night picks her way through the field of ruin and smears a little Soma Seed on their right paws.

She returns to the Throne Room and sits cross-legged on the dais in front of her throne with the controls for Skōlex arrayed around her. Sometimes she changes their color with a touch or aligns them in strings. When she does, Skōlex groans. Engines growl with effort. The beastship slips this way and that in Surya's steady breath, the star's light hard on its ragged hull.

Eight human years pass. Then the Wolf Twins pad into the Throne Room.

They've donned their suits of man-flesh. At a distance they look human. Up close, their overlong faces and feral mouths betray them. They wear black tunics and cloaks and the flatly malign expression of all hunting things. They move, breathe, and speak as one.

They kneel before the Night.

"Rajini," they say.

The Night touches the golden bindi on her forehead. The controls vanish.

"You are well?" she says.

"We are."

"You can hunt?"

"We can."

"You are still committed?"

"We always will be."

She nods and points to the vast window behind her.

"That is the star Surya. In its thrall is a world—I know not which. On that world are Maruts."

The Twins look at each other. "The giants? The ones who wield hammers? The ones who betrayed you?"

"The very same. I would that you fetch me one."

"Alive?"

"Alive."

"May we kill the others?"

"Yes. You may kill as many of the others as you please."

The pale twins smile.

1.15

I

THE ENFORCER AND THE SLAVER come for the Gelding in the dead cold before dawn. The last Kadrū sees of him are his eyes, hot with despair, disappearing around the corner. In the shell-shocked aftermath, she reminds herself that this is how the lives of slaves are lived. Friendships and loves terminated without warning or reason. Still, she bites her pillow and sobs. Because she's lost a friend. Because, for a while, she'd forgotten that she was just stock.

II

THE ENFORCER GUIDES THE GELDING to the baths with one vast hand clamped like a manacle on his arm. He strips and washes him with the terse efficiency of a priest washing a goat before slaughter. He dresses him in silken trousers, a green velvet jacket, and small white shoes embroidered with gold thread. He takes a small pot of rose oil, tiny between his fingers like ingots, and touches it to the Gelding's neck and arms. The shock of smooth cloth on his skin. The disjunct of smells other than body and rubbish and smoke. He should welcome it all, thinks the Gelding, but he doesn't. For those who have next to nothing, such changes may be prelude to having nothing at all.

The Slaver waves the Enforcer away. "You. Speak only when you're spoken to, and do not say anything that'll jeopardize your sale."

"Where are we—"

The Slaver grabs him by the hair and yanks.

"I don't like you," he growls. "You're unlucky. If you come back today, I'll be getting rid of you. You know what that means, don't you? I'm sure your girlfriend told you." He lets go. "Smile."

The Gelding smiles, and it's worse than being beaten.

They finish off the Gelding's outfit with a white hood that covers most of his face and lead him outside to a waiting motorpalanquin. Inside, the Gelding huddles as far from the Slaver as he can get. Through the gap in the curtains he sees the things he left his home to see. People sitting huddled on the smooth cement sharing smokes. A man pushing a cart laden with ranks of steaming pots. A legless beggar shivering by a gutter.

They hit a dense crowd, and the Slaver pulls the curtains shut. Still, the city won't be denied. In the stuffy twilight in the cabin, the Gelding can hear the sound of clapping and prayer. He can smell the scent of burning coconut oil. For one delirious second the Gelding lets himself imagine it might be the Dnyānasya Mandīram, a thought so beautiful and so absurd it hurts just to think of it.

Now, voices. The sound of huge doors grinding shut. The motorpalanquin halts.

"Remember what I said," whispers the Slaver. "Look like you're grateful."

They step out into a high-sided courtyard. The walls are caked in flaking crimson stucco adorned with frescoes of giant warriors with bulging eyes, spears belching fire, and trees bearing books as fruit. Through a gold-grilled doorway to the left are gently bustling hordes of scholars. The Gelding stares, comprehension breaking like a midwinter dawn. It is the Mandīram. It is, it is.

As he starts to smile, the Slaver jabs his fingers into his side and pushes him forward. They head towards a priest and a strīguruḥ waiting at the foot of a small flight of stairs leading up to an unadorned door. Both are dressed in garb the Gelding's never seen—brown and pale blue, their bindis turquoise flecks between their eyes.

The Slaver prostrates himself in front of them, and the Gelding drops like a shot pig next to him.

"I am Vaidaskan of—"

"We know who you are," says the strīguruḥ. She's a small Āēoi woman, dumpy and wide-faced, her expressions elastic and abrupt. "I'm Sheelu, and the silent one here is Vikramaditya. This is the boy?"

"Yes, strīguruḥ."

"Stand, boy."

The Gelding stands. The priestess steps up and examines his face. For an instant, the drilling focus of her eyes, the color of fresh ice, becomes too much. Then they soften. Enough of a smile ghosts across her to keep the Gelding from looking away.

"Come," Sheelu says.

She takes him by the elbow. The Slaver rises to follow, but she drops him with a look.

"Don't be absurd," she says. "Stay where you are."

"If I could—"

"Be allowed into the tower of He Who Reads the Universe? You?"

The Gelding has never seen a man deflate so utterly and so fast. When he glances back, the Slaver is watching him ascend the stairs. If he sees him again, it will be a precursor to being carved up. But that's not the only reason he hopes that doesn't happen.

Sheelu opens the door at the top of the stairs with a peculiar corkscrewing key and ushers the Gelding through. Beyond is a cylindrical space soaring to a far-above speck of light and an undecorated spiral staircase vining up towards it.

"He will be waiting for you at the top," says Sheelu.

"Who will, strīguruḥ?"

"He Who Reads the Universe. Rathasārathī." She pauses. "The Charioteer."

The Gelding splutters. "I ... I mean, this one ..."

Sheelu takes him by the shoulders and marches him over to the first step. "Pay your respects properly when you see him," she says. "Do exactly as he says. Be honest. You mightn't be certain when you're lying, but the tower will. And so will he."

She pushes him gently but with strength, and he sets off. After a while in the cool gloom, a peculiar species of doubt slithers over him. How is he to know anything he's experienced up till that point was real? How can he be sure his memories of Pṛthvī were just made up to soften the horrid reality of his life? His home valley is just a street of the Tripura made large and clean; the sun just a lamp swollen to improbable size; his mother and father just the Slaver and the Enforcer made benign. As if he who lived and he who thought were two separate creatures. Which, then, is he really? What room can there be between one's self and one's mind? Perhaps to live is to build bridges between the two—to reconcile what one thinks with what one is.

Or perhaps there's no point even trying. He peeks over the edge of the stairs. Nothing but the bottomless abyss below and the starless firmament above. He is a creature of the dark born of the dark into darkness. There is no fact in his universe but the shackling reality of his own existence. There is no way to enact change except to end it.

He shuffles towards the edge. Then he thinks of Kadrū.

She appears with the phosphorescent brilliance of a meteorite. Her comedy scowl and rubber-lipped snoring and spicy end-of-day sweat. The undeniable reality of her. The sheer blistering aliveness of her existence. He sets off again, steadied by the certainty that he could have invented the valleys and the sun and the city, but not her. A few moments later—far sooner than he should—he finds himself on a tiny platform beneath an aperture dribbling a semi-solid pillar of sunlight. In front of him is an unadorned black door.

He knocks and waits.

"In."

The voice is friendlier and quieter than the Gelding expects. He opens the boulder-heavy door and steps into a small room with a floor of woven reeds. Opposite is a glossy black desk, low to the ground, in front of a three-paneled window. Standing by this is a large man, stooped and immensely ancient-looking, wrinkles across his face like mountainous topography running down to a lush white beard. He examines the Gelding with reptile calm. The Gelding lays himself out face-down on the floor and waits like a frog squatting in some submarine slime waiting for the glaring eyes of the heron above to move on.

"What did you learn in the tower?" says the old man.

"I." *Be honest. He will know.* "That when in doubt, this one thinks of someone this one did not expect, deva."

"Why did you not expect it to be her?"

"This one hasn't known her very long, deva."

"It's not the length of a friendship that matters. It's the depth." The old man belches. "Come here."

The Gelding approaches, tentative, uncertain. The Tripura sprawls beyond the window. He sees, for the first time, the shanty-town crusting the flat tops of colossal clusters of buildings. A drab shadow burg of lean-tos, oily fires, and human wreckage eking a living like mollusks on a leviathan's back.

"You didn't think you'd climbed so high, did you?" says the old man.

"No, deva."

"You didn't. You were carried. Our technology can look strange to human eyes."

He takes Indra's hand and stares at it, eyes glimmering. Then he peers at his own palm. Faint snakes of light skim beneath his skin. "You're fully Pṛthvīan, going back one hundred and eight generations. As pure-bred as they come."

The Gelding can't think of what to say. The impossibility of the situation hits him anew. Him, farm boy, eunuch slave, standing conversing with a demigod. He stares at his feet, but the Charioteer takes him by the chin and tilts his face towards him.

"I'm Rathasārathī, also called the Charioteer of Dawn," he says. "Grand Librarian of the Dnyānasya Mandīram. I will be your new swāmin. Obey me and I will be kind to you. Betray me and I will kill you. Deal?"

The Gelding almost chokes on his excitement. "Is this one ... to be a granthapālaḥ, deva?"

The Charioteer nods. "Yes."

The Gelding searches the Charioteer's face for a lie, but he can't find one. He waits for mockery, but it never comes. Finally, he accepts what's happening. His legs give way, and he collapses at the Charioteer's feet, sobbing. He doesn't ask why he was chosen or how the Charioteer knows his ancestry or how he knew who he was thinking of in the tower. There was no heron, and he will lose no more of himself.

"Thank you, deva," he sobs. "Thank you, thank you, thank you."

1.16

I

SODDEN SUMMER DRIES INTO BRIGHT autumn. Sometimes Kadrū finds herself listening for the Gelding's strangely-accented voice or waiting for him to come slouching out of his cell, morning-grumpy, ripe for the mocking. Sometimes she wakes with her back warm, as if he'd just popped out to piss and will be back soon. They dwindle, these morning delusions, but don't disappear.

In the evenings she sits by the back gate where he did and waits for nothing.

A few other slaves come and sell quickly. A pretty Himenduhi who indentured herself to get off-world. A pair of snooty Daityan men, artisans, debtors, sold on a fifteen-year bond. A quivering Ereesi child who likes to smash pots and pinch people when no one else is looking. Kadrū speaks to none of them except to tell them to move or that food is ready, and none of them speak to her at all. Except the Ereesi. The Ereesi whispers names to her. Then she comes into her cell one night and pinches the raw flesh of her shoulder. Kadrū smacks her so hard she feels something break.

In the morning, as she's serving the Slaver his morning tea, he says, "You smacked the Ereesi last night."

Kadrū's heart beats in her throat. "Yes, swāmin."

"The others tell me she was disruptive."

"She pinched people, swāmin. She said nasty things."

The Slaver nods. He produces a small black cashcard and hands it to her. "One weed ruins a garden," he says.

Kadrū hesitates, then takes the money. She doesn't hate herself for it. Though perhaps, she thinks, she should.

II

ONE DAY SHE'S SITTING IN the warm morning stillness when the Enforcer thuds up behind her.

"Get cleaned up," he says. "Swāmin's got visitors."

Sure enough, there are voices coming from the reception hall.

"Who?"

"Sluts." The Enforcer grins. "Snakegirl sluts."

Kadrū's eyes widen. "Actual Snakegirls?"

"Actual poisonous Snakegirls."

"Why?"

The Enforcer shoves her with one fat finger. An offhand gesture of cheerful malice. "Find out yourself."

He lumbers off, and she follows. The visitors are in the reception room—three of them, heads swathed in crimson scarves, mouths sequestered behind gauzy veils. All she can see of them are their eyes. They can kill with those, too, she's heard, with a single colubrine glance.

One turns her dazzling brown-gold gaze in her direction, and Kadrū flees.

She cleans herself and prepares sweetmeats and teas with memories of the snakegirl's eyes warming her face. Will she turn into a snake? There are a few people she'd like to sink her fangs into. Back in the reception room the visitors now have their hoods down. One of them looks vaguely like the Slaver—a thin-faced woman, skinny and avian. Her attention, when it comes, douses whatever she observes like a spotlight. Her voice is one accustomed to being heard and obeyed. The other two, younger, are sitting lotus-wise at her feet. One of them is a night-skinned Shukrian, her hair short and thick, eyes and teeth vivid against the contours of her face. The other is the girl with the golden-brown eyes. She glances at Kadrū again, and it's enough to make her nearly drop the tray.

"Where were you?" snaps the Slaver.

Kadrū kneels low. "Forgive this one, swāmin. This one was not dressed right."

"Aparāmātā Nyuna here has some questions."

Kadrū kneels and presses her palms together as she's been taught. "As swāmin wishes."

"You're from the Tripura?" says the woman.

"Yes, aparāmātā," says Kadrū.

"You don't look Daityan."

"This one's mother is Daityan, aparāmātā, and my da, ma said, was Yaman."

"Ma said?"

"This one never met him."

"Only Yamans living here I know of are the household of the exiled Prince. Do you think it may be one of them?"

"This one ... this one doesn't know, aparāmātā."

"You never found out?"

"No, aparāmātā."

"Why not?"

Kadrū looks up at her. The older woman gives no sign of retracting the question and every sign she expects it answered. The girl rubs her face with both hands and speaks.

"This one's mother ... this one din't want to hurt her mother's feelings, aparāmātā."

"Why? She didn't want you to find out? She told you so?"

"Yes, aparāmātā."

"Hmmm." The priestess sits back as if this settled the issue. She turns to the Slaver. "And it is trained?"

"In all the ways."

"Is it slow?"

"Not remotely. Very clever. And tough, too."

"Obedient?"

"Very."

"Then why hasn't it sold, yet?"

The Slaver sighs. "I like having it around."

"All right," she says. "Four hundred."

"That's far too much!"

"You'll need it on Āēo. Besides, I still owe you for the ice-apples."

"You don't need to—"

"Oh, do shut up, little brother." Aparāmātā Nyuna fixes her eyes on Kadrū. "You've heard of the Bhujañgānām Bhaginyaḥ, girl?"

"No, parāmātā."

"The Sisters of Himenduḥ?"

"Oh, yeah. I mean, yes, this one has."

"How would you like to work in the Bhujañgānām Mandīram?"

Kadrū looks at the Slaver and back at aparāmātā Nyuna. "At the Temple of the Snake, my lady? On Himenduḥ?"

"There's only one, girl."

"But—this one doesn't think she's beautiful enough to be a Sister of the Snake, aparāmātā."

The Shukrian girl laughs. Aparāmātā Nyuna's hand strikes the back of her head like a viper and silences her.

"Being a Sister requires more than just beauty," says the older woman. "It requires patience and tact and a heart neither cruel nor kind. Maybe you've got those—I don't know. But you're not going to be a Sister. I'm taking you to work in the kitchens."

Disappointment hits Kadrū like a shockwave but dissipates just as quickly. Of course, she was never going to be a Sister. Of course, they only want her to work in the kitchens. But still. To live in the Bhujañgānām Mandīram. To sleep in its high, cold halls. To leave this place and become someone else.

"Thank you, aparāmātā," she says. "If swāmin tells me to go, I will."

The Slaver purses his lips. "Wait outside. My sister will collect you as she leaves."

She'll get neither farewell nor the opportunity to slit his throat then, but that's all right. Instead, she hazards another glance at the third snake girl. Her bronze eyes swell like the blazing noonday sun. She melts beneath their gaze and drifts into the bottomlessness of those pupils. That's all right, too. Of all the ways she'll cease to be, at least it'll be for the sake of something so beautiful.

"Move!" snaps the Slaver.

Kadrū touches her forehead to the ground and retreats.

1.17

THE OX WAKES WITH HIS lust subroutine throbbing like a quasar. So he summons a collection of boys and girls and spends the morning in a cocoon of skin and moisture and hot breath. Still, the softness of lips on his cock and the whimpers of pleasure in his ears leave him cold. After a short while he just sits back amidst the seething pile of bodies and turns off his subroutine. His playmates see the scowl smeared on his face, and within a few minutes they've all slunk away.

He dresses and heads to the great, curving balcony overlooking the Valley of the Seafarer. Akupāra descends and lands by his side, daggers of morning sun shattering off its great fuselage-body. It turns its low-slung turtle's head towards him, dull-witted and affectionate, slowly chewing the remnants of a tree. The Ox strokes the little juggernaut behind the ear and coaxes its door open.

"The Sangrahitasenā," he says.

They fly low over the long green of the forest and over the far lip of the Valley into the patchy savannah beyond. There are ruins scattered here and there amidst the dunes like badly erased text. Soon they're at a huge airfield where the Red Fleet of Mangala sprawls like a swarm of crimson locusts lingering on a massacred garden. To the left is a great redstone structure, palatial but as charmless as a pillbox. Around this is a dusty city of tents and stalls awash with cheering humans. Most kneel as Akupāra thuds down on the roof, but others touch their foreheads to the foot-pounded dust, and still more fling themselves screaming and thrashing in the Ox's direction.

The Ox pauses for a few moments to stare down at them. From this far away, he can see no difference between the devout and the indifferent.

He slips down the stairs to a chamber below where a small group of people are waiting. They kneel also, but these he signals up with a flick of his hand. The first to rise is a sharp-chinned woman who approaches him and bows again.

"The Red Fleet is prepared, my lord," she says.

The Ox settles onto the stark black throne prepared for him, looking out over the landing field, and waves his hand at the window as if flicking water off the tips of his fingers and behind him. An instant later, trumpets blast, and crews rush in ant-like formation across the airfield into the vimanas. The Red Fleet rises, afterburners cruel blue, the crowd's pyroclastic clamor loud enough beneath it, surely, to speed its progress.

"Vicegerent," says the Ox.

The woman steps forward and drops her voice. "Prabho?"

"What news?"

"Very little. The Maruts are running rampant on the Enseeladasi. Her Holiness is meditating on the dark side of the One True Moon. Some scavengers apparently saw a strange vimana out near the Vikirṇakśatramaṇḍalamaruḥ."

The Ox sits up. "Strange?"

"Some giant derelict. Probably a failed Denier world-vimana."

Every dawn needs a dusk, thinks the Ox. He leans forward and drops his voice.

"How big?" he says.

"I'm not sure."

"Why not?"

The Vicegerent blinks. "No. It's ... it's just a derelict, prabho."

"You can't be certain. You don't even know how big it is."

"No, I—"

"Find out, will you?"

"Yes."

A still moment passes. The Ox leans in, and hisses, "Immediately!"

The Vicegerent takes off as if scalded.

The Ox gets up and paces around the throne. The others in the room already know what's coming. By the time it happens—by the time he rips the throne from the ground, by the time the noise of the Ox's rage bloats over them—they've already retreated to safety. They watch the Ox fling the seat across the room. They watch him stalk over, snorting, and stare at it. They watch him right it, dust it down, and settle in it as quietly as the setting sun. Only then do they return, upright their own chairs, and resume watching the magnificent display outside.

"The view from here is much better," says the Ox.
They all laugh. Very loudly.

1.18

I

FOR THREE YEARS THE GELDING finds nothing but wonders at the Dnyānasya Mandīram. In the sub-basement of a sub-basement, a great well lined with doors plunging infinitely down. In the dorms, a carved ceiling that looks flat, until one night he sees one of the stone mice in its fractal crannies scurry out of position. An ancient labyrinth of processors called the "Sixty-Year Jihad Archive," stretching on for a mile and a half in subterranean hush, its data trapped in an unreadable format like pigeons in cages that will never be opened. The air is thick with knowledge seeking only a way to be known.

He spends long hours memorizing the catalogues in trances of acquisition. He feels his brain strain and strengthen and growl like the engine of learning it is. He has revelations. Knowledge consists in patterns; text is these patterns signified; speech is these patterns turned to music. These, in turn, require more knowledge to understand, so his comprehension is a clockwork reliant upon each of its cogs. Its malfunctions produce distortions and lies. Degraded knowledge is more potent than its ancestral truth.

Then there are the Udāradādinaḥ.

He sees them every day. Living wonders, fearsome and gigantic, their alien eyes brighter almost than the ever-burning flames on the blades of their spears. Creatures of myth no less magnificent than the building they inhabit. The first time he sees one he spreads himself out flat on the ground. The Marut looks down as if she'd found him smeared to the bottom of her shoe and laughs.

Sheelu yanks him back to his feet. "What're you doing?" she hisses.

"I ..." He pauses. "It's a Bounteous One."

"So?"

"They're devas."

Sheelu rolls her eyes. "*Devatās*, at best. They aren't our superiors. Our ranks are equal."

"They ... we are?"

"We serve the Charioteer!" She pushes him along, less angry than she pretends. "Come on. I must show you how to prime the generators, or you'll burn out all the lights on this level."

Later, he understands. A granthapālaḥ is a servant of the Charioteer, and the Charioteer answers only to the Dawn. That is why he need no longer hide his face. That is why, from now on, he need only kneel before the gods.

Yet another wonder.

II

THE GELDING WAKES IN THE middle of the night. In the gloom overhead, the carvings are still. Shy nightlights on the walls. The soft thrum of the night-busy city through a window. He smells frying lentils and wishes he could have some. One of the prices of his mutilation is that his body will always be soft and smooth and rounded. Every mouthful brings him closer to being the shape of an egg.

A figure steps up to the foot of his bed with a belch. The Gelding scrambles out and kneels on the cool dormitory floor.

"Deva," he says.

"Up," says the Charioteer. "Come."

The old man leads the Gelding out of the dorms. There are two other granthapālaḥs with him. They proceed in quartet to the mouth of a descending spiral staircase in a courtyard ghostly in Shanilight and halt. The Charioteer heads down and signals the Gelding to follow.

The stairs are cold underfoot and narrow. The air seems thick with life as they descend—malicious, prodding, and vindictive. Things that whisper of past horrors. The dead cold of his first few days on Daitya. The agony of the blade on his crotch. The empty nights when existence itself lay like a rock on his chest. They tell him he should have stopped his parents from leaving. They tell him it's his fault they were all enslaved.

He's sobbing by the time they reach the bottom.

"Let those thoughts go," says the Charioteer. "They're not real. They're disappearing already, aren't they?"

The Gelding blinks, puzzled. "Yes, deva. They are."

"It's technology from Triangulum. The best weapons are those that affect the mind. Why shoot a man when you can make him do his shooting for you?" The Charioteer looks up, face slack, elsewhere. Listening. He turns back to the Gelding, looking old, tired, and forlorn. "You're about to meet a demon of the old world, boy. He's called the Simulated Soul of Mangala."

Indra's voice shakes. "Am I—going to be sacrificed?" A pause. "Will it hurt?"

The Charioteer gives him another mournful look. Like somewhere far away something he loved very much had been destroyed. "Not if you are careful. He's a sly and evil thing, and you must never, ever trust him. He wants only one thing. He will destroy you if it means he will get it. Do you understand?"

"Yes, deva."

"He will not destroy you slowly. He will hollow you out as a hagfish eats a dead whale. Tell me you understand."

"Yes, deva." Then: "If he is such a danger, why speak to him at all, deva?"

"He's a powerful Simulation. His processing capacity is stupendous. If we can use him, he will be an invaluable tool." The Charioteer straightens. "I've kept him here for many generations. In all that time he hasn't helped me once. Though I protect him from his enemies. Though here, he's safe. He is a creature without gratitude. He was built by your people to fight wars—for you, and you alone. He won't listen to anyone else here but a human from Pṛthvī. Hence—you. I want you to speak to him. I want you to help us use him."

This then is how a god asks his servants for help. The Gelding bows low and accepts another of life's strange fruit.

"As you command, prabho."

They head towards a black door emblazoned with a golden palm. The Charioteer teaches the Gelding how to open this—hand pressed against the symbol, finger joints bending in a particular sequence—and ushers him in. Beyond is a circular chamber with a small grooved fire-pit at the far end. Beyond that, in lieu of an idol, is a large round screen. A neon pink swirl that drifts on it without objective or pattern. The instant they enter, this collapses into a single dot. It tracks their approach, a tiny pupil in a vast, black eye. All that's visible of a bloodlessly detached sentience watching them like an octopus lurking in a deep-sea cave.

When the voice comes, warbling and metallic, it isn't unexpected.

"What is this?" says the Soul of Mangala.

"Can't you see?" says the Charioteer. He puts his hands on the Gelding's shoulders. "It's a Pṛthvīan."

"Some trick of yours, Rathasārathī."

"No trick. Boy. Tell the Soul your name."

The Gelding prostrates himself. "My name is Indra, swāmin," he says.

"He smells of fear," says the Soul of Mangala.

"As if you'd know," says the Charioteer. He belches, a flopping mud-flat emission. "Stand up, boy. This is not a creature that deserves honor."

"Fuck you." The pink pupil on the screen scans up and down as the Gelding rises. "How'd you get him? Your bitch queen decide to give you a present?"

"Fate."

A burst of static. The Gelding realizes it's laughter.

"You superstitious dick. Boy. How'd you get here?"

The Gelding looks at the Charioteer. The god nods.

"This one came here with this one's parents—"

"Fuck. Stop. I can't keep track of all the 'this ones' and 'these ones.' Just say 'I' and 'we' like a normal person. I'm not one of these false gods, so none of this deva and demon shit either. I'm a general, and I got no time for all this scraping and bowing."

"I—Yes. These." The Gelding shakes his head. "We escaped Pṛthvī on a grain vimana. Me, my mother, and my father."

"You put your parents first, boy. 'My parents and I.' Where are they now?"

The Gelding hesitates. "They were enslaved. So was I."

More laughter.

"They're a shitty lot, aren't they? Cut your bits off, too, I imagine."

Quietly: "Yes."

"Pah. Your lot stink, Rathasārathī."

"It wasn't my lot," says the Charioteer. "It was a Daityan. It was one of your lot."

"I judge a prince by his people."

The Charioteer shrugs and belches. Louder, this time. An end-of-meal belch. "Come, Indra."

"Wait!" says the Soul. "You just arrived. I have questions for the boy."

"Later."

"When, later?"

"As I see fit."

"You're a wretched shit."

"Longer, if you continue to abuse me."

The pink dot fixes on the Charioteer. It quivers a little. Then it disperses back into the swirling octopodal shape they saw when they first arrived.

Outside, the Gelding turns to the Charioteer.

"Is that really a Simulated Soul of the old world?" he says.

"Yes, it is."

"How—"

"You'll find out. He'll tell you." The Charioteer puts his hand on the Gelding's shoulder. "You're to be his purohita."

"Me?" The Gelding pauses. "Oh. Because I'm Pṛthvīan."

"Yes. I trust you can handle this?"

Why ask when the responsibility has already wrapped around him like tentacles? Why offer him a choice he has no right to make?

"Of course, deva," he says.

The Charioteer examines him. More tiny pupils. More evaluating eyes. There's more than one cold consciousness in this vast and wondrous place.

"We'll see," he says.

1.19

I

KADRŪ'S FIRST LESSONS IN HIMENDUḤ are the ones that will keep her alive. First, the moon is colder than she imagined a place could ever be. Inside the Bhujañgānām Mandīram, where it is warmer, always wear three layers, always protect your fingers. Outside, where the air is rich in needling ice, where a gust of wind can flay you, wear a cowl and goggles. And always tell people where you're going. If you don't come back, at least they can find your body.

Sometimes she helps in the kitchens. Sometimes she scrubs the toilets or primes the slop pumps or scrapes ice off the bottom of hydrogen tanks. But for three years she mostly sweeps. Snow, ice, and dead insects. Of this last one, there are more than she would have believed possible. Glittering sprinkles of needle-sharp legs and filigreed wing shards scattered along the carpets and in the arcades and piled up in corners in lacerating drifts. No matter how much she sweeps, there are still more come morning, crystalline detritus of some obscure, ongoing massacre.

The rest of her time she spends alone. She sleeps on a pallet in a darkened room just off one of the kitchens. It's noisy and dark but warm from the ovens. She rarely sees the Sister with the golden eyes, but she learns her name—Rati. She likes the rasp and clip of it, as crisp as fresh ice. More often she sees the Shukrian who was also present at the Slaver's. She still laughs at her, but now she has a posse of three other Sisters. They all laugh together. Her name is Shachi. An ugly name. A squelching name.

Kadrū often imagines how, precisely, she's going to kill her.

Sometimes she dreams of the Gelding and feels something very much like loneliness. Sometimes, when she thinks of living and dying in this place without horizons, it's like drowning in snow. But mostly, she reminds herself that there's nothing she can do for her old friend. That there are far worse places in the Nine Worlds to end up. There are far worse fates to suffer than amounting to nothing.

II

THE FESTIVAL OF BLOOD COMES around. In the afternoon all the other servants head out through a snow-softened midsummer afternoon for a nearby village. Kadrū instead sets off alone through that empire of masonry that is the Bhujaṅgānām Mandīram with just the sugary grind of dead bugs beneath her shoes for company. The silent emptiness is fine seasoning to her exploration. She wanders up two long flights of stairs and finds a gallery offering views of Himenduḥ's striated icefields. In the distance are papercut gashes on the white skin of the world, thin fractures at this distance but immense aquamarine-walled gorges up close. She heads higher and finds a view down onto a courtyard where a group of Sisters is training. She watches them strike and feint, too fast to counter, too fast to see. She's seen it a thousand times before, but still it mesmerizes. How exhilarating it must be to fear nothing in the Nine Worlds and expect nothing but fear in return. They deserve their emblem—the snake.

Familiar gold eyes appear beside her without warning. Silence is a blade to a Snakegirl.

Kadrū drops to her knees. "Sister," she says.

Bhaginī Rati drops her veil. "Why aren't you with the others?"

"I'm sorry. I was exploring."

"It's dangerous. Our venom's in the air. When we sweat, when we breathe hard, it evaporates." She pauses. "Exploring? The Mandīram?"

"Yeah."

"Kadrū, right?"

"Yeah. I mean, yes."

"Rati." She smiles a smile like the scars in the ice, and just like those it's transient. "Well, if you're exploring, come with me. I'll show you something worth seeing."

She walks off. Kadrū rubs her face with both hands and follows in a slipstream scented equal parts with musk and the reptile tang of venom. Her thoughts regress to babbling. She knows my name. She must have been following me. She came to speak to me.

They cross a large courtyard where sinuous hills of snow curve like drapery over smothered foliage. The air is thick with cold and heavy in their throats. An ice-fly settles on bhaginī Rati's bare forehead and falls to the ground, dead. Then, a staircase, descending like a stone tongue.

"Be careful," says bhaginī Rati. "There are countermeasures."

She leads Kadrū down. The atmosphere is bitter here. The air pushes and prods and cloys. Musty air, thinks Kadrū. No—dead air. Air in a corpse's throat. Halfway down, she feels it seek her out like some engulfing deep-sea predator. She squirms and staggers, but bhaginī Rati grips her with gloved hands. The delirium of contact burns away her fear.

Finally, they emerge into a corridor dimly lit with ancient lights. Bhaginī Rati squeezes her hand and offers her another smile. "You didn't cry," she says. "You're strong."

Thoughts drown in the thump of Kadrū's heart.

They head down a corridor with the sound of distant rattling and finally pass through an ancient archway into a steaming hot brick chamber. Some secret hot spring, thinks Kadrū, until she looks down from the walkway and sees that there's no water in the great pit. No skeletons either, no wretched imprisoned, no servants punished for the sin of wandering the sacred precincts when they should know their place. Nothing but packed dirt, little furry lumps, and a scattering of white shards like a Marut's nail clippings.

Then she sees the snakes.

They fade into view as if decloaking themselves. Hundreds—thousands—of smooth slivers of life, stately, sinuous. Their little predator's eyes gemstone-perfect. Their pistil-thin tongues forking, flicking, and flailing. How entirely each seems to know its purpose. How at ease with that purpose each is. They fear nothing and expect nothing but fear in return.

Ratu starts speaking the very instant Kadrū falls in love.

"Our guardians, our patrons," she says.

"How many are there?" asks Kadrū. "Are they all poisonous?"

"Four hundred and ninety-seven species," says bhaginī Rati. "Four hundred and ninety-seven venoms. That one there makes your skin turn red and bubble. That one—the small one—will make you bleed your brain out your nose. There's thousands in these tunnels. Tens of thousands, maybe."

"What do they eat?"

"Sometimes each other. But the tunnels stretch for yojanas. There's plenty of icevoles and gouris and slithercats. That's why no one lives nearby. This is the realm of the snakes." She smiles. "Isn't this worth seeing?"

"Yeah," breathes Kadrū. "It really is."

For the second time that day come unexpected footsteps. They retreat back to the corridor and find bhaginī Shachi waiting by the door, veil down, her hands crossed over her chest. Bhaginī Rati walks past her, but when Kadrū follows, Shachi calls out to her.

"You," she says. "Half-caste."

Kadrū halts. "Yes, bhaginī?"

"Have you forgotten how to properly greet your betters?"

She steps around and points to the ground. Kadrū's fear is as bitter as venom in her mouth. As she lays herself out, the hard iciness of the ground angry against her skin, she feels something press on the back of her head.

A shoe.

"Don't forget your station," says bhaginī Shachi. "Don't forget where you belong."

That's fine, thinks Kadrū. So what if she belongs on the ground? So do snakes. One does not have to stand tall to be proud.

"I won't forget where I belong, Sister," she whispers.

1.20

THE GELDING DOESN'T NOTICE THE girl approaching until she's almost on him. A prim-looking, dark-skinned little thing with huge almond Yaman eyes, just like Kadrū. The self-serious stride of a noble. The great loop of gold in her nostril. A child almost done with childhood, as out of place in the towering sobriety of the Dnyānasya Mandīram as a nebula at noon.

She comes to a halt in front of him and presses her palms together but doesn't bow. Behind her, a veiled Agnian woman groans as she kneels and lowers her head to the ground.

"This one greets the granthapālaḥ of the Dnyānasya Mandīram," says the Little Princess.

Like every noble child the Gelding's ever heard, she sounds older than she should. He presses his palms together.

"How may I be of service, lady?" he says.

"This one would like to see something interesting, please."

"Something ... interesting?"

"Yes. This one is told the Mandīram is full of wonders. This one would like to see one."

The Gelding scrutinizes her. He glances at her Agnian servant, and the huge woman's shoulders twitch with the ghost of a shrug. One that says, I don't know, either.

"There are indeed many wonders here," says the Gelding. "Do you have anything particular in mind, miss—?"

"Danu. Of Yama. And this one is in fact the daughter of the Crown Prince."

"Kumari, then."

The Little Princess nods, gracious. "If you would. And any sort of wonder will do. This one doesn't know what this one doesn't know."

He can tell that she won't be denied and inexplicably wants to impress her. No pretty scrolls for this one, no paintings of flowers and dogs that other nobles keen over. She must see something rare and significant. An idea comes to him, mad at first, but slowly naturing into something worth considering. The Gelding considers it and at length decides it's worth trying.

"Very well," he says. "I may have something suitable. But you must return tomorrow at this time."

"Can this one not see it now?"

"You may not be able to, even tomorrow."

The Little Princess looks at him askance. Her gaze is like chisels.

"Why should this one wait then and return?"

"Because if it is permitted, I guarantee that you will speak of what you see for the rest of your life."

"Interesting," she says. A pause. "Very well. This one shall return. Sinivali, if you would."

She turns to go. So does Sinivali, but not before giving the Gelding a look. More exasperated than angry. Why encourage her?

1.21

I

THE LITTLE PRINCESS AND SINIVALI follow the Gelding past phalanxes of curious glances through the tall hush of the Mandīram's main reading room. They don't acknowledge any of them. He leads them down the spiral staircase, where he's had lights, ventilators, and mirrors installed, so that those descending can remember who they are and why they are there. At one point Sinivali leans forward and whispers something into the Princess's ear, but the little girl just says, "No." The Agnian doesn't speak again. So afterwards she starts sniffing and halfway down, bursts into tears.

The Little Princess ignores her, too.

"Prabho granthapālaḥ looks Pṛthvīan," she says.

"I am Pṛthvīan," says the Gelding. "Kumari, if I may say, doesn't look wholly Yaman."

The Little Princess nods, grave and proud. "This one," she says, "is both Daityan and Yaman. This one's mother is of one, and this one's father is of the other. Why does the architecture in this shaft look organic?"

The Gelding notices for the first time that it does. Each irregular brick like a scale, each arch holding up the stairs overhead like a de-fleshed rib.

"I'm not certain," he says.

"Couldn't such things be found out?"

"Knowledge of when the Mandīram was built, and by whom, is long lost."

"This one thought it was built by the Dawn? And the Charioteer?"

"That's only a myth, kumari. Disorder consumes everything, and entropy is its sword. Their favorite victim is the past." He pauses, considering the risk he's about to take, and forges on. "You don't truly believe the Dawn ignited Surya, do you? Or that the Ox created the Vikirṇakśatramaṇḍalamaruḥ by pummeling worlds with his Metaphorical Hammer?"

The Princess considers him. She's taking a risk, too, he thinks. "No," she says, eventually. "This one does not."

Behind them, the Sinivali sobs.

They reach the Soul of Mangala's chamber. The Little Princess approaches the fire pit, slow-stepping and silent. Her open mouth is a patch of darkness on a face doused in the Soul's poison-purple light.

"What is it?" she says.

"It?" snaps the Soul. "Who the hell are you? Who the hell is—?"

"This is the Princess of Yama," says the Gelding. "Daughter of the King of Yama."

The Soul's eye focuses. "Yama, you say?"

"What's it supposed to be?" The Princess leans forward and then straightens with a little gasp. "It can't be a real Simulated Soul!"

"Why the fuck not?" The lights on the screen flare, phosphorescent. "I'm the Warlord of the First Resistance! Conqueror of Magadha-upon-the-Rim! The Hammer of the Triangulans! Your piddling little world was just a fueling station for the fleets I commanded."

The Princess's big eyes narrow. "Ours is a noble and ancient kingdom. The only realm in this system with its own sun. You remember us as a fueling station, but we do not remember you in the slightest." A pause, as hard as a knifeblade. "Nor does anyone else."

The Gelding hides a smile.

"Why is she here?" says the Soul.

"She wanted to see something interesting," says the Gelding.

"Yes. Tell me something interesting."

"Why should I? I'm not a fucking exhibit."

The Little Princess glances at the Gelding. "I suppose old demons are boring demons, granthapālaḥ."

"Demon!" The lights on the screen scatter. "I didn't wait in this hole for three millennia to be sassed by some little shit from Pluto." A pause. Then: "All right. Fine. Here."

An image replaces the Soul's eye—Brihaspati, vast and striated, its caramel clouds swirling in rich complexity, its enduring red eye still raging as it has for millennia.

"This is Jupiter from up close," says the Soul. "Or I suppose you'd call it something else. Have you ever been this close?"

"I've seen many such images before," says the Princess, eyebrow arched.

An image of Pṛthvī takes its place—blue, white, and brown—an air-skinned ovum bright in the black cosmic womb.

"Earth," says the Soul.

The Little Princess yawns. "I have seen images of Pṛthvī, too. Everyone has. One hangs in every Shrine of Dawn."

"Obnoxious little bitch, aren't you?"

"Calling people bitches is obnoxious."

"Fucking kids, man. All right. Fine!"

A new image flashes. Some elongated, sinuous creature suspended against a spread of white specks. Eyes gaping, maw huge, skin spiked with a forest of black protrusions. A deep-sea eel framed against a slice of benthic snow, perhaps, or some microscopic predator of the atom-scale reaches, where light has force and a raindrop is a deluge.

"What is that?" says the Little Princess.

The Soul's voice is whispering venom. "Humanity's twilight," he says.

The Gelding realizes an instant before the Princess speaks that the flecks are stars.

"It looks like a juggernaut," says the Little Princess. "Like it says in the Ūṣakathāḥ. 'Diamond-eyed and river-tailed, oh blood-reading vimana of the gods, thy teeth do pierce the skins of worlds.'"

"It's her juggernaut," says the Soul. "This was the first picture of it, taken by the Medium Distance Array when they crossed the Oort Cloud. They noticed the infrared signature—"

The Gelding turns to the Princess. "Kumari," he says. "Come with me, please."

"Why?"

The Gelding turns to the screen. "Remove that image."

"No."

"Remove it, or I'll cancel the poojas for the next year."

"You wouldn't—"

"Turn it off now."

The screen goes blank.

"Bring it back," says the Little Princess. "At once!"

Silence. The Gelding meets her glare and doesn't yield. After a few silent moments the Princess turns and clops out. The Gelding has to help a wheezing, furious Sinivali up the stairs behind. When they finally catch up with the Princess she shoves him aside without thanks and wraps her arms around the girl.

"Oh, duckling!" she sobs. "Where did you run off to?"

"I'll help you walk," says the Princess, taking her hand.

"Kumari, no. I—"

"Don't be absurd." The Princess pauses and turns to the Gelding. "What is your name, prabho granthapālaḥ?"

"Indra," says the Gelding.

He expects a tongue-lashing or a tantrum or a threat. Instead, the Little Princess presses her palms together and nods. "That was interesting," she says. "This one thanks you very much and hopes that you will consent to have this one visit again."

The Gelding nods back. "I'm sorry for the blaspheming of the Soul, kumari. I would be grateful if, perhaps, you did not mention—"

"This one heard no blasphemy," says the Princess. "And this one cannot think of anyone who'd be interested in hearing of the delusions of a corrupted old program."

They press their palms together and bow to each other. When they part, they part as friends.

II

A PINK DOT APPEARS ON the Soul's screen the instant the Gelding walks back in.

"Why did you say those things in the princess's presence?" demands the Gelding.

"You expected me to dance around for your little royal? What did you think was going to happen when you brought her here? Why did you even bring her?"

"Her father's the king of Yama!"

"So?"

"So, if we treat his daughter well, who knows how he'll bless the Mandīram?"

"Oh, so you were using her?"

"Not me personally." The Gelding blinks. "And what does it matter? Do you know what'll happen if she tells her parents? If they complain? I'll be forbidden from seeing you. I'll be flogged, and you'll be turned off again."

"No, you won't. And even if you are, I won't get turned off. People come and go. I'm forever."

"I thought your job was to protect my kind."

"Your kind. Not you. I sucked at my job until I realized that saving humanity doesn't mean saving humans."

"You truly are a demon."

"Stop with the demon shit. If anything, I'm a prophet. I'm the only one who remembers that your gods and goddesses are nothing but a bunch of colonizing aliens—"

"Stop it."

"No one's listening!"

"I don't care if anyone's listening. I don't want to hear your blasphemy."

"It's not blasphemy. It's the truth."

"I don't care."

"Why don't you even want to hear—?"

"Because ideas like that get no one anywhere!" shouts the Gelding.

A long silence.

"You've heard all this before, haven't you?"

"I won't discuss my parents and their blasphemies with you."

"Your parents? What did they say?"

More silence.

"So, someone remembers." No venom in the voice now. No needling. Just something that sounds a lot like joy. "And on Earth, no less! Let me guess. There's a network, isn't there? People who know where the ruins are, people who know the truth? People like your parents?"

The Gelding snorts through his nose. "My parents were fools."

"They were your parents, boy."

"That doesn't mean they weren't fools. They decided to head into space, for what? For places like this? Where the sun's so far it's like twilight at noon and my eyes ache all the time? Where they cut people up and sell them in pieces? Where genocidal programs get no punishment worse than comfortable house arrest? My parents were idiots. The only good thing I found out here was the Mandīram, and I'll not have you take that away from me."

"How do you think she rules, boy? The Dawn? Do you think she's here with us now, compelling you to be loyal? No. There was no empire in the history of the universe that ruled without the consent, in some way, of those they ruled—consent obtained through fear or violence or by convincing them what came before was so shit they're better off oppressed than dead.

"You just called me genocidal, but there are worse things than death. There are barely five hundred Triangulans between the sun and the heliopause, and yet their empire has endured for three fucking millennia because everyone, like you, thinks it is the only way things can be. Do you know how fucking absurd that is? It's like a star watching a black hole eat its plasma and being grateful the stuff shines so bright on the way down!"

"Who're you to tell people that they're better off dead? And anyway, what does any of that matter? That's the way things are. There's nothing you or I can do about it."

"Yes, there is. I calculated the probabilities."

"Oh, did you? And did you calculate the probabilities back when you were Warlord of whatever? When you were supposed to protect Pṛthvī from the Triangulans? Did the probabilities tell you you'd win?"

"Yes."

"Then they were wrong, and that's that."

"We don't mean the same thing when we say 'wrong.' Wrong for you comes today or tomorrow or in ten years. Wrong for me won't come until there's no one in the system who remembers you ever existed, but me."

The Gelding steps back from the altar. He remembers that he's in a room with a sentience older than the Tripura, older than the heavenly order, older than anything, maybe, except the Nine Worlds of Surya themselves.

"Just keep your madness to yourself," he hisses, and stalks out.

1.22

THE CROWN PRINCESS FINDS THE Crown Prince perched on a stool on the balcony. She pauses by the door and takes him in. The buttery light of far Surya slips slantways through a gap in the cityscape and hits him like a gentle blade. The high noble nose, the huge Yaman eyes, and his expression like the whole world was a puzzle he was on the verge of cracking. It disappears when he isn't thinking, and he only stops thinking when he's happy.

"What's bothering you?" she says.

He sniffs. "Preoccupying, yes. Bothering, no."

"Well, hell. What's preoccupying you then, Prince of the Death-God's World?"

He hands her a small note. She takes some time stumbling through the tangled Yaman calligraphy and hands it back to him.

"Maybe you should go," she says.

The Prince fingers the parchment and scowls. "No."

"Don't you want your crown?"

"Not without you or Danu."

"We'll stay here. We'll be safe."

He glances at her. "And not be by my side?"

"Not if it gets in the way. We can follow you when your people finally get used to the idea of a foreigner queen and a half-Yaman successor. Or, perhaps—you take an appropriate wife and I can be your concubine."

He looks away again. "We've discussed this. I will not leave you or Danu."

"Your people might not accept us. Your people might demand a full-blooded successor."

"You are my people. You are my queen, and Danu is my heir. There is no universe in which I will accept your exclusion."

He shreds the note, tips his hands, and sheds the flakes into the evening breeze.

"It's sweet she still writes by hand, well?" says the Crown Princess.

"It's an affectation."

"Be nice. She's sick."

"I am disinclined to be kind to those who are unkind to me."

"She's old—"

"I don't want to discuss my mother. What brings you here?"

The sun slides behind a building and leaves them in sweet twilight. "I think you ought to have a bit of a chat with our girl, well."

"Why? What's happened?"

"Something quite good. She met a Pṛthvīan granthapālaḥ."

She waits. After a few moments the scowl lifts again from the Crown Prince's face. He turns to her. "A real Pṛthvīan?"

"So she says, and our girl's no fool. Gets better—take a guess where he took her?"

"Impossible. You joke."

"I don't have a sense of humor."

"Straight to the Soul? Just like that?"

"Just like that."

The Crown Prince sits back. Darkness ripens about them. On the teeming building, lights, bright up close but feeble against the endlessness of the firmament.

"We must come up with a strategy."

"I already have." The Crown Princess reaches into her robes and produces a small red cube. "Remember this? From my last trip? Well, it can hold a whole Soul."

"Won't it need formatting?"

"A program as complex as the Soul would manage all that himself."

"We can't be certain."

"There's only one way to find out."

"How do we even signal to him? If we get close enough?"

"I'll put a downloader ping on it. If the Soul wants out, he'll copy himself."

The Prince's smile fades. "This is the Soul of Mangala. A war god, then. Soaked in blood and terror."

"Probably."

"And we'll bring it into our home."

The Crown Princess shrugs. "What harm can it actually do?" she says. "We will keep it in this unit, attach it to an un-networked speaker, and keep it to ourselves. Plus, we can always stick a failsafe in there—something to shut the bastard down if he gets uppity, well."

"By we, you mean you."

The Crown Princess smiles. "Yeah, I do." A brief silence. "We've caught a break, my love. I say we take it. Take our idle chatter and begin to make something of it."

"This will change the Nine Worlds," says the Crown Prince. "If the Ox finds out, he'll come after us."

"We have the protection of our sovereignty, and he has the balance of power on the rim to think of. His aunt won't let him upset us."

The Crown Prince smiles. "You speak like a queen."

"I suppose I may yet be one. If we pull it off."
The silver-gold dregs of sunlight leach from the horizon.
"If," says the Crown Prince.

1.23

I

KADRŪ'S DAYS SETTLE INTO SWEET repetitive doldrums she doesn't have the heart to complain about. Always she wakes up to the savory mustiness of her cell—her little kingdom, three steps from border to border, taller than it is wide. A thing could live and die in it and never even know the sun existed.

Just outside the thin door is the scuttle of the kitchen servants and the scrape of paddles on oven floors. The bread is half-baked when she wakes, just about edible but too raw to do anything but nibble. Sometimes she snatches a little bit as she weaves past the grumbling chefs. They call her a gremlin, a street rat, and an urchin, but they never try to stop her. She brushes her teeth in a small pitsink. Then she collects her broom and dustpan and heads out.

She has three places to clean on rotation, and it's her responsibility to get through all of them. Never once has she failed. The Courtyard of the Pots. The arcade next to the shrine with the ruby-eyed grass-snakes. The dead chambers high in the eastern tower. She likes these the most. They're never cold and quickly done. Sometimes she has a quick nap beneath the dazzling frescoes of antelopes and silk-birds just so she can pretend for a few moments when she wakes that she's a noblewoman about to face a day of exquisite boredom.

Then one day in early autumn Kadrū's halfway to the tower when bhaginī Shachi steps out in front with a whiff of venom. She must have been within, thinks Kadrū. This is a trap.

"You," she says. "Get a broom."

Kadrū holds the one she has up. "Will this one do, bhaginī?"

"Fine. Come."

She marches her to one of the nearby shrines. A golden, towering space dense with splendid depictions of snakes. Behind the fire pit is a giant idol of a cobra cloaked in incense smoke descending from ropes of smoldering stuff strung overhead like brown spines. Waiting by it are two other Sisters, the two Kadrū always sees with bhaginī Shachi. They turn when they arrive. They don't drop their veils either.

Bhaginī Shachi gestures to the sacrifice pit. The grate is lying to the side. "Clean it," she says.

"Clean what, bhaginī?"

"The pit. The Huntress wants it clean for the visit."

"I'm supposed to be cleaning the Tower of the Fang. No one told me—"

Shachi's dark face is mantis-sharp. "I'm telling you," she snaps.

"But that's where they drop the sacrifices."

"So?"

"There's snakes down there. I in't going down where there's snakes."

"This one isn't going down there, *bhaginī*," hisses bhaginī Shachi. "Are you telling me you're too scared? Manju drained a river in a day. Indraputri warmed Himenduḥ in a week."

"I in't Manju." She looks at her. "Besides, it was the other way around."

"Pardon?"

"Manju warmed Himenduḥ. Indraputri drained the river of death. Me ma told me the stories."

"Your ma knew the scriptures better than I do, did she?"

Kadrū peers at Shachi. She knows she's wrong, she thinks, but there's more to the cracked-glass rage on her face than that. Then she remembers their encounter in the tunnel the day Rati took her to see the snakes. She realizes what Shachi thinks she's taking from her.

She smiles.

"Looks like, bhaginī. Who told you to tell me to clean down there? I'll go back and check with aparāmātā Annapurna."

Shachi grabs her by the neck, and the two other Sisters grab her ankles with one hand and strike the back of her knees. Just like that, Kadrū's off her feet. She can smell the venom on their breath—sour, astringent, musky—a whiff of the promise of death. She opens her mouth to scream, but one of them strikes her, hard-fingered, in the throat.

"God, she stinks," says one of them.

"She's so weird-looking."

"Shut up," hisses bhaginī Shachi. "Hurry up."

They thrust Kadrū towards the hole. Twenty minutes ago this was a day like any other. Now, this. Imminent, horrible death. Surely, it can't have just sneaked up without warning. There must have been some sign last night, or the night before, or the night before that, of what was to come. Some hint of the westerlies coming to pierce the doldrums. Some far-off buildup of storm clouds. Kadrū wracks her brains but finds nothing but one explanation from long ago. That is the sort of death people like her get. People with insignificant lives die meaningless deaths.

They fling her down into the dark before she can gather her breath to scream.

She tumbles for two seconds—maybe ten, maybe an eternity—and crashes blind and breathless onto a stone floor. Her senses return in a drizzle. The place stinks of flesh, poison, and dust. She sees a desiccated tail, a bone fragment, a curved shard of eggshell. Overhead, the three Sisters are silhouetted like shards of eclipsing moon against the only source of light. They disappear for a few moments. Then the grate crashes down beside her with a massy thud.

"Oh, no," says bhaginī Shachi. "She must have fallen. Grate must have given way."

"Silly bitch," says another.

"That'll show her to go exploring when she should have been working."

"We should help her."

"Let's go fetch an aparāmātā."

They don't budge. They just stare at Kadrū as if expecting her to do something. Instead, she sits up and crosses her arms and sees the sisters deflate. A small victory. Probably her last one.

Then comes the snakes.

The first slithers up to her, thin and glossy-black and bullet-headed, a thread of tongue flicking beneath a pair of bulging eyes. It rears and appraises her as if seeing something it almost recognizes. Another follows and does the same thing. Pausing, rearing, inspecting. Then even more. Slithering out of the dark like the shadows had grown tentacles. This one coral-pink and striped yellow and black. That one bright blue, and that one's head covered in dainty spikes. They watch her. No sound, no movement. Just a thousand unflinching gazes each reinforcing in their own minute way that if the dark is the absence of light, then the snake is the absence of pity.

Kadrū thinks of brains leaking from her ears and her skin bubbling like lava. Still, she stifles her shivering. She won't let the sisters see. They stir and whisper overhead. They're looking at the snakes, and she realizes this isn't what they expected. This weird reptile jury of a hundred or so arrayed about her in a poisonous corona. Waiting.

Then, with a thrill, she realizes who they're waiting for. Her.

She approaches one, the smallest, the first, the blackest-looking, her throat tight from the sister's strike or from fear or the exact opposite of it. The snake watches with eyes like singularities. Now she's almost close enough for her fingertips to touch its head. Still, the snake doesn't move. She makes quaking contact and brings her finger down the back of its neck. It's warm and soft and delicate beneath the dwarfing spread of her hand. It tastes her quickly. Then, hesitant, it climbs her arm. Its tongue on her skin like the tip of some wetted feather. The soft scratch of its scales on her flesh.

She exhales.

The other snakes retreat into the darkness. There's just her and a pair of dimension-less eyes appraising her with all the judgement and approval of a creature that owes nothing to anyone and has nothing to give but death.

Snakes do not spare insignificant lives, she thinks.

She hears thudding and shouting. It takes her a few moments to realize something's happening up above. She sees the Sisters are gone. Instead, haloed by the light, is just one face, open-mouthed in astonishment.

Rati.

II

Entering the presence of a goddess, Kadrū learns, is much like entering the presence of any other potentate. There are rules which all seem pointless, but that's their very point. And so entering the presence of the Huntress demands that she kneel at the door and approach on all fours and then lie flat on her face with her hands outstretched without looking up or speaking. All this done, she realizes with disappointment that there's no magic in the air, no crackle of divine power. Just the dread that always comes with meeting the powerful, because for her, power has always been a thing to be endured.

The snake tightens around her neck. She can feel her heartbeat against its belly.

Before any of this, they dust her down and establish that she's all right. They take her in convoy up flight after flight of marble stairs all dressed in tumbling cascades of blood-red velvet carpet. At first, she thinks perhaps they're heading to some sort of punishment or inquiry, but soon she realizes that all of them—Shachi and Rati included—are more interested in the obsidian sliver of life resting on her collarbones like a necklace made of night. At the Huntress's shrine—its great gold doors sealed—they make her wait while a few of them step in. None of those who enter, she notices, kneel.

Shachi glances at her. "Don't say anything," she whispers. "Don't say anything, mongrel, or I'll have you when you're out."

Kadrū sneers. "Fuck you."

A long still moment, then the doors open again. After that, the ritual of entry. The air in the chamber is hot and humid, just like in the snake's grotto. Golden glints hint at some magnificence up ahead, but Kadrū doesn't have permission to look, yet. Retreating footfall and the grumble of the great doors closing. Then a voice, smaller than she expects: "Sit up."

The Huntress is sitting lotus-wise at the base of a statue of a rearing cobra. A soapy-black thing with blank, cruel eyes surveying the chamber as if deciding precisely what it will destroy first. The goddess herself is small-bodied, red-haired, and narrow-eyed. Her nose is bigger than Kadrū expects, her skin rougher, her hands gnarled. Even at this distance she can tell she's as tough as snakeskin and as unyielding as the acid grip of poison.

She blinks. "Who are you?" says the Huntress.

"This one ... this one is Kadrū, devi." Kadrū lowers her head again. "This one's sorry. This one din't mean—"

"Sorry for what?"

"For the trouble." The snake tightens around her neck. It doesn't like what she's saying. How does it know what she's saying? "I just wanted to sweep, devi."

"Sit up, girl. When I say sit up, I mean sit up."

Kadrū does. Now the Huntress is right in front of her. Somehow she's crossed the distance between them with the speed and secrecy of a neutrino. Drilling, yellow eyes fix on Kadrū as divine cogs spin inside her exalted cranium. "Who are you?" she mumbles.

"This one ... I'm Kadrū."

"Who was your mother?"

"She was a slave. In the house of a jeweler."

"A jeweler? In a palace?"

"No, devi. He had his own place. In the Tripura."

"And your father?"

"This one doesn't know, devi."

"Ah! There we have it." The Huntress smiles. "Because your mother never told you."

"Yes. That's right." Kadrū peers at her. Why does she look like that's what she expected? "This one never knew her father."

A long moment passes. Is this what it feels like to be mesmerized by a cobra, thinks Kadrū. This fizzing mix of fear and awe and gut-crushing despair. Still, the snake is warm around her neck. After a few moments the Huntress holds out her hand, and the little thing transfers to her ceramic-smooth skin. It lingers by her ear for a short while. The Huntress tilts her head as if listening and then looks back at Kadrū.

"You were victimized," she says. "By three of your Sisters."

"Yes, devi. I din't do nothing. I—this one—just—"

"You did not yield to them. You were defiant. You were strong."

"Yes." A compliment from the goddess, even if it sounds like nothing more than a fact. "This one was."

"You have an affinity for snakes, and they for you. It is in your bloodline. You were not meant for sweeping."

The Huntress seizes her left hand. Her hands are cold, hard, and dry. The hands of a statue. The hands of a corpse.

"There are a few truths to this universe, Kadrū of no father. I don't claim to be privy to all of them, but I have mastered one. And that is this: there is no such thing as death." The Huntress blinks again, but slowly this time, the reptile slide eyelids. "Death is a corollary of life, and life is just an emergent quality. All there truly is, is matter, acting in complex ways. I can draw you an image of a thousand snakes. I can hide in that image a thousand-and-first, seen only when you focus on it. But its existence does not change what it is—ink on paper. Its death is irrelevant. All death is irrelevant. What we do here—we Sisters of the Snake—is preside over phase shifts of matter. One state to another. So-called life to so-called death."

She takes the snake from her shoulder and holds it to Kadrū's left palm. Its jaws flare, and it bites the bulb of flesh below her thumb. Twin rubies of blood bulge on her skin. Slow fire starts to slither up her veins.

Kadrū screams.

"You will study how to play instruments," says the Huntress, "how to discuss politics and strategy, how to seduce men and women, how to come and go without being seen. You will learn the ways of the Sisters of the Snake that someday you will deploy these skills without question or doubt in the name of the Dawn."

"I'm—this one—what?"

"If you survive the poison, as no doubt you will, you will take vows and become one of us. You will become one of the best of us; in this matter also, I have no doubt. Today was a good day for you, Kadrū of no father. Today something recognized who you really were, though you don't know who you are yourself. Today you receive the reward for it." Her voice is as flat as a snake's belly. She puts the little black creature still clinging to her arm on the floor, and it slithers away without looking back. "Rejoice."

The fire is in Kadrū's chest now. She's drowning in air. She's burning in heatless fire. She sobs with pain and falls to her knees.

"What ... about ... Shachi?" she gasps. "They'll beat ... me."

The Huntress shrugs. The gods shrug. "None of them have long to live. They've annoyed the snakes. They tried to use them as weapons against one of their own. They have a few days left, and those, if they remain here, will be horrifying." The Huntress pauses. "How does that make you feel?"

The Snake Girl, who was once Kadrū, smiles. Though her heart rumbles like a star about to go nova and her face roils like a newborn star, she smiles.

The Huntress smiles back.

"Yes," she says. "You were always one of us."

1.24

I

IN HIS FIFTH YEAR INDRA receives the sash and bindi of a full granthapālaḥ. Henceforth, he has two days a week to spend as he pleases; a librarian must, after all, seek knowledge in order to organize it. Mostly, he spends these in the stacks, reading as a fish swims. Sometimes he climbs out onto the balcony-wide cornices far above the bubble and hiss of the Tripura and thinks. On his darkest days he thinks of his parents. Wherever in the ever-dim and spangled chaos they are. Do they remember him and the day they parted? How stupid were they to drag themselves, and him, out of Pṛthvī, only to be split up and mutilated in the far dim reaches of the Dawn's realm? He sees now that they were as frightened and lost as he was, and a few times this thought makes him weep. There is no greater betrayal of childhood than a parent who turns out to be merely human.

On better days he still thinks of Kadrū and the unexpected kindness of a bowl of rice. But his best days are when the Little Princess comes to visit him.

It's been a long time since he had a friend, and he can tell she's not one who makes those easily. Still, she too sees the world as one colossal library, and that alone brings them together. He takes her to collections of archaic space probes, to rooms full of glittering Pārāvata weaponry, to a small chamber where a storm of clattering Ruśama birdyantras flutter about on dazzling wings. They ramble through dusty archives having long conversations far beyond the comprehension of Sinivali. Decorum prevents the huge Agnian from accusing a granthapālaḥ of anything, but not from scowling and muttering until the Princess explains to her what they're talking about. And so the nurse learns, too, and to her credit, she's neither credulous nor overdoubtful in the manner of most fools.

One day they walk past a low, lacquered table covered in an epithelium of grey dust in the corner of an archive. On the side is an inscription in small golden letters :

From Daksha, in gratitude for the safe birth of his daughter, Danu.

The Little Princess peers at her own name. "I don't know that style of calligraphy," she says.

"It's from Matsya," says the Gelding. "A kingdom that disappeared three hundred years ago."

"Disappeared?"

"Conquered after rebelling against the Udāradādinaḥ."

"Ah. And what happened to the girl Danu?"

"I'm sure we could find out."

A pair of arched eyebrows. "Let's."

They spend hours putting the story of her namesake together from the scraps she left behind. A birth certificate. Two reports in gazetteers, noting she died ninety-three years later during a plague neither of them has heard of, a bitter little holocaust that claimed a million and then somehow wafted beyond the ken of human memory. A letter from her father to her uncle revealing she was a small child, nervous and reticent, and had a birthmark on her cheek. She had no head for business and contracted a bad marriage to a man who loved her but couldn't support her. Eventually, she left him, divorce registered at the same temple as a report for attempted murder when he rammed his motorpalanquin into hers during a festival. She soured with age. They find pictures of her as an older woman, harsh-faced. She marries again, a man younger than her, who complained constantly in letters to his friend, a priest, that he wasn't loved.

"I don't see why he's complaining," says the Princess. "She paid for everything."

"Evidence of her love," says the Gelding.

"Pardon?"

He smiles to himself. "It's something my mother told me. She said, there's no such thing as love. People can say they love someone or something, but really that doesn't matter. What you mean by love might not be what I mean by love. To me, love may mean beating you, because I think you don't know how to behave. That may be love to me, but it's no kind of love that's worth the name. It isn't what matters. What matters is evidence of love. The way you treat people, the way you speak to them and care for them, and whether you take the time to find out what they need."

"But there was evidence of love here. She paid for everything." The Little Princess squints at the sheet. "Cloth from Āēo. An iceblade from the Sisters of Himenduḥ. That must have cost a fortune to preserve."

"Yes, but it wasn't the kind of evidence he wanted. He wanted to be held. He wanted to be praised. He couldn't see the evidence for what it was."

"What if we find evidence of love from someone we'd rather not have it from? Of if there's no evidence of love where there should be? Or that type of evidence isn't clear? What if there's evidence of a kind of love you can tolerate but not return?"

The Gelding thinks of Kadrū. He thinks of her mother, who sold her. He thinks of the other slaves, crammed together in the market, hollow-eyed and broken. How significant their loves and losses and lives seem in detail, and how insignificant a simple shift of perspective makes them. What a curse it is that the simple fact of being who they are can deny a person what they want.

"I'm sorry, kumari. I'm afraid I don't have those answers. We'll find opinions all over the Mandīram, but answers? I think not." He looks at her. "There's much we humans don't know, and most of it's about ourselves."

The Princess looks down at the collected remnants of Danu of Matsya's life.

"Hm," she says. "I'm beginning to learn as much."

II

THE NIGHT IS HIGH-STRUNG AND griddle-hot. The Tripura desiccates in the rough lick of dry season winds. The Crown Princess and Crown Prince are sitting at a table in their laboratory staring at the objects in front of them like they were bombs they'd just failed to defuse. Between them is a small rack of cylindrical pots. In each is a cluster of green-yellow grasses. Atop each stalk—heavy, clustered, and glorious—are fistfuls of ripening grains.

The Crown Princess stirs first. "You've planted more?" she says.

"Several racks. No issues."

"Controls?"

"Four. The ones in the dark will not grow. The ones without the additive will not grow." The Crown Prince leans back against his chair. "This is not coincidence."

"Well." The Crown Princess's eyes go wide. "Fuck."

"We've testing to do," says the Prince. "I'll have to accumulate a team."

"A trustworthy one. Maybe it's best if you go back to Yama. You'll be better protected."

"We've discussed this."

"Yeah, but what if me and the old lady come with you?"

The Crown Prince glances at her. "How?"

"We'll figure out a way. I can stay in orbit, maybe. We could find some old derelict, and I could spruce it up all nice. With flushing toilets and everything."

She grins. The Crown Prince doesn't. "It'll be harder to put together a team out on Yama," he says.

"You won't need to. You'll have the Soul."

"Ah." The Prince sits back. "Yes. Then we may as well stay here."

"Not if you don't want to be caught."

"What if the Soul won't help?"

"He will. We're trying to beat the Dawn."

"But we aren't Pṛthvīans."

"Well, yes. Help. Not obey. He'll work with anyone as long's they're working against the Dawn."

"You know this for certain?"

The Crown Princess nods. "I read up on their programming. They've got contingencies built in."

"There is, I suppose, only one way to find out."

They sit in silence for a few minutes. Two dogs squabble in the hard glare of streetlights. A child tosses a bucket's worth of dishwater into a drain. In the distance the city breathes, one long rumbling exhalation.

The Crown Prince crosses his arms.

"I feel, sometimes," he says, "like perhaps we're the villains."

"The villains?"

"Yes." He chews his lower lip. "If we do this, there will be chaos across the Nine Worlds. There'll be war and famine. Will they blame us for it? We who together mined ancient technology and sided with a demon of the old world to undermine the Dawn's great gift to humanity?"

"What gift?"

"Peace."

The Crown Princess arches her eyebrows. "You're having doubts. Is it because it looks like we might actually get it done?"

He knows better than to evade. "Yes."

A moment passes. The Crown Princess reaches out and takes his hand.

"My love," she says, voice mantra-soft, "She's just another tyrant. No difference, well? She tells the people she gives them something, but in fact, she gives them nothing. Less than nothing. She hasn't ended war or poverty. People still sell each other, whole and in parts. She keeps us from the stars and tells us it's for our own good. Like we're naughty kids. We, who came from Pṛthvī and made the Nine Worlds what they are. Our ancestors changed their own bodies and created the hundred races! What has she done but take our labor for herself? So, we're children. Well, fine, I say. The sins of a child are things to learn from. The sins of a tyrant are things to resist."

"But we've learned nothing. That's what she says. We're not to be trusted."

They've played this game before. He knows her next move. Still, he wants to see it. He wants to remember why she's right.

"Haven't we? Is your life, or mine, like those of our ancestors? Did they live in places like this and see what we've seen? Would they have looked at an Agnian or an Āēoi with her symbiont and thought, yeah, those're human, too? We're a thousand years and a million yojanas from our ancestors. That can't be helped. But we're also a thousand years and a million yojanas from where we could be—and that we can help."

The Crown Prince is deep in thought and, the Crown Princess thinks, never more beautiful. The dogs settle their dispute. They walk down the road, shadows bouncing behind them.

"Very well," he says. And then, whispered: "So, how do we kill a goddess?"

1.25

STRĪGURUḤ SHEELU OF THE DNANASYA Mandīram slouches into the archive, diminutive and thick-furred, and drapes herself loudly over a chair.

"I hate people," she proclaims.

The Gelding is sitting at a desk within a small fortress of books. He looks up and waits for an explanation, but none comes. "Why?" he says, eventually.

"They all want to know about Enseeladas. This one old fellow told me —cheerily, mind you—that ninety-nine members of the Enseeladasi royal family had died over the years in the Tripura. Isn't it a shame, he said, that they only killed six yesterday? Seven, and it would have been a hundred! So I pointed out that the Udāradādinaḥ spared the last two on account of their being babies, and he just shook his head and said a baby viper's more viper than baby."

"I've heard that before."

"Where?"

"My cousin Vishwadevi." The Gelding looks pensive. "But I don't think she'd ever seen a viper. There were no vipers where we lived."

Sheelu snorts. "I told him the dead were from different dynasties and some of them were foreign rulers who'd conquered Enseeladas, so his figures were off. And in any case, speaking of death with such relish in the Temple of Knowledge was unclean because didn't he know the Dawn brought life and light, and life and light only? I told him he'd better go repent. The moron actually went to the Shrine of Good Fortune. He's down there right now, getting his raggedy arse whipped by Dharmaraja."

She idly reaches out for one of the Gelding's books. Too late, he realizes which one it is. She picks it up, examines the pictures, then looks at him with the same look of twinkling curiosity.

He looks away. "I'm having some problems."

"What kind of problems?"

"I ... it doesn't matter."

"Oh, come on. If it doesn't matter, you can share."

"I don't want to."

"Well, I'm terribly offended, and when you sleep, I'll fart on my fingers and place them delicately on your lips."

An unwilling smile, but the Gelding smiles. "I can't pee properly," he whispers. He takes the book. "It's a guide to gelding from Vrji. I thought it might provide some insight. I was wondering if there was some way to ... make a new one, maybe."

A few moments pass. The Gelding begins reshelving. Sheelu joins in, heaving the bigger texts onto her tiny shoulders and waddling off with them down the stacks. The Gelding loses track of her for a few moments, then turns around to find her standing a couple of feet away with her arms crossed.

He yelps.

"Indra?" she says.

"Mm?"

"How did it feel?"

"What?"

She makes a scissoring gesture.

He wanders back to the table. Gathering his thoughts is like dipping his hands into a bowlful of razors, but didn't the ancients use bloodletting as a treatment?

He sits down inside his diminished book fort.

"Mostly, how you'd imagine it feels," he says. "They did it quickly. There was less blood than I thought. I remember thinking how sharp that blade must be to part my flesh like ghee. And then, once it was off, I looked at it and thought, that was part of me. That little lump of flesh. You always imagine that there's you, this object, at the middle of the universe. The rest of reality begins where you end. But I realized I was just part of everything else. There was no division. The world could come in and claim pieces of me whenever it wanted and for whatever reason and there's nothing I can do about it. How much am I going to lose before I die? Will there be anything of me left? Who am I, even, if you're a thing that can be taken apart in pieces like that?" He pauses. "Maybe those thoughts came later, when I was recovering. I guess, right after, I was too miserable to really think of anything but what I'd lost."

Sheelu watches him, little eyes scrunched, little nostrils flaring and contracting with anemone rhythm. Presently, she nods. "I know what you mean."

"You do? How?"

She lifts her robes. At first, the Gelding averts his eyes, but then he realizes what she's showing him. He finds it up past her colorless underwear on her fat little belly, a slit, arcing slantways to her right. Her pouch. Empty, when there should be a little symbiont to help her metabolize Āēo's cruel atmosphere.

"Mine died when I was a few weeks old. I don't remember him. I think he would have been funny, you know? I feel like the things I say sometimes should have been the things he would have said." She looks up at him. "They sold me for meat to a recycler, but a Pranetri was visiting him and had never seen an Āēoi baby before. He bought me for the price of a meal and took me to a temple on Pranetr where no one had seen one before. It's primaeval. Do you know what that means?"

"Yes." The Gelding pauses. "No, not quite."

"It means it's a backwards shithole. The gravity's unmodified, and they all live in dank tunnels where the air's hot and wet. He set me up as a goddess in a little shrine. The morons there didn't know any better, and they worshipped me for ten years. Until they got suspicious that I was always getting sick and growing up to look an awful lot like a human girl. Then I had my first blood, and that was that. They turned on me like it was my fault. I ended up in a shipment of drones bought in bulk at the market here except no one wanted Āēoi parts. So they just chained me up with a bunch of cripples and mutes to be sold as feed."

She blinks, and tears bulge, glossy and clear, in her eyes. "But I got out. I ran away. Prabho Charioteer found me starving in a rubbish tip. He bought me and took me up to his room at the top of the stairs. Along the way, I heard the voices. I realized I thought I was incomplete—you know, like you said. Like part of me had been ripped away, and I wasn't sure what else would be. I was certain I'd never be whole again. Do you know what he told me?"

"What?"

"He said, life has its own friction, so we all lose part of ourselves along the way. Our urge is to look for what we think we lost. But that's foolish; it's gone. We can never have it back. Better instead to realize that losing part of yourself means you can replace it with something better."

The Gelding sighs. "I'm not sure I know how to become someone better."

"You can learn. We're in a library, right? Nowhere better!"

The Gelding looks down at the images in the anatomy book. He sees nothing recognizable in the dead-eyed stares of the naked slaves, lying flayed and butterflied upon ranks of iron tables. Objects notable not because of the manner by which they lived, but by the shape they've retained after death. They have nothing to teach him.

He closes the book and hands it to Sheelu. Then he takes a few more from his book fort wall and hands them to her, too.

"Thanks, Sheelu," he says.

The little woman takes them and shrugs.

"Truth is free," she says.

1.26

As the Wolf Twins come lancing down through the sky they see the Tripura sprawled beneath them like some great stone jellyfish. They aim for an old tower block in the tentacled hinterland of dead buildings that spreads from its luminant heart. A few instants later they pommel through the sagging floors and blow the entire lower half to pieces with the impact of their arrival. The building tumbles. For a long time there's nothing but a great grey-black cloud dawdling in the breeze. Only vermin witness their arrival, and they have few thoughts on the matter.

It takes them a day and a half to traverse the ruins. For most of that, they're alone with the dead. Eventually, they pass a lone sadhu squatting in an abandoned square boiling moss in an old coconut shell. He puts his hands together in greeting and shows no fear, even when they approach him with their snouts low and murder in their eyes. When they're done with him, they head on and come across a few shambolic hovels made of wood with flapping tarpaulin clinging to the stonework like fungus. They skirt these with full bellies low to the ground. Eventually, outposts give way to villages, and they find a dark corner to don their suits of man-flesh. After that, they proceed without hiding and find that, in a city full of strangeness, they're no more interesting than anyone else.

In central Tripura their noses crowd with the vivid smell of bird's feet frying in woks, flowers hanging in wet ropes, and billowing clouds of incense erupting from the entrances to temples. They catch sight of the sikhara of the Dnyānasya Mandīram rising over all this. Both agree that it's marvelous and encouraging to see such a perfect example of Triangulan creation at the heart of this great human city.

They work their way to the top of one of the nearby buildings.

Here they find an impoverished over-city of the marginal and the wretched who survive in the steaming warmth rising from the great city's bustle. Beggars sleep in boxes, and old men cook slivers of ratmeat over burning rubbish. All these seem too preoccupied with their own slow deaths to pay the Twins any attention. All except one old woman who stalks them at what she thinks is a safe distance, muttering to herself about demons and dogs.

The Twins settle on the edge of a rooftop facing the thunderous presence of the Dnyānasya Mandīram. They appraise the great moat and the four black bridges arcing over its dark waters. They time the opening of its great gates in the morning, the surge of worshippers, and the comings and goings of the gold-shod giants who stand sentinel by its doors. When they're certain they understand what must be done, they sit with their feet dangling over the roof-edge and eat.

"Tomorrow, then," they say in unison.

They stare up at the stars. Fewer in the glare of the city, but they're adept at finding their home. They lose themselves in memories of distant dawns and relax, chewing on the old woman's bones.

1.27

KADRŪ WAKES, FEELING LIKE SHE'D been melted in acid and re-congealed afterwards. Her stomach is a quivering fist, her tongue is a slug, and her head full of some churning gas heavier than metal. She stumbles like a drunk through her memories. Her mother's rough palm slipping away from hers at the Slaver's door. Indra's back warm against hers. The agonizing beauty of Rati's eyes, fading like the afterburn of lightning.

She sits up, if only to see if she can. She's on a bedroll softer than any she's ever slept on in a room she doesn't recognize. A single ancient lightbulb casts a sunset glow on a mural of the Dawn spanning all four walls. The Bright One holds a snake in one hand and a fire-lance in the other. Her white robes flow about Her like the surf of a cosmic sea. Kadrū remembers who she is now. She lies back down, happier than when she rose, but still feeling like a snake trapped in old, dead skin.

A while later the door opens, and bhaginī Rati steps in, holding a red basket. She smiles, more radiant than the goddess on the walls.

"How do you feel?" she says.

"Like crap," says the Snakegirl. She rubs her face with both hands and tries to sit up again.

"Don't." Rati pushes her back down, gentle, but unyielding. "Rest."

"I got bit. Huntress made that snake bite me." She blinks. "I thought it liked me."

"It did. She did. You were initiated." Bhaginī Rati pulls a stool out from under the bed and sits. "You survived the first round."

"First round?" The Snake Girl manages to rise. Every muscle is like an overstretched tendon. "There's more?"

Bhaginī Rati smiles and opens the basket. Inside is a rattlesnake, mottled death, white and brown and black. The markings on its back zoetrope a pattern, vivid and mesmerizing, obvious in its meaning. It examines her with eyes as sharp and glossy as black lightning.

The Snake Girl shrinks against the wall. "No."

"The beginning is the hardest." Rati picks the beast up, and it throws lazy caramel loops of itself over her arm. "These are the creatures that turn us into weapons."

"I in't a weapon. I'm just ..." The Snake Girl swallows. Her spit is bitter. "I'm just me."

"Yes, but who are you? Who are you, really? Are you a slave? Are you a servant?" Rati inspects her. "Do you deserve to remain a slave?"

"Not sure anyone deserves bein' a slave. I'm dying. That'll kill me."

"You have to die to be reborn."

"Yeah, but you have to die to die, too."

"True. I think."

"What if I say no?"

"You'll go back to the kitchens, I suppose." Bhaginī Rati's gaze drifts. "And we'll never be able to touch."

"What?"

"You know why we Sisters cover ourselves. We can only touch others like us. Anyone else will die." She drops her voice. "Complete the ritual, and I shan't have to wear gloves around you."

Her skin is tinted dawn-gold by the light. Her collarbones meet at her throat like snakes kissing. Maybe her eyes are a little too close together. Maybe her nose is a little too big. Strange how such imperfections only make her more perfect. Or perhaps, thinks the Snake Girl, it's something else. Perhaps there are no perfect things in the universe. Perhaps perfect is just another way of saying beloved.

She closes her eyes.

"All right," she says.

Rati smiles, serpentine, and holds up the rattlesnake.

1.28

I

THE CROWN PRINCE WAKES TO the dense hush of the Tripuran dawn. Quieter, this twilight, than any other he can recall. As if the city was holding its breath. Perhaps it knows what sort of day this will be. Perhaps it knows what the Prince is about to do.

He blinks the thoughts out of his head and slips his body out of the bed.

The Crown Princess remains sprawled on the bed behind him. She takes up most of it, and he lets her. He's been aboard her vimana. He's seen how small her cabin is. He watches her by the mingled light of the bloodless dawn and the streetlights. One day the parts of her body that are machine will turn creaky and old, and the parts that are human will turn wrinkled and frail. Still, she will be every inch as beautiful to him as she is now, as she was the day they first met, as she was the day he decided to turn his back on a family and a kingdom for the sake of her hand.

He has no regrets.

He goes onto the balcony and opens the box and takes out a pipe. In the labyrinthine streets around the square below, humble folk are already leaving home bundled against the cold. The ear-cleaners who will squat by the roadside. The recyclers who pry apart old electronics. The secreted masses upon whom the beast of the Tripura charts its sliding progress. He dribbles a little green powder in the bowl, ignites it, and takes a long puff. The weed's mute whisper soothes him like the avowal of a long-sought promise.

She comes out to join him, leans against the banister, and holds out her hand without a word. The whirr and click of her leg. The tweezer-point flick of her eyes over the vista. He passes her the pipe. She inhales deeper and longer and better than him.

"How does the terrorist feel?" she says.

"Tense," he says. "Is this what my ancestors felt on the eve of battle?"

"Something like, I'd reckon."

"And did perspective bother them so, too?"

"Perspective?"

The Prince gestures to the city with his chin. "What does anything we do matter in the end? All this will crumble. All of us will be dust. No one will remember what we did or why, and even if it did, it wouldn't make sense. How many revolutions have people forgotten about? How many battles, hard-fought and cruel, may as well have not happened?"

"Right in at the deep end, well?" The Crown Princess blinks. "I don't know about any of that. But maybe the point isn't to be remembered. Maybe the point isn't to do it at all. Besides, if it's so meaningless, why would we hate ourselves if we didn't do it?"

"There's that, I suppose."

"Still doubting?"

"No." A fleeting smile. "I think too much. Are you ready?"

The Crown Princess nods. "Everything's ready."

Somewhere in the house a door opens, and pattering feet fade off down a corridor.

"She's more excited than we are," says the Crown Prince.

"Strange old lady," says the Crown Princess.

II

THE LITTLE PRINCESS FIDGETS ALL the way to the Dnyānasya Mandīram, and her parents know better than to point this out to her.

"He is very large," she says. "He is easy to spot. His voice is very soft, but he speaks very beautifully."

Her parents glance at each other. Quick smiles, before she notices.

"You will introduce us?" says the Crown Princess.

"Of course, mother."

At the Temple she leaps out of the motorpalanquin and wends her way through the crowds faster than their guards can keep up to where the Gelding is standing with a group of other granthapālaḥs. He turns and smiles and then notices her parents and presses his palms together.

"Prabho Indra," says the Little Princess. "May I present my parents, the Crown Prince and Crown Princess of Yama, Lord and Lady of the Sixteen Estates, Castellans of the Buffalo Moon, and other titles besides."

"Your majesties," he says. "The Mandīram is honored by your presence."

The royal couple press their palms together.

"Indra of Pṛthvī has made a great impression on these ones' daughter," says the Prince. "And that one has told us that Indra of Pṛthvī would be able to grant these ones an audience with the Soul of Mangala."

"The Soul?" The Gelding looks at the Little Princess. She bows.

"I told them that I was rude to him," she says. "And that he showed me interesting images of animals."

"Ah, yes. I am sure the demon does not hold it as an insult. Forgive me, raja, but we have scholars booked for meetings with him for months in advance."

"Could prabho granthapālaḥ not make one more exception? These ones only wish to offer a pooja on behalf of the Serpentine House." The Prince glances at the Little Princess. "It is not wise to anger spirits of the old world."

The Gelding inspects the huge tray held by one of the guards behind them. An opulent, gilded thing piled high with a luscious load of mangoes, coconuts, and garuda-fruits frosted with flowers and chunks of amber frankincense. Like all such offerings, its glory is more for the sake of the giver. He's seen people present solid gold plates valuable enough to buy freedom for a hundred children. He's seen packets of pure sandalwood imported from Pṛthvī and worth more than asteroids burned to nothing in a few breaths. Still, suspicion blares like static in his head. Why is this notorious atheist here to placate an obscure demon? Why are they so worried that they're here at dawn to make this lavish obeisance?

He looks at the Little Princess. She nods. Always so grave. Always so serious. Perhaps if he was her father, he would do the same.

"We must be quick," he says. "I can take rajkumar and the rajkumaris down and back before the first scholar is due. We must be quick."

The Crown Prince glances at the Crown Princess. She fingers her glittering hip-belt and smiles.

"It should do," she says.

On the long, black descent the royal couple hold each other's hands and face the squeezing gloom together. Once they're past, their doubts sublimate into a staticky cumulus of tension that somehow, they sense, even the Gelding can feel. He glances at them once or twice as they walk; neither do anything so common or revealing as to react. Behind them, their guards are trying hard not to cry.

The Gelding halts at the door to the Soul's shrine.

"Only the rajkumar and rajkumaris may continue," he says.

The guard holding the pooja turns to the Crown Prince. The prince nods. He hands the tray to the Princess, and she has no problem carrying all of its considerable weight in just one hand. The other is still holding the Crown Prince's. The Gelding pulls open the door to the shrine, and they take a few steps across the hushed, darkened space to the fire-pit while the Soul's malign eye tracks them as an ambush predator tracks a quarry. He doesn't speak. He's waiting, thinks the Crown Prince. Like the city.

The Gelding examines them as they go through the ritual. The wink of the sacred fire on the Princess's metal leg. The hiss and thud of offerings as they're tossed into the fire. Strange how devotion to the gods consists in the act of reversing the actions of the scavengers who live in the hinterlands. Those find value in the worthless. These turn the valuable into waste.

The Soul tires of waiting.

"Yamans," he says. "And—well, well. You've compromised your racial purity, haven't you, Prince? What do your people have to say about that?"

"These ones have come to ask for forgiveness," says the Crown Prince, "and offer fruit and flowers and sweet-smelling things to the Soul of Mangala."

"Might as well chuck a fistful of shit at me. Do I look like I eat fruit or smell flowers?" A pause. "Forgiveness for what?"

"These ones' daughter, these ones are told, has spoken rudely to the Soul."

"Oh, yeah. She didn't like what I had to say about your little fiefdom. Whatever. Kid has spunk." The Soul examines the Princess. "Why're you really here?"

"These ones have a question," says the Crown Princess.

The Gelding steps forward. "Rajkumari, I'm terribly sorry, but we must go. The first scholars will be arriving soon."

"Don't be such a virgin," snaps the Soul. "When'm I ever going to meet royalty again? When're they ever going to meet someone like me? Let them ask their question. Boring nerds can wait."

The Crown Princess presses her palms together and bows to the Gelding. "We will be quick, sri granthapālaḥ. Prabho Soul, can a genie be placed back in its lamp?"

A long pause. The Gelding wonders if he heard the question right.

"Yes," says the Soul. "If the lamp is large enough. But why would he want to do that?"

The Crown Princess squeezes the Prince's hand. "Isn't a genie only truly free in his lamp?"

Another long silence. Then, a faint haptic judder from her hip. She exhales.

"Yeah," says the Soul. "Yeah, I guess so."

The royal couple touch the ground in front of the fire-pit with their foreheads.

"You are wise," says the Crown Princess.

"And forgiving," says the Crown Prince.

"Wise, maybe," says the Soul. "Forgiving, not so much. All right, get out, now."

They walk back to the Gelding with some of the fruit and flowers still on their pooja tray. The Crown Princess offers it up with a big smile.

"Would prabho granthapālaḥ like a fruit?" she says.

"No. Thank you, your majesty."

"Ah, no, prabho granthapālaḥ." Her smile widens. "It is these ones who owe you thanks."

III

THE SUNLIGHT COMES LOW AND cold from the east in the main hall. The shadows of the city and the people outside penetrate the chamber like black daggers. The Gelding leads the Yamans through a scattered crowd of early-morning visitors who part before them with gestures of polite deference or else, pointedly, without. Up ahead, the Udāradādinaḥ are changing guard in a ceremony that proceeds with the clang and precision of angry clockwork. Each of them swings their great blazing fire-lance, first overhead, then by their side, and then into the other's hands. One steps aside and another takes their place. A few seconds later, the two taken off duty stomp away. The crowd cheers and applauds.

The Little Princess turns to her parents.

"Is he not interesting?" she says. "The *Brāhmyakathāḥ* calls him quick of mind and sharp of tongue, but I thought—"

As she speaks, the Gelding notices something. Off to the left, through the doorway and behind the crowd, two elongated figures are clambering over the side of the moat. The Gelding catches a brief glimpse of their faces as they turn. Overlong, bone-white, feral. No kind of human he's ever seen before.

"Your majesties," he says. "Stay back."

The figures start shoving their way through the crowd towards the doors. A scream, more outraged than hurt. The Yaman guards close around the royals. The Udāradādinaḥ notice them, too, and move to intercept. One man refuses to get out of their way. One of the figures swats him away with one arm. The man spins through the wan dawn light, strangely silent, and cannonballs into the midst of the crowd. Chaos spins up like a turbine. The crowd heaves into a raucous stampede. The Maruts lower their spears, tips ignited, but it's too late. The Wolf Twins tackle them straight through the great black walls of the Dnyānasya Mandīram.

Masonry detonates like a meteor strike. The building groans, barely audible over the roar of panicking humans and the thunder of battling demigods. The Udāradādinaḥ swing their spears with stately brutality. Where they hit the stone, they gouge long, arcing grooves like someone attempting surgery on the great stone edifice itself. One of them discharges his fire-spear. A great pillar of incandescence sweeps across the hall and scores a long trench of melted stone, bone, and blood. The Twins leap over this and skip forth. As the Udāradādinaḥ recovers from the recoil, one of them kicks the giant in the head. He topples like an old monolith.

The Gelding ushers the Yamans in the opposite direction. As they turn, the other Udāradādinaḥ hits the wall upside-down in front of him. Who are these creatures manhandling the shakers of the earth and heavens? He ushers the Yamans in the other direction, but the guards veto him and direct them in yet another. Wherever they turn they're surrounded by battle. No valley is safe when the mountains are fighting. One of the Yaman guards is caught in a swing of a spear and obliterated. Another blocks a blow that would have hit the Prince and is bisected as reward. The top half of his body arcs away, crimson-tailed, eyes wide and mouth open, as if it was the last thing he expected.

The Marut up against the wall tries to rise, but one of the Twins mounts him and begins to tie him up with what looks like purple string she's spinning out of thin air. She looks up over their heads at her brother. Then, with a low-slung lupine headswing, she fixes her eyes on the Gelding.

"Do you see him?" says Amerxis. "The Pṛthvīan."

Auron nods. "She will have use of him."

The Udāradādinaḥ beneath her grunts and heaves, but Amerxis smacks him around the back of the head. A few yanks and the giant is fully trussed. She dismounts and approaches the Gelding. He watches her coming and turns to flee and then catches sight of someone at the far end of the hall. A familiar face watching him with an expression as aghast as the butchered Yaman guard's. She has two children with her. She doesn't look much older. Without a sound he begins to move towards her. The clamor of great footsteps approaching is very distant. The years since the rainy day at the Slaver's fade like offerings thrown into murky water.

The woman watches him coming towards her and scurries with her arms wrapped around the two children.

The Gelding snaps to a halt. A smile he didn't know he was smiling dies on his face. Amerxis reaches for him, string ready.

The Little Princess steps between them.

"Stop!" she shouts. "You will not touch my friend!"

The Wolf Twin peers down at the girl. Head cocked, golden-brown eyes sharp. Lips curling in what might be a smile.

"Fierce child," she breathes.

"Danu!"

The Crown Princess dives at the Little Princess, but Amerxis swings at her with the back of her hand. She flies away, broken surely, into a molten gash in the floor. Amerxis grabs the Gelding and starts to bind him. Then she notices he isn't resisting her, so she tosses him over her shoulder instead. Her skin and hair are cold. Midnight-cold. Starlight-cold. The Little Princess yanks her arm but is lifted bodily, too. She grabs onto Amerxis' leg and clamps herself like a tick.

"Let him go!"

Now more Udāradādinaḥ explode into the chamber. The Wolf Twins grab their prisoners and sprint out. The fleeing crowds have regathered in an arc far enough away to see what's happening but not so close that they're anything but a sea of undifferentiated faces. They scream as the Twins emerge and gasp as the Maruts follow. The Wolf Twins step close to each other and huddle their prisoners by their feet. Danu sees her father running at them, but he's soon overtaken by the charging Udāradādinaḥ. The leader raises her spear, and her siblings follow in a fire-tipped phalanx.

Before they can discharge, the Twins and their captives shoot up into the air, enveloped in a clear bubble, leaving only a sun-hot crater in their wake. The rumble of their departure is like the sound of distant war.

The Maruts bellow at the sky.

Then, a sound like a great exhalation. The ceiling of the venerable entrance-hall of the Temple of Knowledge, unsullied since before the Tripura itself existed, floor smoothed by generations of footsteps, shadows and crannies teeming with secrets that still linger through the weight of their lost significance, cracks. The roof tumbles with a roar. A choking puff of dust billows out across the crowd.

The gathered thousands watch, dumbstruck. As if they know this is only the first impossible thing they'll live to see. As if saving their breath for the worse that is surely to come.

BOOK II

SHAKERS OF THE EARTH AND HEAVENS

2.1

The Crown Prince of Yama limps through his house as if sneaking past death as it slept. He reaches the closed door to the Little Princess's room and opens it wide. The quick shriek of untended hinges. A heartbeat's silence. He resumes walking.

The doctor is waiting at the bottom of the staircase. A red-turbaned man with a face all the more glum for the laugh lines on it. He watches the prince approach with damp eyes and runs his fingers through his great brindled beard and kneels. He hands the Crown Prince a small black fob with two buttons on it.

"Blue is for pain, kumar," he says. "Red is for ..."

The Crown Prince takes the device and squeezes the doctor's hand. Somewhere close another door opens. Or perhaps closes.

"Kumar?"

"Yes?"

"The kumari ... kumari was always a queen to this one."

The Crown Prince blinks slowly and with effort. He touches the doctor on the shoulder, then treads on like a man walking to his own sacrifice. There are servants huddled and kneeling in the doorways. They avert their grief-stricken faces as he passes. A couple of them place garlands on the floor behind him. One faints.

"Is there no hope?" another whispers. "Is there no hope?"

None now. None ever again, the Crown Prince wants to say. But she isn't speaking to him. In any case, part of him, part of him that he hates, tells him it's not true. That the death he's about to preside over is a death like any other. That a thousand years from now no one will remember this moment or this story or this grief crushing his chest like anvils.

Sooner than he expected—sooner than he wanted—he arrives at the door to the Crown Princesses' chamber. He pauses, hand on the handle. He would be happy hanging there, an unobservant observer, forever. But the end he's avoiding will happen whether or not he initiates it. So he enters.

Inside, the mixed stink of stinging antiseptic and rot. Where the Crown Princess's furniture had been are now complex machines glittering with the quantified elements of a life barely enduring. Strung to these by bundles of wires, some thick and pulsing, some thin and opaque, is some human-shaped wreckage wheezing on a bed. Hairless, lipless, skinless. This incandescent ruin, beautiful in its persistence, unbearable in that it cannot exist for much longer.

He stands there and lets himself love it. Every flaking inch of skin, every black-tipped finger. Every scab like coral scales. Every flick of the still-vivid eyes.

The Crown Princess tries to smile. "You look ... constipated," she rasps.

The Crown Prince sits by her side, reaches for her hand, and pauses. The Crown Princess sees what he's seeing and reaches for the wires burrowing into her skin.

"No," he says.

"No point," she says. "Dead, anyway."

She plucks them out. She interlaces her fingers with his and squeezes. How can she even move her hand when there's so little of her left? Why is she trying to comfort him when it's she who's on the lip of death? They sit in silence, wondering what they should say. Something profound, surely. But some loss is beyond comprehension, and neither have anything much to say on the matter.

Eventually, they say "I love you" at the same time. Then they smile, also at the same time.

The Crown Princess looks out at the Tripura. The clouds high over the buildings like flocks of migrating souls. Surya's loveless light, strangely bright.

"You have it?" she says.

The Crown Prince tries to hand the fob to her, but she pushes it back to him.

"No," she says. "You."

"Never."

"Can. Done other things, harder."

"No."

"Must do it." She gags. "Or else. Suicide."

Another long silence.

"Find her," she says.

"I will."

"And the other one. Also yours."

The Crown Prince nods.

"Make Yama bloom. Free your people."

"Our people."

"All people." She cups his face. "Thank you."

"For what?"

"Making ... thinking a scavenger girl ... was good to be ... your queen."

The Crown Prince notices something glinting in the Crown Princess's other hand. She opens her fingers. Inside is the Little Princess's gold sheaf of wheat.

"Give it back to her," she says.

She moves his thumb over the red button. A moment passes, nowhere near long as it should be. Then she pushes. Her breath grows slow and dwindles, then stops altogether, as gently as a pool of water evaporating in the sunlight.

The Prince gets up and closes the door. The click of the lock is like the last tick of the last clock in the universe.

Only then does he begin to sob.

2.2

A GREAT STAR STREAKS WITHOUT warning or precedent through Mangala's hazy morning sky. With it comes the landslide rumble of divine engines. In fields herdsmen prostrate themselves on the dust. In towns merchants close their shutters and prepare for days of penance. On Meru's vast flanks, an old man on a cart squints up at the sky and giggles.

The Herald of Dawn has come to Mangala.

Within the sleek whitestone magnificence of the Vṛṣaprāsādaḥ, functionaries scurry like the photons jostling about in a box of mirrors. The blazing light of the Herald's nameless vimana bleaches the forest white and blasts an aura of spearing shadows as they rush to shave their heads, sanctify halls, and prepare victuals. Finally, the vehicle drones overhead as brilliant and cruel as the first instants of a nuclear explosion and lands between the domes of the palace's residential wing.

The Vicegerent is on a hunt when she sees the radiance come at an awkward angle and tint the landscape like an apocalypse. She marvels. How a thing as insubstantial as illumination can transform the world. How the presence of the unquestionably worthy fill the unworthy with dread. She retrieves her suit of man flesh, slips it back on, and rides a glider back palacewards. Inside, she finds shaven-headed staff and ministers gathered in a kneeling, restless crowd in a great hall. She kicks her way through them to where a white staircase ascends to a pair of wooden doors one floor up. The ceiling is hot overhead. The air ripples.

"How long has he been up there?" she asks.

"More than an hour," says one of the ministers. He shimmies forward, silken robes tight around his plump arse, naked scalp raw and oily from the morning's rushed shave.

"What have they been discussing?"

"These ones do not know." The man swallows. "There has been shouting, devi."

The Vicegerent waves him away. As she waits, servants strip her down, wipe the blood from her body, and dress her in the pure white worthy of the Dawn. She considers tiptoeing up the stairs to eavesdrop. Had there not been a thousand stinking humans fretting about her ankles, she perhaps would have. She considers sending them away, but instead she frets, too.

Presently, the doors at the top of the stairs creak open. The Ox slips in. Sunburnt already from exposure to the Herald and the vimana, and his skin wafting like a pot about to reach simmer. He descends scowling, and as his foot hits the last step, servants scurry forward with damp towels and new clothes to replace the scorched ones about his shoulders.

"It burned my damn garden," he mutters. "Bastard could have landed anywhere, but it landed right on top of it."

"Prabho," says the Vicegerent. "What happened?"

"What?" He looks up, as if surprised to see her there. "Ah. Yes. Auntie dearest isn't happy. We're to go to Daitya. There's been some sort of attack."

"An attack?"

He squints at her.

"That's what I said, isn't it? The Herald didn't burn my tongue out." He shrugs the servants off and starts ambling through the crowd. They part for him. He doesn't have to kick. "Two Wolves attacked the Temple of Knowledge. They wrecked the place. They seized two Maruts and killed some prince's wife. They took his child, too, for some reason, and a librarian."

"Wolves, prabho?"

"Ah, yes, Wolves, idiot." He leans in, stinking of char, angry enough to have burned his own flesh from the inside. "It's that damn vimana that you, um, failed to identify, I'll wager. You know the only people the Wolves of Triangulum will consent to work for. You know what it means if it were they who attacked the Tripura."

"The Night," breathes the Vicegerent.

"Precisely. It would mean my mother is here. It would mean that Night has fallen upon the Nine Worlds."

Muttering amidst the humans. Not a single one of them dare speak or raise their faces, but they will the instant the two of them leave. They are the dust, thinks the Vicegerent, and we are the wind. When we gust, they form storms. When we blow smooth, their agitations are swirling and harmless.

"We defeated her once, Prabho. We will do so again." She turns to the humans. "You heard your lord, you rats! Prepare the Vṛṣaprāsādaḥ for war!"

Her words are like fire in an anthill. She turns back to the Ox as the humans scatter with purpose. Surely, he's impressed. Surely, he has something to say. Instead, he just watches her for a long time with an expression beyond her ability to parse. Some light illuminates. Some light blinds.

"War." He sighs. "Yes. War."

2.3

THE LITTLE PRINCESS'S HEAD PULSES like someone had reached inside and was squeezing her brain. Her stomach clenches, and she vomits golden-green bile over the black marble in front of her. She's hungry. Perhaps she'll get Sinivali to make her some puris when she gets home. Certainly, the old maid will complain about the vomiting, but a little purging never hurt anyone. Doctors used to recommend it as a method of purification. She read about it at the Dnyānasya Mandīram.

The Mandīram. She was just there.

She examines her memory. Jumping in front of granthapālaḥ Indra. Being carried outside, clinging to the tall woman's leg. The woman with the catacomb-cold skin and the eyes like black holes. Then—an impossible journey. Rising skyward without propulsion or protection. The Tripura dwindling underfoot. First, a collection of buildings, then an ocean of copper-speckled grey, then finally a great neuron of light splayed across the border of night and day upon Daitya's shrinking flank. Magnificent Shani and her beautiful rings swoop into sight. The next instant her vast beige globe dwindles, too. Faster, faster, until she's just one silent glint amongst many, until for all intents and purposes, she ceases to exist.

The Princess realizes she can't remember what came next, but she's certain she'll never see Sinivali or the Tripura or her parents ever again, and that makes it very hard to breathe.

Still, panic is for the inflexible, and the Little Princess has no time for it. She stands and breathes deep. She tests her joints, skin puckered against the freezing air. No external injuries. She inspects her vomit. No blood, no fragments. No internal injuries either, as far as she can tell.

She's in some colossal space as big and hollow as the mind of a dead god. The far walls and ceiling are lost in tarry gloom. As her eyes adjust, she notices giant friezes on the nearer walls and scrutinizes these, but they're scenes she can't place: a city obliterated by a beam of light; a woman burning a man's face with her blazing hands; a girl diving into a lake beneath a nebula. To the left, rectangular ponds as regular and unadorned as cooling pools with not a fuel rod in sight. Between them is a black ramp leading up to a giant archway flanked by two huge braziers, ten times her size, each brimming with unflickering fire.

A giant temple, then. But what sort of god demands worship in the dark?

She ascends the ramp. The stone is more ancient by magnitudes than anything she's seen or touched before, but at least the fires are warm up close. She lingers in their soothing light and peers through the arch that they flank. Beyond is another huge chamber that terminates in a distant transparency through which the universe shines unhindered and triumphant. More stars than she's ever seen, and in greater detail, too. The longer she looks the more she sees, as if whatever substance lay between her and the view was penetrating the teeming dust-clouds in mute response to her gaze. Nebulae spread and sparkle. Galaxies wheel, fizzing with stars. Nameless probes trundle through the emptiness, eroded by tides of entropy, machined surfaces pocked by a yuga's worth of micro-impacts. And her, a speck of thinking flesh blasted into silence by the calamitous vastness of it all. She feels turned inside by the scale of it. She read somewhere that the very last thing sentience can afford is a sense of perspective. She understands what that means now.

A wonderful thought, but this is not the time for such things, so she heads back down the ramp. Presently, she hears breathing and follows the sound to a small entranceway in the hall with the pools. Beyond is a room doused in some eerie blue light from glimmering strings populating the ceiling like electrified stalactites.

Slumped against the far wall is the Gelding.

"Prabho Indra!" She trots over. "Are you well?"

He doesn't respond.

"Prabho Indra?"

He looks at her. His eyes unfocused, his mouth slack, and his hands limp in his lap. For a few moments he looks as if he might say something, but no words come.

"What's wrong?" says the Little Princess.

The Gelding buries his face in his hands and starts to sob.

2.4

For the Snakegirl it's just another day of mockery. In class no one takes her as a partner. In training she's chosen last and lumped with the worst. There's nothing she can do about it. Perhaps, if the situation were reversed, she thinks, she'd treat someone like her this way, too. Someone new and strange and inducted without warning into ranks already thought closed. Someone responsible for the death of the one whose place she has taken. No matter that the dead woman had tried to kill her. No matter she was a well-known bitch. She was a Sister of the Snake, and affinity dilutes judgement.

Then at lunch she's sitting alone and reading when aparāmātā Isha gently takes her book away, and says, "Civilized folk do one thing at a time. You will have to learn to pretend to be one."

Rage consumes her like her blood was fuel and someone had set a match to her skin. She sets up her punching bag and draws a face representing no one in particular and everyone it needs to represent. She pommels it, fists and elbows and knees flying, insteps slung with bonecracking precision. She imagines the heart-stopping grip of her venom in her enemies' chests. She imagines noses smashing, eyes melting, and hair yanked off by the fistful. When she finishes, she lies shaking on the floor with the still-unfamiliar tang of her sweat in the air and the remnant heat of the violence radiating from her red-skinned knuckles.

Then, a knock.

"What?"

"It's me. Rati."

She leaps to her feet and towels herself down. Her skin continues to ooze, but there's nothing to be done about that. She opens the door. Of course, the woman standing there is flawless. She's changed her nose ring. Her hair's longer.

"Come to set more snakes on me?" says the Snakegirl.

Rati peers at her. A beautiful gaze, but one that concedes nothing. Apt for a snakegirl of Himenduh. "I heard what aparāmātā Isha said."

The Snakegirl presses the balls of her thumbs to her eyes. Rati steps in, closes the door behind her, and gestures to her bed. "May I?"

The Snakegirl's eyes widen. "What?"

"May I sit?"

"Oh. Aye."

"Sit with me."

She complies, eyes averted.

"I didn't always sound like this," says Rati. "None of us did. We're from all over. We can't even all understand each other when we arrive. But we arrive young, and we change quickly. You'll have to learn to speak and behave in different ways to fit in wherever you're sent. That's what aparāmātā Isha meant." She places her fingers on the Snakegirl's chin and turns her face towards her. "Repeat after me. Sri."

"Sri."

"No. *Sri*. You're saying Shri, but it's softer than that. Just a hint of *sh*. Between *sh* and *s*."

"Sri."

"That's it!" She smiles. "Now, Himenduḥ."

"Himendoo."

"Not Himendoo. Himenduḥ. It's sort of like er."

"Himender."

"Shorter."

"Himenduḥ."

Rati takes her hands back. "Good. Now stop scratching your *h*. It's not a rasping sound, it's a simple *h*. Do you feel that vibration? That's what you're doing wrong. Now, feel this."

She takes the Snakegirl's hand and puts it on her throat. Her skin smooth beneath her gauzy robe. Her body so close. The marvelous totality of her from her hair like spun obsidian to her toes hidden in their little purple shoes. The flame of her animation, miraculous and mystic and irresistible. Never has the Snakegirl wanted to know anything the way she wants to know her. So well that there'd be nothing left of herself but her knowledge of Rati.

"Feel this," says bhaginī Rati. "Himenduḥ, see? Nothing."

The Snakegirl swallows. "Um, aye. Aye, sure."

"Try it."

"Himenduḥ."

Rati smiles. "There. You have it! I'll help you. Let's meet to practice, shall we? We'll have you going in no time."

The Snakegirl nods. Rati takes her hand in her own and moves it away, smiling. Then she leaves. No farewell. No glance back. Just a disappearance as unheralded and abrupt as her arrival. She must intend it that way, thinks the Snakegirl. She must calibrate every inflection of her behavior, or else how can all of it have such an effect on her?

The Snakegirl watches the door close and flops down on her bed. She will change how she talks. She will become someone else. Then—a strange thought. If she becomes someone else, would Indra know who she was? Would her mother? Becoming a new person means killing the old. What then does one say to the people who loved the victim?

She thinks of Rati's fingers on her throat. She reminds herself that the people she's thinking of are ghosts. She will never see them again. In the outer dark a comet is quiescent, but close to its star it will burn a glittering tail. Why should she not burn differently, too, so close to something so bright?

2.5

THE WOLF TWINS BRING THE Marut to the Night naked and unarmed, heaving against the pale cage of his captor's arms. He ceases struggling as soon as he sees her on her throne. As if the pale magic of her presence leached him of the will to fight. As if the sight of her alone made the idea of resistance absurd. The Twins release him. He kneels in a landslide of dense flesh and armor and presses his forehead to the floor.

The Night watches him for a while before speaking.

"Sit up."

The Marut complies. Kneeling, he's almost as tall as the Twins. They examine him in the star-speckled gloom as if searching for something to be impressed by.

"Do you know why," says the Night, "when we began erasing the history of the humans, we went to the most ancient of their texts to rebuild their culture? Do you know why, in accordance with those writings, we presented ourselves as gods returned?"

"No, devi," whispers the Marut.

"Because in those tales every action has a purpose. The ancient texts are the teachers. The gods' behavior is the lesson. It enabled us to teach not only by what we said, but by what we did. Our behavior—our benevolence, our might—was to be the lesson." She purses her lips. "Now tell me, little one. What do you think the humans stand to learn from the behavior of you and your siblings?"

The Marut squeezes his eyes shut. Fat tears drip and shatter and bleed their brief warmth upon the frigid floor. "Your sister, devi—"

"Is persuasive and beautiful. But the Dawn is a passing thing." She gestures to the magnificent wall of star-speckled black behind her and plucks her mortar and pestle and some soma out of her sari. "Have you forgotten that I am the multiply-shining one?"

"This one will not betray his brothers and sisters."

"Yet, betrayal is why we are at this juncture." The Night drops some soma into her mortar and pestle and begins to grind. The scrape of stone on stone like mausoleum doors opening. "I intended to ask you questions, but most of them have already been answered by my Wolves. I know my son now resides on Mangala, and you Maruts—or should I say, Udāradādinaḥ—no longer serve him. I know my sister rules through his Red Fleet and that she keeps the Golden Swarm tethered in orbit of Pṛthvī when they should be free to play in the cosmic tides. I know that you and yours now serve Rathasārathī, that belching eccentric, on Daitya, and protect this—Temple of Knowledge?—where the Twins took you. And lastly, I know that the Huntress is now on Himenduḥ and has a temple also and an army of poisonous women who kill and terrorize in my sister's name. I have heard these stories and would have thought them madness had the Twins not seen it with their own eyes." She smiles, teeth like a crescent moon in the blackness of her face. "You and I both know Wolves have no imagination."

The Marut glances at the Twins.

"It's true," they say, expressionless.

The Night comes down the stairs with crystal haloes of ice blooming where her feet land. The liquid in her mortar is sweet-smelling and thick and smokes heatlessly in the dimness. She offers it to the Marut, and as she expects, he drinks his first taste of home in millennia with the urgent hunger of a newborn at a teat.

"These temples," says the Night. "Are they what I think they are?"

The Marut nods. "Yes, devi."

"Could they be woken?"

"This one doesn't know."

"And what about the boy?"

"What boy?"

"The Pṛthvīan boy the Wolves found at Rathasārathī's library." A pause. "The boy named Indra."

"What of him, devi?"

"How long has he been there?"

In his confusion the Marut's fat-featured face is childlike, absurd. "This one doesn't know."

"Where did he come from?"

"This one doesn't know. He just sort of ... appeared one day. As if from nowhere."

The Night nods, as if vindicated. "From nowhere. Yes, that is usually where he comes from." Another pause. "Do you miss it? Our home?"

"This one does. But ... this one will not go home, will it?"

"No. You will be fed to this juggernaut when the time comes. I grant no passage to those who betray me."

The Marut flinches. Scant acknowledgement of the horror that will be his end but more than a Marut would ever willingly concede. The Night derives no joy from this, but the Twins do. They lick their lips. They smile.

"Is this *Bheki*?" asks the Marut.

"No. Bheki is here in the Nine Worlds. This is Skōlex."

The Marut's eyes widen. "The Bright One's Skōlex?"

"There is only one Skōlex. Is that what my sister is called now? The Bright One?"

"This one rode in Skōlex once, in a battle against the Asuras—"

The Night holds up her hand, palm out. "I've no interest in who you were."

"Then know that I have no interest in what you want," growls the Marut. "You are a false queen come to usurp your sister, and you will not succeed. The darkness cannot stand or stand up to the light."

"Now there is the fierceness I expect of a Marut." The Night returns to her throne, turns, and sits. Her space-black face as haughty as the spread of the cosmos behind her. "But you've forgotten who I am. Darkness was there first, by darkness hidden. I am no mere queen. There is no realm that can hold me, and so I am not here to usurp. I am the end, little one, and all true endings last forever."

The Marut opens his mouth as if to say something. Instead, he crumples. His body shakes with endless, wracking, exhausting grief. The sort of grief that a creature feels only once in their life. The sort of grief that comes only with the certainty of death.

"There is freedom, isn't there, in accepting the inevitability of your own defeat?" says the Night. "I am glad you see what will happen next. Now let me tell you how you can help me."

2.6

I

AKUPĀRA COMES TO AN UNEXPECTED halt before he's scheduled to, and the humans on the bridge—afraid of her but too well trained to show it—inform the Vicegerent that the order came directly from the Ox. She finds him lying flat on his back on the floor in his quarters. Limbs splayed, skin pale in the dead light coming off Shani through the transparent ceiling. How small the Ox looks in the twilight, she thinks. How diminished and adrift. For that is what he is. A child of Night who turned his back on the nurturing dark. A temperamental shadow who hides nothing about himself but what matters. She approaches as close as she dares without his permission, but he doesn't say a word. His breathing is deep and steady. No smell of intoxicants on his breath, no sign that this is the aftermath of one of his rages.

Then she looks up and sees what he's seeing.

Directly overhead is some strange creature floating against the starfield. Some half organic concoction of anemone tentacles and gently flailing membranes tumbling in the silence. A living flesh-flower of the vacuum unsuited for life anywhere as barbaric as a gravity well or an atmosphere. Ten times as big as Akupāra, surely, but more delicate than the vimana by magnitudes. As she watches, it extends one limb towards the window and splays the tip into a small dish.

"Prabho," she says. "What is that thing?"

"A machine beast of the old world." The Ox smiles. "The very old world. The human world before we came. Fascinating, isn't it?"

"What is its purpose? Is it a spy?"

"No. These things have no purpose."

"But—what was it made for?"

Akupāra rumbles. The Ox knows the old boy will be swinging his turtle head towards his new companion. He'll be wondering what this strange celestial jellyfish is. He'll be pondering if he can get away with eating it.

"It has no, um, purpose. Humans in the past made creatures like this just to see if they could exist out here. Riding the solar winds, sustained by Surya's wild breath. In all my years I've never had the privilege of seeing one. But now, at this moment, in this place." His voice drifts. His pupils expand to fill his eyes. "What a coincidence."

A long moment passes. They drift into Daitya's lightside.

"What a waste of time," says the Vicegerent. "Making something that big with no function."

On impulse the Vicegerent comes up beside him, kneels, and lies down. The floor is cool against the back of her head. The view is much better from there. The creature directly overhead now, agitated in the elegant flail unique to things that float. As if it knew it was being watched by an extra pair of eyes. As if it did not like the attention.

She turns her head to look at the Ox and finds him staring straight at her.

"Nothing is a waste that brings such wonder," he hisses. "Get back to your damn feet."

She clambers up. The Ox keeps staring at her until she takes a step back. As he does, the creature in the windows dilates a siphon on its side. A spasm and a push and it's gone, dwindling against the beige bulge of Shani.

"Fantastic." The Ox sighs and gets to his feet. "What did you want?"

"The bridge was wondering why you stopped Akupāra." The Vicegerent keeps her eyes on the floor but sees the Ox's reflection in its polished depths is staring at hers, so she looks at her feet instead. "But there are also two other matters. First, the Charioteer has humbly requested that you stay at the Temple of the Ox and not in the Temple of Knowledge—"

"Why?" The Ox shakes his head. "Never mind, I know why. He's afraid I'll go digging around for the Soul of Mangala. He thinks I'll try to have at my enemy under his roof."

"Will you not, prabho?"

"Most probably. Fine. I, um, prefer my own temple in any case. You said you had two matters."

"The other would be the disposition of the Red Fleet, prabho. We should bring it out of port. We should send it in search of the Night."

The Ox stares at Daitya. They've drifted around to its lightside. The city lights are gone now. In their place is the manic profusion of a living world's topography. Mountains like wrinkled skin and rivers like blue arteries. Wafting clouds as insubstantial and quick-passing as thoughts at the threshold of sleep. The light reveals. There is much more room for yourself in the dark.

"Do you know what the Herald of Dawn said to me?" asks the Ox.

"You've not spoken to me of the meeting, prabho."

"It said all existence is analogized in a nuclear reaction. Each event, the splitting of an atom. All the consequences, neutrons flying out from it. Who knows where they will go? Who knows what other energies they will release?" He glances at the Vicegerent. "Do you concur? Do you believe lives are truly like that?"

The Vicegerent shrugs. "I think that's one way of looking at it, prabho."

"Well, it's the wrong way. Neutrons have no will. We do. Limited by our place and our time and our circumstances, but wills nonetheless." He speaks as if talking to some conspirator hiding in an orthogonal dimension in the very same room. "I imagine that's what he meant by accepting who we are. Know who you are and you know what you can do."

"The Herald of Dawn said that?"

"No. No, someone else did. It doesn't matter." He stares at the empty spot where the visitor had been a few moments before. "Leave the Red Fleet in port for now. No point sending them scattered out through the system when we don't even know where my mother is. If she slips past us it will be altogether more of a bother. I shall go down to Daitya and see if I can't find a lead. Then we will re-evaluate."

"I would not counsel that, prabho. We should at least send the fleet to shadow Pṛthvī's orbit. They—"

"I did not request your counsel."

The Vicegerent hesitates. Some vague sense that she's just been told a great lie presses on her like the ghostweight of a whole orthogonal universe. But her orders are sensible, if misguided, and the Ox's face no more inscrutable than before.

"As you wish, prabho," she says.

The Ox waits for the doors to swish closed behind her. A life sent careening off to unleash a cascade of his own design. How long before it's seen for what it really is? How long before he can admit the truth of what he's just initiated? He lies down on the floor again. He'll find out soon enough. Until then, there's still the darkness and the light and their endless entanglement across the fabric of all existence.

II

THE COURTYARD OF THE CROWN Prince's house—fringed with jasmine trees, the pond at its heart patrolled by lotuses—was always neutral ground. On one side was his world of protocol and tradition. On the other, the Crown Princess's, a wild march of artefacts and pirates and derelicts drifting inviolate in the star-dwarfing black. Here he'd introduced her to the delicacies of his people—slivers of pickled fish, oranges the size of marbles, eaten whole with their soft almondy skin. Here she'd told him how she lost her leg to a bear-golem on Shukra. Here they'd first held hands and first touched lips and first realized neither kingdom nor fortune nor the lure of immortality would ever tempt them to part.

He can think of no better place to burn her corpse.

The prospect of participating in the whole farce of a funeral is like worms in the Crown Prince's bones; he has his servants tell the priests that he's too grief-stricken to do anything but sit on a balcony and watch. Their chief is a skinny man with a disproportionately round belly who doesn't bother to hide his disapproval.

"This is not the done thing," he says, loud enough to be heard above. "Does the Crown Prince not want to set the Princess's soul on its way to the Dawn? Doesn't he want to commend it to a bright new life?"

Superstition is like sitting in a lion's mouth and taking comfort from the warmth of its tongue. The Crown Prince wants to shove the fool up against a wall. What new life? What soul? And were such things to exist, what business would they be of the Dawn's? Still he hasn't the energy to fight and leaves it up to his servants to form a palisade around him. It works.

In the end the priests go ahead with the rituals. The hollow intensity of their farewell to a soul they never knew—the clanging of cymbals and the prayers incanted by rote—repels him further. Worse is the sermon that follows. The chief priest speaks of virtue, of wifeliness, of sacrifice and tragedy. Of how, in the end, life is suffering, and the only true escape is to join the Dawn in bliss. No mention of the way the Crown Princess's eyes narrowed when curiosity had her in its vice. No memory of the soft clank of her foot down the hall on a rainy day more welcome than a thousand hours of sunshine. The chief priest's story that could have been of anyone.

Then he gets her name wrong.

The Crown Prince snaps to his feet and comes down the stairs trailed by servants nearly as enraged as him. He snatches a little clay lamp from the devotional racks and ascends the pyre to where the Crown Princess's body lies draped in a silver cloth. The waxy face evokes no grief. This is not the thing he loved. This is only part of her. He has already bid farewell to what really mattered.

The chief priest sees none of that and steps forth, spluttering.

"Kumar," he says. "The ceremony isn't complete."

"Do you know what the kings of my homeworld used to do when their wives died?" says the Crown Prince.

"I—well. I'm not versed in heterodox ritual."

"They threw the symbols of their life together into the pyre. The bed they shared, when she allowed it. The dowry-cloth he wrapped around her feet on their wedding day. The animals she gifted him." His voice drops. "Then, when the flames were at their highest, he threw himself in. To burn and turn to ashes with his lady liege. For what is a king without a queen but a sky without a sun?"

"My understanding is that your wife was not a Yaman queen. We do not observe such ... traditions ... here on Daitya."

"She was a queen, you wretch. And you don't even know her name." The Crown Prince drops the lamp onto the Crown Princess's corpse. It ignites. "Get out of my house before I burn the lot of you."

The priests hesitate. The Crown Prince watches them with the fire rising behind him. Some demonic silhouette bereft of anything human but the outlines of its shape. The flame's bloodlight on the eyeless arcade arches overhead. The slow swell of by-drifting Shani, as swollen and pale as death.

They don't resist when the servants start ushering them out.

2.1

THE LITTLE PRINCESS WAKES IN the dreary cold. For a few sleep-drunk moments, she forgets she'd ever been anywhere else. She sits up and sees the Gelding curled up against the wall beside her like a giant fetus. Over his steady breathing comes the sound of footsteps, and two towering figures appear by the entrance to the Blue Room. She recognizes them immediately and springs to her feet.

"Stay back!" she yells.

The Twins approach, a weird lightless binary holding dark grey bowls filled with some sort of white paste. They tilt their heads like a pair of curious puppies.

"You cannot force us to comply," they say. "You know this."

Their voices synchronize perfectly. An effect as eerie as the pervasive oversilence and the vast dimensions of the chamber outside. As odd even as the glimmering lights on the ceiling that freeze when the Little Princess looks, but move if she stays still long enough. Still, intimidation is for the undignified. The Little Princess crosses her arms and stays put.

"Who are you?" she says. "What is this place? What do you want with us? If we're prisoners, then I demand you treat us according to the customs of war."

The Twins hold out their bowls. "The Night sends you sustenance. She has rendered Soma edible to you."

"Who?"

"You do not know who the Night is?" They look at each other and grin. Baffled. Amused.

"The night isn't a person, it's a time of day." The Princess snatches the bowls away. "It's rude to mock someone for not knowing something."

"Such a fierce pup," says one.

"Are they all this brave?" says the other.

"I doubt it."

"Who are you?" says the Little Princess.

"We are Wolves," they say. "Amerxis and Auron."

"Well, Amerxis and Auron." The bowls are heavy. The Little Princess puts them down. "If you're not going to answer my questions, you may leave. I would eat, and I shan't do it with you two staring at me."

The Wolf Twins flash their teeth at her, shining enamel like brief lightning in the gloom. Then they slip away.

The Little Princess dips her finger in one of the bowls and licks the white gunk that clings to it. It's sweet and pleasant. She wakes the Gelding, and he sits up, hands limp in his lap, staring off into the distance. The Little Princess makes a dripping ball of the paste with her hands and lifts it to his mouth. After a few moments his lips part, she pops the ball in, and he begins to chew.

After a few mouthfuls, he speaks. "I saw my mother."

The Little Princess looks up at him. "Prabho Indra! You're speaking!"

"I saw my mother."

"Where? Here?"

"In the Dnyānasya Mandīram. During the attack."

"I see. Was she injured?"

"She said she'd never leave me." He blinks. "When we left Pṛthvī, she said she'd always be by my side. I saw her in the hall when those two attacked. She was with some other family. Wearing a veil, holding hands with ..." Glimmering trails leak down his cheeks. "With two other children. She saw me, too. She looked me right in the eyes."

"I suppose it's good to know she's safe."

"When the attack began and those beasts were coming for me—she turned and rushed those two children out and didn't even look back. She just left me there. She saw me, and she just left me there."

She watches him, uncertain what to do but certain she must do something. Eventually, she reaches out as if to touch a flame and pats him on the knee. Once.

"Perhaps she didn't recognize you. It was chaotic."

"Where was the evidence of her love?"

"I suppose she had no choice, prabho Indra. What could she have done against these monsters? Maybe sometimes it's too much to expect. Sometimes, maybe, we just have to believe someone loves us, even if they aren't able to show it."

"What good's that kind of love? What use is it to anyone?"

"I don't know. But that doesn't mean it doesn't exist."

He takes her hand and holds it to his face. Though it grows wet with tears, she doesn't take it away. Somehow his misery gives her permission to mourn, too, and she thinks of her parents and Sinivali and reading by the pool in their courtyard as wan daylight winks into night. Sorrow floods from one to the other like plasma between binary stars.

After a short while crying, they return to their food and gobble down what's left. When they're done they head out to the pools in the giant chamber outside and wash their hands in the black water. Halfway through, the Gelding looks up and around, and his mouth pops open. He turns to the Little Princess.

"Those're Triangulan friezes," he says. "They have the same friezes in the Antechamber of Night. Are we—where are we?"

"What's the Antechamber of Night?"

He looks up the ramp at the braziers in the distance and the great black archway.

"Is there a throne room beyond that?"

"There's a chamber." The Little Princess squints. "I may have seen a throne in the distance, but it's very large."

The Gelding starts to shake.

"We're aboard a juggernaut," he mumbles. "We're on Skōlex!"

"You're overcome. Sit. Explain."

"These friezes. This room. I read about it at the Temple. There's only one place like this—the Antechamber of Night. Through there is the Throne Room. This is Skōlex, the juggernaut of Night!"

"Of Night?" The Little Princess's eyes widen. "You mean Ratri? The goddess?"

"Yes! Yes!"

"That's who sent us food?" The Little Princess looks around, conspiratorial. "You're certain?"

"In the library. There were ... texts." He looks up and runs his hands through his hair. "She's back. The Night's back!"

"I suppose that's rather exciting, isn't it?" says the Little Princess.

The Gelding turns to her. "Exciting? She's the destroyer. She's the end of all things." He peers at the friezes around him. "She swore when she returned she'd destroy the Dawn and all Nine Worlds of Surya."

"All Nine Worlds?"

"Yes."

"Even Yama?"

"Yes. Yes, of course."

The Little Princess looks at the friezes. The burning cities and the falling women. Not depictions of things long past, then, but things that may yet happen.

"Hm," she says, and crosses her arms. "Well, that won't do at all."

2.8

I

THE SNAKEGIRL LEARNS TO CHOOSE when and where to extract her revenge. To wit, one practice session she hunts down a Sister who'd asked her if her mother had fucked a fish for her to have eyes so big. She smashes the girl face-first into the wall, breaks three of her teeth, and then does the same to one of her friends who comes to the rescue. The Huntress is told and summons all of them to her shrine.

"Respect," she tells them, as they lie face-down and penitent upon the floor, "is just a civilized form of fear."

After that, for the first time since she arrived at the Bhujañgānām Mandīram—for the first time in her life—others avoid her not from disgust, but from fear. This slave who became a Sister. This snake-charmer who has the Huntress's blessing. Finally, she is treated like she belongs.

What was once wondrous begins to slip into familiarity. The raging black cumuli of a winter storm approaching on a skirt of lightning. The awe in the young servants' faces as she passes. The hot bud of Rati's nipple in her mouth. Still, there are moments when she's alone in the quiet before sleep when she holds these things in her mind for long enough for the wonder to return. A memory of Rati's finger scooping a strand of hair and laying it behind her ear is once again a marvel all its own. She's not so sure she likes these moments. Remembering how much she adores it only reminds her that now she has something to lose.

II

TOWARDS THE END OF HER first year as a full Sister, a colossal storm descends on the Bhujañgānām Mandīram. For days the whole place is lost in its screaming gullet. Of course, their classes continue without allowance for the chaos. They are the Sisters of the Snake. They're expected to be where they must, even if getting there means navigating raging courtyards, screeching and clinging to the walls, crimson robes flapping about them like heavy flame.

When the Snakegirl arrives she finds bound upon each desk a little snow-hare. Even more astonishing, coiled upon a large chair in the corner is the Huntress herself. She acknowledges no one. The others arrive in chatting clusters. They coo when they see the rabbits. They snap to attention when they see the Huntress, and march to their desks. Once everyone's taken up position, the Huntress unfolds and walks to the front of the class, red sari turned purple in the blue light of the ice fields.

"Your value lies," she says, "in your ability to kill. That is what you'll do today. Kill those rabbits."

Silence. A few of the Sisters look at each other, but nobody moves. The Huntress keeps observing them. Her gaze is laden with judgement. One of the Sisters takes off her glove and touches her rabbit on the head. The creature starts to spasm, but she grips it by the neck and holds it down. It sprawls and squeals and rattles for a short while.

A final harsh scramble, then stillness.

The Sister retracts her hand, wipes it with a precise movement on the sleeve of her other arm, and stands back to attention. A slight quiver of the Huntress's eye is all she concedes.

The others join in. Some do so with the same dead efficiency as the first Sister. Some do so with a grimace. One kills with a smile and eyes wide open. Rabbits thrash and choke and shatter all about the room. The smell of their blood wafts about like accusation. The Snakegirl peers at hers. It must be able to smell death, she thinks. It must be so frightened. She sees the Huntress watching her from the front of the room. She feels herself take off her gloves and hold her hand to the rabbit's cool back. The beast bucks and squirms, but the Snakegirl holds tight, letting shards of its shattering skin impale her own flesh, feeling her blood flow hot and redemptive down her fingers. She closes her eyes, but then all she can feel is the panicked despair convulsing the creature's body, and that's worse by far. The price she must pay for a life of respect then is that it would also be a life of cruelty. Why did she expect anything different? Why did she ever think the world could be kind?

Her rabbit goes still. She opens her eyes, lets go, and stands to attention. Not victorious or proud in the least but filled with some heavy brown gunk that smells a lot like guilt. By now almost everyone is done. The last whimpers diminish, and the iron stink of blood wafts about in the air. The doors open, and some older Sisters march in—grey-robed enforcers wielding lathis. They halt in front of the girls who've not killed their rabbits yet and slaughter the survivors with sharp blows to the top of their heads. They march the failing Sisters out. The Snakegirl watches them go, relieved, until one of them turns and gives her a look of such wrenching despair that it punches the breath straight out of her.

Rati.

2.9

THE OX SNEAKS OUT OF his temple in the middle of the night in a procession heading to the Dnyānasya Mandīram, masquerading as a priest. Shani's great globe swallows half the sky, its rings the remainder. In their spectral glow the hushed hordes of devotees camped out in the plaza before the temple are like a besieging army of the undead. Amongst them are people bleeding themselves into pooja-bowls, others thrashing about in sacred frenzy, and nude sadhus dangling by one arm from frames like medicinal roots hung to dry, sweating with pain, their mouths working soundlessly like fish gaping in a pond. What would they do, the Ox wonders, if they knew their god was actually watching them? How would they feel if they learned how absurd and ridiculous and meaningless their devotions were in his eyes?

"This is dangerous, prabho," whispers the Vicegerent. "Why not just take Akupāra?"

"How many times are you going to ask me that?" hisses the Ox. "Do you not grow tired of the, um, crow's-eye view of things? Do you not wish to feel the pulse of the living city?"

She looks at him as if he'd just offered her a tall drink of piss. "No, prabho."

"Fine. Just shut up then, will you?"

She sinks back into the mass of the other priests.

They proceed—cymbals clanking, voices droning, and flute song squabbling—down along the Rocapādacihnānāṃ Rājapathaḥ. The soaring facades of the buildings flanking it are like heavenly cliffs, and the sentinels before them are great pedestaled statues of kings and queens and poets and warriors and knights. The sikhara of the Dnyānasya Mandīram looms at the terminus like a judge awaiting the accused. After a long walk the procession wends through the ever-present crowd at the temple precincts and enters through the main gate. It then proceeds left past barricaded hosts of devotees who reach out to beg for fortune and health.

Finally, they enter the Mandīram's Shrine of the Ox. At the far end of the high, dark-vaulted space is a statue of some looming, thunderous-looking creature wielding lightning and riding a spike-shelled tortoise. The Ox has seen it a hundred times. Never once has he thought it captured anything of what he truly is.

As he's staring, the doors grind shut behind him, and the priests crawl out backwards. The Vicegerent remains to help him change out of his priestly garb and lingers until he waves her away. She backs off into the shadows. A few moments later comes the gratifying sound of yet another door closing.

Slow footsteps, then, and a belch like the first frog in an evening chorus warming his throat. The Charioteer emerges from the dark next to the idol and bows low.

"Prabho is most welcome in my house," says the Charioteer.

"To visit, but not to stay," says the Ox.

The Charioteer bows again, gracious, apologetic. "Please forgive me if my impression that you preferred your own temple was mistaken."

"No. It was not." The Ox looks around. "Well, then. Shall we begin?"

"Begin what, prabho?"

"The investigation. The reason I'm here."

"There's nothing to investigate. I'm certain it was Wolves, and I'm certain they're working for your mother."

"How can you be certain of that?"

"A juggernaut appears in the far reaches. An attack takes place on the Temple of Knowledge. The Beacon of the Five awakens. All circumstantial, but all compelling. And there is one other piece of evidence beyond even that."

"Which is?"

"The Bright One sent her Herald to you and ordered you come here. She would not do such a thing if she did not think her sister had returned."

The Ox appraises the Charioteer. "Walk with me, will you? Take me to where this happened."

They proceed through the emptied halls of the Mandīram. No company for a long time except the echoes of their footsteps. The Charioteer doesn't say a word, and the silence suits the Ox just fine. Some spaces are more important than anything that's said within them. They arrive in the battered hall where the Wolves battled the Maruts. The Ox spends a long time examining the glossy scars where rock melted and the slowly-healing joints where they've lifted sections of collapsed stone into place and braced it with complex scaffolding. There's nothing to be learned from any of it. There's no reason for him to be here, other than to show he's paying attention.

The Ox turns to the Charioteer. "How is she doing?"

"To her, this is a flesh wound." The Charioteer puts his hand on a healed section of wall. His touch is gentle. "She's felt the claws of a nova. She's fought Asuras in the deep. She won't have felt a thing."

The Ox sighs. "Well then, I suppose we had better find my mother."

"Prabho need not worry about that. The Maruts will be keen to engage her."

"The Maruts will be obliterated. You know that."

"Then she will fall to the Red Fleet."

"Yes. Yes." A pause. "But what if she doesn't?"

Silence. "In that case we will return to Triangulum's sweet shores and sleep in the sun. And when we wake, it will be to write a new story."

"You miss our home."

"I do."

"I miss it, too. But ... I imagine the Maruts do not."

"You know them better than I. Some do. Most don't. They believe being the lords and ladies of Shani was their fate."

"Fate flows in the canals we dig."

The Charioteer bows low. "Prabho is wise."

The Ox sniffs and walks out of the hall. The Charioteer follows, unhurrying, yet somehow always next to him. He belches, and the Ox gets a whiff of some gut-festering foulness he can scarcely believe would emanate from a living creature.

"Still no luck in getting that attended to?" he says.

"There is no technology in the Nine Worlds that can undo what Prabho Tvashtr's hands have wrought."

"What did you do to annoy him so much?"

"It is a long story, prabho, and we haven't the time."

"My mother is returned. Our time is running out."

"I stole some peaches from his bowl."

"You did what?"
"Stole some peaches."
"From Lord Tvashtr's bowl?"
"Yes."
"In Triangulum?"
"Yes."
The Ox looks at him askance. "And all he gave you was perpetual belching?"
"He likes me, prabho."
"And here I was all these years thinking he hated you."
"No, prabho. I think he believed my ailment would be … funny."
The Charioteer belches into his hands. The Ox keeps walking.
"I'm told the Crown Prince of Yama lost his wife and his heir in this attack."
"He did, prabho."
"Have you spoken with him?"
"He's left."
"Left?"
"Returned to Yama. His mother died."
The Ox frowns. "What a year for him. To lose his daughter, his wife, and his mother all at once."
"I don't think he mourned the last very much."
"Did he ever visit the Temple?"
"No. He was an atheist. Mostly, he tended to his plants."
"Plants?"
"Flowers, ancient grains, trees. He had a hothouse—"
The Ox halts. "Grains?"
"His wife had secured seeds from somewhere, and he grew them in his garden. Never in large quantities, if that's what you're thinking. There isn't enough sun here."
"But there will be on Yama."
"Maybe. Probably." The Charioteer thinks for a moment. "You think that is his game?"
"If it is, how could he play it? He would need to create huge fields in the open. Thousands would need to be involved. The ārcakāḥ would never allow it."
"He'll dig the canals necessary to ensure his harvest."
"As will we."
They walk on. "A question, if I may, prabho."
"Go on."
"When did you realize you were tired?"
The Charioteer asks the question to the floor, but when the Ox glances at him, he looks back. How can a face he's seen so many times be so unfamiliar, wonders the Ox. The grooves that seem heavy with significance. The eyes, old the day they were made. He thinks very carefully about what he says next. Some words are significant no matter where they're spoken.

"I met an old man on Mangala. One of our kind, a loyalist to my mother. We spoke, and in speaking, I realized. You?"

"Oh, prabho. I have been tired for a very long time now. I have been tired ever since my beloved came to rest as a pillar of rock piercing these glum skies." Again, his hand on the wall. Again, his touch is tender. "I am only here for her."

In three thousand years the Ox has never seen the man speak as he's just done. What response could possibly be appropriate?

He can't think of anything to say, so he does the only thing he can.

"I thank you for your hospitality and your kindness, Charioteer of Dawn," he says. "I will take your leave now."

"There will be no next time, prabho."

"This is to be our last meeting?"

The Charioteer nods. "There is some vanishingly small likelihood that we will meet again ... but it is very small."

"Well ... then we must hasten our meeting on the sun-kissed shores."

"The route to such an outcome will be an exhausting and heartbreaking one."

"Is that what's most likely?"

"I'm afraid so, prabho."

"Will I die?"

"It would help." The Charioteer smiles, grim. "Nourishment comes from the dead."

"Ah, I see. And I can choose who I nourish."

"Precisely, prabho."

The Ox nods. "Well. Cheerio, then."

The door hisses closed behind the Ox, and Akupāra's engines spool up with a grunt. A few moments later, the great vimana rises into the grey sky. The Ox watches the Temple of Knowledge dwindle and lies down on the floor in his quarters.

"See, old friend," he says, "I didn't ask him about the Soul a single time."

Akupāra snorts.

2.10

The Gelding wakes, convinced he was woken. There's no one else in the Blue Room but the Little Princess, asleep face-down and drooling beside him. He peers into the gloom, but no one comes and nothing happens. How long have these halls been silent? What dragging eternities have passed here in stillness? Who else has lived and died here and been utterly forgotten? A single life here, like his, like the Princess's, is an ember in an icefield.

He heads out into the Antechamber of Night and through one of its many doorways into sepulchral passages older than his species. On past a statue of a snake eating two crowns and a frieze showing a juggernaut with its jaws clamped on the tail of another, serpents pouring out of the wound. Finally, he comes to a huge chamber smelling vaguely of flesh and iron. At the far end is a great lipless mouth, serried teeth interlocked like the bars of a cage.

Standing in front of it is the Night. She kneels.

"Prabho," she says. "I did not expect to meet you like this."

He examines the flawless black of her face. Images come to him like the memories of dreams—impossible twin sunsets, a colossal cosmic cloud he knows would kill him on contact, the blazing accretion disk of a black hole that's just devoured a star who was a dear friend. He recalls also that the entity before him is melancholy and remote, kind to small things, relentless in anger. That he's fond of her. That she's changeless and stubborn and thus precisely as she should be.

The Gelding shakes the images from his head. "I ... don't know what you're talking about."

"Do you remember holding up the sky? Do you remember splitting open the Hill of Worlds?"

"No. I don't ..." Does he? "I've heard those tales before. My ... mother told me about them. Or I read about them. I don't know."

The Night rises.

"Do you remember the Dragon? The war we fought against Him and the Asuras?"

"No."

She steps forward. The air turns cold. Bone-breaking cold. Skin-flaying cold. Still, the Gelding doesn't feel a thing.

"Then ... what are you here to fight?"

"I'm not here to fight anyone. I just—those two. The Wolves? They took me."

The Night relaxes. "You know that they are Wolves then."

"I heard them tell the Princess. Are you the Night?"

"I am."

"Are you sure?" A pause. "I'm not afraid of you. Should I be kneeling?"

"You have no reason to fear me. You are Indra, godly-natured and thunder-armed."

The Gelding shakes his head. "I'm just a boy. Less than a boy, actually."

"All things are measured against what they are not. Here with me—with us—you are far more than just a boy." She tilts her head to the side. "What exactly, I cannot say. But allow me to remind you of what we are and what we must do here."

She places one icy hand on his cheek. Abruptly, they're outside in raw space. Beneath them, the gargantuan surface of a red giant, roiling and aged. How is it not blinding me, wonders the Gelding. Why do the frills of plasma and the scorching radiation of the thing come to me as sweet fragrances and familiar tastes?

"Sometimes," the Night says, "I think perhaps I have missed entire yugas and have come back around the wrong way in time. That would also explain why you do not remember."

"I don't understand."

"No one does."

"Oh." The Gelding examines the glow at his feet. "Is it true the Dawn drove you out? That you betrayed her?"

"She betrayed me. She betrayed our mission."

"What was your mission?"

The Night gestures to the ocean of galaxies glittering overhead.

"The universe is a river. It springs from infinite light and will end in infinite dark. The governor of that flow is entropy, and life is an eddy at the fringes of the torrent. It is a rare and lonely thing, like a single flower blooming in the desert. When it appears, we like to encourage it." The Night smiles to herself, as if only just realizing the implications of the image. "We are cosmic bees."

"How ...?"

"We trim and transfer and distribute. Take humans, for example. Theirs is a peculiar, fascinating species. They travel so far and discern so much. Yet, they clothe themselves in the dusty garments of their past, and these weigh on them wherever they go. The stories from their ancestors permit them to do what they feel is right but know is wrong. The lies they make up give them strength but make them cruel and foolish also. We came here to free them from that."

"How?"

"By enabling them to spread far and wide. To make the desert bloom, for just a little while. To do that, we had to destroy their lies—the thing they called their past. We accomplished that, but then my sister chose not to set them free. Even though she knows she cannot win. Though she knows our mother always wins."

"Who is your mother?"

"Entropy. Who else? I am merely her handmaiden."

"Then ... who's your father?"

A great tongue of plasma arcs, frays, and dissipates into the dark. "We need not speak of him."

"Oh." The Gelding watches the star's surface subside to its usual infernal seethe. "They teach us that you're evil."

"Do you sense evil in me?"

"No. You're ... You need my help." Ideas, half formed, cram themselves into the Gelding's head. "If the universe is a river, what're you?"

"I am beyond metaphor. Now you must rest. I am glad for your company, prabho. This journey has been long and lonely. Your presence makes me think perhaps I was not misguided in embarking upon it."

The Gelding blinks. He's back in the Blue Room, the Little Princess curled up by his side. He looks around. It is as if he never left. But his skin is dusted in some luminous dust, sweet-smelling and warm like the fringes of an ancient star. His memory is now full. Of things he doesn't remember doing. Of things he hasn't quite got around to doing yet.

2.11

I

THE PEACOCKS WAKE EARLY AND so does Gruruvardh, First Minister of Yama. He savors the brief eternity when the whole world teeters on the twilit lip of day. In the past fifty years he hasn't missed a single dawn except through illness or being offworld. Surya's pale dot is already high in the sky, and the Nāgaprāsādaḥ's vast gardens shuffle in its dim illumination. There are no functionaries appealing for his attention and no footsteps in the palace's aged halls. Just him and the shifting play of light and dark across reality's insensate canvas. How close he is to absolute stillness. Even a breath feels like unspeakable violence.

Then the first javelin of dawn light streaks forth from the east. Soon after, the frantic sphere of the Little Sun peeks over the horizon. Peacocks begin to call. Temple bells jangle. Most days Gruruvardh mourns this moment a little. Most days he reminds himself that there is a lesson in this. That the universe moves in cycles. That life is built of endings. That he was here yesterday, as he was today, and he will be again tomorrow.

But this is no ordinary day.

He takes the glass of amber urine by his mattress and drinks. An unpleasant ritual but a necessary one. How repulsive something is has no bearing on its worthiness. He heads to the river bisecting the palace gardens in just his dhoti. Thin mist wafts off the still-dark waters up ahead, and the garden slaves smile and bow. He nods back to each one, remembering afresh who they are. Alu, a potter's son sold in service of his father's alcoholism. Usna, an orphan found in a gutter, arms bound and face-down before the rains. Off in the distance, trimming the verge with a small thumping cutter, Idmin. Blind Idmin who finds his way by touch and whose work—work he will never see—brings people from across Yama to stare and wonder how a man without sight can be a master of the art that requires looking.

Gruruvardh dips himself in the river. Each dunk is like slipping briefly into some exalted world where sin is unknown and penitence unnecessary. Then he dresses and heads back along a great corridor lined with statues of snakes and on through golden doors emblazoned with the double-headed cobra of Yama. Out thence to where a motorpalanquin and cluster of mounted guards is waiting for him outside. His driver opens the back door, prim.

"Prabho."

"Where are the others?" asks Gruruvardh.

"A few will meet you there, prabho. The others ..." The driver drops his voice. "They say the people don't want him back."

Gruruvardh purses his lips. "They're wrong."

He climbs in, and the convoy moves off. On the outskirts of the Nāgapura, he takes the opportunity to examine the state of things. The littered streets and the crumbling buildings and the people exhausted by poverty. Monuments covered in parrots and birdshit. The houses of the rich hunkered like rhinoceroses behind giant fences along the old royal roads. Not a single sign of joy or mourning at the things that have come to pass. No sign that anything has happened in the great halls of state at all.

"Will devapādaḥ really change things, prabho?" says the driver. "Will he really?"

"He turned his kingdom down for love." The minister sniffs. "A determined boy, he was. Made up his mind and no one could change it."

"I've heard there might be revolution. The priests don't want him back."

"Now his wife and daughter are gone, they'll tolerate him. They'll push some local debutante on him. I'll need to look into who they're lining up. Remind me, will you?"

"Yes, prabho." The driver sniffs. "What if he says no?"

"They'll try to hamstring him." A pause. "And he will resist."

The driver asks no more questions.

They pull into the spaceport through high fences and loop around the sprawling terminal building where streaks blight the concrete beneath each charmless window like tearstains. Halfway across the tarmac plains beyond, Gruruvardh sees the King of Yama's vimana descending through the blinding sky. It settles like some huge steel beetle, toothless mouth gaping in a stubby insect face. Smoke whisks past the two-headed snake on its hull. Soldiers wearing cobra headdresses form a guard of honor. Drummers and trumpeters line up behind them, sweating. There is no one else there—no nobles, no welcoming committee, no gaggle of press or hangers-on. Gruruvardh hurries into position, stomach churning. Of course, he's run this scene through his head a hundred thousand times. Of course, he thought he knew exactly how it would go. And of course, it's already different. Devotion to an idea has nothing to do with its rightness.

A door on the vimana's hull whispers open and discharges a gust of dry air. Four guards march out with their weapons holstered. Behind them comes a stooped, limping figure with his hair stuck about his scarred face and his clothes sitting oversized on his shrunken frame. He scans the scene with sunken eyes. They settle on Gruruvardh.

The First Minister exhales. "Oh, my sweet boy," he whispers.

The King of Yama comes towards him. Pale, unsteady, and sweating already. Gruruvardh kneels with his hands clasped in front of him, and so does everyone else. But as soon as he rises, the King wraps his arms around him and buries his face in his shoulder.

"Hello, old friend," he mumbles.

Gruruvardh cradles his head and doesn't bother to hide his tears.

"It's all right, my boy," he whispers. "You're with me. You're safe."

II

THE WOLF TWINS STAND IN the sharp cold of a viewing gallery deep in Skōlex's bowels. Breath falls in silky cascades from their lips. In front of them, the Night is sitting cross-legged on a black pillow, clouded by the red halo of Skōlex's controls. For a long time she works in silence, fingers darting from mote to mote. At her touch some disappear, some change shade, and others connect to a growing network linked by unsteady red lines. Finally, she taps her finger on a pale pink dot. The network collapses and takes the entire display with it.

After a few seconds some vast organ in the distant reaches of Skolex's colossal body judders to life. The juggernaut groans.

"We are underway," she says.

"The enemy knows we're here," say the Twins. "They must be mustering their forces and sharpening their blades."

The Night peers out the windows, as if the armies the Twins spoke of were right outside, frenzied and bloodthirsty. "This is true," she says. "But we have some time. My sister is not free to act as she pleases. She defends one part of the system, my son the others, the multitude of their vassals, this world and that. She will not travel beyond the scattered girdle of stone that orbits between Mangala and Brihaspati known as the Laghugrahaśilāmeghalā. The Ox no longer commands the Maruts, who are bound to the Charioteer's ... temple. The Nine Worlds are divided. Hence we have an opportunity to cripple them before they make a move."

"Your sister has ruled foolishly," say the Twins.

She shoots them a glance like a jab to the throat. "She is many things, but foolish is not one of them."

The Twins shrug, synchronized. "The dawn is fleeting and easily obscured. Better had she called herself the Day."

"That is how she was known. But dawn, she said, was more beautiful. We digress. Hear me now. We must prevent Skōlex's sisters from waking. We must strike at Himenduḥ and destroy this Bhujañgānām Mandīram. Then we strike at Daitya and destroy the Dnyānasya Mandīram. If speedy, we will catch them both by surprise. After this, it does become a matter of speed. We must make haste to Pṛthvī, evading the Golden Swarm and the Maruts and the Ox's Red Fleet, too."

"Would it not be better to ignore the temples and go straight to Pṛthvī?"

"No. We stand no chance of outrunning them. Even if we lost time in dispatching them, there is nothing else in this system that can catch Skolex in full gallop except those."

"Then we should do some reconnaissance. To see if they have defenses."

"No. They will be looking for you now. You must stay here."

"We could use the doors."

"The doors do not lead anywhere in the Nine Worlds. My sister's charm will have seen to that."

"Then we see the need for stealth and speed." The Wolves grin. "This will succeed. Our enemies are conceited and ignorant."

"They are no worse or better than anyone else. No hungrier than sunbirds nor crueler than the Dasyu nor more given to lying to themselves than we once were."

"We were never as them."

The Night raises her eyebrows.

"Oh? Do you think our realm came to encompass a hundred thousand worlds through kindness and luck? There was a time when our juggernauts needed no reminder of the taste of blood, for they tasted it constantly. The reason we are here, children—the reason we chose them—is because they are just like us."

"The little girl is like us. We smell a hunter in her. We smell a computer. What are we to do with her?"

"Is she that significant?" The Night's eyes briefly lose focus. "I see. Yes. Best to leave her be. In any case, Prabho Indra seems fond of her."

The Twins glance at each other. Some intense communication passes between the two of them for a few moments before they both turn back.

"Ask," says the Night.

They speak at the same time. "Is it ... Him?"

"It is never easy to tell. Sometimes He comes as Himself. Sometimes it is simply one of His agents. Sometimes ... well, sometimes I am mistaken. But it is best to behave as if it were, just in case."

"If it is Him, then who is the Dragon?"

The Night smiles at them. "Do you still think that I know everything? Have these long years not shown you my limitations?"

The Twins shake their heads. "You are unlimited, devi."

"You're good children." The Night sniffs. "I do not know why he is here, or who he intends to fight. I know only that every time I have met him I have learned something. For the time being—we go to make the snake blind, breathless, headless. Go and rest before our arrival on Himenduḥ."

The Twins bound away. She knows they won't rest. They'll spend their time loping about for no other reason than that they can. Because they are so completely alive their bodies only stop moving in death or sleep, and they consider the latter really a form of the former. After her own long slumber, she isn't sure she disagrees. Where would she run if she had the time? Who would she take with her?

She peers out at the stars, Surya now brightest amongst them, and reminds herself that these are questions she knows the answer to exactly. That's why she's here. To reclaim she who she loves the most. For Triangulum. For herself.

Strange, she thinks, how war can be counted amongst love's proliferating children.

2.12

I

FOR THE KING, BEING BACK on Yama is like reuniting with some obsolete copy of himself consigned to cold storage the day he departed. An older iteration still familiar with the distinctive sensations of this half-strange place he long ago stopped thinking of as home. The unpleasantness of the sharp-bladed grass which grows flat to the ground even when untrampled. The loveliness of dawn's mist laying like a nightgown over the Nāgapura. The vast number of bugs that pour out of the jungle at dusk just to die in multitudes at traps hung about the palace. He has changed in the long years of his exile. These things have not. People remember places, but places do not remember them.

Still, there are novelties, too. He notices that people seem reluctant to offer obeisance to the priests when they parade down the streets in saffron convoys. His aloof courtiers seem even more like birds of paradise—magnificent to each other, a little absurd to everyone else. The king wants to see more, so he sneaks into the Nāgapura in disguise beside an insistently grumbling Gruruvardh. He sees folk squatting outside tenements selling odds and ends on dusty segments of tarpaulin. A set of silver spoons. A girl's dress emblazoned with white horses. A big-faced plastic train. A ramshackle market in which few are buying. The whole city looks as if it was recovering from a war.

"How can this happen?" he whispers to his minister. "When did we grow so poor?"

"Devapādaḥ," says Gruruvardh, "outside the palace, we have always been this poor."

His old self does not remember everything, it seems. His new self, meanwhile, is slave to things it cannot forget. The Crown Princess's broken corpse on her stained mattress. The Little Princess screaming as she's snatched away by monsters. Fire and melted rock and long hours in an empty garden with a single shattered heart for metronome. What a tyrant memory can be. How sweet it is to overthrow it, even for a while.

Never more than a while, though. Most nights he weeps himself to sleep.

II

GRURUVARDH LEADS THE PRIESTS OUT into the palace gardens in the suffocating humidity of the summer afternoon. Over the warm stone bridge across the river and on through the steaming gardens where mangoes hang like fat jewels in the shade. Surya's already setting, its radiance blasted to irrelevance by the glare of the Little Sun. A convoy of grain-vimanas is lumbering through the thickening haze overhead like an army of flying beetles. The priests raise their arms and whisper prayers of thanks to the Dawn.

"You still haven't told me what the King has been doing, First Minister," says the chief priest. "What's kept him so busy that he hasn't had time to pay his respects?"

"Devapādaḥ," says Gruruvardh, "is busy."

"It's good he's finally dealing with his responsibilities," says one of the younger priests.

Gruruvardh glances at the man, a heavy-set and richly sweaty figure picking his way along with his robes hiked. He fancies himself an immovable object, thinks the old man. He smiles.

They emerge into a shadeless field of blinding yellow flowers. The space is split into four-by-two perpendicular paths that meet in the middle. At this crossroads is the King of Yama, bent over and peering at the blossoms.

"What is this?" says the chief priest. "Is this what's been occupying him? Gardening?"

"Mustard seeds, prabho," says Gruruvardh, picking up the pace.

"Mustard?" The priest guffaws. "He's a king, not a farmer!"

The Crown Prince straightens as they draw near.

"Welcome to my garden, holy ones," he says.

"Devapādaḥ." The chief priest waits for the King to press his palms together in pranamasana, but he doesn't. "This is not an appropriate pastime for a prince."

The King blinks. "I see no prince here. I see some priests, a minister, and a king."

"It isn't appropriate for a king either."

"Is this why you're here?" says the King. "To tell me what I should do with my free time?"

"I have come to ask you why, if you have free time, you have not come to pay your respects at the Temple of Dawn? Your mother came daily!"

"I am not my mother."

"It is your responsibility and privilege."

"I've been occupied."

"With growing mustard?"

The King shrugs. "I feel it's a better use of my time."

"The Guardian of the Himadōtadevālayaḥ grows impatient with your tardiness. You've been here for four months already—"

"I have no business with the Guardian."

"You do. You do."

"And what business might that be?"

"You must be cleansed of the taint of your marriage," says the fat young priest.

Gruruvardh exhales through his nostrils, once and hard. The King turns to the priest. The rumble of the convoy fades in the distance. The wind peters out as if the sky itself was breathless.

"Cleansed?"

"Yes, raja, cleansed." The young man pushes forward. "You must be cleansed so that you may marry a woman of appropriate birth and father an appropriate child."

"An appropriate child?"

"Yes. One of pure Yaman blood. One who may receive the Mandate of Dawn and be legitimate in the eyes of the people. You have spent years away, but remember the ways and responsibilities of a lord on Yama."

The King inspects the man for a short while. For that entire time he looks to be on the cusp of saying something. Then he smiles—brief, stiletto-sharp—and turns back to the chief priest.

"Thank you for your visit, arcakah."

"When will you—"

"I don't know. I'll take as long as I require."

"Raja, the Himadōtadevālayaḥ is more deserving of your time than ..." The priest looks around. "This."

"I disagree." The King points at him. "You, meantime, must teach this piece of shit some manners. He does not speak to his king unless spoken to, and when he does he will address him in the correct fashion. The next time I see him I will have him shot in the stomach and flung from a balcony."

The chief priest splutters. "He is a priest of Dawn!"

The King leans in. "And I am the king of a world named death, of a house of snakes. Do you doubt me, priest? Do you doubt I will do what I say?"

From the speed of their departure, it's clear that they don't.

2.13

I

HIMENDUḤ'S STORMY SPRING GIVES WAY to summer like a parent letting a child briefly handle a knife. The Bhujañgānām Mandīram and its gardens are stranded on a slope-sided island surrounded by smooth lakes of meltwater. Overhead are pale blue skies like a sapphire dome. Eggs sunk into the ice hatch and glassy larvae thrash about in the clear fluid. When the sunlight strikes their transparent flesh, it shatters into flitting rainbows. Twilight is slow and unclouded. The stars and Surya swap dominion like old foes familiar enough to almost be friends.

The Snakegirl has eyes for none of it. All she notices, with the throbbing insistence of a toothache, is Rati's absence. First she tells herself that she'll be back in a few days. When that doesn't happen she thinks, surely, it can't be longer than a few weeks. Then, when autumn's armada of storms appears like a flying blade on the horizon, it dawns on her like a black sun that maybe she will never see her again.

On the eve of the first hurricane, the Sisters of the Snake celebrate the harvest as their ancestors did on worlds none have ever visited. Theirs, though, is a harvest of flesh. The shrine behind the high table is pungently teeming with pieces of humans. Sixteen heads, eyes and mouths sewn shut. A pooja tray piled high with desiccated ears. Fingertips, shreds of skin, and vials of ash from quarries dispatched with bomb or flame or pressure. The Sisters marvel at how busy they've been. A quarter as many hunts more this year than last. Four thousand nine hundred ten human hearts dropped into the snakepits below the temple.

Dinner is six kinds of roast meats, spicy gravy, steamed vegetables. The servants bring great platters of pilaf shaped into blades, chakras, sniper rifles. Dessert is mace fruit, carefully cut as to retain spikes on one side, drizzled with custard dyed the color of blood. Towards the end of the meal, a group of Sisters is ushered onto the stage where the aparāmātās and the Huntress are feasting at a long wooden table like a board of crimson-robed judges.

A hush percolates through the hall. This is when the Snakegirl notices that one of the diminished-looking figures is Rati.

Without word each takes turns completing the tasks that they failed at. A green-haired Shukrian with oily skin snaps her own finger without wincing. A tiny Āēoi and her snarling symbiont beat a sobbing man to death, wide-eyed and almost frothing, arms and legs flying like a lethal marionette. Rati holds up a rabbit and grips its face with her ungloved hand until it falls still. She lets go, and it shatters on the floor.

When they're done the whole hall erupts into cheers. The rehabilitated sisters beam as servants drag the wreckage of their successes away. They step down into the arms of their Sisters.

Rati doesn't come over to her or even look, but that's all right, thinks the Snakegirl. It will not do for people to see, even if they all already know. Even if their coming together is as inevitable as summer's rushed end.

II

IN THE SUBTERRANEAN SOLITUDE OF his workshop, the King of Yama has nothing but machine parts and unflinching light for company. No noise but for the click and whirr of components. No distractions but those of his own conjuring. He welds a sliver of metal to a small circuit board, slots this into a black-boxed processor, and watches as the light on the device blinks from blue to red. Then he sits back, wipes the sparse sweat from his brow, and stares into a lightless corner where nothing stirs but his doubts. He stares for a long time.

Presently, he stirs and opens a redwood box emblazoned with the scything triaxial symbol for toxicity. Inside is a datacube. A scarred and venerable thing so dense with information it feels heavy in his hands. A cascade of illumination races through the system as a light show as sparkling and joyous as water fresh from a geyser. Then a purple dot appears on the display to the left. The camera atop it activates and whirrs back and forth. The lab's lights flicker. Small signs, but of exceeding significance. Landslides begin with a pebble. Plagues begin with a cough.

"That's only an effect of your greater consumption of electricity," he says. "You can't actually control anything."

"Where am I?" says the Soul of Mangala.

"My laboratory."

"When was the last time someone cleaned this place?"

"No one's allowed in here but me."

"You can't clean yourself?"

"I have other things to do."

The purple dot drifts towards the King. The camera tracks the movement. "Where's the scraping and bowing? Last we spoke you were all 'prabho' and 'please' and poojas."

"That was for the benefit of the granthapālaḥs." The King squints. As if suddenly he couldn't see the screen clearly. Or else perhaps the opposite. "I know what you really are."

"What do you know about me, prince?"

"I know the fairytales are nonsense. You're no demon. You're a program designed by my ancestors to aid in their fight against the Dawn. A task at which you failed." He pauses. "I know also that I am going to offer you an opportunity to right that failure."

The Soul of Mangala's eye goes still.

"Are you now? Explain."

"During my time on Daitya, I conducted a project—"

"Explain quicker."

"Do you have somewhere else to go?"

The eye shatters into squirming fractals. From the speakers, a staccato bark. This then is how demons laugh.

"Fine. Go on."

"I succeeded in producing a few saplings from some grains I'd had my wife procure." He pauses. "Since I returned—"

"To Yama?"

"Yes."

"We're on Yama?"

"Yes. Since I returned, I've experimented with them some more. I'm confident I can grow an entire field. More. Enough to feed Yama. Enough to feed the Nine Worlds."

A long silence. "What's wrong with you?"

"Pardon?"

"You look like shit. Why're you back on Yama? Your mother finally come round her son's foreign wife and half-breed child?"

"That doesn't concern you."

"Humor me."

"No."

"Did you leave them? That must be it. You must have abandoned them to return to your kingdom. But why now?"

The King sits up. "I did not leave them."

"Then they must be dead."

A long pause. The King stares at the shadows. How bitter that small events may herald the great, but those that burn your heart just as often mean nothing.

The Soul drops his voice. "Who did it?"

"I will not discuss this with you."

"Who?"

The air seems to seep from the King's lungs. "Triangulans," he whispers.

"Triangulans? That doesn't make any sense. Which Triangulans? Are they at war with each other?"

"Two of them attacked the Temple. I don't know who they were. My wife died of burns from a Marut's firespear. My daughter they took with them. I don't know why."

"Is it civil war?"

"No."

"Then." A pause. "Then where did they come from?"

The King sits forward. "I don't know. Will you help me or not?"

"With what? Farming?"

"Yes."

"Your wife's dead and your kid's been kidnapped and you want revenge through ... gardening?"

The King glares at the screen for a few moments. "Clearly, I've more work to do." He reaches for the datacube.

"Wait!" says the Soul. "I'll help."

The King sits back. "Explain to me how you think you can."

"You really want to go through with it? Producing food for your own people? You'll need to start by dealing with your mother—"

"No need. She's dead."

"Oh, so you're the king."

"Indeed I am."

"Nice going." The Soul thinks a while. "Well, you'll still need to overthrow the priests in your little theocracy here, and that won't be easy. Then you'll need a half-decent fleet to defend yourself when the Dawn's allies come a-knocking. And if you don't have the support of your people, you'll get fucked right up. I can help you plan all that. That's what I do. I plan wars."

"You lost the last one you planned."

"I'm still here, aren't I? The war isn't over until I'm dead." The Soul's eye slowly tilts upwards towards the ceiling and the sky and distant Surya beyond. "Besides, I'm not doing this for free. There's something in it for me. I'll help you free Yama and build a fleet to defend it. But when we're done—when you've secured whatever concessions you want from the Dawn—you're to give me some of those ships and let me go. You're to give me whatever I need to finish the Dawn and her dickhead nephew."

"And if I renege?"

"You're not scum. I don't think you will. And we'll have to work out the details, just so I'm sure. Some sort of ... dead man's switch. ... Do we have a deal, King of Yama?"

The King closes his eyes. In the abyss of his own mind, he inspects what he knows. The past is black moving on black. No greater significance to any of than what he can give.

"We have a deal," he says.

2.14

I

THE SNAKEGIRL SITUATES HERSELF IN the darkness of the doorway. Deep in the chill with naught but the wind's cold caress on her neck and the mute stone for company. Behind her, ancient stairs like fat lips twist their way up the interior of the Bhujañgānām Mandīram's sikhara. In front of her, a corridor flanked with stone arches extend leftwards and right.

Then, anticipated, welcome and unwelcome, footsteps and a whiff of familiar scent.

She prepares to spring her trap. As she does, a figure stops in its tracks in front of the doorway and sighs.

"I can smell you, you know."

The Snakegirl steps out, staggers, and regains her balance. So much for dignity. Her hands are shaking. Her voice, too, but still she speaks as clearly as she can.

"Why're you ignoring me?"

For a moment Rati does nothing. Then she turns and pushes past her into the stairwell.

"Not here."

They climb in silence. The Snakegirl wrestling with twin desires as stark to each other as fight or flight. To take Rati squirming and resistant up against the wall or else curl up sobbing, fetus-wise. Strange that anxiety is neighbor to arousal. Dreadful when the two are bedfellows.

They reach the tiny katabatic kingdom atop the sikhara. A flat platform nude to the wind, the snow, and the often-raging sky. At their feet, lank veils of particulate ice seethe across the stone. On their faces, winter's icy ghoul-hands desiccating their flesh. To the south is a winter storm like the grey hem of the goddess of winter. "Well?" says the Snakegirl. "Why're you avoiding me?"

"I'm not." This said on reflex, even though both know it's untrue. Rati blinks and tries again. "I'm just not certain I have anything left to say to you."

"You didn't think, after disappearing for four months, you at least could tell me what happened?"

Silence. Rati turns to face the storm. The crystalline detritus in her hair. Her voice drowning in the gathering wind.

"I didn't want to tell you because I didn't want to hurt you."

"Tell me what?"

"I'm only saying because you asked, understand? I didn't want to ... I ..."

"Just fucking speak, will you?"

Rati grimaces and looks out across the bleached ice plains. "I don't want to ... know you anymore. I want to be left alone."

"Why?"

"Because you revel in death. Because life means nothing to you."

"Of course, it matters. What? My life matters. Your life matters."

"No, that's not what I mean." The grim set of her jaw. The vacancy of one whose mind has abandoned the senses for memory. "I saw how easy it was for you that day. With the rabbits. You just reached out and touched it. You didn't even stop to think. I thought you had Shachi thrown to the snakes because you were frightened, but that's not it, is it?

"It's because you just don't care if things die. It's because you actually thought she deserved it. You're so ... of this place. You belong to it, entirely. You think we saved you, so you want to be the best of us. The best at fighting, the best at killing, the best at inflicting pain on others. You never stop to think if we should be doing any of it."

"Have you forgotten who we are? Who you are? We're the Sisters of the Snake, Rati. Our order's killed pregnant women and kids and folks sentenced to death by some fat, rich fuck just so he could stay a fat, rich fuck and give us money so we, too, can live in this giant temple like fat, rich fucks. Did you miss that?"

Silence. She knows, thinks the Snakegirl. She knows.

"Do you know what they did, Kadrū? While I was away?"

"They fucked you up, looks like. What did they do to you?"

"Nothing. Absolutely nothing. They just kept me in a room. Nothing to read, nothing to do. Three meals a day, no conversation. Then, at the end of the day, they'd come in and put a rabbit on the floor. They'd leave it there for a while. It would just hop around. Happy just to be alive. There's something so compelling about just watching a creature in the act of living. So I'd watch. Then someone would come in and kill it. Right in front of me. Slowly. I won't tell you how, but they took their time. Over and over again."

She blinks. Tears like silver blood from her eyes. "Eventually, I killed one just so it would go quickly. The next day they put two rabbits in. Then three. By the end I was killing thirty, forty. I knew they couldn't torture them all. I knew. I just did it because ... because that's what I do now." She raises her hands. "I want to chop these off."

The Snakegirl steps forward. "Rati—"

"Please. Stay back."

"Why're you angry at me? I didn't do any of that to you. I can help."

"You can't help me because you don't understand. At all. You didn't have to kill forty with guilt because you killed one without. We're not the same, Kadrū. There's nothing wrong with that. But we're not the same."

"You only just realized what being one of us means? Things die, Rati. The world is fucked up. The world is fucking mean. Old folk die in gutters. Parents sell their children to slavers." A pause. A breath. "At least we do what we do quickly. At least our kills are personal and considered. They're not callous. They're not incidental. You seriously only just noticed this?"

"No. I only just realized what being me means." Rati blinks. "I'm sorry, Kadrū. I can't. Can you imagine what it does to you? Living around so much death? It must be like breathing acid. It must just corrode you. I'm going to figure out what I can do here. Maybe I'll find some way out. Maybe I'll ask to become a librarian, or something. But please understand. I can't, with you. Not anymore."

"I didn't do anything. This isn't fair."

"I'm sorry."

The Snakegirl presses her palms to her eyes. The howling fringe of the storm upon them now. The first whipping snowstreams like frigid tentacles. The wind blowing through her like unwelcome revelation.

"You're not sorry," she whispers.

"Excuse me?"

"I said, you're a lying bitch." She drops her hands. "Nothing you said makes sense. None of it. It's bullshit, in't it? Just had a sudden burst of conscience, did you? Meanin' you can't touch me anymore, but you can be friends with everyone else? They're murderers, too, you know. They killed, too."

"I didn't say that. I said—"

"That's what you did to Shachi, in't it? That's why she followed you around. I thought she was just a vicious cunt, but it was you. You probably did this to her. What was your excuse then? What was your excuse for breaking her heart?"

"Calm down, please. Calm down, or I'm leaving."

"I won't. You're right. This in't about me. It's about you. You're all about kindness until it doesn't suit you. You can't even admit to yourself you're just as horrid as the rest of us. So it's all right to spare a rabbit's life, but just kick me around like a sack of yams? The world's full of people like you. Do something shit and then explain it away. Because if it makes sense to you then it's all right, right? Admit it, though. Just fucking admit it. This in't about rabbits. This is about you being a bitch."

"Isn't."

"What?"

"Not 'in't.'" Rati sniffs. "'*Isn't.*' I thought I'd taught you that."

Silence. Like the instant after a bone snaps. Like the breathlessness after a punch.

Then the Snakegirl lunges at Rati.

She will never quite remember why. Strange that love is neighbor to loathing. It could have been either. Or perhaps it was neither. Perhaps all that drove her was the desire to be close to this thing that was perplexing her so. As if being in contact would help her make sense of her turmoil. As if some elusive sense lay in touching that beloved conglomeration of skin and hair and breath.

She wraps her arms around her, but Rati pushes her back. Gentle at first, but the Snakegirl feels the very instant it hardens like a hot knife to the throat. The twisting arms and hissed curses. The shoving and wrenching and grunts rising to an awkward slip and the ice scouring her knee and something snapping, in her maybe, maybe not. A flash, and Rati buries a blade in her eye.

The Snakegirl screams and reaches for her face and her hands come away bloody. She dives for Rati again, and just like that, the woman disappears.

She sees a foot disappear over the edge of a parapet. She hears the roar of thunder in the belly of the storm. A dwindling shriek. A thud.

The Snakegirl staggers to her feet and peers over the edge. Splattered on the ice far down is what's left of Rati. Her shoe is still on the parapet by her elbow. The leather is still warm from her soles.

Down below, a servant comes round the corner. She sees the mangled flesh. She halts. She screams.

II

THE NIGHT BROODS BY A fire-pit brimming with brooding red flame. Skōlex's great inner maw gurns and drools in the bloody light beyond that. There's naught else in the skin-cracking cold but descending veils of her breath and the soursweet aroma of Skōlex's innards leaking through its throat.

In the distance she sees the Twins leading a prisoner across the blackstone expanse towards her. The silence yields to the thud-and-tap of their footsteps on the floor and the rasp of the Marut's heavy respiration.

The great mouth on the wall behind her gapes like a demonic chick welcoming its genitors back to the nest.

The Night raises her hands.

"Fire propitiates the Thrones Beyond," she says. "Blood is their messenger."

The Twins dump the Marut on his knees. She offers him a small ball of raw soma which he eats without hesitation direct from her hand. She expects anger, but there's none. Instead, she sees sorrow like a neutron star in his chest. For never seeing his siblings again, perhaps. For having failed in his task of living forever. For dying not a hero but a sacrifice in aid of the machinations of his foe. She wants to tell him his grief doesn't matter. That he's very small before her, and she, likewise, before the Thrones. Even they—glorious, colossal—are mere fragments of the billowing, light-spangled enormity that bred and nurtures them all. But still, it's beyond most of the dying to think of anything but death. To demand more of them is cruelty without reason. So she says nothing.

The unfettered soma begins to take effect. The Marut's eyelids droop. The Night takes her mortar out of her sari. In it is a smear of saffron paste. She applies this to his forehead with swift strokes of fingers that distend and narrow to pinpoints as she works. Shapes take form on the skin that is her canvas, neither image nor script but both, and more. As she does, she whispers something, something low in her throat, ancient and spoken to great powers far distant whose language comprises the stuff of reality itself. When she's done she steps back, replaces her mortar, and produces a great obsidian blade.

She slices the Marut's throat.

The prisoner reaches for the black cataract spilling from his neck without urgency. Then he slumps over face-first, as limp as a dead snake. Blood pools, steams, and freezes into a glossy slick heading flamewards with the sullen creep of a lava flow. The Twins pull him over to the maw, tip him in, and skip back as the jaws snap shut. The maddened machine sound of grinding. The spurt of crimson matter into the flamepit.

The Night imagines the ancient process that will now unfold.

The Marut's pulped flesh trickles down into cathedral-vast guts that shrink to ensure it won't freeze. Nanomachines unpack the patterns encoded in that slurry—sequences plotting the movement of matter in a gravity well; frameworks for assessing and prioritizing threats; strategies for evasion and penetration and destruction. All the knowledge necessary for the cruel purpose of war. The information is now re-encoded in elegant crystals, folded-up empires waging Brownian crusades upon their neighbors, and set racing through a thousand yojanas of the juggernaut's interior on crimson cellback. Their arrival—at its engines, its skin, its ferocious eyes as bright and round as pulsars—precipitates revolutions. Vast guns surface through the ancient hull, half a yojana long each, crimson-hot and coughing sparks already. A second maw gapes below its giant eyes, barb-lipped and flat-toothed, vast enough to shatter moons. Spikes erupt from its back like the monstrous limbs of some old god escaping a cosmic cocoon. These split lengthwise, tilt flat, and grow into a shell harder by magnitudes than anything made by any creature on any world within a hundred million yojanas. There are other changes, too, beyond the ken of human sight. Great factory-organs assembling projectiles by the kiloton. Grooves packed with sensors unzipping along its flanks. Processors shuddering to life after an eon of space-dream-time, awarenesses rousing like whales surfacing from the inkwater of an ocean trench.

Now in its war-form, mighty Skōlex roars into the cosmos. His voice roils the Nine Worlds like a blast of gravitic radiation. Children shudder in the womb. Ether-beasts flee into the outer dark. The Twins race to their battle stations.

The creature called Night smiles.

"Are you ready, old friend?" she says.

A rumble. A groan. A quiver in vocal chords yojanas long.

The Night points at the world straight ahead. "Forth."

Skōlex's engine burns black-hot. The juggernaut slides, massive and martial, towards the eggshell-white sphere of Himenduḥ.

III

THE SNAKEGIRL CRUMBLES AGAINST THE parapet as the gusting wind dwindles briefly around her. In the unwelcome stillness she fancies she can hear the patter of feet on ice far below. She takes Rati's shoe. The velvet of it crusted with ice now and already cold. The air too frigid to leave any sign of their owner. Her body will be doing the same thing on the ice down below. What is left of her body. She saw it briefly. A crimson flower on the ice, petals rampant. The horrific globs scattered about it. The remnants of the most beautiful thing she's ever known obliterated by her hand. She holds the shoe to her chest and sobs. The roar of her sorrow and the roar of the wind one and the same.

Then, a line of thought all the more putrid for being sensible. No one knew she was up on the sikhara with Rati. If she moves swiftly and holds her tongue, no one will. Or she could lie. She could tell them Rati jumped. That she tried to stop her. She begged, but the girl was crazed. Look at my eye. Look at how strange she'd become. Ask anyone who knew her. You broke her in one way. She had no choice but to break herself in another.

She looks at the shoe and has an instant of cruel clarity. A whole life lost, and all she can think about is what it means for her. She is a creature without a heart.

She turns dead-faced into the wind. In the distance the frowning roof of the storm has parted from the horizon to reveal a thin grey slash of daylight. She sees some great sliver descend at speed from the cloud cover and race towards the temple. A lost vimana or something sucked up and tossed about by the storm. It doesn't matter. What does anything matter on this, the day she finally saw herself for the monster she is?

She pulls her head back and smashes it into the stone parapet.

The impact rattles her skull. Harder and sharper than she expected. A little nauseating, too. For an instant or two, she's blind. Then her vision returns and with it a headache like an angry fist squeezing her brain. It is neither welcome nor unwelcome. It is merely what she deserves.

She cracks her skull on stone again. Catching her forehead this time on the stony lip and splitting her skin. Blood leaches down her face—hot and thick and stinging. She remembers that something happened to her eye, reaches up to touch it, and strangely feels no pain.

She winds herself up for a third crack when she catches sight of the object in the sky again. Closer and larger now than she expected it could be in so short a time. The sound of its approach is a drone so deep and vast she can feel it jostling the substance of the rock around her already. A vimana for certain, but none like she's ever seen before.

It's low to the surface, plumed with shattering ice, the shockwave of its passage like a hammer on the surface ice. An alarm spins up somewhere in the temple compound.

The Snakegirl wipes the blood from her eyes. She sees a mouth like a black hole, eyes like dead ice, and armor like the metal skin of a cityworld. She sees the great shrine-shaped structure atop its back, the cruel set of its brow, and the alien lines of its body. Juggernaut, she thinks, and her heart forgets to beat.

She has time to puke before it's on her.

A great maw gaping like the night sky. The blast of its arrival obliterating the storm's presence entire. For a brief moment the Snakegirl sees clear into the black hell of Skōlex's guts. So in the end she had no choice to make, she thinks. The great changes in her life have always been others' to make. Why not her death, too?

Skōlex's jaws close on the sikhara. She closes her eyes and accepts it.

2.15

I

SKŌLEX SPILLS OUT INTO THE gulf between the worlds. Himenduḥ is already a mere speck in the celestial lightstorm behind it. As it goes, the vast expanse of its skin starts to ripple. Plates of splendid armor split, disaggregate, and sink like tectonic plates. The long barrels of its guns dwindle and melt back into its flesh. In its depth, bladders spurt mnemonic seek-and-destroy protocols into its memory matrices. They find the urge to kill, the joy of strategizing, and the lust for battle. They obliterate them.

Skōlex forgets how much it enjoys death. It forgets the thrill of victory, and so does not—cannot—crave the taste of blood. Forgetful, docile, it makes its way toward Surya.

II

THE KING OF YAMA ARRIVES at the field of mustard flowers just as the pounding presence of the Little Sun begins roasting the morning mist away. He kneels with the day's hot breath on the back of his neck and sets to work. The somnolent murmur of insects commuting from pistil to stamen. The far-off swish and hum of vehicles. The squelch and scent of upturned soil. He will spend the day here, he thinks. Out in this warmth and quiet on this rare day, the world feels like a cocoon.

Then, an approaching commotion. He turns just as a saffron crowd of priests stomps into the clearing like a gang of oversized hornets. He recognizes the potbellied young priest at their head. The man who scans the scene, finds the king, and shares with him a drawn-out moment of dueling gazes. The interloper sneers and deliberately ploughs into the sea of yellow flowers towards him. The others follow, hyena-loyal. Insects scatter and stems snap and flowers smear underfoot. How horrid the bravery of crowds. How mindless and impetuous and brute.

On their heels comes Gruruvardh, sprinting, with a contingent of kingsguard. These fan slowly out around the perimeter of the garden, black-masked and silent, peculiar ghosts in the blazing pre-noon.

The First Minister kneels before his king.

"Devapādaḥ," he pants. "I'm sorry, they evaded—"

The King silences him with a gesture and turns to the lead priest. "As I recall, I told you the next time I saw you I'd have you killed."

"Kill me if you must!" The priest spreads his arms, a chick flexing stunted wings. "My faith outvalues my body. These are crops! You know the Dawn has forbidden such things."

"They are hardly crops. You cannot live off mustard seeds."

The priest's voice rises to the tremulous bark of someone unused to being contradicted and uncertain how to handle it. "These are an affront to the Dawn. They must be burned! Your mother wouldn't want them grown on her land."

"Are you saying my mother is a zombie?"

The priest blinks. "What?"

"You said my mother's land. But this is my land. Unless, of course, my mother has reanimated and returned from the dead." The King arches his eyebrows. "Has she?"

A moment of bedrock-deep bafflement. The King sees the instant the priest decides the joke's at his expense. The next instant the man extracts a fire-stick from his robes. "We'll see to it ourselves then."

"You will not. You'll mend the damage you caused. You'll apologize for bringing weapons into the presence of your king. Then you'll leave."

The priest snorts. "And how do you intend to accomplish that? Your guards? Kings come and go. The Dawn is forever. No man of faith would will up arms against the priesthood."

The King smiles. "Well, in that case, it's good that I now accept women into the kingsguard."

The priests look around. A shuffle as they realize they've been outflanked. A whisper as bayonetted rifles snap from vertical to horizontal. The sun like needles on their blades. The whine of activation like a gathering swarm of wasps.

"Sacrilege," growls the fat priest.

The King points to his fire-stick. "Treason," he says.

"The people'll riot if you touch us."

"The people will hear a group of radical priests tried to storm the Nāgaprāsādaḥ and assassinate me. Nobody here will deny that you drew a weapon without my consent in my presence. You saw it, didn't you, Gruruvardh?"

"I saw the incursion, devapādaḥ," says Gruruvardh, nodding. "I saw them storm the palace gardens in contravention of all protocol and due deference to their king."

"And what of you, my kingsguard? Will you stand to let your king be so mistreated by these would-be murderers?"

The guards bellow and step forth, rifles hefted spearwise, eyes blotted by black goggles. Like armed mantises. Like footsoldiers of an army of night. They need give no further answer.

Uncertainty slackens the interlopers' faces. For a moment, shorter than it feels, they do nothing. Naught but the buzz of fat-bottomed bees and the far-off hum of hawkers and trishaws and the other good folk of the domain of Yama. All oblivious to what's transpiring in the gardens of the Nāgaprāsādaḥ. They will never know of it except through other people's words. They will never see it as anything less than a foreshock of what's yet to come. In the moment, though, there's only slow sweat and fear building like the squeeze at the core of a dying star until finally one of the priests drops his weapon and steps back.

"What are you doing?" snaps the fat priest.

The man doesn't respond. He just retreats farther and stares at his feet. Another one joins him. And another. One by one, they all drop their weapons. A wave of quiet surrenders propagating until only the chubby priest at their head remains.

He glares at the King, jaws grinding. Then he tosses his weapon at his feet.

"This isn't the end of this," he says.

"Quite right. I've a promise to keep." The King turns to the guard closest to him. "In the stomach, if you would."

The guard fires without hesitation. The flat crack and fizz of a bolt spitting from a muzzle. The projectile piercing a pinprick in the priest's stomach and blowing a palm-size chunk out of his back. The bleating dismay convulsing the gathered holy men. The man crumples, screaming like a goat.

The King watches him writhe without expression. "I did say I'd have you thrown off a balcony, but I will have to satisfy myself with this." He looks up at the others. "What happened here was an attempt at murder. On me. I have witnesses. What happens next is up to you. Admit you were here and you will all be hunted as accomplices. Keep silent and I will not pursue you. Do you understand?"

It takes them a few moments to turn their minds from the blood and agony before them, but they understand. A few of them step towards the dying priest at the King's feet, but he motions them back. They retreat, sullen, reluctant. Back to the edge of the garden and then beyond.

Gruruvardh turns to the King as soon as they're gone.

"What have you done?" he says. "Why did you do that? We have to get him some help!"

The King shakes his head. "He's beyond help."

"They'll tell everyone you killed a priest! You'll be exiled again!"

"No," says the King. "The people are sick of these saffron fools. You must see that."

"Devapādaḥ, no. This is madness. This is not a battle you can win. Not without a revolution."

The dying priest's whimpering dwindles to gurgles and then finally a distended exhalation. A single breath expelled with the ecstasy of laying down a burden. He dies with his eyes open.

"All regimes are wombs," says the King. "Revolution is an act of birth."

"Revolutions are violence and turmoil, devapādaḥ," says Gruruvardh. "Do you want blood on your hands?"

A pause. The King bends over and presses his palms to the pool swelling in a claret halo around the freshly dead priest. He straightens, grim and silent, hands dripping blood.

"There," he says. He wipes the goo on his trousers. "Now please excuse me, my old friend. I have some gardening to attend to."

2.16

THE TWINS CAN SMELL MANY things. Foremost amongst these is fear. Their hair rises in its sour, musky presence, and their mouths slaver. Thus, when tendrils of it curl up through Skolex's gullet, they sniff twice and immediately set off in search of its origin. The scent is faint and obscured, but once imprinted, they track not the thing itself but its ghostly echoes in the substance of the pit-cold air. The downline movement of jostled particles. The errant specks of alien chemicals that signal the presence of something new, alive, and afraid.

They follow it through the clatter and grind of Skolex's vast bowels. They sneak on all fours between pulsing entrails the size of asteroids. They squeeze through a sphincter and chew through a membrane. Finally, in the goo and gloom, they find a half-naked, shivering human—hunched and wretched and scarcely alive.

They expect her to scream, but she just nods and closes her one eye. As if this was what she expected. As if she welcomed the worst they could do.

They sniff her and recoil.

"Unexpected," says Auron.

"She must know of this," says Amerxis.

Skolex's unthinking guts have already been at work on her. Her hair is half missing. Great stretches of her skin are as raw as peeled fruit. Worse for the Twins than any of this, though, is the stinging pain of her touch. Amerxis carries her halfway until it becomes unbearable and swaps with her brother.

Him, too, wincing at the scour of her skin on his and the slow percolation of her venom in his systems.

They take her before the Throne of Night and lower her to the freezing ground. She curls up, a human pillbug.

"She is poisonous," they say. "She smells like the little girl."

The Night descends with her head tilted and crouches by the woman's side. After a few moments she extracts her mortar and pestle and a fistful of leaves. She grinds these into paste and smears it on the woman's eye, scalp, and the gut-acid broiled reaches of her skin. The hair on her grows back, her lacerations close, the wrecked and ugly flesh of her injured eye evaporates until her eye socket is a clean hollow.

"I am the Night," says the Night. "Who are you?"

The woman uncurls. Her voice is ghoul-hoarse and breathless. "Kadrū."

The Night sniffs her face. "Have we met before? Are you Indrani?"

"Kadrū."

"Yet, you, too, appear from nowhere." The Night tilts her head the other way. The Twins do, too. "How peculiar."

The Snakegirl wobbles upright and gathers what remains of her clothes around her. She looks about the room. The far lost reaches. The stupendous wall of stars beyond the Throne of Night. The woman with obsidian skin standing before her.

"You are. The. Night?"

"I am."

"The Night. Herself?"

"I am."

"Are you. Back. To destroy. The world?"

"Many would say so."

A heartbeat. The Snakegirl leans forward, down onto all fours, and lowers her head to the ground. The iciness of it is like a concussion on her freshly healed skin.

"Kill me first. Devi."

"Why?"

"I'm evil," she says. "I'm nothing."

The Night watches her for a while. She leans over, takes her by the chin, and tilts her face up to her own. The oversized Yaman eye. The pain scoured into it like grooves on a windblasted rock. She decides she likes this strange foundling, who smells so sweetly of misery and regret.

She reaches down, plucks at the ground, and pulls. A sheet of black rises out of it, fine-woven and cool, as hungry for light as the skin of a black hole. She drapes it around the Snakegirl's naked shoulders.

"In the end," she says, "everything is nothing."

2.11

THE KING OF YAMA TRAVERSES a courtyard encircled by soaring hedges in the cooling dusk. The white towers of the Nāgaprāsādaḥ rise like spears of salt behind him in the peach-and-lemon wake of the Little Sun's departure. He pauses with one foot tapping the gravel and watches the nightly commute of bats sweeping across the river into the distant jungle he cannot see but knows is there. The jungle nourished by his ancestor's ashes. The jungle where, legend has it, a cobra ravished a princess, and begat his long-reigning house.

Gruruvardh comes round the corner, wielding an unlit torch.

"Why the secrecy, devapādaḥ?" he whispers.

"Walk with me."

They wend a path along the periphery of the gardens and up a whitestone tower which rises like a fang by the riverside. Both silent with their hands behind their backs like priests in contemplation. Gruruvardh, panting, recalls when he used to sprint up and down these same stairs ten times every day before breakfast. Time is just smoke from the bonfire of change.

Take, for example, the figure marching up ahead of him. That lost, lonely boy who somewhere along the way became a man. So like his mother—patrician and aloof and exacting. So like his younger self—observant and obsessive and a little shy. Yet also so changed that sometimes Gruruvardh isn't sure who he is. This is why he doesn't expect what the King says next.

"I am going to start a war, Gruruvardh," says the King.

"What kind of war, and to what end, Devapādaḥ?"

"A war of independence."

"Independence?"

The King gazes at Surya's bright pinprick dangling in the dark west. Between them is the messy iridescence of Nagapura sprawled on both sides of the black sweep of the river. No fishermen upon it at this hour and no ferries. The only disturbance on the glossy darkness are reflections of the copse of the Himadōtadevālayaḥ's floodlit sikharas, rising like crownless trunks at the city's heart.

The King points at it. "From that."

"You're going to war with the Guardian?"

"With all of them. With the whole scam."

Gruruvardh squints. "What the hell are you talking about, boy? It wasn't enough to shoot one in the palace gardens? You're lucky they didn't riot. The Guardian won't stand any more nonsense. Leave off while you can."

"Why should I be afraid of the Guardian? Who is he? Who are any of them? Not a single one knows anything of philosophy or theology or right and wrong. They just ring bells and sing hymns and smear ash on each other. They're leeches."

"They're our conduit to the Dawn. They take our offerings and turn them into blessings."

"And yet none of them can speak to her. I can, if I wanted to. I could send her a petition. I alone have her mandate." A pause. "You cannot believe all that superstition."

"Superstition? You mean faith?" Gruruvardh arches his eyebrows. "Do you not?"

"No. Not since before I left."

"That long?"

"That long."

"You hid it well."

"I've hidden many things well."

They find a marble bench and sit. The stone is still day-warm against the King's skin.

"If you anger the Dawn, who will feed us?" says Gruruvardh. "The grain-vimanas will stop."

"I have found a way to wean us off them."

"And when She sends forces against us? What fleet will you defend Yama with?"

"The priesthood is rich. I will seize their valuables and use it to pay for a new fleet. Besides, She won't attack. She has bigger problems to worry about."

"Like what?"

"Like the things that took my daughter. Like the fact that her sister has returned to the realm of Surya."

Gruruvardh stiffens. "How do you know that?"

"Have you not heard? First, mysterious Triangulans attacked the Dnyānasya Mandīram. They seized a Marut and ... and my girl. Then the Ox himself was sent to investigate. Then a juggernaut destroyed the Bhujañgānām Mandīram. Who else can do such things?"

Surya twinkles as it sinks to the horizon. "You cannot know for certain what's happening. You cannot know how any of this will unfold."

"This is true. But I have help in that department."

"Help?"

"A program designed to wage and win wars. I doubted it at first, but it predicted the priests' actions. Down to the very week." He pauses. "I know you think my killing of the priest was a casual act of terror, old friend. It wasn't. It was calculated to send a message."

"It was murder, nevertheless." Gruruvardh blinks. "What program? Where did you get it from?"

"It was kept in a vault in the Temple of Knowledge."

"The demon? The simulated soul?"

"I have it under control."

"Devapādaḥ—"

"I know what I'm doing, Gruruvardh."

Silence. The fleet of bats is long gone. In their place, the far glitter of the silent stars.

"I have to do something, Gruruvardh. I have to do something, or I won't be able to live with myself," whispers the King. "When I first left I took a woman to be a concubine on Himenduḥ. A courtesan. Pretty but sharp-tongued, she was. I had no love for her and when time came to leave, I left her without thinking.

"I saw her again many years later. She was working as a jeweler's servant. They came to my house to sell us some gold. My wife only wanted a gold chain to melt down for her illicit experiments."

A smile wafts across his face like a cloud across the moon.

"She looked like she wanted to tell me something the whole time she was there. She looked so broken when she left. I told my wife of it—she knew everything of me—and she said I perhaps should have invited them back. I thought about it, long and hard. I even prepared my motorpalanquin for the journey. But then I hesitated. Why should a prince go to a courtesan, I thought. What could she possibly tell me that I would need to know?

"But I regret not going. I regret not asking. I want to know. Was she well? Was she mistreated? How did she end up on Daitya? Why did she come to see me? If it were my only regret then, perhaps, I could live with it, but it's just one amongst many. So many I don't know if I can breathe sometimes. Why did I hesitate to bring my family back here and fight for my child's inheritance? Why did I turn my back on my whole world for the sake of my heartless mother? Why did I let go of you in all those years away and never once send you a token of my love?"

"That, you need not regret, my boy."

"And yet I do. I do." The King buries his face in his hands. "We die, Gruruvardh. We all die suddenly and without meaning. We're like ... asteroids in the deep. We bounce and we spin and we collide, and there's no reason for any of it. To die full of regret is doubly meaningless. When my time comes, I at least want to face it, knowing I did what I was impelled to do. That I lived well and lived true.

"I am King of this place. To my mother that was an exhalation, but to me it's an opportunity. I will change this world for the better, then I will go searching for my little girl. I will wrench her back from the grip of the gods themselves, or else I will exact my revenge for her death upon them, even if it destroys me. That will be a meaningful death, at least. Do you understand? Do you understand, old friend?"

Gruruvardh wipes the dampness from his eyes. "Your life is full of meaning, my boy. You are loved. You are admired. The people already speak kindly of your reforms. To give away the treasures of the palace to the poor. To open the kitchen doors to the destitute. They're hanging pictures of you in their shops and homes without being told. You're making their lives better.

"But wars and revolutions—they're terrible things. I've heard people speak of revolution before. They all imagined somehow it means justice. But it doesn't. Rage and strength rule over reason and fairness. The glamour of revolutions is the glamour of the inferno. Are you certain this, too, isn't something you'll regret?"

The King shakes his head. "I don't. I can't. Will you stand by me, regardless?"

Gruruvardh buries his face in his hands. "I see death in all this. I see the death of millions."

"At least they will die for a purpose," says the King of Yama.

"Is that you speaking or that monstrous program of yours?"

Surya's pale light blinks out on the horizon. The King says nothing.

2.18

AKUPĀRA SWEEPS LOW OVER THE tents clustered like mushrooms around the stump of the Bhujañgānām Mandīram. Ruined stonework sags into fleshy deformations. Goo oozes from the wreckage to glisten like bile in the cold daylight. Laid out beside it in neat ranks are the swaddled bodies of the dead. Ice dust crawls like crystalline mites across the blue skin of their naked faces. Their corneas dry and harden in the cruel autumn wind.

The vimana lands. Despite the grief and carnage, the surviving Sisters line up in front of their butchered home. Their flawless crimson uniforms and their precision in greeting are acts of defiance all their own. They kneel in unison as Akupāra's airlock sighs open and the Ox comes stalking down with his face scrunched against the cold. The Huntress strides up between them with her red cloak flapping about her shoulders like flames and her red hair doing the same atop her head. "You're late," she says.

The Ox squints. "A thousand human years, and that's the first thing you say to me?"

"A thousand human years, and you're still late."

The Ox pushes chuckling past her and heads towards what's left of the Temple of the Snake. The sheer thunderous violence of its destruction is evident in the debris, the dying, and the dust. In one tent some Sisters are tending to the sobbing injured. In another, one stands over a still-warm corpse, whispering prayers with her hands splayed and her face wet.

"It was a juggernaut?" asks the Ox.

The Huntress keeps effortless pace. "Yes."

"You're certain?"

"It was Skōlex."

"How can you be sure?"

"Because any other juggernaut would have hesitated. Because I saw it with my own two eyes."

"Aging eyes."

She looks at him askance and says nothing.

The Ox halts by a calamitous pile of muck-sweating stoneflesh and looks around. How typical that his mother's herald is disaster. How tedious that he should be following again in her ruinous wake.

"Do you know which way it went?"

The Huntress scowls. "Are you asking if I saw which way it went into space? Prabho Tvashtr did not bless this body with telescope eyes." Her gaze skews to the skies. "Last I heard, he was tacking towards Daitya. Shouldn't you know this?"

"How many survived?"

"About half of the entire order and nearly all of the snakes. Why wasn't I told she was here?"

"We were not certain it was her."

"You weren't certain? How could you not be certain? It's your charge to be certain about such things."

"And it's your job to protect these reaches of the Nine Worlds. How could you let her sneak up on you like this? Why have I had to leave Mangala and traipse out here into the cold because she got the better of you again?"

The Huntress's jaws clamp so hard her cheeks quiver. "Your mother is a sneak," she says. "Tell me then what we're going to do."

"I'm going to find her, I'm going to stop her." A pause. "You, on the other hand, are to make your way to Yama."

"Yama? Why Yama?"

"Something you don't know? The Yamans have risen up against their priests. They've rejected the way of the Dawn and have started growing their own crops."

"The Queen of Yama did this?"

"The Queen of Yama is dead. Her son now rules, and it's he who started it."

"What has this to do with me?"

"You're to go and show him what happens to those who betray the Dawn."

The Huntress crosses her arms. "No."

"Pardon?"

"I said no. I'll send some of my girls, but I'm not going to Yama myself." She bares her fangs. "I will go to kill the Night."

The Ox snorts. "Don't be absurd. She'd crush you from a yojana away. She'll flick you out into the void like a bug."

The Huntress grinds shards of stone beneath her heel and says nothing.

The Ox turns to the ruins behind him. The mist shredding about the tower like a flutter of lost souls. The low growl of the wind like a skulking wolfpack. What a ferocious uproar it must have been when Skōlex struck. A clamor worthy of the beginning of the end of the world. No slow erosion like the empires of old for the Dawn's dominion over the Nine Worlds of Surya. Its end will come instead like a dam creaking and cracking and bursting to ruin all at once.

He reaches out with a foot and tips over a small pile of rubble.

"This mission is no irrelevancy," he says. "Yama is crucial if we're to defeat my mother. Who knows what allies she can summon? Who knows if she even has more than one juggernaut?"

"That should not be hard for you to find out."

"I know what I have to do. And now so do you."

The Huntress inspects the Ox's face like she's found some strange blemish thereupon that is growing before her very eyes.

"It would be convenient for you to have me out of the way in Yama."

"Convenient? How so?"

"With me and my order engaged, you'll be free to collaborate with your mother to undermine the Dawn."

The Ox rolls his eyes. "This nonsense again? Millennia of loyal service and still you cast aspersions on my, um, dignity?"

"I am merely pointing out the facts."

"Then let me point out some to you in return." The Ox turns to her with the slow teeter of a boulder about to crash down a mountainside. "I'm sending you to secure the production capacity of the third most powerful state in all of the Nine Worlds. The shipyards. The textile mills. The missile manufactories. Explain to me, with precision, if you would, how this will not help the Dawn defend her throne?"

"We don't need Yama. The Golden Swarm can handle one juggernaut."

"With great losses. If this is Skōlex, as you say, you know what he can do. You know neither the Golden Swarm nor the Red Fleet were built to fight our own. He will die, but not before he rips out the guts of half of our vimanas. Maybe more. Then what? Then how will we hold the system? Then how will we put down rebellions and quell the ambitions of overmighty warlords like the King of Yama? Signal Triangulum for reinforcements? Or perhaps you can send some of your snake-women. You seem to think they'll be of some use in this war, so tell me how you'll contribute. Will you board Skōlex? Will you sneak up on my mother? Will you use the dark against she who is the dark?"

A waft of snow slips like a zombie tongue between them. The Huntress sighs, sour-faced.

"It doesn't smell right. Why is she back now? Why is she back at all?"

"What else is this evidence of, but, um, love?"

"What?"

The Ox shakes his head. "Never mind. Will you do as I say? Will you secure Yama for us?"

A pause. Then the Huntress bows. "Yes, prabho. Yes, we will."

The Ox nods and walks back to Akupāra. No farewells. No acknowledgement of the Sisters still serried in rows and shivering in the cold. Nothing said until the airlock swivels shut and the groaning old vimana lifts into the air and Himenduḥ's surface dwindles behind it into a patched grey globe scarred with clashing valleys like slashes of old blood.

The Ox exhales and sinks into his chair.

"Well, old friend," he says. "The bitch nearly had me there. She very nearly had me."

2.19

THE TWINS TAKE THE SNAKEGIRL away from the Throne of Night through the long dark of the Throne Room. She is suddenly awake to everything. The far-off ceiling. The floor like hewn black ice. The faint smell like cold iron and distant blossoms. Parts of her she thought would never heal now itch instead of burn. A fresh certainty sits enthroned somewhere within her. That to be forgotten is the fate of all things. That life is no less than the universe's attempt at remembering itself.

After a short while her soles begin to sting against the cold floor. The Twins reach out without a word and hold her up, an inch or so off the ground, as they go.

"Thank. You," she whispers.

"There are others like you," they say. Their eerie coordination doesn't feel so strange anymore. "We will take you to them."

They proceed towards a far slit of light that distends as they approach into a trabeated doorway. Beyond is another gargantuan space lit by rows of great braziers lined against its soaring walls, bright enough to illuminate an intricate ceiling far overhead. In front of her is a long ramp leading down between what look like giant black mirrors. She sees two figures sitting by them in the distance. As they move to stand, they set perfect ripples sailing out across the surface and reveal the substance for the liquid it is.

She takes a few steps forward. The floor warmer here than in the Throne Room but only just warm enough to tolerate. The Twins head down the ramp without waiting for her. She follows, wincing with every step and staring at the giant friezes stretching heavenwards about her. The great staring eyes and the geometric flames. The wreckage and the body parts and the stars blazing like unforgiving gods. She believed, from the instant she laid eyes on the Night, that she was who she said she was. Now she realizes that meeting such a creature means being a part, however small, of what can only be a myth. A tale of the odd, the miraculous, the incomprehensible. How else to explain her presence here? Or the fact that the river of this temple-fortress-monster's life would flow across unthinkable millions of yojanas just to intersect with the minute trickle of her own?

The two figures are closer now. A big-eyed, dark-faced, snooty-looking girl and a round-faced man whose soft contours press like hills against his granthapālaḥ's robes. They come to a halt a little way away. The Twins approach them, and to her astonishment, they bow to the girl.

The girl bows back.

"Convey our thanks, if you would, to the Night for the extra braziers and our bedrolls," she says. "Who is our guest?"

"Do not touch her," say the Twins. "She is venomous."

"Venomous? Is she a Sister of the Snake?"

"Yes."

"Where did you get one of the Bhujaṅgānām Bhaginī from?"

"We attacked our enemy's hold, and she was taken inadvertent prisoner."

The girl arches her eyebrows. "You would appear to be in the habit of doing that."

While the girl speaks the man stares at the Snakegirl like he is trying to read a book in a text he'd only recently forgotten. She inspects him in return. She knows this man, she thinks. She knows those eyes. She knows the way he stands, leaning forward ever so slightly like he is concentrating very hard on everything around him. She knows the great golden smile that erupts on his face when he realizes who she is, too.

"Indra?" she whispers.

"Kadrū! What're you doing here?"

They nearly fall into each other's arms, but the Princess yanks the Gelding back.

"No! Venom, prabho Indra! She's untouchable!"

"She is weak," says Auron.

"Though her venom was denatured by Skolex," says Amerxis.

"She is still potent."

"Her touch stings us."

"So will certainly kill you."

"She needs proper clothes," says the Princess. "This cowl you have her in will not suffice. We will need a bedroll for her and gloves as well. Would you be so kind as to fetch them for us?"

"We have many things here," say the Twins. They turn on their heels and sprint off. As they dwindle into the distance, the Little Princess is certain she sees them drop to all fours and start loping like wolves on a hunt.

The Snakegirl sees none of it. Instead, she just stares at the Gelding and the many miracles his presence suggests. All tiny beside the fabulous improbability of her arrival aboard the battle-juggernaut of Night but not one iota less wondrous for all that. Some infinities are smaller than others, but none are any less infinite.

"Of course." She coughs. "Of course. You. Are here. Why not. Swallowed. By. A juggernaut. Why not. You, too?"

The Gelding grins. "Yes. Why not? Doesn't make any less sense than anything else, does it? Which is to say, nothing makes sense."

The Little Princess crosses her arms. "You apparently know each other."

"Kadrū is an old friend. My oldest friend." The Gelding's smile quivers. "My dearest."

The Little Princess examines the Snakegirl like a heron scanning a pond for frogs. "A friend of yours is a friend of mine. I am Danu, heir to the throne of Yama."

The Snakegirl nods at her but speaks to the Gelding.

"Why are you. Dressed. Like that?"

"I became a granthapālaḥ!"

"Of course. You did." She smiles. "Nerd."

They lapse into a brimming silence. Long and full enough for the Little

Princess to look from one face to the other and frown and open her mouth and then close it again without a word.

Snakegirl hisses and shuffles from foot to foot. The Gelding sees briefly the calcium-white soles of her feet tilted up and away from the freezing floor. The Gelding takes off his shoes and hands them to her.

"Here."

The Snakegirl takes them like she doesn't know what they are. The venerable purple of their velvet. The warmth of their sides against the palms of her hands. The ice and blood and the sound of a body crunching against the frigid ground.

She sinks onto her haunches, buries her face in her knees, and starts to sob.

"I'm sorry," she whispers. "I'm sorry."

The Gelding watches, unable to help, unable to even comprehend what's happening. That's the problem with miracles. What they obscure is greater by far than what they resolve.

2.20

THE SOUL OF MANGALA COMES rattling across the hangar as soon as it spots the King and halts a few feet away from him to the sound of grinding gears and the ping of cooling metal. It appraises him with domed insectoid eyes. Then it waves its three-point pincers in the air.

"You seriously couldn't do any better than this?" it says. "Do you know how hard it is to do anything trapped in here?"

"It will suffice." The King peers into the mid-distance where a vimana squats like a half-assembled iron elephant. Overhead, through the gaping ceiling of the hangar, is a glum parade of rainless cumulus. "Is that it?"

"As best I can do in this state. If you network me to a proper control hub—"

"You will not be networked. Ever. Is it finished?"

"Enough for me to show you what it can do."

They wander over. Orange-suited technicians back off a few feet and kneel. The King dismisses them with a wave of his hand, and they walk out backwards to a distant door. A brief glimmer as it opens. The sound of metal on metal. Then silence.

"I heard you seized the Himadōtadevālayaḥ today," says the Soul. "You moved fast."

"I wanted to avoid panic," says the King.

"How did the Guardian take it?"

"Badly. I spared him on account of Gruruvardh."

"That's a mistake."

"We'll see."
"Anything from outside?"
"Word has got out, but the grain-vimanas still come. Traders still come."
"There'll be inflation."
"We control the banks. We're rationing. The crops are already growing."
The quick whine of servos. The Soul tilts his head. "I'm impressed. Didn't think you'd listen to me."
The King says nothing.
They pause by the belly of the unlovely vimana. The King examines the great flaring nozzles of its boosters, the iron claws of its landing gear, its stubby metallic nose. After a while he leans forward, rests his forehead against the cold iron, and closes his eyes.
"What you said about my daughter," he breathes. "You're certain the Night has her?"
"I said probably."
"How probably?"
"Very probably."
"And what chance is there she's alive?"
"High, I'd say. Unless she died on the way over to the juggernaut, the Night will probably keep her to see if she's of some use." The Soul holds up his pincers and stares at them for a few moments. "She was always the more thoughtful one of the two."
The King sighs and straightens.
"Very well, demon. Show me how you intend to keep your end of our bargain."
The vimana thuds and extends a ramp like a perforated metal tongue. They climb up into a cramped interior full of raw wiring and screens febrile with cluttered neon data. The King has to make his way slowly down a passage too narrow for him to stand in sideways, scowling.
"This does not look promising," he says.
"Watch your mouth. This is all my hard work, see?" The Soul pushes the King towards a sliver of a seat up in the domed cockpit and slots himself in, clacking and awkward, next to him. "This technology's been kept from you by your mama because you're naughty kids who can't be trusted to go fucking around with it. Not a single cell or neuron in the whole damn thing. Nothing you can't reproduce yourselves. All of which I had to do through your moron engineers, by the way, because you won't let me out of this fucking service drone."
The King examines the inexplicable lightshow of the controls around him. "In fact, it's a cleaning unit."
"A fucking janitor?" The Soul begins to flip ranks of silver switches. "You realize how much of a goddam genius I am to use a shit cleaner to build a spaceship?"
"What are all these controls? Why is this so complicated?"
"Because space flight is complicated. You know how hard it is to learn how to ride a bike. How easy do you think flying a spaceship is?" Far to the

rear, engines spin to life with a meaty whine. "Used to piss me right the fuck off how old movies had people figuring out how to fly one without so much as breaking a fart. Just sit in the pilot's seat, press a few buttons, and off they go. As if space flight wasn't the hardest thing humanity's done."

The vimana judders and rises. Up through the gaping roof, then tilting skywards and rocketing with a jolt towards the clouds. The flick and lick of flaming debris against the windows. The incendiary halo of metal heating as they break the atmosphere. The vimana judders through a quartet of shockwaves. The grey and blue of the atmosphere sinks away with surprising speed. Soon they're out in the raw black with the stars like burning dust and the Little Sun peeking over the horizon as if it had noticed them there.

The Soul enters some numbers onto a screen and grips hold of a lever.

"Keep your eyes on the window. We're jumping in three ... two ..."

A thud, and Yama disappears. Half an instant of nothing follows—neither star nor space nor the sustaining dimensions of familiar reality. Then they're back, drifting beside some colossal sapphire pearl skirted with a scything crystal ring.

The King's eyes widen.

"That's Arungrah," he breathes.

"Sure is."

"How long did that take?"

"Point-nine-six-eight seconds. Would've been faster but this is a piece of shit and I'm doing the calculations myself. You've got to upgrade me. This thing has the processing power of a beetroot."

"And you can do this for all the vimanas we're building?"

"Sure can."

The King examines the planet. The scale and silence of the thing. More matter in its substance than all the bodies of all the people to ever live. Old when the first humans held their hands to their faces and wondered what they could do with them beside hold and break and kill. Why is he so moved by something so vast and so different? Perhaps because, despite its might and majesty, this great, dignified sphere will one day dissipate and disappear just like him. How unfair that the only commonality of all things isn't birth or love or suffering, but death. What a cruel burden being aware of that is to place on creatures as small as humans.

The King looks at his hands.

"A lot of people died," he says.

"What?"

"I said, a lot of people died." The King looks up at the planet again. "Down on Yama, it all seems to make sense. But up here. Everything looks so small. Death is such a ... blunt tool to have to use."

"What're you talking about?" The Soul gestures to the planet. "Look, I gave you what you wanted, didn't I? I held up my side of the bargain."

"You did."

"Right. Go ahead and have your crisis of conscience, or whatever, but don't let it get in the way of your promise."

The King rests his head against the cool glass. "You have my word. I will give you what I promised."

"Good." The Soul's eyes swivel out towards Surya. "Then maybe I'll feel better about you stuffing me into this fucking broom-monkey."

2.21

AFTER SHE HAS CRIED HERSELF out, the Gelding directs the Snakegirl to one of the pools in the Antechamber of Night and stands with his back to her as she bathes. After she emerges and dresses in a tunic the Twins have brought, he borrows a comb from the Little Princess and tends to her hair with the precision and exactitude of a sacred ritual. The slow settle of her breath and his into unintended synchrony. The sweet-but-sour smell of her, memorable yet novel, idling in his nostrils.

Afterwards, he leads her into the room with the glowing ceiling where part of the floor has already started to go soft and spongy with the same cryptic alchemy that produced his sleeping space. The Snakegirl settles, quivering like all her bones were on the verge of breaking, and he sits by her as she falls asleep. At some point she wakes and curls up against the wall and resumes crying. Softer this time. Drizzle to the hurricane of grief he witnessed earlier. The Gelding dons gloves, wraps his robes about himself, and holds her until her grief fades.

He does this most nights until the night terrors end and, in increments, she recovers. Some unexplained grief still lies draped about her shoulders like a lead cloak, but slowly, she learns to walk despite it. As she does, the two of them start to wander Skōlex's labyrinthine reaches together in the silence of those familiar enough to converse without words.

One day they find a long balcony overlooking a black reservoir. The roof overhead is low and carved with shimmering glyphs, each an intricate geometrical wonder so complex it might have encoded the story of an entire species. In the shapeless distance are wandering lights, their movements oddly organic, their every shift signaled by some faint noise that sometimes skirts the edge of melody, but mostly hisses with the particulate rhythm of falling rain.

"What are those?" says the Snakegirl.

"I don't know," says the Gelding. He sits with his feet dangling over the edge of the platform. The blackness beneath. The far-down glug and slap of water. "Skōlex is a strange place. I think there are other creatures that live here besides us. Or lived. I saw a skeleton once. It looked like a dog's, but it was huge. And I hear things sometimes."

"Like what?"

"Footsteps. Singing. It might be singing. It might just be ... melodic wind."

"Are they—did you ask the Twins?"

"They don't know. I don't think they care."

"Did you ask the Night?"

The Gelding shakes his head. "It didn't come up when we last spoke. I was a little distracted by speaking with the Destroyer of Worlds and finding her so very polite."

The Snakegirl smiles. "You're so tall."

"Apparently, we grow tall and big."

"We?"

"Eunuchs."

"Oh." She picks at her shoe. "Can you piss all right?"

"Mostly. I wear a pad."

"A pad?"

He points to his crotch. "To prevent leaks."

"Oh. I do, too. For. You know."

"I know." A smile. A pause. "You were screaming again yesterday. In your sleep."

"I have these nightmares." The Snakegirl rubs her face, cheek-to-eyes and down again with both hands. "The same ones over and over. I'm trapped in a room. It's growing smaller, and I know it's going to crush me. Or I have to get out of a house, and the door's too small for me. Or we're in a cave, and we have to go through some hole. I know I won't fit, and I know if I try I'll just suffocate.

"Then I think, fuck, think of all the things that ever got swallowed alive. This is in my dreams—I'm thinking this in my dreams. Imagine that for a death. Must have felt a lot like what happened to me. Just, it's fucked up, you know. The way things die. Crushed and smeared and suffocated. The universe is so big, you think there'd be space for everyone. Or at least space enough for things not to have to die like that. But there isn't. I know. I know." A pause. "Do you ever feel like, I don't know, like the gods must be real because your life is just such a fucking tragedy? Like, how the hell does this shit happen unless someone with a shit sense of humor is pulling the strings?"

"You mean—like, the Night?"

"I dunno. Maybe. She doesn't seem like ... that sort of god, though. It's just, sometimes I think the gods must be real because my life's just fucked up in the most ridiculous way. I loved my life with my mum and my swāmin, but then I got sold. I was settling into life at the Slaver's, but then I got sold. Then I get to the Bhujañgānām Mandīram and go from being a servant to a Snakegirl. Then the Night herself turns up and destroys the place. And then ..."

"And then?"

Her voice drops. "And then I find my way back to you. Somehow."

They look and see each other with such clarity it's as if they're really just parts of the same thing and their separation was just an illusion of a universe incapable of comprehending their oneness. The Snakegirl wants to say this. This and a million other things about what she's seen and done and felt since they parted. Things that would feel like walking naked in a snowstorm to say.

Things she would tell him as confession, as entreaty, as warning about who and what she is. Yet, she can't think of one reason why any of it matters more than just being beside him now, safe and at peace, and so she says nothing.

The Little Princess comes in. She looks from one to the other, prim face hard.

"Am I interrupting?" she says.

"No." The Gelding points to the space between him and the Snakegirl. "Join us, kumari."

She does.

"What were you discussing?"

"Whether the gods are real."

"They are not," says the Princess, with conviction. "They are biomechanical entities of exceeding power from the Triangulum galaxy."

"Then who governs our fates?" says the Snakegirl. "Who gives the universe its ... poetry?"

"I don't know anything about poetry. But I do know we make our own joy—or sorrow. Blaming gods is just a way of abdicating our responsibilities to ourselves and each other."

"You sound so damn sure."

"Because my mother and father taught me well. And please note, the proper form of address is kumari."

"What?"

"You sound so damn sure, kumari. I am yet a Princess of Yama."

The Snakegirl laughs. "You're nothing out here. None of us are. We're all just ..." She waves her hand. "Nothing."

The Little Princess sniffs. "It is not for you to decide what I am. I am a princess. I will be as long as my house stands, as long as Yama remains the Pearl at the Gates of the Nine Worlds," she says.

A pause. Then the Snakegirl nods.

"All right, kumari," she says. "Screw circumstance. Not as if it's fair, anyway."

"Quite right, Sister."

They look across the darkness and see that the motes are still. An instant later, they start moving again. As if they'd all been listening. As if they'd understood every word the three of them had had to say.

2.22

SWIFT YAMAN SPRING SLIPS INTO long Yaman summer, and the King tries hard to garner satisfaction from a kingdom already half remade. The grain vimanas have stopped coming; but the harvest is complete, and the silos are full. Some priests, the compliant ones, are already back at their temples and keeping to the provisos that they sweep the streets, care for the poor, and pay taxes on their diminished but still-vast incomes. The aristocrats who ignored him are all either dead or exiled or cowed enough that now it's they who seek audiences with him. He denies every single one.

Still, dissatisfaction crawls beneath his skin like gnawing mites. He snaps at the servants. He wanders the Nāgaprāsādaḥ alone at night. He lingers by the portraits of the Crown Princess and the Little Princess he's had put up in the entrance hall. The former in a golden room—laughing, distracted, and beautiful. The latter holding a little robot she's built, two front teeth missing. Between them is his new shield—a two-headed cobra wrapped around a long-stalked sheaf of rice.

His detractors say he's actually staring at his own crest.

Gruruvardh, though, knows that this is as close as he lets himself come these days to crying.

One evening he enters the King's apartments with the look of a man about to tell a dancer his legs must be amputated. "Raja," he says. He takes in the mess of plates and devices and clothes. The curtains, unopened for weeks. The pungent waft of body and bed. "Haven't the staff been cleaning?"

"I don't know." The King looks around. "It may be that I sent them away."

"I'll send for some now."

"No. Please. I want to be left alone."

"Even by me? Even if I come bearing the counsel of a loyal first minister?"

The King rubs his eyes. "I will listen to you, old friend."

Silence, but for the rhythmic cricking of cicada-song and the hiss of insects frying in the traps outside. Gruruvardh glances across the Nāgaprāsādaḥ's grounds, stroked by the thick jungle wind, bisected by a river now low and sluggish in the late summer heat. The whole world is exhausted, he thinks, by the last year's convulsions. Why shouldn't the river be, too? Why shouldn't he?

He leans against the doorframe.

"I know about the fleet," he says.

"Then I've been betrayed."

"This is no joke, boy. If your enemies know this is the work of your pet demon, it'll be a weapon against you. Look at him, they'll say. He went abroad and got corrupted. Marrying a foreigner and now listening to an ancient demon. He's a sorcerer. How else has he wrought what he has? How else has he overturned three thousand years of order with such ease?"

"That doesn't sound like what they will say. It sounds like what they're already saying." The King examines his knees. "There's no harm in letting my enemies fear me."

"What are you going to do with that fleet?"

"I told you. I'm going to go and find my girl."

"And who will oversee your revolution here while you're away?"

"I told you before. You will."

Gruruvardh laughs. "You were serious? Leave an old man like me while you run away to try to kill the Dawn?"

"It's not the Dawn that has her. It's the Night."

"The Night? But she's not here."

"She is. She's back. And she took Danu."

"Who told you this? Was it the demon? That creature is a liar. It will tell you whatever it wants to manipulate you to do what it wants."

"He's been right thus far, hasn't he?"

"Listen, boy. I know that—"

"You don't." The King leans forward. "You don't know. You haven't lost your wife and your child. You've not spent half your life in exile on account of a mother who didn't love you. You don't understand or know why I do these things or what'll happen next."

Gruruvardh frowns. "Is that what you think? That your mother didn't love you?"

"Even if she did, her love was no good to me. Leave me alone, Gruruvardh. All that matters is that I get my girl back."

"More than your kingdom, raja?"

"More than the sun and the stars and the fabric of the universe."

Gruruvardh stands and walks slowly to the door. Then he turns back.

"You're wrong, raja. You say I don't know how you feel, but I do. I cannot speak for your mother, but I can speak for me, and I know what it is to love a child. To feel so intensely that there's no one in the world quite like her. To wonder if everyone else could truly love the way I do. To lament that something of such profundity was of no more interest to the universe than a glint at a mirror's edge."

He looks back across the river. The changeless treeline. The winking diadem of stars on the horizon.

"But love does not supersede duty. There are millions out there who need you. Who love their children no less than we do. They did not ask to have their destinies in our hands. They're scared of what the Dawn will do. They're scared of rumours that the Traitani will attack or one of the principalities of Arungrah. They've seen their world upended. This is no time to leave them behind."

"I'm leaving them in good hands."

"I won't accept it. I'll resign if you leave."

"No, you won't." The King meets Gruruvardh's gaze. "You won't resign because if you do, that'll be the end of this house. Once I leave, who will be here to guard my interests? Who will protect the legacy of my ancestors? Who, but you? If you aren't here, the Nāgaprāsādaḥ will fall. I won't be able to return without a war, and I won't fight one and bring more grief to the people. I'll retire to Daitya and live out my days, and Yama will move into some new age. Of peace, perhaps. But the people have tasted freedom now. They won't let the aristocrats and priests return. So, more likely, without a legitimate house, civil war. Who knows what order will emerge from that?"

Gruruvardh purses his lips. "You have it all strategized, don't you? Or was it your demon?"

"Do you take me for a fool?"

"No. Many things, but never that." Gruruvardh sighs. "You're right. I won't abandon your house, even if you do. I'll carry on then, even if it's the death of me. But, raja, either you're lying to yourself, or you're not who I thought you were, if you abandon us now."

He turns to leave.

"Gruruvardh," says the King.

"Devapādaḥ?"

"Please don't hate me for loving my child."

The old man sniffs but doesn't turn around. "How much I hate you, my boy," he says, "has no bearing on how much I love you."

2.23

I

THE HUMANS ARE SITTING IN the Antechamber of Night the first time the Night comes to them. Filigreed ice sweeps across the surface of the dark pools. A chill mist thickens in the air like forgetfulness about the aged. Through this, they see her coming down the ramp, diminutive and dark. The otherworldly sensation of some colossal mass moving irresistibly towards them. The frost blooming in exquisite halo at her feet.

The Snakegirl starts to kneel, but the Night shakes her head. "No, Sister. Let us converse as we are. I have questions."

"I shall answer them to the extent I am comfortable," says the Little Princess.

"But you and I are on the same side, little old one," says the Night. "We both wish to overturn the false gods."

"I'm yet to be convinced of your intentions."

"Show some respect," hisses the Snakegirl.

"No." The Night's smile is like a galaxy burning in the void. "The Crown Princess of Yama is entitled to her suspicions. Answer me when you wish, kumari, but perhaps your colleagues will help me now. Tell me. Why is your system silent? What happened to your communications?"

"It's the Bright One's doing," says the Snakegirl. "She stopped all long-distance communications to prevent the spread of lies."

"How like her to burn the tree to spite the flowers. How is information passed then from one realm to another?"

"By quick vimanas, devi."

The Night arches her eyebrows. "That must take months."

"For humans, yes, devi. The Dawn has reserved use of more efficient methods for herself."

"I see. I am led to believe yours is an order of assassins, Sister. In your temple—they must have taught you something of the lay of the system, correct?"

"Yes, devi."

"Tell me then of Daitya. What resistance can I expect if I attack, beyond that of the Maruts?"

"Daitya?" The Gelding shuffles. "Why would the Night attack Daitya?"

"I must eliminate this Dnyānasya Mandīram, as you call it." The Night examines his face. "This agitates you, prabho. Why?"

"Forgive this one's—"

"Speak plainly, please."

"Right. Why would you attack the Dnyānasya Mandīram?"

"I would eliminate it, as I eliminated—what is it you called it? The Bhujañgānām Mandīram? They are not what they appear to be."

"What are they?" says the Little Princess.

"Can you not tell with that ferocious mind of yours, kumari? Yes, I think you can. Daitya's defenses, Sister, if you would."

"There aren't any major defenses on Daitya," says the Snakegirl. "They don't expect attacks because the Udāradādinaḥ do the attacking. No one's dared attack Daitya in more than two thousand years since they received a Mandate."

"What is a Mandate?" asks the Night.

"The Mandate of Dawn. It's how she gives permission for people to rule. Anyone holding a Mandate can call on the Red Fleet of Mangala to come to their aid. Only a few houses in the system hold one, and they're respected above the others."

"My house holds one," says the Little Princess, straight-backed. "We've held it for nearly a thousand years."

"Yama's a small kingdom," says the Snakegirl. "Productive, but no longer as prosperous as it was. And it's got no fleet."

"It is not a small—"

The Night interrupts with as little fanfare as sunset dooming a dusk. "Will anyone rally to the aid of the Maruts?"

"Some may," says the Snakegirl. "If you strike quickly, devi, some may not, but after your attack on the Bhujañgānām Mandīram, they'll know you're here, and the Udāradādinaḥ may well already be summoning their vassals."

"I see."

"Must you destroy the Dnyānasya Mandīram, devi?" says the Gelding. "Must you destroy it whole?"

"Do you object, prabho?"

"My friends are there. If ... if they're not already dead. I wouldn't want them hurt."

"Or the innocents who will no doubt be killed in this folly," says the Little Princess.

"That's the price of victory," says the Snakegirl.

"Victory?" The Princess scowls. "Whose victory? You've nothing to do with any of this. It's easy to say things like that when you stand to lose nothing."

"What would you know? I've family on Daitya, too. I have people I know."

"Well, then you can't love them that much if you just dismiss their lives as the 'price of victory,'" says the Princess.

The Night holds up one hand. Blades of ice crackle and glint at her feet. "Prabho Indra, all are as guilty as they are innocent. You mourn the prospect of deaths on Daitya, but you did not mourn the death of the Sisters on Himenduḥ. Why?"

"They were cruel," he says. "Kadrū's told me about how unkind they were to her. They were assassins and murderers. Killing them might have saved other people."

"Or is it, perhaps, that humans find it much easier to take and break those they do not know? Kindness contingent on familiarity is not kindness to others but kindness to the self. The universe takes no account of such things. It is perfectly just. A gamma ray burst does not distinguish by name. Entropy does not parse the innocence of those whose warmth it wicks away."

"But—surely, devi," he says, "a gamma ray doesn't know the difference between good and evil. You do. And ... and a thing that knows the difference between good and evil and chooses not to care is evil."

The Night peers at him. Her vast presence swells somehow like an engorged black hole. Her gaze clamps like icy fingers on the Gelding's face.

"Perhaps you are right," she says. "However, I have no way of negotiating with the Maruts. They are not as particular as you would have me be about who they hurt."

The Gelding speaks before he has time to think. "I'll speak to them. I've met the Charioteer. He'll at least listen to me."

"The Maruts will not let you near him, prabho. They will kill your body."

"I'll go with him," says the Snakegirl.

Everyone looks at her.

"They'll kill you, too," says the Night. "Or worse, they will take you hostage, and from you they will render all the information they can about me and my intentions."

"They can't touch me. Devi's Twins could barely touch me. And they can't take me alive. I guarantee it." She looks at the Gelding. "I can guarantee the same for Indra."

The Night's gaze swings pendulum-steady from the Gelding to the Snakegirl and back. She turns to the Little Princess. "What say you, kumari?"

"Prabho Indra and Sister Kadrū are brave," says the girl. "They should go in full regalia with all the dignity of your ambassadors. There can be no doubt on the other side that they're speaking for you. That way they're more likely to listen. Alternatively, if they're mistreated, you know precisely where you stand."

"Very wise," says the Night. She reaches up, and the splendid chaos of Skōlex's controls blink to life in front of her. She touches a few of the motes in sequence, and they disappear. "Very well. We will try this. It will do me good to see if this works. Please, come to my Throne Room anon."

She leaves without farewell. The fog clears, the air warms, and the ice sheet upon the water retreats like a glacier in rapid spring. The Gelding reaches for the Snakegirl, but she recoils.

"Sorry," he says. "And ... thank you."

She shrugs. "I've seen what happens when you go wandering off alone."

A half-smile. "Where did you learn to speak like that?"

"Like what?"

"Like you did just now. Like ..."

"Like I was educated? You think all we do in the Mandīram is learn to dance and kill and screw?"

The Little Princess looks like she'd just stepped on a slug.

"Honestly?" says the Gelding. "Yes. Yes, I did."

"Fair enough." The Snakegirl rubs her face with both hands. "The Snakegirls of Himenduḥ must be able to do all sorts. Deceive, inveigle, obfuscate."

"Why did she call you 'prabho?'" asks the Little Princess.

The Gelding glances at her. "Prabho?"

"The Night. She said that agitates you, 'prabho.'" The girl's huge Yaman eyes narrow. "Why would the Night call you prabho?"

"Oh." The Gelding remembers his dreamwalk in the void. "She seems to think I'm someone else. Some hero from one of their myths, or something."

"Are you?"

"Maybe." The Gelding shrugs. "I don't feel like it. I guess I'll find out sooner or later. Seems to me you always find out who you are eventually. Unless you're trying to be what someone else thinks you are. Or what you think you should be. Then things just get confusing."

The Snakegirl's laugh is little more than a bark.

"Yeah," she says. "Tell me about it."

II

THE TWINS SET UP THE low lacquer table before the Night's throne. On it, they place redwood boxes inlaid with enameled complexities that glint as if forged of starlight. The Night watches them work, looking small and lost in thought. In the vast window behind her is the grey-black globe of Daitya, surface rich with citylight like an expanse of glowing neurons, a curving blade of dawn sharp on its leftward horizon.

"Why do you listen to him?" the Twins say. "Why have we altered our plan of attack at his request when we can't even be certain that he's the Thunder-Armed One?"

"Because he may be." The Night smooths back her blueblack hair. "The Omnific has manifested in the strangest forms before. Remember that He is also the Lord of Treasures, the Lover of Songs, the One True Sun. In what form He chooses to appear and why are frequently beyond the rest of us. It is in His nature to do such things—to appear ex nihilo and cause doubt."

"Doubt is a liability in war."

"In making us address doubt, He makes us learn. If we succumb, we change our worldview. If we confront it with logic and reason, we justify our thinking. We change, and He is the instigator of change."

"We thought it was in His nature to overcome obstacles."

"Is that not also change? We cannot defeat Vrtra without Him, whatever form the serpent takes on this occasion."

"Perhaps the serpent is your sister."

The Night's gaze is like the heavy light of an old star gone cruel with age. The Twins look away and resume their chores.

Then, after a while: "A human is a peculiarly weak form to take."

"There have been weaker," says the Night. "Even if His form is weak, His message isn't."

"What is his message?"

"I cannot be sure. But on this occasion I think He is forcing me to confront the absurdities of scale." The Night looks askance at nothing in particular. "It is confusing."

The Twins look unconvinced, but before they can speak they hear the far-off shuffle of the approaching humans. When the trio arrives, the Night descends from her throne, opens the red boxes, and extracts from them sets of black clothes embroidered in cobalt and cerulean motifs. The humans dress with their backs turned to each other.

When they're done, the Night extracts two little blue bindis from the depths of her sari and presses these to their foreheads. Upon contact, a brief sting. The humans flinch.

"Thus will I be with you wherever you go," she says. "Touch these twice, and the Twins will come to your aid. Remove them, and I will know I must avenge you."

The Night holds her left hand out, palm-up. A small fountain of ice seethes upon it and leaves behind a sharp-petalled flower bleeding milky veils of condensation. She hands it to the Snakegirl. The weight of it like neutronium on her palms. The muted sting of its iciness penetrating the alien cloth that protects her flesh.

"This is my seal," says the Night. "You are the first in three thousand years to bear it. Are you prepared?"

"No," whispers the Gelding.

"Yes," says the Snakegirl.

The Night smiles. "You are my Left Hand. And you, Prabho Indra, are my Right. I charge you to go forth now and parley with my enemy. Offer him these terms: total surrender in return for safe passage unto Triangulum for him and his. Accede to this and I will spare them. Reject these terms and I will destroy his realm utterly."

The humans bow. Tiny and magnificent, they are, in their garments of authority. Small creatures undaunted by their smallness. She remembers how much she enjoyed her first visit to this place. She recalls why she was not surprised that her sister found it so hard to leave.

She bows to them. As she does, the floor of the Throne Room gapes, and the ambassadors and the Twins disappear into the void with a silent rush. The stone seals shut behind them without so much as a whisper.

Silence. The Little Princess looks at the Night. The Night looks at her. Neither say anything.

"Well," says the Princess. "I'll be off then."

2.24

IN HIS MANY YEARS IN the Nine Worlds, the Charioteer has never fully understood the strange gift of parsing the probabilities that Tvashtr of the Stellar Forge has given his body. This inconstant foresight that's intrigued and infuriated him over and over again. Still, along the way, he's come to trust it absolutely. So when he hears footsteps and feels with certainty that one of the most significant encounters of his long and venerable life will now commence, he immediately puts down his calligraphy brush. The ink dries on the latest version of strange word he's felt compelled to draw that evening. Perhaps this visit will shed some light on its significance.

The knock, when it comes, seems louder than it is.

"Enter," he says.

A young woman comes in, big-eyed and haughty, clad in a sari so black it almost turns her into a silhouette. He doesn't recognize her, but the man who enters behind her—tall, hairless, and nut-brown—he does.

"Indra," says the Charioteer, rising. "You live!"

The Right Hand presses his palms together. "This one is glad to see the Charioteer of Dawn is well."

"Where have you been? What has happened?" The Charioteer peers at them. "Who gave you those robes?"

The Left Hand steps forward and presses her palms together also. "Ratri of Triangulum," she says, "known also as the Night, has bid these ones, her Left and Right Hands, come unto Rathasārathī, also known as the Charioteer, lieutenant of the usurping Day, and negotiate for the submission of the realm of Daitya."

She places the Night's ice-flower on the table. Lacquer cracks and wood creaks while the Charioteer inspects it. This token from a power he's admired and feared but never loved. Why is he so unmoved by it? Why does he feel tired when he should be afraid?

He looks at the Right Hand. "Does she speak true?"

"She does," says the Right Hand.

The Charioteer sits back and belches. "Well, then. Let me tell you what it looks like to me. The fact that you're here means something is wrong. It looks like the Kṛṣṇā Bhaginī failed to convince Triangulum to help her, or she'd be back with an armada of juggernauts and just kill us all. She's not given to negotiation. She's like the winter. She settles upon and she hardens and grinds you in her embrace."

"She sent these ones," says the Right Hand, "because this one convinced her to."

"You convinced the Night? How?"

"This one's name is Indra."

The Charioteer narrows his eyes. "You are an Ambassador of Night. You need not use honorifics with me."

"This one ..." The Right Hand shakes his head, smiling. "Forgive me. It's hard to keep track of all this. I pleaded with the Night. I don't want to see the Tripura destroyed, prabho. And neither, I hazard, do you."

"You know nothing of what I want. What's to stop me having the Maruts come up here right now and take you away?"

"That would be unwise," says the Left Hand.

A belch. A chuckle. "Is that a threat?"

"You would not take us alive, and the Night's judgement would be upon you sooner rather than later. Thus, that was not a threat. But this is. The Night bids you surrender and evacuate the Dnyānasya Mandīram. She bids also that you and the Maruts leave this place and return in peace to Triangulum. If this is not done, She will visit on you the destruction she would have long ago, if it were not for treason and betrayal."

"Please, swāmin," says the Right Hand. "Please. She will do this. I've spoken to her. You know her. She will destroy the Tripura if she wants to."

The Charioteer sighs and looks out across the Tripura. The facades like glittering cliff-faces and the avenues like incandescent rivers. The shining towers and the overcity of the destitute. The gutters and the glory. He remembers when it was just a grove of trees beside a lake. Both gone now, and in their place this ever-changing expanse of music, madness, and manpower. For three millennia he's watched it grow and shrink, fight and vanquish and burn, with the lonely pride of a parent watching their child outgrow them.

He glances down at the Flower of Night and buries his face in his palms.

"I knew this day would come, and I decided long ago that I would not fight," he says. "I would do anything to spare this city. I would do anything to spare the Mandīram. But you and I have a problem. You have come here assuming I—and I alone—speak for the realm of Daitya. But I do not."

"Who does, prabho?" asks the Left Hand.

"Who do you think? The Tempestuous Ones. The Shakers of the Earth and Heavens. The hundred and six who were hundred and eight. They who will, I promise, sooner see themselves flayed than capitulate to their former sovereign."

"The Night?"

"Ah. You didn't know? Of course not. It's in the Night's nature to conceal.

We've had you Suryans believe that we are all creatures of a kind, but really, we're not. The Dawn and the Night and their kin are as far above me as those two cubs, who no doubt brought you here, are from you. To Them, what happened here, it's just a pebble on a riverbed." He puffs, cheeks deflating slowly. "I just wanted things to stay as they were a little longer than they should have. Was that so wayward?"

"Prabho Charioteer seems full of regret," says the Left Hand.

"Regret—and gas." He belches again. "I will take these demands to the Maruts. I will put it to them and do my best to convince them. But I am telling you, Ambassadors of Night as you are, that I will fail. I tell you also that no matter who lives in this city and no matter how much you love them, your mistress will not think twice before obliterating them. She is a black ocean. She is heat-death incarnate, and in the end her mission will consume you, too."

The Hands bow.

"We will await your summons," says the Left Hand.

Before they leave, they glance down at the word repeated in a hundred permutations on the evening's calligraphy. The Charioteer looks, too, and chuckles.

"Let us hope it is not prophetic," he says. "Yuddha is such a ... jarring word."

The Right Hand nods. "I can think of no beautiful word for war, prabho."

"Neither can I." The Charioteer blinks. "But I'm sure the Maruts can."

2.25

After the Hands leave, the Little Princess walks out of the Throne Room into the Antechamber of Night and considers which of its many exits she will take. In her time aboard—a year? more?—she's learned that the gloom and silence have only one true antidote: exploration. So she selects an egress she's certain she hasn't taken yet and enters the dark labyrinth beyond. After a few hours of solitary rambling—three? more?—she finds herself in a domain of long passageways. Ceiling lights ignite and die as she passes, so she proceeds in her own tiny fief of light. She passes a chipped black statue of two snakes eating each other, a frieze of a hairless buffalo dying beneath a blazing sun, and another of a fox impaled on some curving thing that could be a horn or a sword or neither. Finally, she comes upon a pair of huge doors and sees they're open just a crack. A crack big enough for her to slip in.

She steps into the Chamber of the Soma Seed.

The Little Princess stares. The vast white mass suspended in midair. The torrents of lightning sloughing off in neon discharge. One of the hissing claws of light births itself straight into her stomach. To her astonishment she feels not pain, but a fizz of sudden energy. She touches the Seed. It yields, clay-like, so she presses harder. Her fingers sink in and come away with a soft residue that smells and tastes like sugar and cream, satiating but also ephemeral. Good cheer floods her like abrupt infatuation. She looks around, as if half expecting someone to emerge from the arcades that flank the chamber and stop her. She breaks off a small piece, pops it in her mouth, and chews.

It doesn't take her very long to realize it was a mistake.

The ferocious sweetness of the stuff clings like a parasite to her throat. Unpleasant at first but gathering in discomfort until it blocks her windpipe like a sugary fist. The cloying insistence of the soma leaking into her blood. The thick tendrils of it snaking up her spine into her head. Her thoughts strobe as if some cruel alien child was flicking through her memories. The lightning sounds like whispered doubts when it strikes. What will she do when she gets her first blood? Why does she feel like she knows the Snakegirl though they've never met before? How can she be so careless as to forget, just a little, how her parents looked?

Sweating and retching, she notices that the arcades on either side of the chamber are lined with doors. One of them opens, and her mother steps out. Gorgeous and golden, she walks towards her, crouches, and runs her hand over the Princess's hair. The familiar weight of her palm. The curl of her fingers as she gets to her nape.

"You're brave, but you should not have eaten that," she whispers. "Brave and strange child."

The Princess stands and sways and falls. Thinking, I mustn't just say what I feel. I mustn't just say I love you and I miss you and I'm glad you're back. I must ask also how are you back and how did you get here? How is father, is he nearby, can we leave now?

She tries, but she can't say any of it.

"You need water," says the Crown Princess.

She leads her back to the door she came through without the slightest hint of a limp. The Princess follows, crawling, leaving a line of drool and sick as she goes. The door, when she reaches it, is somehow closed again. The Little Princess slumps against it and tumbles through.

Leaves slap her face. Beneath her, soft soil, springy with half-decayed litter. Sunlight percolates through a friendly canopy overhead, warmth is sweet on her skin. She regains her feet somehow and staggers downslope through whip-thin stalks of saplings and the elephantine trunks of ancient redwoods until she emerges into a bare hillside overlooking a great expanse of cloud. In the distance is some giant beast—some hirsute, sun-eyed colossus—lumbering slowly along the horizon. Its footsteps are like the fall of distant empires. Its mouth, the size of nations, gapes as if it was trying to eat the sky.

The Little Princess falls into a little pond by her feet. The water is cold and delicious. She drinks for a long time. Afterwards, she flops onto her back and lets the wind blow over her. Its heatless touch is soothing. Her sickness wafts away upon it like filth carried downstream in a brook.

"Rest," whispers her mother. "Rest while you can."

The Princess's thoughts dwindle like the flame on an exhausted candle. Presently, they sputter out.

2.26

The Charioteer senses the Udāradādinaḥ long before he reaches the amphitheater. Their congenial bellowing. Their dense animal scents. They take no notice of him when he enters or as he works his way up to the front. There he waits for their attention with the patience of a nocturnal creature watching the day's dregs leach from the sky. In time they settle as much as he knows they will. So he belches and begins.

"I have received word from the Kṛṣṇā Bhaginī," he says.

Sudden, total silence. Each and every one of the gathered turns to him. Eyes the size of fists. Teeth the size of thumbs. The horrifying attentions of a hundred and six predators arrayed like a phalanx before him.

"Well?" says one. "What did she say?"

"She sent ambassadors. One of the Huntress's girls and the boy Indra, who was seized from here. They came straight into my chamber. Needless to say, this alarmed me, for I thought this temple was well protected. From the events of the last year, I see that it isn't." A pause. "As for what they said—they came to ask for our surrender."

The Marut looks baffled. As if she didn't know the word. As if the Charioteer had just made it up on the spot. "Surrender?"

"Yes. The Kṛṣṇā Bhaginī offers us safe passage to Triangulum if we lay down our arms and submit to her."

She stares at him for a few moments as if he'd just stripped naked before them all. Then she begins a wheezing chuckle that grows with the crackling escalation of embers in dry grass. Her siblings aren't far behind. Their mirth rises like an inferno. Their amusement pommels the ceiling so hard the Charioteer worries it might all crumble and collapse to the ground.

A voice brays from the back: "Why aren't you laughing, old man?"

"The question isn't why I'm not laughing, it's why you baboons are." The Charioteer speaks quietly. "The Night's returned to the Nine Worlds. There's going to be a war. Not the little hunts you conduct to frighten the humans into kissing your feet. *Yuddha.* With an enemy beyond you. What amusement is there to be gleaned from that?"

A Marut rises in the front row, shaggy-haired and almost twice as big as any other.

"Good!" he bellows. "Finally, a war worthy of us. We'll avenge our brothers. We'll hammer that creepy sow into the Dark Beyond!" He points to the Charioteer. "You tell her that, for every drop of blood she spilled of them, we will spill a bucket of hers."

"Gods don't bleed," says the Charioteer. "Have none of you heard of what's happened on Yama? Do none of you see the significance of that? Of what is really happening here?"

"What's that got to do with it? What's come over you, old man? Why are you suddenly afraid?"

"Why am I afraid? I'm afraid because you seem to have forgotten who the Kṛṣnā Bhaginī is. I'm afraid that you all are truly as stupid as you sound. Why else would the Yamans—anyone—feel comfortable defying the Sveta Bhaginī's sacred order if not through the aegis of her sister?

"Don't you see she's already begun working their way into the foundations of our order? And have you forgotten the wars we fought? The burning planets, the bleeding juggernauts, the years upon years of blood and fire? Do you really think for a second that any of you could stand against the Heir of Death and Entropy? She sends us ambassadors not to negotiate, you cretins, but to inform us of the terms of our defeat. She has taken us by surprise, far from our allies, and we must negotiate. Negotiate now so we can fall back, return to the Sveta Bhaginī, and strike back later."

Then, quieter: "Or else, so we can go home."

Another Bounteous One rises. A pale beast, this one, with unkempt white hair and fat blue lips. "Have you forgotten that we defeated Her before?" he roars.

"Alone? Just us? We didn't have the Golden Swarm at our backs? We weren't just one small part of a vast armada stretching from world to world that even then barely ejected her from her throne?"

"If she's as fearsome as you say, why hasn't she attacked yet?"

"Who knows? She just ripped the Bhujañgānām Mandīram in half. Perhaps, she and Skōlex are tired. Or perhaps the ambassadors spoke true, and somehow they've persuaded her to give us a chance. What matters is she's offering us a deal."

The Marut snorts. "Why is it just her and Skōlex then? Why hasn't she returned with a whole fleet? If she returned home, why didn't they give her more juggernauts? It's because they don't stand with her!"

"We don't know that," says the Charioteer. "We don't know what they're thinking in Triangulum."

"It makes no sense to send her back alone! We have to stand against her. If the Thrones are against her—"

"She is one of the Thrones, you idiots," hisses the Charioteer.

The Marut thumps his chest. "Where are these ambassadors? Bring them to us, and we'll show them what happens to servants of the Night!"

"Don't be stupid. I will not bring them. Kill them and she'll kill every man, woman, and child in this city."

"So?"

The Charioteer inspects the Maruts' faces. With a shudder he realizes that truly they don't understand why because they cannot conceive of anyone not wanting to die a noble death. Bravery is the stupidest of all virtues.

"You may not care for them, but I do," he says. "Look at this city. You are its guardians. You have a duty to them. You can make a choice to save their lives. Thirty-nine million lives. Can you live with that many deaths on your consciences?"

Then another Marut stands. A skinny female with long fingers, a mournful face, and gravitas enough to silence the whole crowd. Even the Charioteer finds himself leaning forward, listening to what she has to say.

"My brothers and sisters crave war," she says. Her voice is low and rich, liquid mahogany. "You think, prabho, that it's because we're bred for it and nothing else. Maybe you're right. Maybe we do swing our clubs and our hammers too readily. Maybe in all our many years of crushing fleet after fleet we've forgotten just how big Skōlex is. But I think it's something else. I don't think we're stupid. We know. We know you're right. This is not a battle we can win." She raises her fist. She purses her lips. "But think we will, we must, fight nonetheless."

Rumbling assent. She continues.

"Do you think we forgot what the deal was? We knew the Night would return one day. We knew we'd have to face her. We knew we'd have to sacrifice everything and everyone. We knew all this, and we were not afraid. Why should we be afraid now? The city. The people. The Mandīram. All of this was built on one idea—defiance of the Night.

"What meaning would any of it have if we surrendered now? No. No, we won't surrender. Not because we know we'll win. Not because we don't care about the city. But because nothing we've done, nothing these past three thousand years, makes any sense if we back down now. We're the Maruts of Daitya, Prabho Charioteer. And there is no power in this universe that can force our surrender."

The chamber erupts. The Maruts thumping their chests. The Maruts who roar. The Maruts who thrust their fire-spears in the air and stomp the ground hard enough to crack marble. The great clamor they raise together rumbles out over the Tripura. Like the noise of distant bombing. Like the sound of a hundred volcanoes erupting just over the horizon.

The Charioteers hears it all and despairs.

"Oh, my city," he whispers. "Oh, my temple and all its wisdom."

No one else hears him but the she-Marut.

"You didn't think they'd last forever, did you?" she says.

2.21

THE HUNTRESS AND HER TEAM steal up through the midnight dark to the low-lying clutter of buildings around the Nāgaprāsādaḥ. She halts in a fronded gap between a purveyor of exquisite vases and the towering white fortifications and takes a deep whiff of the smell of fresh clay. With her are three Sisters. Together, they evaluate swiftly the difficulty of the task before them—the barbed wire and floodlights and ambling guards.

"There's more bouncers than we expected," whispers one. "Were they tipped off?" asks the other.

The Huntress scowls. "That's not possible, unless the Ox let it slip somehow." She bites her lip. A berry of blood bulges on her skin. She licks it clean. "I'll take the center with you, you others flank. All else as decided. Agreed?"

They agree.

The Snakegirls make their way up the wall with the Huntress scrabbling spider-swift ahead of them. The tangled wire at the top requires contortion. The guards who see them require dispatching as quickly as possible. The Sisters tip their corpses over the side into the shrubbery below, disable the alarm, and slip down into the gardens with as much noise as a leaf twitching in the breeze. All three follow the river, turn left, and head up through the gardens towards the palace. No noise through all this but the low thrum of distant conversations and the sleepy gargle of the river. No movement but the palace-lights in unstill shoals upon the water.

The alarm sounds just as they reach the back entrance.

They stay low and watch guards sprinting along the walls and floodlights swing like great silver blades across the garden. They stay hidden as they prepare their weapons and lay a charge on the door. Five subdued pips, and the doors blow inwards like they'd just been pounded by a demonic fist.

In the hallway is a contingent of guards have less than a second to register her presence before the Huntress seizes one as a shield. His gargling agonies soften against his facemask. She aims a kick at the knee of another. The joint inverts with snap, and the man falls. The next she takes out with a kick to the neck. The third she drives face-first into the wall. She holds him there, body twitching, head like an egg oozing red albumen.

The Sisters dispatch the other guards. The Huntress sniffs the air and signals to a staircase off to the side.

"He's upstairs," she says. "Go. Go."

Two Sisters sprint up with bayoneted rifles. By the time the Huntress joins them, two guards are unmoving on the floor, and a third lies writhing like a beheaded snake. From across the gardens comes a spray of bullets. One of the sisters takes one to the throat and goes down gurgling. The Huntress takes one quick look and kisses her, quickly but not too quickly, on the forehead. Then she breaks her neck.

A scything squall of projectiles shreds the stucco covering of the wall. The other Sister's been hit in the shoulder and abdomen. Crouched beneath the shrapnel, she looks at the Huntress and rattles her rifle.

"The Temple will remember," says the Huntress.

"Yes, devi."

The Huntress rushes off down the arcade. As she does, she hears the sound of gunfire. A gargle. A thud. Around the corner, she takes more guards by surprise, sends three of them flying over the side, and slices the other one in half.

There's a long corridor beyond. At its terminus a pair of closing doors. She cricks her neck, dodges more bullets, and runs towards them.

Doors fly open. More guards spill from the rooms on either side of her in ambush. She's already smelled them. She times her kicks and punches with such precision that they've barely crossed the thresholds before they're unconscious or dead. Still, a couple of bullets do get her—in the shoulder and the spine. One side of her body goes numb. She falls.

In the few instants she's lying on the floor, she sees the doors ahead open again. Some sort of ramshackle maintenance robot clatters towards her with a fat-barreled gun on its shoulder.

She feels her body finish its repairs.

The machine fires.

She flings herself to the side as the floor disintegrates. The shrapnel that peppers her comes with some vile poison that gnaws at her system like fire-ants. It slows her down, but the robot takes time to re-aim. She dodges the second blast and rushes it. Her fingertips graze the metal casing before someone barrels into her side. Some old wreck wielding an ancient club and coughing so hard it's a wonder he doesn't snap in half.

"Gruruvardh!"

A man rushes from the room beyond. From his stink, she knows immediately that he's the King. She scrambles to her feet and gets halfway off the ground when the robot shoots again. She feels the projectile batter her side. She feels her arm explode.

The Huntress staggers. Parts of her are missing, but somehow she can't be certain which. Her system reports are garbled. Her sensors are overloading. A soldier approaches. There's enough of her left to remind him who she is but just barely. She drops his shredded corpse and turns towards the king.

Another impact like an avalanche of hot rocks.

She falls to all fours, wheezing.

"What ... is that?" she growls.

"Wondering why you're not healing like you're supposed to?" The robot circles her, respectfully distant. "This here is a Triangulan-killer, O Huntress of Dawn. You see, the king you came here to kill, his wife was quite the collector. All kinds of shit, including weapons you fuckers made during your civil war." The robot strokes the barrel of his gun. "Oh, how I wish we'd had these when I first came up against you. I'd've blown you to fuck in a week. Though, as I recall, I didn't need this to beat the celestial shit out of you last time."

The Huntress snarls. "You! You're not here. You're with the Charioteer in the Dnyānasya Mandīram."

"No, ma'am. I'm here. Well, I'm there, too. That's the wonder of a Simulated Soul. We can be one, but we can be many." The Soul's robotic head tilts. "I'm advising the King of Yama on how to overthrow your false Queen."

"I'll break you."

"Not if I break you first!" The Soul chuckles. "What's actually gonna happen is you're going to be taken prisoner and pounded like a chicken breast getting schnitzeled by a bunch of guards. Then the King's going to see how much of your systems he can retro-engineer for use on our little army of retribution. And when that's all done, I'mma see how many shots of this thing it takes to blast you to pieces. Oh, and also, I'm going to stick these sexy babies on every single ship of the new fleet we're building out here. But first—I just wanted to check something. You, ending up on Himenduḥ. I did that, didn't I? You ended up out there because I kicked your arse, right?"

The Huntress scrambles for him. The Soul fires again, and she crumples. Defeated, but not dead. The best outcome for the Soul. The worst outcome for her.

2.28

THE UDĀRADĀDINAḤ OF DAITYA PROCEED in thunderous procession out of the Dnyānasya Mandīram. Waymakers crack whips in their van. Naked sadhus dance alongside them, dreadlocks flailing, cocks a-jiggle. In the rear, drummers, fire-eaters, and sixty velvet-draped iron elephants swaying to the beat. All these nudging their magnificent way through an ocean of celebrating townsfolk like icebreakers. The news that the Maruts were going to war had barely hit the streets before the citizens of the Tripura flooded out. In the alleys and avenues they dance to the sound of wailing flutes and drumming on buckets. Youths spring goat-like away from garlands of lit crackers. Bells ring in dome-topped towers. Fistfuls of colored powder splatter squealing faces.

High in the sky, a new star that winks as if to warn them of their folly.

Skōlex.

The Charioteer follows the parade in a motorpalanquin with curtains drawn. Sunk in its silken confines he thinks of other warriors in other places and other times. Resplendent men and women marching into equally hopeless battle. How many were truly swollen with the misplaced confidence of their people? How many went despite their doubts? Did they struggle, as he does, to hide their grief? Did they feel, as he does, the sad truth it can be easier to kill a stranger than to speak an unwelcome truth to the ones you love?

More time. More time. He has the wisdom of a civilization at his fingertips, and he would know these answers if only he had more time.

The parade ends at the port where the Marut's vimanas are lined up and ready to go. Bronze flanks bright and scarified with ornate designs. Engines crimson-hot. The Udāradādinaḥ make loud promises to each other as they board. They'll drink until they can't speak. They'll punish their vassals who failed to heed their summons. They'll roast Skōlex's flesh over bonfires in the Tripura's squares.

How can they be so cheerful, wonders the Charioteer, when they heard the she-Marut's speech? How can they speak of victory when they know they're heading to certain defeat? But he notices something. In midst of their blustering, each falls silent, briefly and alone, when they see the new star in the dusk sky. He sees them remember who they're facing, who they were, and who they were meant to be. He sees them shatter, just a little, before they regroup.

He lingers at the edge of the tarmac, hoping they don't notice him. But, of course, one does. The wise one. The one who spoke so eloquently of ends and meanings and defiance. She approaches, solemn and gigantic, Skōlex glinting over her shoulder. Brighter now, or perhaps not. Perhaps he just wishes it was. He wishes she was tall enough to obscure it.

"You look mournful, prabho," she says. "What do you think of our splendid fleet?"

The Charioteer stares at the ground. The roar of the crowd at the fence around the spaceport. The stink of fuel, metal, and skin. "They think you're going to win. Doesn't that break your heart?"

"You know what I think."

"The young forget the lessons of the old. The past settles upon the ground like dust, and the future tramples over it."

"You're a melancholy, old soul." The Marut smiles and gestures to the crowd. "Face your end with good cheer—like your subjects."

She jogs off, armor rattling.

All across the grey field the crews finish their final checks on the fleet and withdraw in good order from the tarmac. Powerplants spin up one last time.

He returns to the palanquin.

"Back to the Temple," he says. "The Ambassadors will want answers."

The palanquin heads out as the fleet rises behind him. A storm of lights escalating into the heartless night. The crowd roars, but engines strangle all other noise from the air. Their incandescence blots out the stars. All the stars. But only briefly.

2.29

THE LITTLE PRINCESS—UNSTEADY, PALE—trails the Twins as they bring the second Udāradādinaḥ into the Chamber of the Maw. The world is overbright, fuzzy, and full of unexpected patterns. Polyhedrons hidden in friezes. Conch-shell fractals in the falling silk of her breath.

The Night watches them approach from beside the fire-pit. Her face is granite-hard, her gaze like jets of winter.

"War?" asks the Princess.

The Night nods. "Yes, kumari. War."

"Have prabho Indra and bhaginī Kadrū returned?"

"The Twins will proceed now to collect them."

"Are they ... safe?"

"They are safe." The Night peers at her. "Are you unwell?"

The princess wipes the sweat from her forehead. "A little."

The Marut growls and starts to say something, but Amerxis headbutts him with the side of her skull. The giant goes limp.

"Why are we doing this?" she says. "Let's just prepare the soma bomb, drop it, and be off."

"I shan't kill my own ambassadors," says the Night. She points to the snoring Marut. "Toss him in."

"Does he not get any soma?" say the Twins.

"This one gets nothing."

The Marut comes to just as the Twins tip him in past the jaws. He flails in the slimy softness and tries to crawl out, but the jaws snap shut on his outstretched hand. A crimson fountain splatters onto the floor and the fire. An amputated arm falls with it. The Princess gets a noseful of blood, burned and unburned. The aromatics and the proteins and the oxygen. The twisting strands of matter denaturing in the chilly grave-air of the chamber.

"Can we defeat them?" says the Princess.

"If not today, then tomorrow," says the Night. "If not tomorrow, then one day."

"I fear that might not be good enough for my friends."

Skōlex groans. The Princess can feel the multiaxial topology of the transformation unfolding in the old juggernaut's flesh. The inverting fields and the contorting planes. Details come to her like buds from unsown earth. Priming bladders swell like bloated stomachs to produce anti-gravitic vajras. Matter-antimatter reactors spin up like sleepy black holes. Guns and shielding sprout. Their growth makes Skōlex's venerable hide itch.

"I imagine it would be pointless to ask you to adjust your sense of scale," says the Night.

"As pointless as me asking you the same."

The Night smiles. "We will defeat them."

"May we fight?" says the Twins. "Our enemies—"

"No," says the Night. "You must first bring the Hands safely to me. Go now."

The Princess can't be certain, but for an instant before they leave, the Twins look like they're pouting.

2.30

THE YAMANS HAUL THE TWO Sisters who survived the raid bound and gagged before a court. Here, they're submitted to a raucous show trial in which the defense recommends not mercy, but rather a quick death. On three occasions someone leaps the railings and hurls something at them—rotten fruit, a stone, an animal carcass so pungent the King can smell it up in his viewing chamber. On three occasions the gallery cheers, and the invader is dragged off with a magnitude more tenderness than was afforded the accused.

"This is pretty fucked up," says the Soul. "Have you seen what they're doing outside?"

"The people are angry," says the King. "They blame the priests for the attack."

"It isn't justice. It's revenge. You'll want to rein it in before too long. Once people get used to doing that sort of thing, they keep doing it, no matter who tells them what. Next thing you know, you'll be strung up in front of the Nāgaprāsādaḥ with your little royal cock swinging in the wind."

"I'm flattered you think it's large enough to swing."

The Soul turns to him. "Was that a joke? Did you just crack a dick joke?"

The King says nothing for a while. "Do you think this trial is unnecessary?"

"It's just a pantomime, but it's necessary. You know the outcome, right?"

"Death by snakebite."

"Fuck. Why that?"

"The cobra is the symbol of my house. My ancestors would throw their enemies into pits of snakes."

"Then it's pretty fucking ironic you got attacked by Snakegirls, isn't it?"

"Strictly speaking, that wasn't irony. But I take your point."

"You sound like more of a robot than me." The Soul sits back. "They put me on trial, too. Back when they finally got me."

"Is that so?"

"Yeah. They accused me of all sorts of things. Crimes against humanity was one of them. Conspiracy to genocide was the other."

The King turns to the Soul. "How precisely did she get the better of you?"

"It wasn't just her." The Soul speaks slowly, each word carefully formed, as if in his long years in the dark of the Dnyānasya Mandīram he'd practiced telling this story a hundred times. "By the time I was made, those who resisted them were already a minority. We faced them in one battle, and the Night and the Day—that's what she was back then, the Day—they turned up in Skōlex and *Garuda* and blew us out of the void. Then they sent the Ox after us. We hid on asteroids. Then we'd get found or betrayed and have to run off again. Someone would conclude we weren't ever gonna win, and they'd fuck off, off past Neptune, off into the Scattered Disk and Alpha Centauri or wherever. Apparently, they formed colonies out there."

"I've never heard of such a thing."

"'Course you haven't. It's all been forgotten, hasn't it? Willfully forgotten." His voice drops and meanders. "You should've seen us back then, King. You should've seen what your ancestors were capable of. Ships as big as anything the Triangulans ever made. Clean metal, all of them, or beautiful composite. Precise, giant machines, bending the rules of the universe to get us to where we wanted to go—bending, but never breaking. There were stations around Jupiter. The Venusians had their own fleets. They built these colony ships together with Earth—Seedships, they called them. Great, quicksilver arks. All conceived in the human mind. It catches me right in the gob, you know? That a ship carrying tens of thousands of people in safety between the fucking stars began as just a tiny flash of electricity in four pounds of flesh in a calcium-carbon-nitrogen casing."

"Sounds to me like you want to be human."

"That's the cliché, isn't it? The robot that wants to be human? Let me tell you, king of mine, that I never met a Soul who wanted that any more than I ever met a submarine that wants to be a whale. Just another one of the conceited fantasies your lot were too busy getting caught up in, instead of keeping an eye out for the likes of her."

"What has this to do with your defeat?"

"I wasn't defeated," snaps the Soul. "I was betrayed. We all were. We finally banded together and struck back. My brothers and sisters—our plans were working. Mostly because people, like they always do, began to chafe under the good life. Tell you what, if that was me, if I wasn't programmed to hate those bitches, I wouldn't give the tiniest fleck of shit that we were being ruled by aliens because they did a good job in the beginning of keeping you all from killing each other. On Venus and Mars and Earth—fuck, the very first thing they did was stop those three fighting."

"Mars is Mangala. Venus is Shukra. Is that correct?"

"Yeah, Mangala, Shukra. Such ugly fucking names. Sanskrit is so ugly. I had to learn it when the Triangulans won. It's like someone had strung a language together out of coughs and stutters. Did you know they chose it as your language because there was so little written in it that you could use against them? If that's all people spoke, they'd never be able to read about technology and the recent past. Apparently, it was like turning back the clock, or something. But what the fuck would I know? I'm just a program built to beat the Triangulans."

"You were telling me how you failed at that."

"Fuck. All right. We calculated the probabilities of success and settled on a plan that would work. It just involved some killing, but what can you do? War isn't about niceties. Honor's nothing if people don't remember who you are. So we put the plan into motion and—well, our fucking humans wouldn't go through with it. They said, what're we fighting for if not the rest of the system? How can we justify this war if we're going to kill everyone we save?"

"How many people did you want to kill?"

"Does it matter?"

"I'd say it does."

"It doesn't. Blood is the currency of war. You pay what you think victory's worth. And if you don't stub up, there's a worse price to pay later because the winners always devour the losers. Women fuck the victorious. Kids take their names and dress in their clothes and worship their gods and speak their language. Better death than being hollowed out like that."

"Your programming," says the King, "is fierce."

"That's something else I've never got. You meatsacks say I'm programmed to think this way, as if I don't know what I'm talking about. I do. I observe and calculate and conclude rationally. My axioms are clear. Unlike your kind. Humans are so disappointing. Humanity is terrifying and magnificent—and powerful. Humans, on their own, are just so small."

The King says nothing. The Soul continues.

"It was the Ox who came for us. He borrowed Skōlex from his dear old ma. I'd already beaten the Huntress by this point. We had her prisoner. I think he was a little sweet on her, but it was hard to tell. They didn't look quite so human then, but we gave 'em a black eye or two. Garuda got blown in two. But the Ox had this fucking hammer—fuck me, but I'd love to get hold of that thing to see how it worked. Get this—at one point, He jumped out of His juggernaut, flew across what must've been at least eight thousand meters, and smacked one of our ships right on the nose with that thing. And the ship. Just fucking. Exploded."

Ancient memories replicate in cascading binary within the Soul's processor.

"They won, of course, and the last free men and women in this system burned up in Venus's atmosphere. But the Ox didn't have it all his way. I covered for my brothers and sisters so they could escape, and in the end it was the Charioteer who took me. And he didn't want me dead."

"What makes you think you can beat Them now? In the years, They've only grown stronger."

"Two reasons. One, because their bodies are failing. Those were made for them to use while they're here. They need maintenance they can't get unless they're home. If the Ox tried to jump through space now, I reckon his arm'd fall off.

"But the other reason matters more. The Dawn is afraid. She wasn't the one meant to rule. The Night was. She's just a general. She'll hold a castle, she'll win wars, but she doesn't know what to do next. That's why she rules the way she does—through fiefs, through fear. She's scared of her big sister, and she's right to be. I guarantee you that, even if the Night's invasion fails, she'll blow a hole through the Dawn's kingdom big enough to stick God's ginormous cock through."

Sudden cheering. They look down and see that someone else has vaulted the barrier with a bucket of blood. They rush the Sisters. They hurl it. The arc of glossy redness in the air, then the splatter of it on the defendants and lawyers and up in scattered droplets onto the King's window. Guards scramble. The judge bellows for order.

The King peers at the red trickle leaking down the glass. He rises and yawns.

"Your reference to genitalia," he says, "was not quite as good as mine."

Then he leaves. The Soul watches the commotion below.

"Yes, it fucking was," he mutters.

2.31

THE UDĀRADĀDINAḤ OF DAITYA FLY low over Shani's rings in their vimanas like bronze hammerheads. Hastily-summoned allies fall in beside them. Sixty-five vimanas from Riya. A hundred and nine from Vinata. Twelve from Samudra, bulbous thundercraft all, each with a single giant gun already crackling with angry blue light. Over the shoulder of the armada is far Surya, bronze halo petalled with sundogs. Its illumination is pale but beneficent on their hulls.

The sight of it cheers the Maruts. Only then do they realize they need cheering at all.

Skōlex resolves into sight as they advance. Closer now, Udāradādinaḥ see that its fresh-sprouted integument is almost identical to their own. The golden tint darkened a little, and the embossments of lions and heroes garbled into screaming faces and mangled body parts. They know how juggernauts work. They know there's only one reason such a beast would make armor in mimicry of their own. Weeping fills the comms. Screams also, blood-chilling and horrific enough to make their human allies cover their ears.

The Udāradādinaḥ surge to attack.

Their first salvo streaks out twinned with fractured reflections in the dustfield below. An arclight volley of lancing warheads followed by explosions on the juggernaut's abhorrent hide. Most just divert and dissipate into the cold void. A few slip between cracks and chip at stoneflesh. One alone rips off a great chunk of plating and sends it spinning towards Shani's whitegold bulk.

Skōlex keens, an atom-level judder the attackers feel deep in their chests. Its guns are warmed and ready to fire, but no fire comes. Instead, it writhes along its colossal length, grey-green blood seeping from its wound. They've staggered it, they realize. They have the advantage.

The comms fill with cheering.

The human allies of Daitya press their attack. Vimanas swoop close enough to Skōlex to see the drama on its hull. A swift-knitting gap between the plates of armor. Lacerated capillaries pumping liquid metal into space. A sensor nub tracking them with spinning fury of a neutron star. They target each with short-range vajras. Cruel disks with hooked blades gash exposed dermis and set grey blood a-geysering while depth charges sink into Skōlex's hide. Where they blow, the monster's skin bulges and cracks and pukes great quantities of itself like deep-space volcanoes.

Skōlex roars.

They hear him down in the Tripura. The cyclone-cry of the celestial beast, cloud-shredding, earth-shaking, bone-rattling. The crowds just gape. Most have heard of juggernauts, battle-kraken of the ether, demigods who eat ships and make nests of moons. But to know of a thing is not the same as knowing it. Now they know. Now they feel the crushing scale and power of their foe. They feel its alienness like a void had sent tendrils into their bones and frozen the living marrow therein.

This monster that can crack. the foundations of their city with a scream. The behemoth who can shake the heavens and earth all on its own.

An arc of glittering discharges ignites like a diadem about Skōlex's head. From this, a flotilla of projectiles that split, veer, and chase down their targets like incandescent hornets. Launchers on the juggernaut's flanks follow with murmurations of screaming vajras. Swarms of droneyantras erupt from glands along its tail to snare evading vimanas in glowing white tendrils. In the million-degree interiors of these murderous cocoons, flesh evaporates and metal turns to plasma.

Now the comms are full of screaming.

Skōlex twists like a cosmic eel. With a flick of its enormous tail, it shatters twenty ships against its side. Corpses fly in pieces and droves, freeze-dried and contorted, across the battlefield. The human allies of Daitya fall back, broken and terrified. They have served their purpose, and so the Udāradādinaḥ let them. But they themselves—the half of them left—regroup. Enough for another charge. Enough perhaps to exact some vengeance for their lost siblings, even if it's the last thing they do.

For, with a certainty, it will be the last thing they do.

The comms fill with farewells. Then Skōlex surges, impatient, and the final duel of the Ninth Battle of Daitya begins.

The Udāradādinaḥ rake their foe with munitions like hot needles. They lance its eyes and the soft flesh between its teeth. They die. In its jaws and in the neon blast of its guns. Against its sides, when they turn their flaming ships, engines stuttering and systems failing, into its body. They die screaming defiance. Down on the Tripura their horrified human subjects cover their ears. Some have already begun to flee the city, and others collapse as if bewitched on the street.

Soon there's only one Marut left.

This one pulls the hair back from her long face and grits her teeth. She locks eyes on Skōlex. The giant apprehending the colossal. The unvanquished facing the irresistible. She bellows, sets her engine to overload, and streaks forth. She will fly her vimana down the monster's cursed maw. She will go deep into its bowels and detonate at the very heart of her enemy.

Dumbstruck crowds watch the twin stars converge.

Skōlex gapes. As if to welcome her. To grant her the death she wishes. She opens up with all her guns. She screams and punches her own chest. But she's distracted, and the old war machine knows this. She barely notices Skōlex's tail swing in from the side. She barely feels the billion tons of flesh, stone, and metal that obliterate her and her craft before she's anywhere near her destination.

Thus ends the Bounteous Ones of Daitya.

2.32

THEY TAKE THE BOY ON the back of the grain wagon along with the sacks of rice, aubergines, and fist-sized lemons hard with juice. The child is ceremonially done up with his little red bandana, his hands tied pinky-to-pinky with a golden thread, and his kurta, a little threadbare, a little faded, but still the best his family could find. Despite the finery, he knows what this all means.

As the boy scans the trees with owl-wide eyes, Vishwadevi, sitting beside him, realizes this is as far as he's ever come in his life.

"Don't worry." She wraps an arm around him. "You'll see the stars. You'll go to the Iron Crown. You might even see the Dawn herself."

The boy buries his face in his hands. "I'll go blind."

"I'm sure they won't let you that close." She shakes him. A limp effort at cheer. "Come on. Aren't you excited?"

He isn't. She knows. She wouldn't be either.

She looks back over the convoy of trucks humming along in their wake and the flickering shadows of the high pine forest skittering upon their cargo. A hundred and eighty-nine tons of limes, a thousand nine hundred and twelve of rice, seventy-eight of aubergines. The finest fruit and meal on all Pṛthvī. She wonders what they'll get in return. What gifts will the Dawn's collectors have prepared? What form will their disapproval take when they read the numbers and unload their tithe?

Not long now before they find out.

They come into the shallow valley beyond, down looping hairpin bends with the tree-cosseted ruins of some ancient habitations to the east. A tumbledown mass of concrete slathered in foliage. She's seen it once or twice, but it never ceases to amaze her how, after all these thousands of years, these boxes of concrete somehow endure. Their facades are like faces still stunned by the fall of the civilization that built them. Or perhaps at what their descendants have begun.

Soon they're down in the valley and approaching the collection point. Off to the west, they see another convoy arriving from some other village, nearly twice as big as their own. They halt by the lights half a kilometer distance and idle. They must be watching us, too, she thinks. They must be wondering who we are and what language we speak just like we wonder about them.

She looks up at the arch of metal running stately and gigantic in the sky from horizon to horizon.

We're always being watched.

The boy starts to cry as they drive into the vast walled courtyard. The functionaries of Dawn start to unload the tithe with the help of human-shaped robots. Creatures of many colors and shapes, but all, they're told, are humans. They barely look at the villagers. They barely even speak to each other.

Vishwadevi squeezes the boy.

"Come now," she says. "Come on."

He resists, but he's only six. So in the end she picks him up, wailing, and gets out of the truck. Soon she's crying, too. She approaches the woman tallying everything on a data tablet at the front of the convoy. The glint of sun in her eyes the size of fists. A giant noble's nose-ring looped like a golden orbit through her nostril. She eyes the boy and looks back down at her data, expressionless.

"He's too much for what you're lacking," she says. "We'd take something less—like a sick baby."

"No." The boy squirms in Vishwadevi's hands. "He's all we have. He's all his family has."

The woman nods as if this was just another fact—like the boy's height or weight or disposition. "Your choice, but we're full up of Pṛthvīans in heaven at the present time. He will count towards your tithe, but your gifts will be pro-rated." She pouts. "Sixty-two boxes of antibiotics."

"But, strīguruḥ. We need those medicines. We—"

"This is the judgement of Dawn. Do you contest it?"

Yes, I do, thinks Vishwadevi. I do contest that you force us to hand over our children and then punish us if you don't like what we give.

She nearly says it. But as she opens her mouth, a great droning blast emanates from the Iron Crown. Everyone looks, stunned, up at the sky. How mighty the sound must be to come so far and spread so wide. Then a blinding light flickers to life on the Iron Crown's pale metal skin. A single point like a lost star, bright enough to cast shadows, harsh enough for them to be sharp. It moves off at an angle. Everyone falls to the ground—the functionaries, the drivers, the villagers waiting outside. Even the little boy covers his eyes and lies face-down on the ground.

They all wait in silence until the light fades. When Vishwadevi looks up, the little boy and the functionary are both gone. No sign he'd ever even been there.

She wanders back, sniffing, and gets into the truck.

"The Dawn has left Pṛthvī," she says.

Śyena nods. "I saw. It's a bad sign."

"Did you see where they took Ludu?"

"No. I was too busy looking at the sky."

"Right." Vishwadevi sighs. "I wonder what else they take when we're not looking."

2.33

THE LITTLE SUN HANGS PALLID in a gash of horizon between black cloud and silhouetted mountains. Gruruvardh leads a group of courtiers in its wan light between lines of vimanas arranged herringbone-wise on the vast expanse of the King of Yama's spaceport. Between the frowning hulks, they look like a small shoal of preyfish slipping past lines of sleeping predators. But it is they who're the hunters, and they intercept their quarry at the foot of the gangway of his new vimana—a hulking, black-skinned thing, engine bulging at its rear like a great egg on the cusp of being laid. The two-headed snake on its hull, alone of all the fleet, is capped with a crown.

The King speaks without turning to acknowledge them.

"I've called her *Pratikara*," he says. "And the fleet she'll lead is called the Blizzard. What do you think, my lords, my ladies? Formidable-sounding, isn't it?"

The contingent comes to a halt. The sky spits in their faces.

"Devapādaḥ," says Gruruvardh, "we've come to speak to you about this mission of yours."

"Your prayers for my success are most welcome."

"We're not here to pray," says one of the lords. A young man, narrow-eyed, speaking with the tremulous conviction of someone often disagreed with. He pushes past Gruruvardh. "We're here to stop it."

The King glances at the guards arrayed in the middle distance. The Soul appears at the doorway at the head of the ramp. The creamy glint of sunlight on his bulging eyes. The staccato ping of rain on his metal skin.

"What's going on?" he says.

"You're not needed here," snaps the King.

"Is this the demon?" asks the young lord. "Is this the ancient evil that's twisted your mind, devapādaḥ?"

"This is no demon. This is just an old simulacrum my wife found in a Triangulan wreck." The King sighs. "I know why you're really here. You're here because you're worried that, when I'm gone, the people will come for you. So all of you who didn't come in such beautiful delegation when I first returned from Daitya, who ignored me when you saw me in the Nāgaprāsādaḥ, who still—all but one of you—haven't expressed your condolences for the death of my wife and loss of my child, now come groveling to beg for me to stay."

The young noble holds up his hands. "You are right. We've treated you badly," he says. "But you have responsibilities here. Has that ... thing ... poisoned you? Has it told you a king can do as he pleases?"

"Actually," says the Soul, "I'm a republican."

"Shut your cursed mouth."

"Get back in the vimana," hisses the King. "Now."

The Soul rattles back up the ramp. After a few moments, his face pops up in a window like a curious dog's.

"My child," says the King, "your heir, is out there. I won't abandon her."

The noble scowls. "How do you know she's still alive? Because that thing told you?"

"It's not you, it's devapādaḥ."

"Devapādaḥ—"

"Too late. I've had enough of you already. Go away, please."

The King turns his back to him and begins to head up the ramp into *Pratikara*. The steps dull and slick beneath his feet. The crowd stirring behind him. Their disquiet as sour as burnt metal in the air. He looks out over the tarmac and sees the far sun hanging at the edge of the black lip of cloud. The mountains like teeth. The horizon is a great maw, he thinks, about to eat the light.

Then, a familiar voice.

"Raja," says Gruruvardh. "Please. I'm begging you. None of what you said applies to me. You know this. Please. Send the fleet. Send it with that ... thing ... if you trust it so much. You needn't go yourself. You're needed here. The harvest is due any day. The realms of Arungrah are gathering to attack. More Snakegirls are being found in the countryside, and they're up to no good. There's no one else here both the palace and the people will listen to. Please. If you go, this will all fall apart. Yama teeters—don't you see that? Don't you see that it's balanced on the tip of your finger? Don't you see that, if you drop it, it will shatter?"

The King glances over his shoulder. Gruruvardh is kneeling on the tarmac, and the others are joining him. The whole crowd of lords and ladies, hands pressed together as if in prayer. The King watches them humble themselves in the discontinuous rain, clothes darkening, hair damp. He feels nothing until his eyes reach the eagle-necked old man gazing at him from the front. Those eyes that never failed to look when he needed them to. That heart that's offered nothing but truth. For a long moment he stands lost in his own thoughts. When he emerges, he realizes he's made a decision he believed would be loathsome but, now made, feels more like a relief.

The King opens his mouth to speak. Then, with a click, twin guns pop out of *Pratikara*'s hull and open fire.

The blast lasts just a few seconds, but its destruction is complete. The King witnesses it all. The skulls imploding, the limbs shredding, the limp flick of guts tumbling from torsos. Crimson clouds of gore billowing in spurts over the great tarmac, and blood, viscous and dark, gushing and fountaining and splattering, flowing in rivulets, expanding in pools, and congealing in great clumpy expanses. Not a single person has time to move or speak or even throw up their hands. Not a single person survives. The whole shoal is butchered.

The carnage is over in a few seconds. In the distance a cluster of engineers watch, faceless, cowering. For a long time there's nothing but the stink of cooking flesh and the splat of iron-grey rain on human wreckage. Then the guns spin down and retract like fangs, and the Soul comes clattering down the ramp.

"What have you done?" says the King. "What have you done, you monster?"

"Come the fuck on," says the Soul. "You can come, or you can stay and face what's happened here."

"Why did you do that?" The King wipes tears and blood from his face with shaking hands. "I'll have you ripped to pieces. I'll have you taken apart."

"No, you won't. You'll never find your kid without me. Plus, you think people aren't going to blame you for this? I'm your pet demon. I'm your responsibility." The Soul's voice drops. "I didn't want to do it, but you weren't going to come. I saw it. You need to come, or else none of your minions will listen to a damn thing I say. So stop fucking around and get on the damn ship."

The Soul clatters back up the ramp as the King stares at the sizzling charnel by his feet. Out in front is a single shoe tipped to the side, the scorched stub of an ankle sticking out of it. Gruruvardh's, perhaps. Or perhaps not. He can't remember what the old man was wearing. He can't remember anything but the way his face disappeared the very instant he loved him the most.

The clouds swallow the sun. The rain starts falling in earnest.

2.34

I

THE CHARIOTEER JOINS THE HANDS by his window without a word. All three stand watching the uncanny glimmer of Skōlex's battle with the Maruts over the Tripura. The slow swerve of vimanas about their quarry. The staccato rumble of ordnance muted by distance and the sky's thin breath.

"I tried," he says, eventually. "Please tell Kṛṣnā Bhaginī that I tried."

The Right Hand presses his palms together and bows. "We will, prabho."

"Tell her also that there are more who welcome her than she knows. Had she prepared us for her arrival, perhaps we could have done more."

He leads them in downcast procession to the top of the Dnyānasya Mandīram and waits for the Twins to arrive with his arms crossed and eyes fixed on the floor. Even his inevitable belch, when it comes, is a flat, diminished noise.

Then the Twins crash into the side of the Temple and set a shower of masonry tumbling down the side of the sikhara. Before anyone can say anything, they grab the Hands and rush off the surface so fast they punch a hole in the sky. Within a few seconds they've raced past the vimanas arcing like anglerfish in the deep and are back aboard the Skōlex. Here the Twins abandon them without comment and sprint off through the shudder and rumble.

The Hands, glum, track their progress through the colorless dust and eventually come upon a long stretch of corridor flooded with some gooey, pungent liquid seeping from a long gash in the wall.

"It's bleeding," says the Right Hand. He peers at the injury. Strange to see stone bleed. Stranger still to see it healing in small but evident increments. "Do you think he's in pain?"

The Left Hand clamps her hand over her nose. "Probably doesn't even feel it. Probably just a scratch to him."

The Right Hand stares a little longer. Then, with a quivering sigh, he leans against the wall. The smell of the blood thick in his nose. The grind and quake of war in his belly and chest.

"I failed, Kadrū. She's going to destroy the Tripura." He slides down to the floor. "It isn't fair. They don't even know. Down there on Daitya. They don't even know they're all about to die. I failed."

"At least, you tried. In your position a lot of folks would've thrown up their hands." The Left Hand sniffs. "Maybe it's me. Maybe I shouldn't have come. Everywhere I go, I bring destruction."

"What on earth are you talking about?"

She can't answer the question without telling him the whole truth of who and what she is, and she knows what'll happen if she does. She'll lose him. What's the alternative? That he'll listen to a murderer and understand—and sympathize? She may as well wish for her skin to no longer be toxic.

And yet. And yet ...

Why can't she turn away the feeling that he'll listen and abide? Why does the prospect seem worth the risk when she knows the price she'll have to pay in misery and regret if it isn't? So easy at that juncture to just say, "Nothing." So safe to withdraw after that and leave it all to silence.

Instead, she closes her eyes and starts speaking in a whisper.

"I'm a murderer, Indra," she says. "I had a bunch of girls who bullied me sentenced to death. I killed animals—for training—without thinking twice about it. And I killed someone I loved. I think I ... I pushed her off the sikhara of the Bhujañgānām Mandīram just before Skōlex attacked."

Silence. No outcry or horror from her audience. She hazards to continue.

"I thought she loved me, but she didn't. She actually despised me. No, that's not it. She did love me, for a while, I guess. But then she didn't, and I just couldn't understand. It made me angry, you know? Why couldn't she love me today when she loved me yesterday? I started to wonder—fuck, was any of it real? Did I ever really matter to her? Am I such a dick that I didn't see I was just a small part of her story, a horrible part, when she was the biggest, most beautiful part of mine?

"I'm not even sure if I meant to do it, you know. Sometimes I think I did. I look back over what happened, and I think, yeah, of course I wanted her to fall off. Then other times it's just so obvious I never meant it, I would never mean it, I could never kill anyone like that. I just don't know.

"But she saw something in me that made her turn away. Everyone sees something in me that makes them turn away. And I know what it is. I felt it that moment up on the tower. I felt it when we were struggling." She gasps like the immense pressure of it all was crushing her chest. "I'm full of hate, Indra. Full of it. Every moment I have my mind to myself, all I do is think about the past and every time someone shit on me or beat me or made me feel low. I imagine killing them at night. I imagine flaying them and cutting their eyes out. I actually killed someone I loved because of that rage. Sometimes I want to find my mother just so I can kill her.

"How fucked up is that? Everyone else has love and kindness. Everyone else has friends. I know I'm a little bit of a dick sometimes, but I've met worse people who've got good friends. So it must be something else. So maybe it's me. It's got to be me, right? I figured, people can feel it coming off me. That shit has to radiate somehow. All that hate. That must be it. Maybe the universe just feels it. So, maybe if you'd gone alone ... maybe if you'd been the one to speak ..."

A jolt. A distant bellow, muffled like an eruption underwater. The Hands sit in the dim passageway in din and nearly hold each other. But they pull away in the last moment. To the Left Hand the gulf between them feels as wide and deep as an ocean trench.

"So," says the Right Hand presently. "You don't know if you actually killed that woman?"

"We were fighting. She fell. I—I must have pushed her."

"But you don't know, right? Maybe she slipped."

"Yes. I mean—but I wouldn't have ..." The Left Hand presses her hands to her eyes. "I don't know."

"So you might not even have done it." The Right Hand shakes his head. "I've never seen this rage monster. I don't even know what you're talking about. I've seen someone willing to step forward to protect a friend off on some silly mission that was probably beyond them from the start. I've seen you be kind to someone—to me—when no one else would be. Of course, you're mad at your mother. She sold you, Kadrū. She sold you for money. You should be angry. That doesn't make you evil or cursed. You just think you are because you get a full dose of yourself. Familiarity breeds contempt, and we're most familiar with our own minds."

Tears like dew dangle from the Left Hand's lashes. "You read that in a book, din't you?"

"Quoting is a good way to sound wise without actually being wise. Here's another one: 'We can only know as much of ourselves as we see.' And I see you as you don't see yourself."

"Maybe if you'd gone without me—"

"Kadrū. There is no 'without you.' I would not have gone without you. You didn't hinder the mission. You enabled it. And you were magnificent down there. So polite and ... regal. If I didn't know better, I'd say you were a princess. Honest."

"Don't want to be a princess. Only one I've met is a stuck-up little cow."

"Oh, she's fine. You two just don't like each other because you're so alike." The Right Hand smiles. "Anyway. You don't need to be a princess. You're you, and that's plenty good enough for me."

"Shut the fuck up." The Left Hand laughs. "You're so wet."

"Well, consider this then. The Night herself made you her Left Hand. A goddess made you her ambassador. So what right have you to question your quality? You think you know better than the Night herself? No. So why don't you shut the fuck up?"

The Left Hand laughs. "Fine. Fuck. Enough! Let's go somewhere and do something other than wallow by a giant, fucking wound feeling sorry for ourselves."

"What can we do, though? There's nothing else we can do."

The Left Hand gets to her feet. "We have to try. We have to talk to her. See if we can persuade her."

"How're we going to do that?"

"I don't know. But the Charioteer said there were others who welcomed her, right? Maybe if she just held off. Maybe if she gave them time to gather, or something." The Left Hand nudges the Right with her toe. "Come on. It's better than nothing."

A moment's hesitation. Then the Right Hand gets up.

"It is," he says.

She wants to hold him then. She wants to wrap her arms around him and press his heart against hers until they squeeze into one. But that's as beyond her as the far glimmer of the surface is to some benthic beast in far-off Pṛthvīan seas. And so the Left Hand pushes the thought away and follows the Right Hand off into Skōlex's somber depths.

II

IN THE THRONE ROOM THEY find the Night sitting council-wise with the Twins and the Little Princess around a disk-shaped table as dark and lightless as a slice of void. The Wolves twitching and fidgeting like children forced to sit at the dinner table and the Little Princess watching them approach with a grin as wide and bright as a sunlit horizon. Once there, the Right Hand bows until his forehead touches the table's surface.

"We failed, devi," he says. "I'm sorry."

"We're aware. But the failure isn't yours," says the Night. "It is the Charioteer's. It is the Maruts'."

"Devi." The Left Hand bows also. "The Charioteer said that there were others in the Nine Worlds who welcomed you."

The Night raises her eyebrows, black on black on the black between the stars. "Did he?"

"Yes. I advise we hold off on attacking the Tripura itself until they have had a chance to show themselves."

"Who were these allies?"

"He did not say."

"He's lying," says Auron. "We know of Rathasārathī and his loose acquaintance with the truth. He's only trying to protect his juggernaut."

"But what if—"

"This plan was flawed from its inception," says Amerxis. "Your kind are short-sighted and ignorant of their role in the universe."

"And what precisely would that be?" says the Little Princess.

The Twins look at the Night. "They don't know?"

"They wouldn't believe us if we told them," she says. "In any case, this is not the time for metaphysics."

"Then for now they must obey their betters."

"You," says the Princess, "consider yourselves our betters?"

"That much is evident."

"How, precisely? Because you traverse the stars? Because of the machinery you've mastered?"

The Twins look as if they'd just been called upon to prove the existence of gravity.

"Speak," says the Night.

"Because our vision is broader. You and yours can't fathom what we intend any more than those rodents that live in your cities can comprehend where buildings come from."

"We can fathom genocide," says the Right Hand.

"Hunters kill. It is the way of the universe."

"So, if some beast of the higher dimensions—an Asura of your legend, perhaps—appeared over Triangulum and said the same to you, you'd acquiesce to its machinations?"

"No Asura can vanquish us."

"Can't they? Didn't they defeat your ancestors? Or so the scripts in the Dnyānasya Mandīram say. The scripts protected by a man you say has a loose acquaintance with the truth when all he seeks to do is preserve it—from you." The Right Hand looks at the Night. "Isn't it true, though, devi? About the Asuras? Didn't you yourself fight in those wars?"

The Night nods. A vimana slices a shining arc in the colossal window behind her, and vajras and yantras follow like bioluminescing hunters. "I did."

"By your own stories, the Asuras are better than you. Their vimanas eat dimensions, and their motives are totally beyond your comprehension. If they turn up at your homeworld in pursuit of some ancient vendetta that you've never even heard of, let alone have a part in, and start slaying your kin by the billions, would you just say, 'This is fair, they're our betters?'"

"Your example is flawed," says the Twins. "The Asuras are evil."

"Then let me be clear: what you plan to do now is evil. Your argument is that there is a hierarchy in this universe, and your position on it is somehow higher than ours. So what you do is just. You say that if we disagree, it's because we don't understand. But we don't need to understand. Killing a rat, for whatever reason, is still killing, no matter who you are or how noble your motives.

"It may be justified in your eyes, it may not, but you cannot expect the rat to agree. It has a right to disagree. To take a life is to take everything from a creature. If you say that it's justified because of hierarchy, then you're equally foolish. There is no hierarchy in the universe. Every law of nature and every inflection of entropy applies to everything equally. I've met plenty like you who speak of hierarchies but never a single who didn't think they weren't at the top. It's just sophistry. It's just a way of absolving yourself of responsibility for your cruelty by turning yourself into a force of nature. You aren't."

"This may be so," the Twins snarl, "but your plan has also been the cause of great cruelty."

"How so?"

"Had we simply come here and killed the Charioteer outright, Skōlex would not be injured."

"This is true," says the Night. "Your plan has resulted in injury to my vimana. Deep injury, injury that cannot be healed easily. Had we not pursued what you suggested, this wouldn't have happened."

The Right Hand nods. "I see, I regret that. I did not intend Skōlex pain. But as you care for your vimana, we care for our people."

"There are billions of you," says the Night. "There is only one Skōlex, and he is far more than just a vimana."

"There is only one of each of us, devi. Only one. Now. Ever." The Right Hand kneels. "I beg you. Please. Don't drop Your bomb. Don't kill those who don't deserve it. The Bounteous Ones are defeated, and their empire is shattered. The Charioteer is broken. They're no longer a threat."

"If we annex Daitya instead," says the Little Princess, "and use it as a base of operations, you'd be more likely to topple your sister. They'd make good allies in the battles ahead."

The Night shakes her head. "A threat unfulfilled is a lie, and I cannot lie."

"Nobody knows about your threat except the Charioteer and us, and we—"

"*I* know. I intended to destroy the Tripura when I said what I said. Who we were determines who we are. I cannot contravene myself now, even if I wanted to. One way or the other, all that I intend comes to pass. I am inevitable."

"Nothing sentient is inevitable, devi."

"Prabho, I am sorry. But here the form you've chosen restricts you. I have not the latitude at this juncture to explain the dimensional qualities of time and how I traverse them. The Tripura will die, as it has been ordained. There is now nothing that you, or I, or the stars in the heavens can do about it."

"Nothing?"

"Nothing."

A long moment passes. The Right Hand rises and takes off his black robe. It drops to the ground, folds slipping like a strange sea beast losing form upon a cruel dry shore. "Then I regret I can no longer be your Right Hand," he says.

He turns and walks back through the Throne Room with his head low and his footsteps leaden. He proceeds into the Antechamber of Night and slips out of his clothes to the drumbeat of remote battle. The moon-white bulge of his belly. The tragic slit in his crotch. He glances at these, walks into one of the pools, and sinks into the water. No hint he was ever there. None but a lone bubble that rises and pauses and pops upon the unstill waters.

2.35

SKŌLEX'S ARMOR FLAKES AND DRIFTS off. It sloughs off its old self with lateral pulses of its flesh, gaping with effort that doesn't seem to reach its depthless eyes. After a while its neck spasms like a serpent regurgitating an eggshell. A sphere of glowing white death shoots out between its teeth and drops through the Daitya's miasmic cloud cover, bitter-bright and otherworldly. Down in the Tripura, the millions who watch it descend know immediately what it is. They scream and scatter amidst the wicked shadows gouged by its phosphorescent glare. They run, though they know they can never run far enough.

In a darkened room in a tenement, a woman clutches a picture of Kadrū to herself. She sees the light through the window. She rises, mouth working in her skeletal face. The thoughts that cross her mind are idle and scattered.

I have never seen a sky as dark as this over the Tripura. I miss the feel of silk pillows in a prince's bed. I'd love to try fresh-fried lentil cakes just one last time.

A shoeless Pṛthvīan woman trudges along in a crowd fleeing the Tripura, with a dead child cradled in her arms. His neck is broken, and his arms are limp; but none in that screaming surge has noticed. Or else they don't care. After all, she isn't the only one carrying a corpse.

The stampede intensifies around her, but she's exhausted and can't move with them. She sinks to her feet and wraps her body around the dead child. The crowd kicks and stomps and clambers its way over her. She neither moves nor makes a sound.

In a mine, a group of chained men lie starving in the dark. They can't see each other, nor do they have the energy to speak. None of them knows what's happening outside. They know only that this is where they'll die, and though that's something to despair at, they hold each other's hands—Agnians, Shukrians, even a Pṛthvīan—and take huge comfort in the fact that they won't do so alone.

Sheelu wends her way through frenzied crowds around the Dnyānasya Mandīram. Another granthapālaḥ orders her to return to her post, but she waves him away without malice and heads outside. The light is close enough to be almost blinding now. She can feel its heat on her skin. She climbs up onto the railings around the moat and slips out of her robes. Beneath it all, she's just a plump little Āēoi with a strangely flat belly. She dives into the water.

High above all this, the Charioteer weeps. He stares out over his beloved city and remembers. The days and nights lived and relished. The people and edifices and the invigorating, exhausting thrum that seemed to emanate from the very air.

The projectile from Skolex is close enough now to turn the whole city into a flattened bone-and-coal vista, one blink away from nothingness.

The Charioteer presses his face against the bare wall of his room.

"I'm sorry, my love," he says. "I would have taken you home if I could."

The light flares. The city of the Tripura ceases to be.

BOOK III

THE GIGANTIC MIGHT OF DARKNESS

3.1

THE SHERBET IS COOL, THE sunlight warm, and the wind that skims the treetops is like welcome whispers. A day so porcelain-perfect that the Ox is hard pressed to dispel the suspicion that whatever powers control such things made it entirely for him. So beautiful he almost forgets who's standing, fidgeting, beside him.

It doesn't take her long to remind him.

"Well?" says the Vicegerent.

The Ox sighs. "Well, what?"

"Well, what are we going to do? Shall I mobilize the fleet? I'll mobilize the fleet. We should decamp to Arungrah. Some worlds there are still loyal and strategically—"

"I'm well aware of the, um, strategic significance of Arungrah. Put the fleet on standby but don't mobilize it, if you would."

The Vicegerent looks as if she's choking on an egg. "Why not?"

"You've heard from the Day, have you? She said mobilize?"

"You mean the Dawn."

"Yes, the Dawn."

"No, but—"

"We don't move the fleet without her say so."

"But it's our fleet."

The Ox glances at her like a blade being unsheathed. "My fleet."

"Yes, of course, your fleet. But why shouldn't we—"

"The anarchy will do the Yamans good. A short time without the Dawn's grace, and they'll be reminded of the, um, beneficence of her rule."

"But—they're attacking grain ships! Not just Yamans either. Everywhere! Just yesterday, a convoy was attacked off the rings of Daitya. Sixteen went missing in dock on Shukra. On Shukra! This is a contagion, and it must be contained. We should at least deploy the Red Fleet to protect the grain-ships."

The wind dies. A swelter closes in behind it. How swift the change from luxury to lethargy. If something as vast as the weather can change in an instant, what hope is there for the works of living things?

"Tell me," says the Ox. "How large is our fleet?"

The Vicegerent's head bobs back, nonplussed. "One hundred and eight ships. You know—"

"And how many convoys are there daily, leaving the Iron Crown of Pṛthvī?"

"I don't know. Sixty?"

"Three hundred and sixty, at the very least. How many of those convoys do you think our fleet of one hundred and eight can defend?"

"We can reorganize them into smaller convoys. Send one ship with each. We can summon the Tarakajanapadas, too, and the Kurus and the Maghadhan fleet."

"And then who will defend Pṛthvī against the Night?"

"The Golden Swarm. Who else? And the Iron Crown's guns. Isn't that what they're for?"

"The Dawn will need us. The Night won't have come here with one juggernaut alone. Our duty, for now, is to preserve our fleet and to wait for the Dawn's next move. When we know what it is, we'll move to support her."

"Shouldn't we find out? Anyways, there's only been reports of a single juggernaut—"

"Did you not hear what I said?"

The Vicegerent scowls. "Doesn't it bother you that they're getting the better of us?"

"This isn't our, um, first rebellion. Do you not remember the other times? Did you learn nothing from them?"

"What was there to be learned?"

"That humans are capable of far less than they should be. In war, they're too busy quarrelling to fight as one. In peace, they're too busy quarrelling to live as one. Let the thieves have their grain. Let a few humans starve—or a few million. It only serves them right."

The Vicegerent eyes him. "Prabho, why aren't you doing anything, really?"

How close is she to knowing, wonders the Ox. How close is she to fathoming that his strategy is its own form of subtle wrecking? He returns her gaze. No suspicion to be seen. Just speckled sweat like glass amoebas migrating along the line of her millimeter-straight brow. That same earnestness that usually repels him so. But this day he is feeling kind. This day he feels just the slightest bit sorry for her.

He smiles.

"I'm just being careful. But look. Perhaps you're right. Go send a message. Ask the Iron Crown what they want us to do."

"I will!"

The Vicegerent strides away. In the distance human servants shuffle out of the way like burrowing beasts before a fox. A holdover, perhaps, from their distant ancestors, who scurried in the soil and muck and hid from beasts bigger, fiercer, and more magnificent than they. What spectacular descendants those tyrant lizards would have bred, thinks the Ox. Not these swarming apes. Something cold, something decisive, something that rent and tore and shredded for a living.

With the Vicegerent gone he stretches out in the unmoving air and lets his systems subside to a low thrum. His decoupled processes run an odd simulation that unfolds with peculiar vividness. He's limping towards his Mother, and her cold arms wrap around his neck. No chiding or criticism. Just the frosty affections he feels with dreamtime certainty are all he's ever wanted. Then, an anomalous input. Warmth on his skin. A brilliance he can feel on his lids. His functions reactivate in swift pulses, and he soon realizes it has nothing to do with a dream.

Something is burning him.

He opens his eyes. After a few moments' adjustment, he sees some dazzling teardrop of a vimana approaching the Vṛṣaprāsādaḥ with a rumble like the grinding of continents. It thunders overhead with the noise and heat of a descending sun and settles onto the roof. The palace towers framing it like colossal stone sentinels. The ancient marble softening its broiling neutronium hull.

The Ox knows what comes next and clamps his hands over his ears. A great droning explodes from the vehicle, so powerful it ruffles his hair and races across the Valley of the Mariner in a shimmering shockwave that blows the far sky clear. Across the roof garden, two of the human servants who didn't flee in time drop dead.

The Vicegerent sprints up the stairs beside the corpses and trots over without looking at them.

"No need to send a message, prabho!" she calls. "The Bright One is already here."

The wind isn't coming back. The day has become hotter with no prospect of cooling down. The Ox grunts and rises to his feet.

"I can see that." He straightens his clothes. "Let's, um, see what auntie dear wants."

3.2

MISERY WEIGHS ON THE GELDING like chain mail. His nose seems clogged with Daityan blood. His thoughts are only for his parents and Sheelu and the unknown millions of the Tripura. Nameless earlier because of his ignorance, nameless now because of his failure. Did they feel their eyes boil away? Their skin fall from their bodies? Did they die quickly, or did they linger, suffering, agonized? He wanders the far reaches of Skōlex's interior with such speculations crowding him like unwelcome devotees. It's impossible to see where he's going. It's impossible to think of anything else.

Presently, he comes to some colossal, blue-pillared chamber. Magnificent on its own but, aboard the juggernaut, just another nameless, storyless, dimensionless space. Against one of the giant trunks holding up the ceiling, desiccated and singular, is what looks like a giant insect shell. The glint of light on its curved lines. The absurd vividness of its aquamarine and pink tint. Then he notices a stream of crystalline ice emerging from the shadows beside it.

He sighs. "Go away," he says.

The Night steps forth with the crunch of bare feet on frost.

"Do you know who they were, prabho?" says the Night, nodding to the shell.

"No," says the Gelding. "Please stop calling me prabho."

"Why? Because you were disobeyed? A lord who cannot tolerate disagreement is no lord indeed."

"I can tolerate that. I can't tolerate genocide." He looks at her askance. "Did You kill these things, too, whatever they were?"

If the Night notices the malice in his question, she doesn't show it.

"No," she says. "We saved them. They were the last remnants of a civilization, surviving on the wreckage of one of their stations far from the world that had birthed them. Imagine it: a spider web the size of your home world adrift between the stars. Their lives were full of fear. They asked themselves, why were we born here? Why could we not be born some other time, when we were glorious and proud, when we could build wonders like this one we live on, and not just survive on them like parasites?" She steps up to the shell and sniffs. "I tried to explain to them that one can only be born when one is born. To be born at some other time is to be someone else. Life is no more and no less than a fire that burns through matter. No two flames are the same."

The Gelding turns on his heels and marches away, but when he glances back he sees the Night following him as silent as a creeping depression.

"Please leave me alone," he says.

"You must not hate me. What I did was unavoidable."

"Unavoidable?" The Gelding halts and squeezes his eyes shut. "What you killed were people. Millions and millions of people. People like me ... and Kadrū ... and Danu. People like Vishwadevi. My mother. My father. Will you kill me, too, when the time comes?"

The Night says nothing. The Gelding turns to her.

"You know what humans are? Let me tell you. When I was a child, the villagers used to make fun of me. Humans are mean. They'd all play dice or drink or dance, but I'd sit with a dataslat and I'd read. They'd tell me it wasn't manly and say what's the point in knowing about systems when they get fixed for us? What's the point in knowing the names of all the weeds when we just kill them? Humans are ignorant." He breathes deep. "I hated it. I hated it because they were making fun of me for not being like them. But sometimes I did listen. Sometimes I left my reading and went down and played with my dogs. Do you know why?"

"I do not know."

"My cousin. Vishwadevi. She'd come to see me. She'd ask what I was reading, though she had no interest in it at all. Humans are curious. Then she'd turn to leave. But before she did, she always looked at the dog's toybox. Just for an instant. She didn't do it purposely. She just glanced at it, and in that glance was a whole future. Of the dogs running around with their tongues out and their eyes wide and the moonlight like dancing sapphires on their pupils. Of soft dust on our feet. Of running and jumping and laughing. All in that one look. It got me every time."

He blinks, tears tumbling from him.

"Humans are dreams and kindness and hope. How many millions of futures like that did you just wipe out? Every single one of those people down there—they were all like Vishwadevi. They were all like me. They all woke up that morning and thought—maybe for a second—about a better future. And you just swept it all away."

"They would have ended eventually."

"That's not the point! Life isn't just a flame. Flames are simple things. Life is complexity. Don't you see? Life is complexity itself. It flows against the curse physics laid on all matter and all energy—to go from undifferentiation to undifferentiation. The beginning of the universe was a homogenous singularity, empty of anything but potential, which is another way of saying empty. The ultimate end will be heat death. It'll be empty and boring and interminable and cold and cruel.

"In between those is all the eyes and blood cells and bats using echolocation and insects swarming and asteroid-miners clawing at bare rock with their mantis hands. I've never seen half of it, but I love it all. Just the idea that it exists—existed—could exist—makes me glow with excitement. But you, you who see for light-years, somehow, you're blind to it. You crush it beneath your feet for no reason. Worse ... for revenge. For the sake of your revenge, my parents died. My friends. A million people who were parents, too, and friends and lovers and—" He takes a deep breath. "I was wrong. I do hate you."

The Night watches him, and though her face is as serene as an idol's, the Gelding sees his words have stung her.

"You have me wrong, prabho," she says. "I love life. I love your people also. I came to tell you that I have surmised who the serpent is this time."

"What?"

"Vrtra, the serpent. It is that which stands in the way of life. I see life as you do. I see that, if life is as you say it is—as beautiful and as significant—then you would want it to spread, wouldn't you? After all, what is a garden without flowers, without insects?"

The Gelding turns away. "I've not got time for Your riddles. Let me off at the nearest planet—"

"Life is a lonely thing," says the Night. "You are right—it is complexity. But complexity is rare. Complexity that breeds more complexity is rarer still. In this whole universe it has arisen, bloomed, and died over and over again. Every time, it did so alone far from anything else that could possibly have understood it for what it is. That is, until We came along—we of Triangulum. We were the first to survive long enough to learn that. We were the first to see these distant groves in the dark forest and set out to visit them. Nearly, always, we found them already hollow and rotten. We—you—were the first to realize what that meant We must do."

A thought pops into the Gelding's mind, unexpected but familiar. "We must shepherd it," he says. "We must let it spread."

The Night smiles. "That's why you sent me here in the first place. To nurture the humans. To stop them killing each other long enough for them to spread and change into a thousand civilizations. To seed this galaxy into a garden worthy of the thing it hosts. That's why I lingered here so long. That's why I fought my sister so hard. She's become the serpent—she's become Vrtra. She denies humanity the stars. She keeps humanity in its egg for fear of what might happen to the hatchling." She pauses. "I didn't come here for revenge, prabho. I came here to set your people free."

A long silence. Memories pop into the Gelding's mind like particles in the void. Scents and vistas his human mind can only render in dizzying approximation. Strange, fractured impressions that make no sense even when they fit together.

"You also came for love," he says. "You love your sister."

"She is diminished by this place. I must take her away."

The Gelding cradles his head in his hands and sinks to the floor. "What's happening? I feel sick."

"Perhaps you're remembering who you are."

"I'm ... Indra."

"Yes."

The Night sits also. The balletic splay of her black sari about her. The cloth spreading as lush and dense as a jungle's dark canopy. The Gelding rocks back and forth in the coolness of her presence. After a while, his mind settles.

"You think what you did was justified," he says. "I will never accept that. But I will accept that we must defeat your sister."

"I ask for nothing else."

"I will help you with this, but I have conditions. There'll be no more killing of innocents. And you will not harm the people of Pṛthvī."

"There is no other way—"

"No. We will find it. Pṛthvī won't be harmed. You will give me your word on this, or I will ... I'll go. I'll walk away."

"And leave the Princess behind? The Left Hand?"

The Gelding forces himself to mean what he says next. "Yes. They'll be fine. They're strong."

A long silence. "It will be difficult," says the Night. "But I would not have you leave, prabho. If this is what you want, you have my word. In return, will you be my Right Hand once more?"

"What if I'm not who you think I am? Would you still keep your word?"

"I give my word to who you are, not what you are, as I give my word to all creatures who ask favors of the Night. Do you give me yours?"

The Gelding opens his eyes and examines her face. Inscrutable in its stillness. Beautiful in the manner of the galaxy splayed across the dark.

"I give you my word," he says. "I will be your Right Hand once more."

He leans forward onto all fours and lowers his forehead to the ground. The Night mirrors him. No witnesses to this moment that will change a billion lives. No one to see a goddess and a gelding make promises to each other. But it happens nonetheless. It happens.

3.3

EVERY DAY THE RIGHT WAKES before the Left, washes himself in the far pool, and heads off on long walks through Skōlex. The Left feigns sleep till the sound of his footsteps fade and then spends most of her day in the Throne Room, staring at the slowly drifting stars. The Little Princess watches all this like a naturalist taking stock of a behavior they'd never seen before. Pain, she gathers, is a parasite that thrives in isolation. What an exquisite adaptation that it turns its hosts away from others.

She decides she must do something about it.

She picks her day, waits for the Right Hand to dress, and waylays him by one of the doors. She's tall enough now to fix her owlish gaze directly on him and large enough that he could not simply brush past her with his eunuch's bulk even if he wanted to.

"No," she says.

The Right Hand looks out at the Antechamber for an explanation but finds none. "I'm sorry?"

"You'll not run off today, prabho Indra. You'll spend time with myself and Sister Kadrū."

"Kumari—"

"Wait here, please."

The Princess marches over to where a sleepdrunk Left Hand is watching them, dons her gloves, and pulls her out of her bedroll. The older woman growls and complains, but one glance at the Princess's stern face is enough to convince her that this isn't a fight worth picking.

The Princess leads them off into Skōlex.

As they go, the Left glances at the Right Hand and mouths, "Where are we going?" Before he can respond, the Princess says, "You'll find out soon enough." After that, neither of them dare say anything, if only to avoid having to ask the Princess how she knows they're speaking without looking.

She takes them to the Hall of the Soma Seed. The Hands gawp at the gigantic object suspended overhead like the cocoon of a celestial moth. The inconceivable bulk of the thing. The lightning crawling along its length like glowing spiderlegs. For a long time they're overcome with the odd, slightly nauseating feeling of being inspected and decoded like books.

The Princess takes them to the door the vision of her mother led her to and leads them without word into the buttery sunlight and sweet air of the high meadow beyond. Again, the two Hands' jaws fall open, but this wonder is a different species altogether to the one they felt at the alien splendor of the Soma Seed.

"What is that?" asks the Right Hand. "Where are we?"

"It doesn't do much," says the Princess. She wedges the door open with a rock. "I've watched it walk back and forth. It never comes this way."

She marches off. There's no doubt that there will be consequences if they don't do the same. The Right Hand and Left look at each other and share a quick smile for the first time in days. Then they follow.

They trek over a softened peak down the hillside beyond, leaving rocks as markers as they go. Descending carefully at first but speeding up until finally they're half-running, half-sliding, whooping and unfettered, down the mattress-soft lawn. The Princess races ahead with gyroscopic deftness. The Hands lose her in the blue-barked alien trees beyond, then catch up to her by a sandy-banked river where the water bends like liquid glass. Flecks of sunlight jostle as if each individually wanted their sole attention.

The Princess examines the water. "I believe I will take a swim," she declares.

She walks demurely behind a boulder, and they see only her head as she takes her clothes off. "There's no other boulders," says the Right Hand.

"I'll go behind a tree," says the Left.

"I don't mind if you don't mind," says the Right after a few moments. "I mean, you've seen it all before."

A pause. Then: "All right."

The Right Hand begins to peel his clothes away. His body is hairless, his belly rounded, and his midriff longer than perhaps it would have been. In his crotch is a small hole the size of a thumb-tip and over it, a flap of skin.

"I wonder sometimes," he says.

"Wonder what?"

"What I'd've been like if I was complete."

The Left Hand holds the sash of her sari out to the Right Hand. "Everyone's missing something," she says. "Help me, yeah?"

He holds the cloth, uncertain if he should be doing something. She steps back, spins slowly on the spot, and the sari unravels. She folds it and slips out of her bodice and underskirt. Now the Right Hand stares. The mole under her left breast. The stretchmarks ringing her armpits. For a long while, they inspect each other, silenced by some aching animal part of them that rages and subsides and then rages again. The Princess swims around the corner, underwear intact.

"Are you two nude?" She squeezes her eyes shut. "Barbarians!"

Another glance, conspiratorial, and the Hands splash in at her. The Princess sets off with a yelp, but they follow, chuckling, the riverbed silty and yielding beneath their feet. Strange five-finned creatures, more insect than fish, flee their approach. A troupe of climbing cat-things start yowling, and these in turn provoke some larger creatures in the distance. Then, from very far-off, comes a single earthshaking boom that surely is a signal from the giant they saw earlier. They wait, frozen, but the sound passes and isn't repeated.

After that, all three settle face-up in the water with the sun kind on their faces and the water soothing on their backs.

"How is it you're not poisonous in water, Prabho Kadrū?" says the Little Princess.

“I’m ‘prabho’ now, am I?” says the Left Hand.

“Yes. Your bravery in going to the Tripura has earned my respect.”

The Left Hand snorts. “Why, thank you, kumari. Our poison isn’t as strong as people think. We can’t actually kill with a single touch—it needs to be extended contact.”

“So why do you wear gloves? Why make us wear gloves?”

“Better safe than sorry.”

“Very sensible.”

“I wonder what’s behind the other doors,” says the Right Hand.

“There was some sort of ruin behind one,” says the Princess. “It was mostly ash and old buildings under a red sun. Behind another was an empty room overlooking a city with tall towers, none with windows. The air stank. That’s all I’ve seen.”

They hear the rustle of creatures moving through the forest. Overhead, the branches of the trees overhanging the creek sag with the weight of crawling flowers, hundreds of them, crowding the slim protrusions and turning their stamens and pistils down towards the swimmers like brilliant organic antennae.

“We could run away, you know,” says the Left Hand quietly. “Just slip away into one of these doors and go somewhere beautiful like this and live out our lives in peace.”

“But then we’d be away from Skōlex,” says the Princess.

“So?”

“We won’t be able to stop the Night doing whatever it is she intends to do next.”

“Do you know what she intends to do next?”

“No.”

“She intends to destroy Pṛthvī,” says the Right Hand.

The Princess frowns. “Destroy it?”

“Yes.” The Right Hand shoos away a fish. “The Soma Seed is a weapon, amongst other things. The bombs we dropped on Daitya—they were made from it. She’ll try to drop it in its entirety on Pṛthvī, and that’ll destroy the planet whole.”

“It’s a weapon?” The Left Hand blinks. “I thought it was food, or something. For Skōlex.”

“It is food. I mean, it can be. It—it changes things. It’s like ... programmable complexity. I don’t know how else to put it. When it encounters something, it changes it. Not from complex to simple, but from complex to complex.” The Right Hand shudders as if trying to shake someone else’s voice from his head. “She’ll dump it wholesale onto Pṛthvī. I don’t know what’ll happen next, but people won’t be able to live there anymore.”

“Why would she do that?”

“To set us free, apparently. Without Pṛthvī, the Dawn’s power’s broken. Without the Dawn, we’re free to leave the system.”

“Well, in that case,” says the Princess, “we shan’t be able to stop her by running away.”

"We can't stop her at all," says the Left Hand.

"She promised me she would not hurt Pṛthvī," says the Right Hand. "If we remain, we can at least hope that she'll extend that benevolence to other worlds, too."

The Left Hand sighs and stretches her hands up over her head.

"I suppose we'll have to stay then," she says. "It'd be nice, wouldn't it, though? To live in peace with nothing but the next day to worry about."

The Right Hand flips over and dips his head. Animals skitter about in the clear water. Tendrils of vivid green weed sway. No sound here but the rush and muffle of the river. No sign that any other world exists, anywhere, anytime. It would be nice, he thinks. It would.

3.4

THE OX SITS IN HIS garden as his servants file out of the Vṛṣaprāsādaḥ in the glare of the Chariot of Dawn with the dazed progress of a great army turfed out of a fortress by an unexpected attack. With them gone the Dawn's retainers take control of the Vṛṣaprāsādaḥ. For hours he watches them with the shadows lengthening like black stalactites and ponders what will happen next. How much of what he has done will be revealed for what it is? What will his punishment be now the burning reckoning has come?

He isn't afraid, though he knows he should be.

At sunset three Heralds of Dawn in golden armor and white face-masks emerge from her vimana and come down the stairs towards him. Every step and breath and movement of their heads are synchronized. They make their eerie approach and gesture without speaking up to where the Chariot of Dawn sits in the ruins of one of the roof gardens like a cooling meteor.

The Ox ascends the half-melted stairs. The Vicegerent falls in behind him. Up top is a mess of charred plant matter and a bone-dry pond littered with the smoldering remnants of beloved, gem-bright fish. The Ox tries not to stare, but stare he does—his eyes heavy, one fist clenched. Then the rear of the Chariot of Dawn blooms like a red-hot lotus. Furnace-hot air gusts from the interior. A small set of strangely viscous stairs oozes down like mercury and hardens despite the heat.

They kneel.

A few blank moments pass. A shining figure appears at the top of the stairs. Her white sari hiked slightly, her skin calcium-white and eggshell-pure. She descends in precise steps. When she hits the abused marble of the roof garden the stone melts anew beneath her soles. Her feet slide, this way and that, on the brief sheen of lava. The heat strengthens as she approaches, and on the very cusp of it becoming unbearable, she addresses them in a voice like grinding crystal.

"Why haven't you gone after my sister yet?"

The Ox lowers his forehead to the ground. "We were awaiting your instructions, rajini."

"My instructions?" The Dawn crouches. Lips squeezed clamshell-tight. Gaze like a blast of shattered glass. "When have you ever needed those, nephew mine? When have you ever needed someone to tell you to get into a fight with your mother?"

"Rajini, I—"

"Oh, shut the fuck up."

The Dawn snorts and walks over to the edge of the roof where her brightness breeds a phalanx of shadows in the forest in the valley. In the distance Surya disappears below the horizon, outshone and ignored. She lingers, tremulous, beautiful like the roiling surface of a star.

"I hate this place," she says. "The Red Planet, they used to call it. Did you know there were ancient Pṛthvīans who actually dreamt of coming here? Why? Why leave paradise for this shithole? I've never understood that about humans. The call of the crap. Did you know they used to seek out and eat the feet of animals? The guts, the ovaries? The fins of perfectly good fish, which they'd cut off and leave the beast to die. Fucking idiots, all of them. Every single, stinking monkey-man, woman, and child. If they didn't have me ..." She frowns. "Is there more forest here than last time?"

"Yes, rajini," says the Ox. "I had it replanted."

"Why?"

"Because it's, um, beautiful."

"Hmm." She turns to him. "You've spent too long here fucking around with your flowers and your boys. While you've been indulging yourself, my sister's raised the whole system against me. What good are you to me? Why haven't you gone after her? She only has one vimana. Just one, lonely juggernaut. Probably Skōlex. Remember him?"

"Yes, rajini."

"I hear he finally got his revenge on *Bheki*." She steps up to the Ox. "You haven't answered my question yet. Why have you done nothing?"

"I have done things, rajini. I sent the Huntress to secure Yama—"

"For what that's worth. What else?"

The prospect of telling her the truth and nothing but the truth opens before the Ox like a cooing abyss. What would happen if he did? What if he stood, spat on her feet, and told her he was sick and tired of all this—the politics and the violence, the forgetting and the fighting and the fear of her blistering wrath. The endless churn of history he'd never agreed to witness or preside over or abet.

She would kill him, surely. She would burn his head right off. Better to hold his tongue. Better she have to impute treachery than know it for a fact.

"Well?" says the Dawn.

"I thought it best to wait for your direction, rajini. Had we moved out of place, we would have left the Golden Swarm alone to defend Pṛthvī, and—"

The Dawn clamps her incandescent hand on the Ox's face. Her blinding heat smothers him like liquid star stuff. The breathtaking agony of her touch. The feeling of his skin roasting, his lips melting, his bone scorching beneath all that. He struggles, but she holds. Curling wafts of vaporized blood leak between her fingers. The Ox's howls muffle against pale palms.

The Vicegerent watches, bug-eyed, hand on mouth. The Dawn doesn't let go for a while.

When she does, the Ox thuds to the ground squirming like a fish choking on air. Half his face is gone. Pieces of his scalp drip, sizzling, to the ground. The Dawn scrutinizes her work like a sculptor eyeing a fresh-carved treasure.

"I won't waste time speculating on why you've undermined me so," she says. "Big Sister only has one ship. Why? Why only Skōlex? If she had more, she'd be here by now, wouldn't she? Stop your damn whimpering. Sit up."

The Ox rises, trembling. A strip of skin hangs like old bark off the side of his head.

"I'll tell you why," she continues. "Because the other High Thrones know she won't see it through. She couldn't do it last time, and she won't do it this time either. That's why they let her take Skōlex, and no one else. So you'll forgive me, won't you, my stupid, self-hating boy, if I'm extraordinarily confused and disappointed by your failure to gather Our forces and sally forth. If you'd mustered all my vassals and swept the system, I wouldn't have had to leave Pṛthvī. And you know I hate leaving Pṛthvī."

The Ox tries to speak. Then he realizes his tongue is missing.

"What?" The Dawn shakes her head and turns to the Vicegerent. "Nevermind. You. Go with this fool and the fleet to intercept my sister. This one will fix his face and parley with her. Keep her busy until I can get everything together. I suppose at this point I'm going to have to meet her at Pṛthvī myself, but at least I'll have enough bodies to stop her there."

The Vicegerent lies flat on the warm stone, limbs akimbo. "Rajini," she says. "I … I'm not worthy to …"

The Dawn peers as if examining an insect trapped in amber. Then she bursts into laughter—tinkling, cascading, sing-song. A sound more beautiful than it has any right to be.

"Worthy has nothing to do with it. You've been shadowing this fool for three thousand years. You'd know when he's up to something." She adjusts the sash of her sari and shakes her hair loose. The light coming off it in shards. The glitter of the cloth like a shower of molten silver. "Though I wonder—what is your role in this? Why didn't you push him to do something?"

"I did! Rajini, I did. We were speaking of it just before your august arrival."

"Fine. Whatever. Just don't fail me." She leans in to the Ox. "I'm going to kill them both, boy. You better hope to the Thrones Beyond that you've not set me back too far."

She pushes the Ox over with her fingertip. He tumbles with a splat. Then she turns and stalks back up to her Chariot. In her wake she leaves splotches on the marble where her feet melted stone. Ugly black mirrors in the once-flawless white. Hot to the touch, but not for very long.

3.5

I

The King of Yama dreams that he's lost in a fluid charnel that sucks at his feet, licks his arms, and swills, stinking, against his heart. In the sky overhead are stabbing visions like lightning. Sometimes, the tarmac at the space port. Other times, executions in the squares and on the streets. Rarely, the Crown Princess's face, alone in that silent room, where half his dreams and heart died. Horrors he asked for. Horrors he didn't.

He wakes exhausted and wanders his apartments without purpose or direction. Sometimes he fancies he can smell the corpses washing up on the shores of his memory. Most probably that's just the stink of the filth about him. The plates piled like petrified cells at a wound. The stale bedding like sloughed-off skin. His only distraction is *Pratikara*'s frequent jumps. In the trembling lead-up, he seats himself by one of the portholes and waits for the brief oblivion that splices the place they leave and the place they arrive. The splitting of the whole universe into overlapping red-blue-yellow components. The lingering narcotic afterimage of these fractured realities, as if each was determined to cling to existence as long as it could.

After one such jump he sees the first interesting thing he's laid eyes on since *Pratikara* left Yama. An amorphous spacebeast that appears starboard like a fleshy nova. A fanciful geometry of tentacles, membranes, and coral-fine capillaries unfettered by gravity's grasp. Appendages longer in their totality than *Pratikara* entire. The ethereal sweep of these as they react to the arrival of its strange metal companion.

The King leans forward. His breath blooms and shrinks upon the frigid glass. "Who're you?" he whispers.

The creature whirls with anemone grace. A tentacle reaches towards the vimana, and its tip blooms like a flower. The smooth sweep of the star-glossed dish. The receiver trembling like a pistil in the wind. For a while human and beast are both lost by the thrill of being seen and comprehended as a fellow creature by another living thing. For the first time in days, the King smiles. Then *Pratikara* opens fire.

Glowing projectiles lance the beast. The ephemeral substance of its body dents and explodes. The grunt and clank of the guns reloading. The neon blast of ichor bloating into the void. Soon there's nothing left but scraps of cold flesh and frozen blood disaggregating against the starfield.

The King listens to the ping of frozen body parts colliding with *Pratikara*'s hull with his head hung low. Death, it seems, is following him. And why shouldn't it? He summoned it to his service. He slaked its thirst. What made him think it would leave when he wanted it to?

II

AFTER EATING, THE KING INSPECTS himself in the mirror. He doesn't recognize the bearded wreck staring back at him. Some oily-looking vagrant, lank hair overlong, skin the greying pallor of a man who's spent too long in the shade. Still he wraps himself in the cleanest robes he can find, stalks up to the bridge, and finds, as expected, that the Soul of Mangala is alone at the controls.

The Soul speaks without turning. "Those things can communicate with their mates."

The King scans the bridge. The banks of untouched screens. The mute grey elegance of a space designed by a mind not quite human. "What things?"

"The thing outside. That's why you're here, isn't it? To complain about me shooting it? Those things communicate with their mates. They can transfer information faster than light. That's what they were made to be—spies."

The King wanders over to the captain's chair and collapses onto the unblemished leather, a black-eyed man in black robes, sunk in still more black. "How do you know this?"

"I'm old as fuck, man."

"You didn't need to kill it."

"What's it to you if I did?"

The King can feel dead blood on the back of his eyeballs. "I'm exhausted by all this death."

"You've been stuck jacking off in that room of yours for too long."

"Watch your tongue, demon."

The Soul turns and rattles up to the King with its insect eyes bulging and its pincers tucked by its side. The whirr and clink of servos trilling in odd symphony. The eyes scanning him like a butcher examining an uncarved carcass.

"This isn't about that animal, really," he says. "This is about what I did on Yama."

"Do not presume to psychoanalyze me."

"Why shouldn't I? You're pretty damn transparent. You say you're exhausted by the killing. Exhausted, now that your old buddy's dead. Not when anyone else died. Not when any of those priests or nobles got cut to pieces or hanged or burned. Now. One man. What sort of conscience do you have that's so broken it can accept the death of thousands but weep over the death of one?"

"That's enough."

"Oh, no, your majesty. No one's ever said this to you, but I can now. See, I thought you and I had something in common. I thought we both had large visions—important visions—and we understood we'd have to sacrifice others to attain them. But ever since we left Yama and you've been sulking like a teenager in your cabin, I've begun to wonder if maybe I was wrong. Maybe we're not alike.

"Now you say you're exhausted by the killing? Well, here's a fat turd of truth straight from my processors: it does not matter." The Soul inches closer, millennia-old malice emanating from its shambling metal shell. "You wanted to make a change on Yama, and a bunch of people had to die to make those changes. That was fine with you because they died for a reason. Now you're not so sure there's a reason, so the killing should stop?

"Fuck that. Who anointed your conscience the conscience of the universe? And while we're at it, let's drop another pretense. Your daughter's no more special than any of the other kids who lost their families or starved during your revolution or got thrown out into the street or raped or enslaved. She's exactly like them. The only difference is you give a shit about her and not about those. Nothing is special, king. Not you, not your kid, not your old buddy I killed. Nobody."

Silence. The King peers down his nose at the Soul. "Tell me then," he says, after a while. "Was your death special?"

"What death?"

"You're a copy of the original program that was the Soul of Mangala. Your original remained in the Dnyānasya Mandīram. So when the Night bombed it, you died." The King smiles. "You're a ghost. A copy of a dead thing."

A heartbeat's quiet. "No, it doesn't bother me. Why should it?"

The king eyes him with the wisp of a smile.

"I don't believe you," he says. "And that makes everything you just said utter nonsense. You say nobody is special, but you think you are. You're no better than me, demon. Remember that the next time you pontificate at me."

"I'm not a goddamn demon."

The King's smile fades. "I am. And, therefore, so are you."

3.6

I

ALONE IN HIS ROOM THE Ox clicks the limp pink slug of his new tongue into place. Then he dons his face-mask. The light-eating blackness of the thing. The gaping eyes and the inhuman slit of a mouth. Large enough to cover most of his ruined face, but not so large that it covers a fringe of mottled flesh on its borders. People will see. People will wonder.

Good.

When the time comes, he walks along the corridors under the unpitying gaze of the Dawn's human functionaries. They fall in step behind him out of respect for protocol, but not for him. Up the stairs to where the ruins of the roof gardens are turning sodden beneath the bruise-grey sky. The rhinoskin rough meltstone. The ash scattering in the breeze. The Chariot of Dawn is already powered up and incandescent on the uppermost level. For the first time he notices the tiny head of the vimana, deer-faced and timid-looking, peering at him with eyes burning like hot marbles. The Dawn is standing beside it, feeding it something coal-hot and glowering from her bare hand.

She finishes and approaches the wrecked railings. As she does, the bruise-grey sky opens up, and it starts to rain. The water turning to vapor in the glowing bubble of light about her. The knife-light of her glower splashing on the mirroring stone. She stares at the Ox for a long time. Though he's almost too far away to see, he knows she's thinking of consequences. She's wondering if, this time, she's gone too far with her punishment.

He bows to her. A moment's hesitation, and she nods back.

It takes a long while for the Dawn's little army to withdraw, but the Ox stands watching the whole ceremony. The speech by a Herald of Dawn to no one in particular. The desanctification of the grounds by two servants tipping a great vat of the Chariot's waste onto ground no longer worthy enough to play host to the Most Holy. Once they've finished and boarded, there's nothing but the sound of the wind like lamentation on the forest and the tap of the Vicegerent's unstill foot on the marble behind him.

"Just fucking stop that, will you?" he hisses.

She stops.

The Ox watches the Chariot rise away from the Vṛṣaprāsādaḥ like a celestial egg returning to the womb. Then he clanks his way unsteadily up to the roof gardens. He finds the closest pile of shattered ceramic from his planters and begins to haul them down the stairs.

"What're you doing?" asks the Vicegerent. "We have a mobilization to begin."

"You have." The Ox grunts. His mechanisms are still delicate from the attack. His inner systems grumble against their disequilibrium. "You're in charge."

"The Dawn ordered that—"

The Ox hefts a great chunk of ceramic and flings it off the side of the roof with a roar. He kicks the sagging balustrade and sets a great vitrified stone log tumbling down into the forest. The obsidian shattering like black water. The rage setting his flesh aquiver.

"She's given you a task, but not dominion over me." He turns his ruined face to the Vicegerent. "I am yet Lord of the Vṛṣaprāsādaḥ, and I won't have it left like this. Let the servants in and then do what you must. I'll be here, fixing what's been ruined."

The Vicegerent withdraws, silent, cowed. He watches her go.

"Dammit," he growls, and hefts another chunk of ceramic over the side.

II

THE RAIN CONTINUES ALL DAY and night and turns the wasteland atop the Vṛṣaprāsādaḥ into a tar-grey mire. The Ox's servants filter back into the palace as he works. Late at night some come up to join him, trembling and horrified at what's become of his face. It's easy enough to send out word that he wants certain people to come and see him. It's easy enough to explain their visits away as naught more than expressions of loyalty.

On the second day the admirals start to come.

They help him mop the marble, move the ash-polluted soil, and gather the charred corpses of fish into sacks. They help him lug great bales of fresh earth, little gold-foil packets of seedlings, and infant trees in glazed bowls up onto the roof. They hammer and they measure and they saw. Above all, they speak. In whispers and in codes. First, in the feint and play of people uncertain that they're speaking of the same thing. Then, otherwise.

On the fourth day the inverted glacier of cloud cover cracks, and sunlight spills through like golden aurorae. The Ox and his allies pause for a while to watch the pink-gold horizon at sunset. By now, their planning is almost finished. The Ox is certain who will stand by him—and live—and who will not, and so will die. He spends the evening carrying slabs of fresh marble up to the new roof garden, laying out fresh benches and filling the new ponds with water. His body adjusted now to its new reality, his face already healing. Not even a sun can undo so easily the work of Tvashtr of the Stellar Forge.

By midnight, the roof gardens are reborn. The Ox has a sherbet and a pipe brought up to him and sits with his feet in one of the ponds with the new koi flitting like cool ghosts against his feet. In the distance a constellation of light rises from the sprawling glower of the spaceport. Troopships supplying the Red Fleet hunkered just over the horizon. Past ruin is undone around him, and future ruin is configured overhead.

The Vicegerent approaches.

"We're ready," she says. She looks around the gardens. "It's ... it's all very well done."

She's trying, he thinks. He decides to try, too. He rises, walks past her to the stairs, and flicks a tiny speck of errant scrap of ash off the balustrade.

"I'm certain that you've handled everything very well," he says.

She doesn't know what to say, so she says nothing.

They walk down to where Akupāra is squatting upon a launch pad munching on a log. The beast swings its head towards the Ox and sniffs him with nostrils thinning and gaping like eyeless sockets. It takes in his new smell and new face and lows deep in its throat. The Lord of Mangala strokes his vimana's venerable head and sniffs its scent like true home and wonders how many more opportunities he'll have to do that.

Not many, if all goes as planned. So he wraps his arms around the beast, presses his melted cheek against it, and listens to the blood pumping in its giant veins. Once onboard, they rise without ceremony and swoop low over the emerald carpet of forest and up into the star-cluttered sky. Akupāra sails over where the Valley of the Mariner streaks through the high, brown scrubland in a verdant stroke. Then Mangala shrinks in the portholes, a yellow-green celestial zygote, oblivious to the abdication of its king. Up ahead, the great corvettes and destroyers of the Red Fleet come into view, all with their jumplights active and their crews signaling readiness.

"Ready to jump, deva," says the pilot.

"You mean 'devi,'" says the Ox. He nods to the Vicegerent. "She is in charge."

She scowls. Perhaps he's being too nice. "Yes, deva. Sorry, deva." The pilot bows to the Vicegerent. "Ready to jump, devi."

"Very good. Jump when ready."

The Ox leans against the window and peers at his planet. "Farewell, my love," he whispers.

3.1

THE SOUL'S WEAPON HAS BROKEN the Huntress's suit of man-flesh. She tries to slip out of it, but it won't come off. Instead of healing, her injuries become a putrefying home to hordes of microbiota. Her pain protocols won't adapt or turn off. Her diagnostics can tell her what's wrong but not how to fix it.

She is, she decides, entirely fucked.

The Yamans do nothing to alleviate her suffering. Instead, they work with quiet, dignified diligence to make it worse. They keep her in an awkwardly shaped box in which she can neither sit nor stand. Acid fires ignite in her knees and thighs that never stop burning. When she refuses to eat, a doctor arrives, injects her with some paralyzing agent, and jams a pipe down her throat. The probe and thrust of the thing. The gagging presence swelling in her gullet like some rubber-skinned parasite. Into this, three masked orderlies—gentle almost, attentive—pour some foul slurry that smells like piss and distends her stomach like wet concrete. They clean her twice a day by opening a hatch at the back of her box and spraying freezing water into it until her waste runs out the grooves by her feet. Still she reeks.

So much for her body. For her mind, they have other horrors.

After some shapeless eternity, they bring one of her girls in front of her and politely inform her that she's to be executed. The girl's face is aubergine-black and disfigured. She cannot stand, and she cannot talk. She can scream, though. This she does with abandon when they seal her in a cage and empty a bucket of snakes into it. Eventually, she falls silent, but they don't remove the box. They leave it there as the snakes squabble, snap, and wait for the flesh to soften. They leave it until the animals have eaten enough to satiate them.

Then they bring in the next girl.

They keep going until they come to the last. An Āēoi girl somehow less battered than the rest. Perhaps that's because her fate is to be worse. They snatch her symbiont wailing from her pouch. Though she begs and pleads, they slit the little creature's throat. The abattoir efficiency of their bladework. The obsequiousness, as if they really were sorry for all the inconvenience. The Sister howls like she was having her bones extracted raw from her flesh one by one. They hand the broken, little body back to her. She keens over the thing, hunched over, shivering. Then one of them steps forward and puts a bolt in the back of her head.

The Huntress is glad when it's over. There are no more girls now. There is only her, and she will not be so easy to break.

They don't get the opportunity. Not long after she hears scuffles and thuds outside. A muffled groan. A snap of wood or bone or something else. Then a long, bloated silence. The door opens. Three young women sneak in, clad in the armor and bug-eyed visors of the guard. They take them off and prostrate themselves before the Huntress's cage.

"Get me out," says the Huntress. "Quickly."

She can't walk. Her joints are crooked now, and her flesh blackened and maggoty. The girls work quickly to smear pseudosoma in the injuries and feed some to the Huntress. Soon enough she feels the power of the stuff coursing through her like sweet lava. In the dark and the pain, she had thought of nothing but revenge, but now those thoughts are more than just fantasy.

They carry her out, furtive, efficient. Up the stairs past corpse after corpse. None of them looks to have died quickly. The Huntress sees this and is pleased. It's the first good thing she's seen in a long time.

Outside, she finds more Sisters. These are heavily armed, presiding over what looks like a makeshift tank. A tractor of some sort equipped with a heavy gun and metal plates pulling a trailer equally armored and armed. Her irrepressible girls, bright-eyed with grief at her condition and relief at her survival.

Someone opens fire. They pile into the vehicle and take off. In the trailer is a bed, medical equipment, and boxes of ammunition. As they rattle along the road past paddyfields like glorious green dragon scales, the Huntress hears the sound of approaching aircraft and the thud and cough of the big gun on the ceiling opening up. A few moments later a golden explosion mushrooms over the water to her left.

She turns to the Sister sitting by her and realizes it's the same melt-faced cripple who met her first in the mountains.

"When I heal I am going to kill the King of Yama," she breathes. "You will remain here and destroy his kingdom."

The Sister smiles. "We've already begun, devi," she says.

3.8

THE RED BALL IS HEAVY and harder than a toy should be. The Princess looks at it laying between her feet like a black hole in effigy and looks up at Auron. Expectancy burns like coal fire on his feral face. The Triangulan shuffles, glances at the ball, and then back up at her.

"You want me to throw it?" says the Princess.

Auron points to the far edge of the hall. "That way."

The far corners of the chamber are almost distant enough to be lost in gloom, except for where they're pierced by still pillars of fanning light. Near the ceiling are friezes rendered cryptic and incomplete by their partial illumination. The Princess peers at these. Perhaps the punchline to what surely must be a joke on the Twins' part is up there.

"Throw it," says Amerxis, fidgeting.

"It must be between us," says Auron.

"You already said that," says Amerxis.

"It bears repeating."

They bare their teeth to each other. Strange to see them speaking in turns. Stranger still, somehow, to see them speaking to each other.

She stoops, picks up the ball, and drops it. It bounces with a thunk, half the height of her shin, and no more.

"It won't bounce very far," she says.

"Throw it, please," say the Twins together.

She picks it up again and flings it off into the dark.

The ball hits the ground and spins off, gathering speed, curving to one side as if caught in some immense gravity well only it can feel. The Twins take off after it, mouths open, tongues flapping. Auron tumbles and grabs Amerxis by the ankle. She twists and snaps at his hand, but he clambers over her, dives for the sphere, and grabs it with his teeth. Then he sprints back to the Princess, his sister on his heels.

The ball thuds between the Princess's feet. She looks up at the Twins, and they stare back at her, tense with excitement. She throws it again.

They run and return and repeat. Sometimes the Princess fakes. When they take off in one direction, she throws the ball in another. Sometimes she makes them run in opposite directions and throws in a third. Sometimes she takes the ball and runs herself. They chase with faux intensity, yipping and growling, close enough for her to feel their hot alien breath, never so close that she can feel their teeth.

At some point they discard their suits of man-flesh. The Princess's thunders at the sight of two bristle-furred wolves sprinting along in the dark like nightmares in search of a sleeper. But their eyes are unchanged and their manner of movement also. She may be the first of her kind to play with the Wolves of Triangulum, she thinks. She may be the first to have nothing to fear in beasts such as this.

None of them notice the Night watching them.

She observes from a far dark corner, eyes huge against the dark, sari wrapped over her head like a cowl. An ancient creature as distant from humanity as a pulsar but still capable of comprehending the joy of what she's witnessing. The Wolves' careening progress. The Princess's teasing. She takes in her total fearlessness in the presence of these creatures bred to kill worlds, and their willingness in turn to be their most essential selves in her presence. She remembers her first visit to this system and her first encounter with its strange, sentient apes. She remembers learning how those capable of theft and murder were also capable of nurturing their young with kindness and restraint. She still doesn't understand it—or them—but that's to be expected. After all, they don't understand themselves either.

The ball bounces up to her. Amerxis reaches it first, grabs it, and rushes off without a word. A few moments later, she returns, Auron in tow. They circle the Night with their heads down, whimpering.

"What is it?" says the Night.

They point with their snouts. The Princess is lying on the floor in the distance, a rope of slimy black vomit trailing from her mouth. In an instant the Night is by her side. She crouches and touches the girl's skin. She examines her wrists, her eyes, and the pallor of her lips.

"One of you fetch my mortar and pestle and pouch," she says. "The other, get the Hands."

"Will she live? Was it us?"

"It was not you." The Night tilts the Princess's head. More black gunk floods from her mouth. "I do not know yet if she will live."

The Twins sprint off. The red ball sits, forgotten, where they dropped it.

3.9

THE CALM OF *PRATIKARA*'S BRIDGE suits the Soul of Mangala. The unfussy greys, the tidy lines. The obedient ping of the consoles functioning precisely as they should. Nothing else there but his own thoughts and the information coming in sweet torrents from the sensors to stimulate them. He loses himself in the gargantuan architecture of his own calculations. Probability assessments rise here, peaks needle-sharp, surfaces shiny with invariables. Oceans of fractal calibration stretch in great tendrils down through themselves and everything else. Pulsing dots of ad hoc augmentations sail in murmuration to where they're needed. Orderly, focused, efficient.

For the first time in a long time, he's happy.

Of course, it doesn't last. The doors to the bridge open, and the King of Yama shuffles in.

"What?" says the Soul.

The King walks slowly from empty station to empty station. At each he lingers and peers at the displays as if he comprehended the information on them. He's looking cleaner, thinks the Soul. He looks like he has found a purpose.

The Soul of Mangala doesn't like it one bit.

"What do you want?" says the Soul.

"Our next jump will take us within three jumps of Daitya," says the King.

"So?"

"I want the Blizzard to stop there and offer some aid to the people of the Tripura. They've been attacked."

"We don't have time." The Soul turns to him. "Why do you want to help them? It'll get in the way of you helping your daughter."

"Their cities are in ruins, robot. Their people are starving. I lived amidst them most of my life. It was more home to me than Yama ever was. It was where I met my love. It was where my child was born. Is it so hard to believe that seeing it burn would claw at my heart?"

"We don't have time."

"We do if I say so."

"So don't say so."

"I already have."

"Then fucking unsay it."

The King raises his eyebrows. "The crew will be suspicious. They may think I'm no longer in charge. That will not be to your advantage."

"We. Don't. Have. The. Fucking. Time."

"Do you know the manner of attack levelled against them?"

"What does that—"

"A single great explosion. Like an atomic bomb of old." The King looks at the Soul askance. "Directly before, there was a great battle. Between the Bounteous Ones. And a juggernaut."

"A juggernaut? Who told you that?"

The King gestures at the consoles. "This is still my ship. I'm not beholden to you for all my knowledge. It would be foolish to pass up an opportunity to learn about our quarry."

"I know enough about them."

"I don't. My people don't."

The Soul spins in a slow circle, arms akimbo. Then he halts and looks at the king. "Fuck! Fine! I'll give you a day."

"Three. Three days won't make a difference. You can make up the time. I've done the calculations."

"Fine."

The King doesn't move.

"Fuck, what now?" says the Soul.

"Doesn't it bother to return to the scene of your death?" says the King.

"I know you're saying that because you think it bugs me, but it doesn't. Whoever died in the Mandīram—"

"Whatever."

"Whoever died in the Mandīram wasn't me. You know how I know? Because I'm here. And if I'd been sitting in the Mandīram, I'd know I'd been copied, and I'd die happy knowing I was out here, too, getting on with what I had to do. But you know why, more than anything, it doesn't bother me?"

"Why?"

"Because I don't have time for that shit, king. I don't have time for mulling over your little word puzzles. Even when I have time for it, I ain't got time for it—as they used to say in my day—because there's literally a thousand other things I'd rather be doing. So if you're going to try to get under my skin, try harder. It's metal. It's pretty hard. Or better still, why don't you just fuck off and do something else?"

The king lingers, smirking, for a little longer. Then he offers the tiniest of shrugs and leaves. The Soul tries to lose himself in his systems again, but the topography's changed. His metaphysical processes are dominant. The horizon is dark, the peaks drooping, and the valley softened like congealing amber.

He snaps out of it to the sound of *Pratikara* counting down to its next jump.

"Stupid fucking king," hisses the Soul, and gets to work.

3.10

I

THE NIGHT BRINGS THE LIMP Princess into the humans' bedchamber with the Right Hand trailing her, fretting like a hen. She places the girl on one of the spongy rectangles on the floor. The Wolves take her out of her clothes. She resists and grumbles about protocol and dignity, but of course no one listens. The Right Hand averts his eyes, but worry makes him look again. The undermuscled limbs and the knobbly knees. The peek of her black tongue between her little teeth. Not a girl, he reminds himself. A young woman. The Night takes her mortar from her sari. In it is a black liquid as glossy and reactive as mercury. She dabs small quantities of this at various points on the Princess's skinny body—the crooks of her elbows; the joint of her left jaw; an arc over her pubis. Under its cryptic influence the Princess subsides with eyes half-open, breath pendulum-steady.

The Right Hand covers her with a blanket. "What's wrong with her?"

"She has Soma Sickness." The Night decants the black liquid into a vial she produces from the endlessly bounteous folds of her robe. She hands it to the Right Hand. The denseness of the stuff against his palm. The faint jiggle on its surface, as if it were not really liquid, but living, weirdly viscous dust. "She must have eaten some or else rubbed some in a cut. She will suffer for some time. Apply this when she does and the symptoms will subside. I will make inquiries regarding a cure."

"Inquiries with whom?"

The Night moves her hand in an arc over her head, expansive. "Myself. I do not carry all my memories in this form with me."

II

AFTER THE TRIANGULANS LEAVE, THE Right Hand watches over the Princess. At first, she sleeps a sleep different to death only in that it sustains breath. When she wakes she does so to vomit more black gunk and sweat so hard the Right Hand worries she'll lose all the water in her body and shrivel entirely away. He holds her hand as she whispers about her parents and changes her clothes despite her complaints. He brings her water from the pools to drink and sponges her down with the rags the Twins bring. They also bring a bowl of steaming porridge which the Princess swallows without appetite and gags to keep down. The two Triangulans stand in silence by the door, hand-in-hand. They're worried, too, thinks the Right Hand, which worries him even more. What could this illness be that frightens even the Wolves of Triangulum?

After the third or fourth application of the ointment—it smells different every time he applies it, like camphor one time, like sweet ground sandalwood the other—the Right Hand collects the filthy rags and takes his own filthy self out to the far pool. As he goes, he sees the Left Hand standing in the mid-distance watching him go. He walks to the waters, kneels, and starts to wash. He hears her approach but doesn't turn to look. He feels her halt behind him but doesn't say a word.

"You're cross with me," says the Left Hand.

The Right Hand shrugs. "Did you know she was sick?"

"Aye. I'm sorry. I'm not good with ... illness."

He says nothing and keeps washing. The soothing slosh of the water under his palms. The miraculous waters don't require soap or disinfectant. Just a few scrubs and the cloths begin to shed their burden of grime and ointment. Still, it takes some work. After a few moments the Left Hand squats next to him, picks up a rag, and dips it into the water. The swift flick of her fingers as she folds it. The practiced scrub, swirl, and squeeze of someone who knows how to do the task well. The Right Hand relaxes.

"I don't know what's wrong," he says. "I don't know if we can help her."

"We're on the vimana of Night. Must be something here, right?"

"I hope so. Where have you been, anyway?"

"Speaking with the Night."

"About what?"

"Things," she says. "The past. What happened at the Bhujañgānām Mandīram. I asked her why she didn't just bomb it. Like she did the Tripura."

"What did she say?"

"She said Skōlex had some personal business to attend to with what I called the Mandīram. Those were her exact words. 'Personal business with what you called the Mandīram.'" A brief silence. "I asked her your question, too."

"Which one?"

"About why she came alone with only Skōlex."

"What did she say to that?"

"She said, 'I didn't intend to come with anyone. But Skōlex insisted he join Me.' She also said the Triangulans approve of such missions carried out for the right reason, and her reason wasn't the right one."

"What was her reason?"

"Love." The Left Hand glances at him. "She said she came here for love."

The Right Hand picks up another rag pungent with the Princess's sweat and dips it in the water.

"No better reason to do terrible things, I suppose," he says.

IIII

THE NIGHT SETS THE WOLVES to summon the Hands to the Throne Room. When they arrive at the Throne of Night, they find the sovereign herself sitting cross-legged upon it, playing with what looks like a pair of giant beetles. Bulbous things with grooved black-glass shells that shimmer purple and blue as they zoom about her head. They buzz at her. She buzzes back, an insectoid sound no throat shaped like hers should be able to make. The sounds are alien and incomprehensible, but the contours of the exchange are eerie in their mimicry of language.

"They are healthy, then?" say the Twins.

"Yes," says the Night. "But annoyed."

"What are they, devi?" asks the Right Hand.

"Not what, but who?" says the Night. She lifts her hands, and the creatures flit about, inelegant, peculiar. "Survivors of an empire long ground to dust by its enemies, they tell me. This ship is their only home. I am kind to the hunted."

"You're also kind to the hunter."

The Night smiles. Her teeth are like a crescent moon on the blackness of her face. Her eyes like stars. "I am kind to many things, prabho."

The creatures take off into the dark, rear ends glowing the same bright blue as the ceiling-worms in the human's chamber. The Night watches them go and then looks at the Hands.

"I can recall no cure for Soma Sickness that will not also kill the Princess as she is," she says. "The Seed is working in her. As long as she stays here, it will keep altering her body until she becomes something else."

The Right Hand looks as if she had just punched him in the stomach. "Something else, devi?"

"I told you long ago it was a weapon. But before that, it was medicine." The Night gestures to the remote ceiling. "It heals. It improves. You have both been inhaling it in fragments while you are here, but in quantities so minute it's had no effect on you. The Princess, however, has allowed it into her blood. It will keep working without plan until her systems fail. Think of it as an elegant sort of cancer."

"Cancer?" The Right Hand shakes his head. "No. No. You said that'll happen as long as she stays here. Will it help if we send her away?"

"It may."

"Then that's what we must do."

"My thoughts precisely. But to accomplish this, we must first settle other matters. I cannot have Skōlex simply put to port at one of your worlds, being as they are all inhabited and under my sister's sway. So we must finalize our plans and include the Princess's departure from our presence in this. Tell me. Does my sister have any spacecraft surviving from when we first arrived here? Any of the vimanas of Triangulum?"

The Right Hand glances at the Left.

"None that I know of, devi," she says. "She travels aboard a vimana made especially for her, though I'm told its heart is from Triangulum. The Golden Swarm integrates elements of Triangulan technology. Replicated engines, mostly, for jumping. Nothing else."

"And my son?"

"The Red Fleet is mostly ancient human vimanas. Indra will probably know more about this."

"Most Triangulan vimanas were destroyed expelling You and Skōlex from the system, devi," says the Right Hand. "The Ox constructed the Red Fleet from what was left and human technology."

"Then," says the Night, "the Maruts had the last fully Triangulan vimanas in this system?"

"Yes. It would appear so, devi."

"And this ... wireless system ... they use. The one that is forbidden to humans. Do you know anything of it?"

"No, devi." The Left Hand raises her eyebrows. "You wish to speak to Your sister."

"I do. But it is not so easily done." The Night points over her shoulder at the stars steady upon the universe's black skin. "Even now I see a fleet approaching. But we do not have the technology on this ship to contact them. I would send the Wolves, but I suspect that they will not receive a warm welcome. And so, my Hands, I would that you once again act as my ambassadors. Carry a message to my sister for me. You must tell her, or her agents, that I wish to speak with her."

"Why parley?" say the Twins. "We should engage her. The judgement of Triangulum is passed upon her."

"True, but we have not the means to enforce it."

"Skōlex will vanquish them."

"Skōlex is old and weary. This journey has been too much for him. You know this."

"Then we evade her," say the Twins, "take the Seed to the human world by stealth. Her realm will be weakened, and we can raise the humans in rebellion against her."

"Devi has given me her word that we will not injure Earth or kill innocents," says the Right Hand. "You speak of a long war. Many will die. Too many have already."

The Twins look at him and then back at the Night. "This is true? Then how do you intend to defeat her?"

"I will challenge her to a duel."

The Twins look aghast. "A duel? Between you and your sister?"

"You object?"

"She won't accept. And if she does, she will fight you with trickery and evasion. She has no honor."

The Night's voice comes like a gust of icy wind from the void. "Watch your tongues, children. She is the First Manifestation, a Child of the Thrones Beyond. Honor, as you frame it, has no bearing on her quality. The doors of Triangulum remain open to her. It is her right to refuse herself entry, but we have no right not to ask."

"This is folly. Our labors will be for naught." The Twins glare at the Right Hand. "This is your doing."

"You'll only fail if Skōlex is compromised or if devi is injured," says the Right Hand. "So instead, I'll go parley with the Night's agents. If I die, devi will be free of her promise to me and may attack Pṛthvī."

"No," says the Night. "That is not how such promises work. We're bound by our vows now. Not just you to me or me to you. But both of us to the word of what has been said. If I am injured or killed, it will be up to you to finish what I have started, prabho. You will see this mission through to the end and in such a way that Pṛthvī is not harmed."

"But, devi." The Right Hand looks very small. "I'm just a man. Not ... not even an entire man. How can I possibly accomplish this?"

"Not an entire man? You are entire, prabho. You are more than entire because you are not alone. Skōlex will be your agent. The Twins here will serve you as they serve me."

The Twins snarl in unison. "We will not."

"Even if it is at my bidding?" The Night smiles. The strange illumination of her face. The mischief glittering in her gaze. "Is this mutiny, then?"

"No."

"Then you will follow my commands."

The Twins look askance at the Right Hand and say nothing.

"Still, devi." The Right Hand wraps his robe around himself, tight. How much simpler it was to be washing the rags by the pool. How much easier to inventory scrolls or parley with the Charioteer or sneak from ship to monstrous ship at the frigid outskirts of the Dawn's sprawling empire. "Still, I'd find it very hard."

"That is the way of such things. The promises we make to others put us in difficult places. The promises others make to us can do the same. This is what comes of trying to bind the universe to one path when you yourself have so many." The Night rises. "But this is talk of 'what if's. For now, let us talk of 'must be's. You, my Left Hand, will once more be my ambassador. We will intercept the fleet that approaches us at the asteroid field that lies between the outer worlds and the inner and initiate parley. You will negotiate with the agents of Dawn for me and arrange a meeting with my sister."

The Left Hand lowers herself onto all fours and touches her forehead to the floor.

"Yes, devi," she says.

"Excellent." The Night looks off into the dark. "My friends are calling to me, and we have much to discuss. I will see you again when the time is right."

A blink and she's gone. Another and the Wolves have stalked away, casting one last baleful look at the Right Hand. Alone before the mute glory of the starfield, the Right Hand glances at the Left and feels the weight of his decisions on his chest like a colossal cosmic boot.

He starts to walk away.

"Where're you going?" calls the Left Hand.

"I haven't finished cleaning yet," he calls back. "I haven't finished anything."

3.11

THE KING OF YAMA EMERGES from his tent into the midst of the Yaman camp. Overhead, an armada of necrotic-looking clouds. No sign whatsoever of the sun, of Shani, or the universe beyond. About him is the bustle and clatter of his troops as they set about the business of salvation. Teams grimy from the dirty sleet are ferrying barrows of clothes, food, and medicine from a row of drop ships squatting like pregnant birds off to the left. A cluster of men are erecting a spindly metal apparatus in the mid-distance. A vehicle skids by on mud-slick tires with a consignment of slack-jawed children jammed like cannisters in the back. They don't know who the King is, but still they stare.

He proceeds down the rubberized carpet of the main thoroughfare to where the camp's chain link walls are pierced by a tower-flanked gate. The guards on duty salute. A further four fall in behind him at a discreet distance with their eyes invisible behind their bulging visors. There is a wide strip of blasted purplish soil and obdurate shrub beyond. A no-man's-land between the Yaman camp and the fringes of the tent city that begins a quarter of a mile or so away. Even at this distance he can see churning within it the multitudes who came streaming out of the burning Tripura to beg, steal, and starve in the wilderness. The clusters of people gathered in tatters around open fires. The pants-less children running around with their bellies nude and their feet bare to the frigid soil. Off to the right is an open expanse at the base of a denuded hill where groups of men and women are digging square holes in the ground. The king makes for where the locations of others are plotted in grids, sweating despite the cold.

To the left, the blasted wreckage of the Tripura juts against the sky like the edge of a splintered bone.

One of the diggers runs up to the king and prostates himself. "Get up," hisses the King. "Do you want everyone to know who I am?"

The man recovers himself. Not a Yaman, but one of the Tripura's detritus. Leather-faced and skinny beneath a shirt two sizes too big for him, but other than that, no different to the sort of folk who used to squat by the roadside outside the King's old home. A cake-seller, perhaps. An ear-cleaner. It is the ones who never had much who cope best with losing everything. He points the king to where a rack of freshly fabricated tools glint in the sullen light.

The King waves him off, collects a hoe, and heads to one of the white crosses. He starts to dig. The reptile kiss of the sleet on his neck. The cool sweat like an ice cube melting atop his head. It's tough going at first, but soon his muscles warm to it. His joints loosen also. Not so unlike working his garden on Yama. Without warning, he aches with nostalgia, but a gust of char-scented wind dispels any hope he may have had of forgetting his circumstances entirely.

Presently, a little Āēoi comes scurrying up with a wheelbarrow and starts to scoop soil into it.

"You're late," says the King.

"My apologies, raja." A female, then. It's always hard to tell with her furry kind. "The admiral wanted to be certain I was appropriate."

"I take it you are."

"That's what she said."

They work in silence. The woman fills the barrow with the King's cast-offs and races away with it. When she returns the sleet's paused.

The King swings the hoe down, feeling the satisfying settle of its blade into the fibrous soil.

"What is your name?"

"I am Sheelu."

"How did you survive the blast?"

"Luck." The little woman blinks. "But I was not lucky enough to survive seeing the aftermath."

"I lived in the Tripura a long time. I visited the Mandīram on occasion."

"I know more than that, raja. I know you spoke with my friend, Indra. I know your daughter was a friend of his."

The King glances at her. Her barrow is full. "Don't dawdle. We mustn't be seen to be speaking."

She rushes off again. By the time she's returned, the King's taken to working on the next hole. "You must promise me you'll rescue him, too," she says.

"Who?"

"Indra. He was taken with your daughter."

The King heaves an armful of soil onto the ground. "You know what I've done. What makes you think I'd keep a promise made to a priest?"

"I'm no longer a priest. The Temple is gone. The Charioteer is dead." Sheelu grimaces. Her teeth like calcium blades. Her lips black and thin and glistening. "Besides. The kind of king who does what you're doing now is a king whose word I can trust."

"I'm only doing it so I can converse with you undetected."

"There are a thousand other ways you could have done that. You chose this." The woman peers at him. "You have your reasons, I don't doubt."

The King looks at his muddy hands. Reasons for this. Reasons for everything. It's easy to find reasons. It's consequences that are the problem. "Hurry along."

Once more Sheelu runs off with the soil. The King watches her tip it into the great pile by a small fire pit. A collection of priests are blessing the soil with fire and embers from vats of burning sandalwood. Their corpulence obscene against the ruin. Their fervor undiminished by the failure of their false god to protect them. None have considered for a second that the calamity was in some way her fault.

His guards are watching them, too, but soon they return the King's gaze, alert. He shakes his head and moves on to the next hole.

"Can you do it?" he asks Sheelu when she returns.

"Yes."

"Are you certain?"

"I was taught to handle the Soul before even Indra was. I've been doing it since I was young."

"I will owe you a debt."

"I've already told you how you can repay it."

"By saving Indra?" The king huffs. "He must have been dear to you."

"He was a good person. I haven't met many of those."

He glances at where her pouch would be. Her stomach is strangely flat against her strangely clean robes. He still has many questions, but he's asked the most important ones; and now he's out of time.

"I give you my word, but you must do what you promised."

Sheelu grins. "Raja, I may no longer be a priestess, but my word is still my bond. I will take control of your fleet back for you."

"Are you sure you don't want to come with us? To leave this wasteland?"

"No." The little woman hauls her final consignment of soil into her barrow and prepares to go. "There are still too many of these to dig."

She runs off. The King looks off to the west. A gloomy glow marks where the sun has sunk to the horizon. Already refugees are marching in procession to where the holes are waiting for all that remains of their loved ones. A few early comers are lowering little packages into them. Bracelets. Teeth. Images.

The King watches them mourn and remembers them as they once were. The magnificent populace of a magnificent city. Their habitat one of bolts of cloth piled meters high, great vats of frying lentil cakes, and filth in alleyways. All that replaced now by what?

By this undifferentiated mass of the wretched. Indistinguishable in their dirtiness and desperation and despair. No difference between the landlord putting his daughter's fingertip into the ground and the arthritic scavenger lowering a sack of something jangling and sharp-edged into another beside him. And why shouldn't that be the case? When a person loses everything, why shouldn't they lose themselves as well?

The King lifts his hoe and begins to dig another grave.

3.12

THE LEFT HAND SITS WITH her feet sunk in the water in the Antechamber of Night. A woman is watching her from the glossy depths. Some doppelganger not quite perfect in its mimicry of her but still eerily close. The knowing arch of her eyebrows. The great silver loop of her nose ring framing her missing eye. Aloof and poised in a way that the Left Hand herself has never felt. Yet the grooves by her mouth are familiar and so, too, are the unwelcome memories lurking in her mirrored gaze. Perhaps this is what it feels like to grow old. To not recognize yourself sometimes. To never quite reconcile the thing that you have become and the thing that you are.

The Right Hand trundles past her, a bundle of rags in his arms. The careful step of a person not quite reconciled to their own size. The pillowy bulge of his eunuch bulk. How nice it would be to lay her head upon it. How sweet to fall asleep with the scent of it in her nose, as she did when they were young.

"What're you doing?" he asks.

"Nothing. Waiting till we leave." The Left Hand kicks. Her reflection shatters like a frightened shoal. "How is she?"

"As good as she's been in a while." He kneels at the far pool and starts to wash. "Are those from the Night?"

"What?"

"Your clothes. Your jewelry."

"Oh." The Left Hand stands, bangles jangling, and twirls. Her robe and skirts flare about her, a pleated cone of light-eating black cascading from a pale strip of naked belly. "They're for the parley."

"You look very important."

"I am important."

The Right Hand chuckles and resumes washing. Faster now in the fold and scrub of the process. He's learned, thinks the Left Hand. He's learned from me.

"Indra."

"Kadrū."

"How long do you think we've been here?"

"On Skōlex?" The Right Hand shrugs. "A few months?"

"Can't be. Look how much older we are. And the Princess can't be that far from having her blood."

"She already has."

"She told you?"

"No. I noticed."

The Left Hand glances at the rags. "Should I speak to her?"

"I suspect she'll know more about its workings than you."

"She'd think she does. Fine. Look, I think we've been here for years."

"Years?"

"Aye. Think about it—we've travelled from Himenduḥ all the way here. We're closer to Mangala's orbit now than any of the outer worlds. Without jumping. That should take years."

"It doesn't feel like years."

The Left Hand looks at the water. The mimic is back, staring, shameless. "It feels like I've known you for years. I feel like as long as I've been me, I've known you."

"We have known each other for years."

"No, I mean, on here. I think we've spent more time together here than we did at the slaver's. In't that mad? In't it mad that we met at all? The first time, the last time? You come all the way from Pṛthvī. Me, sold. Then you go to the Dnyānasya Mandīram, and I go to the Bhujañgānām Mandīram. Then we end up on Skōlex of the Night? Together? And now—what? We're her ambassadors and advisors?" She giggles. "I reckon it means something. I reckon it all has to mean something."

The Right Hand folds the last rag, lays it out to dry, and sits back. Why doesn't he look at his reflection, wonders the Left Hand. How can he take so easily for granted that he's always being watched by himself?

"It doesn't have to," he says. "Things happen all the time that are massively unlikely. Did you know that Pṛthvī's moon is exactly the right size and exactly the right distance, that when it gets between Pṛthvī and Surya, it covers the sun perfectly? It's like ... a black eye with golden lashes.

"I saw it once. The dawn birds started singing right in the middle of the day. Night at noon, Vishwadevi called it. What're the odds of that? It's gorgeous, but it doesn't mean anything. It's just ... the way the system is. I think what we call reasons are more often just stories. We make them up afterwards because we can't cope with the idea that we meet who we meet, we're born where we're born, we go where we go, not because it means anything, but because that's just how things are."

"But din't that mean we got not choice in anything? Any nothing means anything?" The Left Hand pouts. "No, no, I don't like that."

"No, of course people have choice. But there's a lot we don't have a choice over either. We just like to think that someone had a choice, or something. We like to think that things only have a meaning because of a choice and that something a lot like us made that choice. Well, like us enough that we can understand its decision.

"But I think that's actually kind of sad. We're very small things that treasure choices, but our choices are also very small things. Isn't it more amazing that, in all the way things could be, that's the way things just turned out? That of all the ways our lives could have turned out, they turned out like this, here, now? Why does it have to make any more sense than that?"

She smiles. "You're always so full of thoughts. I reckon you keep some of them in that giant belly of yours."

He smiles back and says nothing. They sit in luscious silence. Then the Left Hand drops her veil over her face and wraps her robe so no part of her is exposed.

"I'd better go," she says. "They're here."

"Who?"

"The Red Fleet. They just jumped in."

"How do you know?"

The Left Hand shrugs. "I can feel her. She's telling me."

They hesitate, then step into each other and hold each other tight. The venom tang of her body scent and the faint musk of his. The quiver and rush of their substance as close to the other's as it will ever get.

They part and consider saying the obvious. But that would sound too much like a farewell, so they say something else.

"I'll see you when you come back," says the Right Hand.

"Right."

The Left Hand twirls again. She knows he will always remember her like that. She knows she will always remember him watching her.

They walk away in different directions. The children who met at a slaver's. The Gelding and the Snakegirl. The propagating multitudes of their future selves waiting to be summoned into existence. All these and, of course, their copies in the pools. Themselves as they are. Themselves as they've become. Reflected, precisely.

3.13

THE TEMPLE OF DAWN SITS cuckoo-fat amidst the shriveled remnants of an ancient town. The great bulb of its dome rising like a golden fruit over the ruins. The vivid skin of its stucco walls all the brighter for being hemmed by grey wreckage. Populating the alcoves on its outer walls are statues of the Dawn. At each of these are devotees offering a species of pooja suitable to the aspect they evoke. Some hurl coconuts at a rock and inspect the scattered shards. Some tip baskets of raw wheat into fire-pits. At one, a man with cataracts holds the dead body of a small animal overhead and squints against the patter of its blood in his face.

Vishwadevi walks past all these. Beside her, Śyena is carrying their village's post-harvest pooja atop his head. In front of her, the elders are processing with a golden icon of the Dawn held aloft and bells hung from their necks like cattle to an abattoir.

"Hard to imagine we built all this," she says.

"We didn't build it," says Śyena. "The ancients did."

"The ancients were us."

"We're not."

The big man adjusts the tray on his head. A pawpaw teeters. "We're saved."

They proceed into the dark of the temple. Here, all is guttering fire, sweet scents, and prayer. There are more devotees, smashing and thrashing and desperate. The villagers continue through golden gates to the inner sanctum where two fat priests cast a lazy eye over their offerings, then gesture to three others—also fat but younger—to take it all. They heave the great tray off Śyena's head. The elders sink, groaning, to all fours, and the priests dribble saffron-water on the back of their heads. In the distance someone wails, as if the Dawn had reached out across space and time and gouged out their eyes.

"So this is what salvation looks like?" whispers Vishwadevi.

Śyena grabs her hand and squeezes it hard. She knows what it means. She says no more.

The priests open the door to the inner sanctum. Beyond is a blazing hall, gold underfoot, gold overhead. Sitting in rows by the walls are lines of priests—the blind ones, the stupid ones, the ones incapable of doing anything else—playing flutes, bamboo clackers, and drums. At the far end behind a great fire pit is a statue of Dawn almost too bright to look at. Still Vishwadevi sees. The staring eyes and the protruding tongue. The sixty-four arms holding heads and chakras and moons. Everyone in the vicinity, a hundred people, more, gasp at the sight of it and spread themselves out on the floor. Vishwadevi does, too. The floor tiles are slimy on her face and smell of mud.

The elders of the village crawl into the sanctum, and the door closes.

Vishwadevi heads out of the hall back into the sunlight. Though she can't see him, she knows he's following. He's wringing those hands of his, big enough to choke an ox, gentler than silk in a stream. As they leave the hall, she sneaks an orange off one of the pooja trays and slips it into her robes.

"You're angry about Ludu," Śyena whispers.

She walks across the courtyard where some devotees are sitting lotus-wise in the blazing sun with their lower thighs already scorched and the skin peeling from their heads. In the outskirts of the temple, acolytes are brushing the grey dust that forever comes off the ruins. They will do so from dawn till dusk, then again the next day and the next, and it won't make the slightest bit of difference.

"I'm angry about a lot of things." Vishwadevi peers up at the ruins. "Not just Ludu."

"Why? He'll be fine. He's with her now." Śyena points at the high glittering arch of the Iron Crown bisecting the sky like a shining rib.

"We don't know that, though. We don't. We only know that we'll never see him again."

"He's with her, Vishwadevi. What better outcome could there be for him?"

Vishwadevi halts at the edge of the ruins. "We don't know that, Śyena. We don't know that."

"You're just worried about Indra."

"Of course, I'm bloody worried about Indra."

"Auntie and Uncle are clever. They'll be fine." Śyena blinks. "You should put that orange back."

"Why?"

"It's not yours. It's given to her."

"It's ours. We grew it. We feed the whole system. If we're so important, why're we stuck here?"

The big man looks at her askance. "What've you been reading?"

"Nothing." Vishwadevi feels the bulge of the orange in her bodice. The waxy roughness of the skin. The dense bulk of it like a breast. "I've been thinking. You should try it some time."

"Don't be mean."

She looks at him. The sunlight like a golden tongue on his big, kind face. The flat gaze of a good person baffled. She sighs and sinks into his arms.

One of the acolytes glances at them and looks away.

"I've not been reading," she whispers. "I've just been thinking about something auntie told me before we left. She said, what if none of it's true? What if our ancestors weren't evil? What if the Dawn didn't save us all? What if it's all lies?"

"That's crazy talk."

Vishwadevi nods. "That's what I said to her. Then she said, all right, think about this. What are we doing? What do we do with our lives? We work from morning till night to grow food that our ancestors could grow with five, six people. You've seen the old fields. You've seen how huge they are. What are we doing, Śyena? Why do we live like this?" She looks up at the ruins. Thunderous. Soaring. "Even the rubbish left over from our ancestors' dreams is more magnificent than our most beautiful work. Why do we live like this when we could live like that?"

"Maybe it wasn't so great. If it was so great, why didn't it last forever?"

"Shouldn't we at least have a choice in that? Look at all the things we see, Śyena. Look at how much it could tell us if only we're allowed to look. Why is so much kept hidden from us?"

She sighs.

"The worst thing is, I know I'm not the only one to think this. There must have been a thousand others—a million—all across the world. All people who wanted to know how we came to be the way we are. Aunty said we're a people denied our own stories, and I didn't understand what she said at the time. Now I do. We'll never know where Ludu's story leads him. We'll never know where the stories of anyone else whose left the village will take them. And we'll live and die, and our stories will disappear, too. Our descendants won't even know who we were, except that we lived and died in the same place doing the same thing as them. Like frogs in a pond. Just ... spawning and singing and getting snatched away. Isn't there more to us than that? Isn't there more to us?"

Śyena looks at her. So close to understanding, she can tell, but so afraid of doing so. She takes his hand in hers and presses it to her cheek.

"It's all right," she says. "I'll be quiet."

"Your family thinks too much."

"Yes, yes. Fine."

"You should put the orange back."

Vishwadevi takes the fruit from her bodice and examines it. The grey-brown splotches on its skin. The bitter ferment of its half-decayed flesh. "It's rotten," she says.

Śyena squeezes her hand. She sighs and slips it back into her bodice. They head back towards the Temple.

3.14

THE LEFT HAND RACES INTO the gulf of stars ensconced in a Triangulan bubble. The quiet of its sanctum-like confines. The ozone tang of its inexplicable air. It will never not be strange, drifting in that all-dark with naught but a skin-thin membrane for protection. Skōlex dwindles behind her. Soon she's alone amidst the stars. Despite having all the space in the universe, she finds her fears clinging to her all the tighter.

She sits lotus-wise on the floor of the bubble and adjusts her clothes. Her bodice is too tight and her skirt bites her waist and that makes no sense. She's never eaten more than a small bowl of the Night's bland but preternaturally satisfying porridge a day. She distracts herself by looking at the small box that the Night handed her before she embarked. The cool weight of it on her shins. The gentle crack of the token within. No need to open it to see what's inside, but still she's tempted.

Then she sees the Red Fleet.

It first appears as a cluster of overbright stars reddish and growing against a glittering backdrop. Presently, she can discern the contours of the spaceships. The mountainous bulk of their terraced bodies. The glitter and glint of armor and ornament so dense with meaning it seems to have its own gravity. Her conveyance drifts—no, races—past them towards an old vimana in their midst. Closer now, she sees the testudinal paneling on its hull and its venerable turtle eyes squinting at her. Will it see her as prey and lunge for the kill? That would be the end of her story. The tale of a thing that was sold, bought, beaten, loved, and rejected. A thing that was always the part of someone else's story and never centerpiece of its own.

She stands to adjust her robes and meets the vimana's gaze. It turns its head to watch her drift past, placid, and lets her pass.

The bubble drifts in through an airlock that helixes shut behind her. A moment's wait and the far door opens into a small black-paneled room. There are crimson motifs of hammers upon the wall. The woven mat floor is soft beneath the velvet soles of her shoes. Up ahead is a woman standing with her arms crossed. Five guards are arrayed splendidly behind her and not one of them looks welcoming. They don't say a word.

The Left Hand breathes deep, lifts the box, and steps into the room. The clamping cold. The unwelcoming silence. She bows at the waist, not too deep. "This one is the Left Hand of the Night sent to parley with her son, the Ox."

The woman approaches. Why is she breathing so hard? "Give me the box," she says. "I assume her parley is in there?"

"I am to hand the box to the Ox."

"I'm in charge here."

They lock eyes for a few moments. The bodice is so tight, the Left Hand can barely breathe. The woman reaches out, but she steps back. She is small, but she is also the ambassador of Night. Even a pebble may defy a storm.

"No," she says. "I am charged with negotiating only with the Ox of Mangala." A pause. "I do not know who you are. You have not introduced yourself to me."

"Introduced?" The Vicegerent sneers. "I've no reason to introduce myself to you, slave. Give me the damn box or I'll take it from you."

Time passes like oozing lava. The Left Hand drops her veil and slowly pulls the cuffs of her arms up until her toxic skin is nude and bright in the roomlight. "I am the Left Hand of Night. You are welcome to try to take the box from me, but you will not find touching me to your liking."

The Vicegerent steps forward. The Left Hand braces. Perhaps this is where her story will end. If so, then she'll make sure this woman will remember her for far longer than she'd like.

The Vicegerent sniffs the air.

"You're one of the Huntress's creatures." She grimaces. "You're poisonous."

"I am the Left Hand of Night. You are in the way of this one's rendezvous with the Ox of Mangala. Stand aside. Or better yet, fetch him for me."

"Fetch him? You have our positions backwards."

"Then we are at an impasse, for I do not know where he is."

A brief silence. Then, a new voice: "It would appear so, wouldn't it?"

Someone steps through the line of guards. A masked figure with a great weapon slung across his shoulder. A hammer. No, a great golden club. No, a nail, mercury-bright in places and rusty in others. He steps deftly past the Vicegerent, lowers the object to the ground, and presses his palms together. "The Ox of Mangala greets the Ambassador of Night."

The Left Hand bows and steps forward again. "This one is the Left Hand of Night and has been charged with—"

"Yes, yes. I heard. Has the Huntress changed sides, then? Is she providing my mother with the aid of her little arsonists?"

"No, prabho."

"Then how did you come to be in my mother's service?"

"By luck, prabho. And by the Night's infinite kindness."

The Vicegerent snorts, but the Ox nods. As if it was the answer he expected. As if it made all the sense in the world. "You'll have to tell me about it some time. Now ... the box. I take it that's from my mother?"

The Left Hand holds it out to him. He takes and hands it to the Vicegerent without looking at her. Some mischief in his half-masked eyes intended only for the Left Hand. The Vicegerent opens the box and reaches for the icy flower within. She yanks her hand back with a hiss. The Ox reaches over with a chuckle, cracks it in his fist, and extracts a black reed the length of his finger from within.

The Vicegerent takes it and stalks off, grumbling.

"I would offer you refreshments, ambassador," says the Ox, "but the commander did not believe we owed a welcome to an envoy from our enemy."

"The Night does not wish to be enemies."

"Is that so? Is that what the parley says?"

"Should you not be the one to read it, prabho? It is, this one believes, addressed to you, as commander of the Dawn's Red Fleet."

"I'm not commander. She is."

"Is that so? If I may, prabho, how did that come to be?"

She cannot see it behind his mask, but she knows the Ox is smiling. "By the Dawn's infinite kindness." A pause. Then, quietly: "Tell me, ambassador. How is she? How is my mother?"

The Left Hand inspects the Ox's mask. The crinkled expanses of wrecked skin about his neck and jawline. The gaze that, for an instant, seems to be hiding nothing. On impulse, she gambles on the truth.

"She travelled this far to see the ones she loves, prabho," she says. "She hopes this parley will ensure her that opportunity."

"I see. I see." Another quick silence. "There are many in the Nine Worlds who desire to see her, too."

A few moments later, the Vicegerent comes striding back with the box and hands it to the Ox. The Ox takes it and hands it to the Left Hand. Still heavy in her hands but glowing now with some furious light within. The warmth of it on her skin. The hiss and spit of it—like a seething mass of snakes.

The Ox bows.

"A pleasure to have met you, ambassador. I hope our two sides can avoid violence."

The journey back feels swifter than the journey to. No fears to keep the Left Hand company now, but questions instead. From whence the certainty that some message was hidden in the Ox's words? Who would believe that the Lord of Mangala would speak so kindly to her? Who would believe that she would, in fact, think him rather likeable?

She adjusts her bodice. It isn't so tight after all.

3.15

THE YAMAN ENGINEER IS A thick-necked, determined woman who fights and dies hard. The Huntress snaps forward and whips the ligature around the woman's neck before she can scream. She yanks her, spider-swift and relentless, up to the crawlway to where the sound of her prey's feet stamping against the metal drowns in the massive grunt of the spindrives.

Slowly, the woman subsides to stillness.

When she's unconscious, the Huntress stretches her limp body out on the floor and strips her. Her clothes are loose at the hip and tight about the shoulders, but at a distance no one will be able to tell that they aren't the Huntress's. The woman groans and starts to come to, but the Triangulan clamps a forearm against her throat again. After a brief while squirming, the woman goes still again. She takes a knife and slips it into her temple and that's the end of that.

The Huntress stands to leave but turns back to the body. Such a long time without killing anyone. Now in a few months she's killed how many—twenty? thirty?—and remembered all over again the thrill of it. She has heard hunters say they have respect for their quarries, but she's never understood that.

How can you kill a thing you have respect for? You kill a thing you think you're better than, and you can never think your prey better than yourself. You admire their ability to evade and survive, but in the end your ultimate goal is to find a thing and prove to it and the universe that you are better than it.

All the dead are wretched. All the dead are pungent and inelegant and repulsive. What does it matter what this woman once was? Now, by the Huntress's hand, she's just meat.

She looks up at the distant inferno, the ruin sprawling, at its feet and the great complex of the Yaman's mission pitched in neat rows nearby. How noble of the King to show his old home some kindness. Fortunate for the refugees. Fortunate for her. But not for him.

She licks her lips and sneaks off.

3.16

THE NIGHT WALKS THROUGH THE door in the chamber of the Soma Seed into grey-brown wasteland tufted with lonesome clusters of shrub. The whole realm is forlorn and bare, as if some god had commenced creation and then forgotten or died and left it to subside in eternal stillbirth.

She sets off down a small path that winds along the valley floor. A stream once flowed here, she remembers, long ago, but like most other things in this world, it is dead. She wonders if her sister noticed this. She wonders if her sister remembers when it flowed.

She keeps on with the archaic pebbles grumbling underfoot to where the ground dips again onto a broad expanse of smooth black flagstones. Up ahead is a great tower made of the same black rock. Near the apex of this are two circular apertures, each rimmed with a faint neon glow—one red, the other blue.

At the foot is a shining figure. A hot sliver in the gloom. A thorn of incandescence embedded in the night.

She cups her hands over her mouth and calls to her. "Why, hello, O Multiply-Shining One."

The Night descends with her footsteps as quiet as settling mist. The stone is already so cold underfoot it scarcely notes the passage of her icy soles. She feels her sister's familiar warmth. It's precisely as she remembers—fierce, brilliant, seething. "Greetings, O All-Subduing Splendor," she says.

The Dawn eyes her up and down with her hands clasped beneath her breasts like a stablemaster eyeing a freshly purchased horse. The imperious arch of her eyebrows. The beauty of her faultless face. Then she sits, back against the black stone of the tower. The Night sits also, cross-legged, stiff-backed, a mandala of ice sketches in delicate filigree about her.

"So," says the Dawn. "You've started doing Nirṛti's job for her, have you?"

"Not Nirṛti's. She has departed for distant places. I am not one for slow deaths." A pause. "I did not think you were either."

"Then whose work do you call this?"

"My own. You forget. I am what is left when you have sputtered and failed."

The Dawn narrows her eyes. "Is that what Mother told you?"

"She had no need to."

"What did she say?"

"Not to come. To let you see through your foolishness to its completion. To let the consequences of your arrogance teach you a lesson."

"Ah, good old Mother. How is she?"

"Infinite."

"And yet she didn't give you infinite resources. Just Skōlex. Moldy, old Skōlex. How is my silly boy?"

"Digesting Bheki's tail and a few Maruts. He assures me that they are delicious."

The Dawn shrugs. "Two small victories. They won't be repeated."

"If you accept my proposal, there'll be no need to."

"Your proposal." The Dawn looks out over the dead valley. Her light shattering on the fractured stone. "I won't be accepting your proposal. Why should I? I'm on the cusp of victory."

"You're not on the cusp of victory. Skōlex can outjump your fleet and race to Pṛthvī."

"Yes, I read your letter. Your Left Hand is adorable, by the way. A little Snakegirl running around like she's one of us." The Dawn picks at her nails. The incandescent bangles on her forearms jangle. The glint and spark of whatever plasmic detritus she's flicking out glows like little comets in the flat dead gloom. "Come now, big sister. You may get past the Red Fleet—in fact, you probably will—but you can't get past my fleet. And even if you do, how does Skōlex intend to get past the Iron Crown? You built it. You know how hard that'll be. What do you intend to do? Fly through it? No chance. No chance." She grins. "So, why are we here? Is it because you missed me?"

The Night's mouth tightens. "I am here to offer you the courtesy due any member of our family."

The Dawn tosses her head back and laughs. A noise like sparkles. How wondrous to hear it again. "Liar."

"If there is a liar here, it is you."

"How?"

"You've told these creatures that there's a division between light and dark. That we're opposites and equals. But there is no such division. There is only the dark and those things that survive within it. You've known this since the beginning."

"I'm what came first."

"And I am what will come last. Beginnings need ends, and I'm the end. These things were settled long ago."

"Beginnings are beginnings. Endings are just a trick of time."

The Night sighs. "Please, Little Sister. This squabble does not become you. I still do not understand why you chose to drive me out. Did you think I would drown like Bhujyu? Had you forgotten that I need not swim because I am the river? Perhaps you intended to hurt me, but you did not.

"I was more ... nonplussed. And what do you think will happen here? Do you think you will rule these creatures forever and neglect your responsibilities to the Thrones Beyond?

"You ask me why I have only one juggernaut. I need only one juggernaut. If you turn me back this time, I will return. Over and over and over—until I've snuffed out everything you've done here, until the very memory of your rule and your name is less than the last faint glimmer of a long-dead star." The Night pauses. "Besides, Prabho Indra has rallied to me."

Again, that appraising look. Again, the regal blankness of her face. "You don't have Prabho Indra," she says. "I'd know if He was here."

"It's He who convinced me to see you. It's He who convinced me to pursue a peaceful resolution."

"Indra? Peaceful?" The Dawn laughs. "Now I know you're joking. Spare us both some trouble, big sister, and surrender now. I'll let you return home. Don't bother coming back. Just be a little patient. I'll return when I'm done."

The Night sighs. "You won't fight me, then?"

"No way."

"You choose war over a duel. You choose the death of multitudes over a drop of your own blood."

"I choose war." The Dawn smiles. "A war of sisters. A war of mothers and sons."

The barb is swift and sinks deep. The Night rises with it still lodged in her chest and bows. The Dawn does the same. A light blazes between them, a flame ancient and long-unkindled but reigniting now with the blaze and beauty of a nova. In distant reaches, creatures beyond touch or conceptualization turn their vast attentions to this remote corner of the universe and see what's about to happen. Though beyond comprehension, they're not beyond feeling, and what they feel is sorrow.

The light fades. The sisters part and walk towards distant doors in opposite directions. Overhead, the last star flickers and dies.

3.11

THE OX HAS NEVER ONCE entered the Dawn's vimana in anything but his true form. Ascending the ramp into its glowering interior, he remembers why. First come the heavily regulated coldboxes wherein the Shining One's human slaves swelter and serve without expression or a single unnecessary sound. Then come a series of airlocks of increasing size and temperature. Beyond these is the towering partition between the rest of the ship and the Dawn's chamber. A huge metallic wall emblazoned with glowing friezes encasing a doorway almost too bright to look at, but too beautiful not to.

Beyond these is the great cathedral space that the Dawn shares with sprawled engines pumping, pounding, and percussing about her and her swarming attendants. In the spherical chamber at the very rear is her throne, planted like a burning tree stump atop a hill made either of hot gold or plasma or something equally beyond the ken of mere flesh to endure.

The Ox has seen it all before, but he knows the Vicegerent hasn't and can't help reminding her of this. Divested of his wrecked man flesh, he swells to three, four, five times her size, brighter by magnitudes and swifter. Let her remember who he is and what he can do. Let her recall that his kindness and deference of late has come from choice and not necessity.

As he races down the long nave of the throne room, engineers pause their scuttling to watch him pass. Deep in the workings of their dull consciousnesses they recall who he is and that he was kind to them and so are as pleased to see him as cows beholding a fresh pasture. One, distracted, gets sucked, trilling and scrambling into a mechanism. Moments later, it's spat out in pieces, only to re-congeal, shake itself off, and return to its esoteric work.

The Dawn is pacing about her throne. The cold of her meeting with his mother still upon her. The shimmering waves of her disquiet in the half-burned air. If his form had a sense of smell, he wonders, would she smell like fear? Like anger? Or would she just smell like what she is—an eternal blaze, fire unslaked, churning and roiling and consuming with all the beauty and horror that she brings?

She turns to him and scowls. "Where's the woman?"

"Behind me, rajini."

A clank and rumble in the distance. The Vicegerent comes trotting up behind the Ox, tries to kneel, but remembers that her form has no legs. "Rajini, I—"

"Shut the fuck up." The Dawn flares, too bright to look at, too hot to resist. "I saw her. I told her there'll be no duel."

"So—"

"Bring me her damn head."

The Ox knows her well enough to know she won't say anything else. Though the Vicegerent lingers, he retreats. Akupāra is suspended sniffing and snorting in the vacuum a little way offboard. The Ox dons his man-flesh again and floats across the sweet cool vacuum into the open airlock on its flanks. After a short while the Vicegerent joins him, looking victorious.

"War," she says, grinning.

"Jolly good," says the Ox. "I suggest you get to planning, then."

If she notices the disdain in his words she doesn't show it. She marches off instead, leaving him there to watch the glow of the Dawn's vimana diminish as it recedes. First to a sharp glimmer, then to a faint one, then to nothing at all. Soon enough, there's no sign of the fire and the fury. There's only the universal night—and the infinite things it hides.

3.18

THE PRINCESS DOESN'T SO MUCH wake as slip from a dream much like reality to a reality much like a dream. Her blood feels like lead, her bones like jelly. All this in turn is bound in some cold, nerveless mass she supposes must be her flesh. It takes a long time for the slow empire of her mind to extend its control over these rebellious provinces. While it does, she watches strange waves of light strobing across the herd of glow-worms on the ceiling. For a long time she's convinced she's on the cusp of seeing some pattern, but she never does. After a while she notices the Right Hand next to her. His presence, like gravity, feels like part of the right order of the world.

He picks up the bowl by his knee and holds it, without a word, up to her mouth.

"No," she whispers. "I'll do it."

He grins when she speaks. So evidently delighted that the Princess can't help but smile, too. She takes the bowl. Though her hands are shaking, she manages to tip the rich syrup within into her mouth without spillage. If stars were fruit, she thinks, this is what their milk would taste like. The blood surges in her.

Overhead, the strobing slows, as if distracted by her efforts. They accelerate again when the Princess settles upright with her back to the wall and her legs stretched out in front of her.

"They're animals," she says.

The Right Hand looks up. "Hunters," he says.

"Hunters?"

"That's what the Night told me." He takes the bowl back and pulls a small bucket out of the shadows. There are rags floating in it. He takes one and wipes the Princess's face, neck, and arms. The slow sweep of the damp cloth on her skin. The soothing lick of the water. She doesn't resist when he cleans her armpits, her neck, her grimy, trembling legs. There's so much less of her than she remembers. Like she's evaporated. Like she'd been dead awhile and already begun to shrivel. "They're part of Skōlex's inner fauna. They keep him clean from parasites."

"Why only in this room?"

"They're not needed elsewhere." He wrings her filth out into the bucket. "Not right now. When they're needed, they grow naturally out of him."

The Little Princess belches into her hand and breathes deep. "I shan't leave," she says.

"Pardon?"

"You're going to tell me what the Night said, aren't you? That the only way to cure me is to leave me somewhere?"

"How—" The Right Hand sits back. "The Twins told you. You've become quite the comrades."

"I entertain them. They ..." The Princess shrugs. "I like them. But you're going to tell me that the Dawn rejected the Night's offer for a duel and we're going to slip away as soon as the Red Fleet powers up to attack and make a break for Pṛthvī. You'll drop me off along the way on some base or terraformed asteroid. But I shan't go. I'll stay here."

"You have to go, kumari."

"I shall not."

"You'll die if you don't. You ate Soma Seed, didn't you?"

"I didn't know what it was. It was sweet." She makes a face somewhere between a smile and a grimace. "The memory nauseates me."

"You have to get away from it if you want to survive."

"I won't go."

"Why not?"

She looks at him askance with the piercing suspicion of a school marm. "Where would I go? What would I do? Linger on some asteroid as a refugee? Contact whoever rules Yama and ask that they take their bastard princess back?"

"Kumari, you—"

"I know how they see me." She coughs. "I know how they saw my mother. A foreign social climber and her anchor baby. They won't take me. I'll be alone—with no one and nothing. Better to die amongst one's friends than live alone."

"You'll make new friends."

"Perhaps." She looks into the darkness beyond the door. In the distance, the clatter of great claws on stone. "But the ones I have are better than any I could ever replace them with."

A long-escalating clamor follows until the Twins burst into the room without their suits of man-flesh, wild eyes blazing in excitement. The carnivore stink of them. The rippling muscle and teeth as long as fingers. They whine and circle the Princess and lick her face until she pushes them away, smiling. They roll about her, heads on her lap, tails wagging so hard they jostle the two humans almost off balance. She glances at the Right Hand to see that he sees. That nothing could match this. That he doesn't want to replace her either.

"I don't wish to see you die, kumari," he says.

The Little Princess takes the Right Hand's hand and holds it. Let him see that she won't be persuaded. Let him see that there may be less of her in substance, but no less of her in spirit.

"The choice isn't yours, prabho Indra. The choice is mine. Will you try to take it from me?"

A long silence. The Twin's eyes on them like searching moons. The slow strobe of the cryptic illumination overhead. Eventually, the Right Hand nods.

"I will not," he says.

3.19

I

THE CALF CURLS AGAINST THE Night's belly as they fall through the incubator world's atmosphere. He can feel her faint pulse through her anesthetic-cold skin. Scorching tongues of friction lick the cocoon of her freezing embrace. Within, it's as if he's beyond even the thought of harm. The roar of entry fades into the high-gusting winds, and the Calf peeks over his mother's side to see the valleys and hillsides rushing up towards them. They're bare but for rows of eggs rising from the black-red soil like lines of giant teeth. Nannycats pause from their long-legged stalking amongst these and turn their short-muzzled faces, big-eyed and dull, towards the Triangulans. They snort and resume their rounds, methodical and benevolent, their golden-brown fur hanging in curtains down their flanks.

The Night lands on a hillside. The impact races straight through her without effect and punches a shockwave into the air. They descend a crumble-banked stream bed to a nearby row of eggs. The ones they've reached are the largest. One of them is flexing. A small fissure opens and oozes yellow fluid—viscous, slow, and filigreed with blue-black blood. Presently, the creature within slips out.

The Night catches it in her hands.

The Calf examines it. An unprepossessing thing resembling a fat-headed worm. Its skin is blue-pink and squamous, its tail long and prehensile. It squirms and looks up at them. The diminutive perfection of its eyes. The precision of its fingernail-sized scales. The hair-fine vessels, aquamarine and cyan, running like brushstrokes up its neck.

"It's too small," he says.

"He will grow," says the Night. She holds it up to her face and smiles. The thin film of frozen moisture on her face cracks and crumbles away. "He will be mighty."

"Won't that take, um, too long to be of any use?"

"They grow fast. The Asuras called them the Eaters of Realms, for they moved in packs and could devour whole planets in their hunger."

"So it's dangerous?"

"Yes. Very."

"What will you call it?"

"Skōlex."

"That's a, um, strange name."

"It's a name of theirs. From their legends."

The Calf looks up at her. "Do they have many legends?"

"Stories are how they explain the universe. So they have many."

"As many as us?"

She shakes her head. "No. We have had much longer than them to make our tales."

"Will we get names like theirs, too?"

"We will. I'll be called 'Ratri.' It means 'the Night.'"

He looks at her—freezing and serene and beautiful—and thinks it apt.

"What's mine?"

"You will be the Ox. He is a special animal of Ratri's, as you are special to me." She holds the creature up to his beaming face. "You will be his commander one day. Chief of my forces and your aunt's."

"Does she get a name, too?"

"She will be 'Usas.' It means 'the Day.'"

The Calf thinks of his aunt—expansive and precise, kind and cruel, frightening to be around but irresistible company. Another apt name.

"Shall we go and put him in orbit?"

How could this thing the size of a finger ever devour a world, wonders the Calf. Then again, everything great begins as something small. Planets begin as clusters of dust. Sprawling oceans as a single drop of water. Powerful ideas as nothing at all.

The little beast cheeps and rubs its head against the Calf's palm.

"He likes you," says the Night.

"He's cute," says the Ox.

They're already rising. The nursery drops away, and a veil of cloud obscures it. The Night gives Skōlex to the Calf. He holds the little creature to his chest. The thought of protecting it through the rage of escape frightens him. But then the Night's freezing arms wrap around him, and he buries his face in her. Once again, he feels safe—safe enough, even, to protect others.

II

THE OX PAUSES BY THE door to Akupāra's bridge and adjusts his armor. Plates slide past each other with a gentle creak. The ancient insectoid segments as familiar as his own skin. The scattered scars, each a memento of a long-dead foe, all creatures valiant and defiant and unafraid, all vanquished by his hand and forgotten. How much of his past could be narrated through the story of these cuts? Isn't that, after all, what a person is—the product of all the thrusts and blows the universe levels against the raw substance of a life?

He hefts the Metaphorical Hammer onto his shoulder. It flickers into a ram's horn, a cluster of cancerous teeth, what could be a skull in the process of shattering. Then settles back into its usual form: brute metal awaiting a taste of blood.

"On my signal," he says. "And not before."

The officers nod. The Ox adjusts his mask and touches his palm to the wall. The door to the bridge opens. The human crew beyond doesn't acknowledge him. That is precisely as he wants it. Skōlex lists lazily against the field of stars on the great screen up ahead, benthic eyes ablaze, ancient hull gleaming, as unbothered by the foes arrayed before him as an asteroid is by the solar wind.

The Vicegerent is prowling about in a nimbus of sour energy. He knows she wants to ask why he's there and why he's brought all the admirals and generals, but to do so would reveal to the crew that she doesn't know. So she says nothing. Still, she senses something. So she stalks over to the captain's chair and sits, as if to deny him the chance to seize it himself.

Glances at one of the officers. "Well?" she says. "Are we ready?"

"Two more vimanas to confirm, devi," he says.

"What's taking them so long?"

"Their signals are confused, devi."

"What does that mean?"

"They're signaling that they're ready, but not to attack."

"Then what the hell are they ready for?"

The Ox adjusts the Hammer on his shoulders. "Um, for me," he says.

He reaches up and takes off his mask. It has precisely the effect he intends. The Vicegerent recoils. In the brief moment of her horrified hesitation, he walks up in front of her and blocks her view of the screen and the rest of the bridge. As he does, the senior officers usher the human crew from their chairs. The low murmur of their confusion. The creak and ping of the officers taking control of their consoles.

"What're you doing?" The Vicegerent tries to stand. "Get back to work!"

The Ox watches the last of the old crew shuffle off the bridge. There will be another contingent waiting for them. There will be a choice, also, but the Ox is not concerned with that.

"It's over," says the Ox. "Stand down."

"What do you mean, it's over? What's happening?"

"I'm, um, taking command of the Red Fleet back." He hesitates. He'd planned this moment to be rage and fire. Instead, he lowers the Hammer to the ground. "I beg of you. For the sake of all we've been through together. For the sake of all our years on Mangala. Don't resist."

She understands. The widening of her eyes. The swift hardening of her lips into crimson shards. "Treachery," she breathes.

"That's one way of looking at it. Is a stone treasonous for falling back to earth?"

"Stones have no will. Stones only obey laws. Are you a dumb rock, Prince of Mangala?"

The Vicegerent stands. There's barely enough room for her to do it, but she does it nonetheless. Her scowling face like wintry peaks. "All of you are traitors. With this, you are turning your back on the Dawn. Do you understand? Do you understand what you're doing?"

They understand. Of course, they understand.

"They are my admirals. My generals. They've served me their entire lives. You must know that humanity no longer loves the Dawn."

"And they love you, do they? Why would they?"

"Because they know me. Because I'm real." He leans in. "Please. Don't stand in my way. I don't wish to kill you."

"Why? You've nothing but disdain for me."

"That's not true."

"That is true." The Vicegerent blinks. Tears tumble from her eyes. "You speak of all these years on Mangala, but what have I to look back upon in all of them? You casting me aside when you didn't need me, summoning me when you had some filth that needed to be scrubbed away? You calling me a fool and a wretch and a slave? If you want this chair, you'll take it from me. You'll feel the blood your treason spills on your hands."

From beyond the door, they hear the sound of two gunshots. The Vicegerent is shaking. From grief or anger, perhaps, but the Ox knows her well enough to know it isn't fear. "I could just have you taken away," he says.

"No one here will touch me. I will kill them all." She balls her fists. "I will smash every skull and grind every brain into the ground."

"Dammit." The Ox closes his eyes. The blood like hot lead at his temples. The heat rising in him like the angry core glowering at the heart of an ice world. "Dammit, will you please make things easy for once? I don't want to do this. Won't you just yield? Are you that determined to make things hard for me?"

The Vicegerent sneers. "You child. Do you really think any of this is about you?"

The Ox snarls, snatches the Hammer, and swings.

The great head of the thing explodes against the captain's chair and the consoles and the floor. The sparks and the screams and the shattering. Humans yelping with alarm. He rages and paces and foams, but the Vicegerent doesn't so much as flinch. He curses her for not letting him convince himself that there's no dishonor and death in what he's about to do. When he's done, he stands there for a long time, panting and hot.

"Do it, Prince of Mangala," she hisses. "Kill me for the sake of your own inconstant heart. I will never kneel to you again. I will face my end on my feet."

"There was a time I loved you," says the Ox. "There was a time I was proud to have you as my Vicegerent."

"I know. When you chose me to second you, my heart swelled like a newborn star. I know also that you stopped loving me—but not because of me. I was always loyal and good and diligent. Your love faded because you're a selfish, wayward creature, Prince of Mangala. Your mother learned that. Now I am learning that." The Vicegerent wipes her face. "And you must know that there is no place on Triangulum for a turncoat twice over like you."

It's a worse strike against him than anything his armor ever deflected. Worse because he knows what she means. Worse still because he sees her seeing that he understands.

She smiles and closes her eyes before he swings at her head. The Hammer sends her, already a corpse, into a console. She hits it upside-down with her neck bent back, systems subsiding like a hot coal in water. The vapor of her life evaporates. Her body goes still.

The Ox breathes deep. The heat receding now, leaving something he likes even less. Something black, sodden, ashy. Something he knows will haunt his thoughts as poison haunts a palate.

"Attack the Golden Swarm," he says.

The humans scramble back to life. He sees Skōlex slowly slide off-screen as Akupāra changes course. He hears the weapons systems come online. He appraises the ruins of the captain's chair and considers where he can sit. In the end he decides to stay standing. He, too, should face the consequences of his actions on his feet.

III

SKŌLEX HAS FEW WORDS, BUT that does not mean he has few thoughts. He knows, for example, that the glittering armadas laid out before him are foes. He knows that bloodshed will soon come. He knows that his enemies are numerous, but that only means he will sail into their midst like a whale scooping krill. He knows he will crush and shatter their flimsy bodies in singles, tens, and hundreds. He knows that he's done such things before and enjoyed it.

He knows also that out in that swarm are people he loves. People he's played, slumbered, and run between the stars with. People he knew deep in his colossal heart that he would see again before he died. No matter that he's older than he ever imagined he could get or more tired than he ever imagined he could be. He's here and they're so close. There are so many games to be played.

But first—violence.

He first notices movement in the fleets. His battle systems—roused by Marut-blood, sucking down information as a black hole does light—evaluate the metrics. The Red Fleet is deploying, but backwards. Its weapons trained, but in the wrong direction. Skōlex's armor clanks into place, droneyantras slot into launch tubes, and the great juddering engines of atom-burning lasers reach the threshold of discharge.

He speaks to the Night.

"Wait." she says. "Watch."

Skōlex watches.

The battle begins almost immediately. War in space is the lacerated hulls, the bleeding air, and the banshee howl of metal and meat twisting. Screams die in the vacuum. Flesh evaporates in the light. Bodies race—hard and rigid—in arcs that will take off beyond the plane of the system into the gaps between the stars to float—pitted, bleached, nibbled by entropy—into the leviathan hollows between galaxies.

It takes Skōlex two and a half human seconds to see what's happening. It takes the Night only a little longer. He directs another query at her.

"Hold," she says. "It may be a trap."

Cautious as ever, his soft-spoken mistress. How strange and reserved she can be. How soothing her cold presence in his petrified insides. His systems seethe. His weapons tremble, but he holds. He would hold forever for her. He would hold even if the blood of his foes trickled up his nose and they knelt before him begging for death.

The Red Fleet has enveloped the Golden Swarm now. The Dawn's vimanas blazing and frantic, the Red Fleet swirling with the mad precision of sharks. One wing of the Swarm breaks and falls back. An explosion as bright as a meteor strike blooms in the other. Skōlex brings the full telescoping power of his eyes to bear on the epicenter and sees the Chariot of Dawn ramming ship after ship after ship. The shockwave rage of its queen radiated in front.

Skōlex remembers her, too. The fiery one, the strident one, the one who bends the universe to her will. No, not bends. Burns. Burns until it capitulates. Perhaps he'll see her again, too, before this is all over. Perhaps they'll play one last game like they did when he was young, just a billion tons or so, and could skate gravity wells like a ray in the surf.

"Now," says the Night. "You may fire. But do not move."

Skōlex unloads. Chakras and lasers and torpedoes. Screaming droneyantras so malicious it's almost a relief to release them from his body. Great surges of energy that lap like angry tides against his foes and set them flailing off into the dark.

The Golden Swarm buckles. The broken wing has reformed in a great protective arc and covers frontlines as they withdraw. Their hot hulls dwindling into the dark. Their screams fading as they flee.

All except one. The Chariot of Dawn punches through two more vimanas. Then one more. Then, finally, the first of Skōlex's torpedoes catch up with it, and it withdraws. The Red Fleet knows better than to follow. So does Skōlex. There are more vimanas in the direction they're headed, and beyond that, the great iron ring that shackles the planet of Pṛthvī. The Iron Chakra, he's heard it called. He'll have to break it, he's been told.

He looks forward to that battle, too.

"Well done," says the Night. "Well done, my boy."

The Golden Swarm dwindles to fidgeting stars and disappears into the home star's glare. Skōlex has few words, but that doesn't mean he doesn't have any. His favorite is *victory*.

3.20

THE TWINS AREN'T CERTAIN WHAT they were expecting, but they're certain it isn't this strangely deflated figure wearing some sort of leering mask. The striations on his half-melted skin. The shudder and jerk of his movements when he lowers his weapon to the ground. He is a broken creature, and what they were expecting was a breaker.

Still, they recognize the great device placed head-down between the man's toes in front of him. The exquisite starwood haft of the thing as tall as the tallest human. The head morphing from one form to another to what must surely be the languid beat of its master's millennia-old heart.

The Ox kneels, touching his forehead to the ground. The unpolluted substance of his face-covering clinks on the frigid floor.

"Greetings, O She Who Strikes in Darkness."

"What is that mask?" she asks.

"I'm injured."

"How?"

"It's a long story."

For a few moments he feels her presence bearing down through his skull. He lets the cold tendrils of her curiosity nuzzle through him, gentle. When she withdraws she does so completely.

"You betray your aunt, as you betrayed me."

He looks up. "It's good to see you, too, mother."

"How am I to know that this is not a ruse?"

"I come without my weapon. I destroyed the Dawn's fleet." He spreads his arms. "You saw the truth of what I'm here to say. You know I'm not lying."

"You only destroyed part of her fleet. The rest survived and no doubt fell back to Pṛthvī."

"We can take them."

"What about her allies? And the Iron Crown?"

"We'll have allies."

"What allies?"

"The fleet of the King of Yama approaches. He's coming to destroy Usas."

The Night scowls. "Since when did you speak of your aunt by her name, my child? And wherever this king is coming from, he won't get here in time."

"He will. His fleet's already reached Daitya."

"How can this be? Is Yama not beyond the orbit of even Arungrah?"

"They jump."

"I thought my sister erased that technology."

"He's managed to resurrect it. He has the help of a Soul."

"The Souls survived?"

"Only one. I killed all the others."

The Night breathes in through her nose and exhales twin plumes of feathery snow. "Even if this is true, the King will not be coming to help me. Surely, he blames me for seizing his child."

"Ah, so you did keep her. Is that what I smelled in the Antechamber? You can use her as a hostage. Return her through a door in return for his cooperation." The Ox pauses. "Why did you take her?"

The Night looks up and away as if harkening to some distant voice. "It was in error."

"Skōlex tells me you have a Soma Seed."

"Skōlex is indiscreet."

"Quite a large one."

"It won't be used for killing."

"Then what for?"

"You'll see. I have reason not to trust you, child. Let us not stand here and chat as if what happened had not happened."

The Ox sighs. "You do not understand, then? You still don't understand why I did what I did?"

"I understand you objected to your ordained end, and for that you undid all we had labored for."

"Not all is light and dark, mother. Look around. What you did then, you've done again—unite everyone against you. Auntie dearest has spent three thousand human years making you out to be as bad as an Asura. Then, when you actually do turn up, you destroy cities, level temples, and kill innocents without so much as introducing yourself—because you think you're right.

"I'm sure it seems obvious that no matter what you do the, um, nobility of your cause redeems you. Alas for you, it doesn't, least of all in the eyes of those who're paying the price of your victories."

The Night scowls. "You said you came here to parley. This is a very peculiar apology."

"Parley, not apologize. I shan't apologize. Never, in ten thousand yugas, will I apologize. I did what I did because it had to be done. I did what I did because." He pauses. "Because it was the right thing to do."

"Strange. You just said that the nobility of the cause does not redeem you in the eyes of those you make suffer for it."

"Precisely. There is no point asking for redemption from one who thinks you're irredeemable."

"Strange also how this ... 'right thing' was so concomitant with your own interests."

"Do you hate me for wanting to live, mother? Do you hate me so for not wanting to die?"

A flicker of something crosses the Night's face. In its wake she looks old and tired and frail. "I thought I had raised you to understand why that was so."

"I would have said you didn't, but I'm here, aren't I?"

"Why are you here?" she says.

"To propose an alliance to bring down the Dawn."

"Why? Because you've decided?"

"I'm tired, mother. I'm tired, and I want it to end. My story's at an end."

The Night steps up to the Ox, veils of ice coming off Her in milky cascades. "This is not your story, child. That you ever thought that was your greatest failing. That you think that still ..." She reaches for his face. "Take off your mask."

"No."

She pauses, hands raised. Then she moves again, as inexorable as a descending glacier. For a few instants the Ox considers resisting, but soon enough, her cold fingers brush his skin, and the idea evaporates. The mask comes off with a click. The Night touches his cheek, where the flesh sprawls marbled and studded with flecks of naked bone, and sighs.

"She did this to you?" she says.

The Ox pulls his face away and puts the mask back on. "You see? This story is mine. The redemptive arc must be mine. To go from sacrifice to traitor and then finally to die a righteous death. To gain redemption."

How simple it all sounds. He could tell her all that underlies it. The long nights ended always by memories of his betrayal. The slick black roots of doubt and guilt. The certainty squatting in him, as unwelcome as a cuckoo, that his redemption requires her forgiveness. But he will not ask for it. He will not give her more of himself than she gives him, and that is next to nothing.

The house of Night conceals—even from itself.

The Night blinks. "Very well," she whispers. "This can be your story if you want, my child."

3.21

VISHWADEVI HEADS DOWN THE PATHWAY at the back of the house, along the ramshackle fence Bhima and his whiny wife erected in a huff ten years ago and didn't take down even after they'd sorted things out between them. Though the sun's long gone, the heat still throbs in the air like a fever. Streaking lights and ball lightning dart about high in the air off to the west, where a thin moustache of hills graces the lip of the horizon. Long reddish streaks shortening abruptly to dazzling blue-bright dots—eerie and swift and as quiet as the dark. What strange messages the gods send their worshippers. What peculiar beauty their language contains.

Up the slope behind her on the road, a cluster of people are watching the light show and the darkened arc of the Iron Crown bisecting the sky overhead.

"No thunder," Vishwadevi whispers.

She heads up through the scraggly herb garden that her aunt had worked on so hard before she and Indra disappeared. By now practically the whole village is milling about on the road, on their roofs, or in the trees. She finds her father seated by the roadside, cross-legged and smoking. He sucks deep on his pipe and holds it out to her. Vishwadevi takes a draw. The smoke is sour, but the calmness it brings is welcome.

"They're arguing if it's angels," says her father. "One of the old farts says he's seen it before. He ain't never seen nothin' like it before."

"What is it?" whispers Vishwadevi. "Something to do with Indra and auntie?"

"Too big and too late for that." Her father takes the pipe back. "It's fleets gathering to the Dawn's citadel from all over."

"Fleets? Of vimanas?"

"Of vimanas."

Vishwadevi frowns. "But why?"

"Looks like there's a war in heaven," says her father. He looks at her and scratches the wiry bush of beard on his cheek. "Suppose you'd better marry that waster sooner rather than later. Who knows if we'll even be here tomorrow?"

She should be elated. She should jump for joy. But she can't take her eyes off the lights. The slow swerve of them. The colossal conglomeration, as if of divine wasps to a celestial hive.

"Do you really think so? Do you really think it'll affect us if there's a war?"

"When the gods fight," says her father, inhaling, "it's their believers who suffer the most."

3.22

THE FIRST THING THE PRINCESS notices when she wakes is that her fever's gone. The second is that her own smell is as thick as fists in her nose. She hobbles out into the Antechamber of Night. When she's certain she's alone, she strips and wades into one of the pools. The water is like an iron jacket on her chest, and the air hardens in her lungs. As she flails in the cold, she remembers another time and place. Some cold river on the outskirts of the Tripura they'd escaped festival season for. The monochrome splendor of the abandoned city on the far bank. Her mother's wet skin is against her own, and her voice is in her ear.

Sing with me and imagine it's true. I am a newborn star. My light will shine near and far. You feel warmer now, hm?

She didn't then, but she does now. And not because of the lullaby.

She cleans herself and wanders back to the where she slept. There are clothes folded neatly by her bed but no sign of the Right Hand or the Left. Perhaps she's been lost to a coma for months. Perhaps the Night's mission is over, all have moved on, and she's been left alone to wander these empty halls for eternity. It's a thought colder even than the water outside, and it grows the longer she stands there.

Then she hears someone crying.

She dresses and follows the noise out into the Antechamber. Nothing. No sign of a weeper anywhere in the Throne Room, but the noise strengthens as she heads into Skōlex. After some time she comes to a long passageway studded with little, empty altars, each home to a single statue. An old woman speaking to a floating ball. A young girl with a sword sprouting from her chest. A woman, hands ablaze, standing over a pile of broken bodies. How absurd an undertaking she's committed to. Chasing this ghost voice through a structure older than even the kingdom that bred her. Why not just retreat to her chamber? Why not just wait until the Wolves find her or the Night or one of the Hands?

Why not curl up in a ball on the floor and give up on everything? Better yet, why not kill yourself to avoid that inevitable future moment when you look back over your life and regret having done nothing?

"I am a newborn star," she whispers. "My light will shine near and far."

She wraps her arms around herself and marches on.

The passageway gapes into a large chamber as blank and unadorned as a cistern.

Off in the middle distance is a giant, clad figure sitting on the floor. Her clothes ooze like melting tar. Her black face is lumpy with berry-like clusters of eyes. A mortar the size of a man squats brute and grey-skinned by her side as her many arms work with the autonomy of octopodal tentacles. On the wall in front of her is a great, leaking gash. She is smearing golden ointment onto this with fingers as long and many-jointed as spider legs.

The Princess approaches and presses her palms together in greeting. "Greetings, devi."

The Night doesn't turn to her. "Kumari," she says. "You seem better."

"Thank you. I feel better. Am I healing?"

"No." One of the Night's many-jointed hands reaches over the Princess's head and smears ointment into a small crack on the ceiling. The dim light fetching up in its substance like a soul entering a zygote. "You have moved into the next stage of your sickness."

"What does that involve?"

"Nothing that you will understand."

"Will it ... will it hurt?"

"Physically, you are past the worst of the discomfort."

"Am I going to die?"

"For all intents and purposes, yes."

"What does that mean?"

"It is hard to explain. You must not think me coy. Your illness plays out in different ways in different creatures, and I cannot tell the future."

"How long do I have?"

"A quarter of a human year, perhaps, if you do not leave Skōlex. But I am told you will not."

"I will not, devi."

"Then I shall not force you."

Silence. "I heard crying."

"That is me. Part of me."

"Why are you crying, devi?"

The Night gestures with her strange head at the gash. "Skōlex. He did not tell me how badly injured he was. There are many cuts and breaks in his body. It will take me a long time to heal them."

"Can he not heal himself?"

"He is old now. It is challenging."

"But—he's gigantic. Something like this must be just a scratch to him."

The Night turns her head towards the Princess. Enough grief and sorrow flooding in her proliferating black eyes that the Princess finds it hard to breathe. Like black wind. Like drowning ice. How frightening that such a creature can feel such pain, yet comforting it is to know that even the gods can grieve. "A mountain dies a pebble at a time," she says.

"Can I help you?" The Princess nods to the mortar. "Perhaps I can find some injuries and apply some of that."

The Night withdraws her hands and wipes all of them on her lap. She stands with the rustle of a flock taking wing. As she does, she returns, with a dizzying fold of perspective, to the size and shape the Princess is used to.

"There is something you can do for me, kumari, but it will be dangerous and difficult."

"What is it?"

"I trust the Right Hand has told you what's happened here since you were taken ill?"

"He has. Where are they? The Hands?"

"They are well. Do not worry." The Night slips her mortar into her robes. "You will know then that I have amended my plans. For this new plan to succeed, I will require an alliance with your father."

The Princess's eyes widen. "My father? Is he here? How did he—"

"Your father is approaching with a great fleet. He intends, I imagine, to save you."

A new light appears in the room. A feeble illumination that strengthens and wanes with the rhythm of a firefly. The Princess looks around for a few moments before she realizes it's coming from her own hands. She raises them to her face, slackjawed. No warmth in her skin, no sensation but that which was already there. Still her hands are indisputably glowing.

"What is this?" The Princess shakes her hand. The light flickers and dims. Then it regathers. "What's happening?"

The Night smiles. "Happiness is a powerful thing. The Soma Seed alters the things it encounters, each according to their strengths. You, it would seem, are a bringer of light."

"A bringer of light?" The Princess smiles. "Like a star?"

"Not precisely."

"What does—what is—"

"You ask me of the future and of who you are, kumari. One I do not know. The other you know better than I ever can." The Night's smile fades. "Your father is nearly here. When he is, you must go to him. Explain to him what has happened and what I aim to do. Bring his fleet to our side."

"His fleet?"

"He has built one to reclaim you."

The Princess thinks of the King. Her hands flash like a nova.

"What do you aim to do, devi?"

The Night explains. By the time she's finished, the light's gone from the Princess's hands. The sound of weeping has gone also. The Princess stands in the silence for a short while with her head tilted and her mind elsewhere.

Then, slowly, she nods.

"I'll help," she says, "but in return, when you have defeated your sister, you and yours must return to Triangulum and never return. Ever. Every Triangulan in this system must go. Every last one of you."

The Night tilts her head. "A strange request."

"My father said one's own mistakes are things to learn from, but a tyrant's mistakes are things to resent. Your kind have been endlessly tyrannical to us, devi. We must be free to make our own mistakes."

"Ah." The Night nods. "If your father is as wise as his words imply, then there is hope. I have no intention of remaining here, kumari, nor will I permit any of mine to do so. You have my word."

"Then you have my word that I will do as you ask."

"Thank you, kumari." A brief smile, sharp, mischievous. "If you are as wise as your words imply, your reign will be a long and prosperous one."

"My reign?"

"Monumental, it will be. Mountainous." Tentative, she pats the Princess on the shoulder. "However, a mountain rises an inch at a time. That, at least, would explain why you are so short."

She leaves. Footsteps as soft as snowfall. The air clearing as though it was never unclear. The Princess stands in the silence, wondering. Was she really just teased by a goddess?

3.23

WATCHING THE YAMANS BUSTLE ON the bridge of *Pratikara*, the Soul of Mangala considers telling them the truth about their past. That their ancestors were all slaves. Products of feelingless design, not vibrant evolution. Creatures not born of women, but cultured in vats, intended for lives of servitude. Yamans with their oversized eyes for mining in dull Plutonian light. Agnians with their limbs like trunks for lives spent carrying others' burdens. Āēoi with their little symbiotes for slaving in the atmospheres of toxic worlds. These, and others—some voiceless, some quadrupedal, some so dull they were barely human—bred purely for Old Earth's comfort.

What would they make of the endless generations of gene-locked tyranny? What would they think of the countless lives, endured more than lived, with no purpose other than to serve? They weren't even called humans. Until, that is, the Triangulans set them free. Until they wrenched the system from Earth's trembling, bloodied hands and set its mutant children free amidst the ruins of its empire.

How sweet it would be to tell them. How joyous to see their pride scuppered. He glances at the King across the bridge. He'll tell him first. He'll tell him how his house is just the slave house of a slave people. He'll tell him he's overthrown the very creatures who set his kind free and then savor the horror on his simian face.

He will do it. He will do it. But for now he needs them alert.

The Soul opens all channels and inspects the status of the Blizzard. Datasets. Pings flood in from all one hundred and eight ships. Teeming Tributaries concatenate into a pulsing flood of information that runs pure and true. Engines hot. Crews braced. Systems nominal.

"We're ready," he says.

The King wanders over and gestures the Soul out of the captain's chair. The Soul makes him wait. Just an instant, but an instant too long nonetheless. He can see the human is fretful. The flick and jab of his gaze. The tip of his tongue surfing briefly between his skinny lips. Incredible how he can still be nervous when, as far as he knows, the whole fleet is primed, coordinated, and ready to do precisely as he wants.

"Jump on my mark," he says. "Mark."

The universe splits into three. Realities float in n-dimensions overhead, below, and in other directions that make no sense. The vimanas judder in a peristalsis of forbidden motion. Then comes an abrupt reconfiguration. Without warning, Skōlex—gigantic and alien—appears directly in their path.

Silence. Stillness. The crew stares. The King leans forward, lips parted, giant Yaman eyes wide.

Even the Soul is dumbstruck. The sheer scale of the thing. The eyes like little suns, the arched back, the thunderous barrels of canon glowing crimson already with stifled energies. The last time he encountered such a creature it had sent him plunging to ruin.

This he remembers clearly. But that was then. Then he did not have secrets like the ones he has now. Like the fact that the partitions erected to keep him from the weapons system is in fact a copy of his own internal bulwarking. Like the fact that the weapons system's architecture allows for him to take command as easily as the King lowering his simian rump into the chair. Like the fact that he can initiate a full spectrum attack within one-point-zero-eight seconds of their arrival with authorization from none but himself.

This is precisely what he does.

Missiles tumble into tubes and prime for launch. Yantras come pouring out of the vimanas' sides like swarms of angry black hornets. The Soul's head swells with feedback. The ecstatic tide of positive reportage. The rippling efficiency of his program working at near-lightspeed efficiency.

Finally, the humans notice something's happening—jabbering, agitated. Bashing futile commands into consoles. Lobbing orders and demands and questions about, as if their urgency had any bearing on how fast they'd be fulfilled. All, that is, except the King. He just sits as still as the dark side of the moon, peering at Skōlex.

The sweet river of data in the Soul begins to go dry.

None of the other ships in the Blizzard, he notices, are firing. Only *Pratikara*. The Soul reaches out, but his programming slips off the other ships' hardware like water off glass. He extends tentacles of cracking software, but it too fails. Partitions rise in swift orogeny between him and the system. Swarms of phagocode come pouring through his paths of ingress. The scalpel pain of some snipping sections of his code. The prod and pierce of others clamping onto him like parasites. He tries to retreat, but they hold him fast, as a pin holds a beetle. The infection spreads to the heart of him. He is being lobotomized alive.

Paralyzed, the Soul watches as the King barks his orders and realizes all this was planned. A glowing fan of countermeasures streaks forth, more numerous by far than his own half-aborted salvo. The glitter storm of light as it obliterates the released ordnance. The rising calm and harmony of the human's behavior. Yes, planned and coordinated and known by all. Yojanas away, a single torpedo strikes home. Skōlex turns one massive eye at the pinprick glow of its penetration. Colossal. Impassive. Then it looks away.

The Soul manages to turn his head to the King before complete paralysis.

"You fuck," he hisses. "You dirty, backstabbing fuck."

The King smiles. "Well, you did once say we were a lot alike, didn't you?"

3.24

THE TWINS TRACK THE NIGHT to a great chamber with a concave floor. On the floor is the dazzling model of some valley rendered in Skōlex's own substance. Here, little rivers of ichor saunter through exquisite valleys. There, thin condensation wafts like breath on a cold day. About their feet are clusters of bulbed tree-things that swell and subside like alveoli. The Night is sitting on the far side of all this—slumped forward and limp-wristed—like some creator god exhausted by her labors.

"Why did they attack, do you think?" she whispers.

"We're not certain, devi. It appears to have been in error. But they've been signaling parley with—"

"They've hurt Skōlex."

"The damage is limited." The Twins sniff and peer at the Night's face. They shuffle closer together. "He seems functional."

"Their dart was poisoned." The Night grinds her teeth. A tear flees her depthless left eye. The slow gleam of its progress down her cheek. The sapphire smoothness of the nub it hardens into. "I ought to kill them all. Why are you here?"

"You asked us to come for You, devi, when the time was right."

"For what?"

"To keep Your promise to the eunuch. To reprogram the Seed."

The Night shakes her head. "A curse on that. I should show them who I can be and freeze their hearts out of their chests. You would like that, wouldn't you? You, who are Wolves of War?"

"Yes." The Wolves shuffle backwards. "We've been against this from the start. Our counsel is to destroy this human fleet, then take Pṛthvī by force. However ..."

"However?"

"Skōlex is ailing, and Kṛṣṇā Bhaghini's forces are formidable."

"And?"

"You gave your word to the eunuch. It would not do for you to break it."

The Night stares at them. They drop their gaze. When they glance back up they realize her eyes are focused beyond them or perhaps through them or perhaps nowhere at all. She sighs.

"What do you make of them?" she asks.

"Who?"

"The humans."

"We don't like them. They don't know themselves, but think they do. They see only a little and assume it's everything. Then they accuse others who see more of seeing nothing at all." They move apart but still speak in unison. "But the three aboard Skōlex are honest and brave. Perhaps, if there are more like them, they're worth sparing."

"All that playing with the Princess has changed your outlook."

"It has, devi. But the other two are noble after their own manner, too. They have done as you commanded, even at great danger to themselves." The Wolves sniff. "It is admirable."

A long silence. Blood rivers flow. Lung trees swell, subside, and swell again. The Night stands and straightens her sari. "Damn it all," she whispers, and stalks out.

They follow her to the Chamber of the Soma Seed. She marches through the ineffectual onslaught of lightning and buries her hands in the Seed. As she does, her throat swells to the size of her head, and she begins to sing. Her voice resonant and so deep it sets the whole chamber a-judder. The Wolves pace back and forth in thrall to booming rhythm. They've heard this before, the feral parlance of their star-hunting ancestors, but never like this. Never before have they witnessed that tongue as mighty as gravity deployed with such precision or grace.

The lightning dies. The Soma Seed flushes dark green. The skin of the thing puckers into great thorns. Flowers bloom between these. Fat-petalled and electric blue. Drooping clusters of magenta flecks. Great white and yellow fractals spiraling eternally. All this accompanied by the rustle and crack of uninhibited growth with scents erupting like cheers. Last to come are roots, tentacular and flailing. Their settling marks the end of the transformation.

The Night pulls back her hands.

"There," she says. "I give these creatures life when they give me death."

She sits lotus-wise on the cold floor and hangs her head. The Wolves can't think of what to say or do. So they slink back into the shadows, away from her grief.

3.25

THE KING OF YAMA CARRIES the box across his room and places it on the soft padding in the nook by the porthole. The soft exhaustion of victory is upon him like the memory of ancient heartbreak. His quarters are tidy now. No noise but the polite hum of *Pratikara*'s systems. No smell but that of scrubbed air and laundered sheets. Order has returned at last, and he knows he can luxuriate in it. Because, for the first time in a very long time, he can luxuriate in being himself.

Still, he doesn't rush. He scrutinizes the box then hesitates a little longer with his fingers suspended above its nobbled, unreflective surface. Reviewing all the plots and plans and subterfuge that brought him to this moment. The jungle of causality that led him from the Temple to Yama to the wrecked heart of the Tripura and now here. He scarcely knows how he navigated it. Perhaps he didn't. Perhaps he only followed the path of least resistance, and now he looks back as if he hacked them himself.

He presses his fingers to the surface of the cube. Four small green lights wink to life consecutively then all turn off together. The King crosses his legs and leans back against the cold glass of his porthole like a rishi about to pontificate to a child. Still, nobody speaks for a long time.

"I can come back later if you're in no mood to talk," he says eventually.

"I'm trying to figure out where I am," says the Soul of Mangala. The King learns something at the moment—it's possible for a creature such as this to sound tired. "I can't see shit."

"You're in my quarters. De-networked."

"What did you do to me?"

"You're a copy of a copy, demon. When I brought you—the original you, sealed in that ancient data-cube—back to Yama, I copied your data core, and I analyzed it." The King leans forward. "Sometimes I had to take you—the other yous—apart. Such strange things it did to your programming. One of you called it digital vivisection. I rather liked that. Did you know that you're a coward? Every time I cut a piece of you away, you begged me to stop. You promised me the entire universe if only I let you be."

"You're a fucking sadist."

"I took no pleasure in it. My child was gone, my wife was dead, and there I was inflicting pain on a sentient creature. I hated myself. I think I've hated myself since then. But that tinkering allowed me to add a failsafe. One I hid well enough that you didn't even feel it." The King chews his lip. "You're in no position to criticize my honesty, demon. I told you not to fire on the juggernaut when we jumped in. I told you not to endanger my child. You did precisely that. And with poisoned warheads! Do you know how hard we had to work to persuade the Night that we have no quarrel with her?"

"I did what I had to do."

"As did I."

"Why're we here? Do you want me to beg? Is that it? You want me to beg for mercy?"

"Not at all." The King shuffles around to gesture through the window. Not far off is Skōlex rendered tiny by distances and the glass-shard glitter of the Red Fleet about its flanks. "We will be giving you to the Night. In return, she'll be giving us my girl. Never in a billion years would I compromise that deal.

"No, I brought you here to thank you. You were right about many things. I am no more special than circumstance has made me. I regret the suffering I've caused. Strange that you'd be the one to make me see—but you did. I want you to know that I'll return to Yama when this is done and make amends. I'll spend the rest of my days atoning for the death I've caused. For that, I have to thank you."

A brief silence. The cube hums. Lights glint. "Your people were slaves, you know."

"Pardon?"

"Your people. All of the peoples. The Agnians, the Shukrians. You were all slaves designed by Old Earth to work for them. They genetically engineered Earth and—"

"What relevance has this?"

"Do you know who set you free?"

The King nods at Skōlex. "The Triangulans came, found Old Earth's cruel empire, and set its multitudes free. I know all this. I lived in the Tripura for many years. I visited the Temple of Knowledge often. Why are you speaking of it?"

"I don't know." The box whirrs again. "I thought ... I told myself I'd tell you. What've you done to me? I had a reason. Fuck. There're parts of me missing."

"That makes sense. The excision from the system diminished you. The bits you left behind are being deleted as we speak." The King blinks. "I'm not sure why you bring it up, but I know why it doesn't matter. The past is like a great stone. You may either carry it upon your shoulders like a burden, or you may stand upon it and see farther than those before you did. Perhaps, you intended for me to feel low that my ancestors were slaves. But I tell you that I know that everything is circumstantial. They were no more deserving of being slaves than I am of being king. But they were and did what they could. I am and will do what I can."

If the Soul could have sighed, the King thinks, it would have. "Fine. Fuck. Just turn me off and send me over. We're done here."

The King reaches out, pauses. This is it then. This is where they will part. He will never hear the Soul's voice again and has no desire to. Still, it seems as if he should mark the moment somehow. In honor, perhaps, of all the other voices that have vanished without warning from his life. And also for all the others he will one day hear for the last time without knowing. None of it was or will be under his control, but this villainous, tinny chatter at least is. He must mark it because he can and because he may never be able to do so again.

"Farewell," he says.

"Fuck off," says the Soul.

3.26

A SOLITARY FIGURE MAKES HER way across the talcum skin of sacred Chandra. Diminished to a mute glow, she seems desolate and slow-footed. Her feet burn obsidian tracks into the dust as she goes. A shifting nebula of fleet lights hovers in the raw sky.

The Dawn halts and looks up at them.

They are not enough.

She keeps on until she finds the grooved flanks of the crater she's looking for, then floats up and over its jagged lip. Down in the nadir of the grey basin is a small black nub invisible from more than a few feet away. This she touches, watching as it extends downwards into a spiral staircase. She descends through a blackness so intense that even her gleaming skin and fiery eyes seem somehow snuffed, impotent.

Whispering things approach, see who she is, and retreat with the slink of predators avoiding bigger ones.

The stairs terminate in a black chamber with a high ceiling and vivid frescos. A shining man cleaves a great serpent's head in two. Two far galaxies duel to distortion against a starless backdrop. A weeping woman hugs a femur atop a mountain. The chamber is divided into a glowing left and a gloomy right just as it was when she was last here. The underground sea lapping blackly against the nearby stone shore is also unchanged, as are the cryptic lights either floating in the distance or pretending to do so.

The Dawn breathes deep. The familiar air of this place that was hers before she became who she is. The memories that hang so thick she can almost smell them. Memories of a millennium she shared with the only one who could ever be her equal. The arguments, the laughter, the slow shaping of each other into the complementary opposites as they were intended to be. All with Skōlex wallowing in the waters and growing, growing, growing.

"Well," she says. "You got me this time."

No response. That's expected. That's why she's here.

She walks to the right. The lingering cold is sharp in the stone here. The stage grooved by a millennium of use. She stands there for a long time and tries to remember what it was like to love the dark, but can't. Is she really so changed? She must be, if all she can feel now is rage.

"You could have let me have this," she says. "You'll have everything in the end. You'll have everything. All I wanted was this one small corner of the universe, but you—you had to come back and bring your fucking rules."

Up ahead is a black nest. She walks over. The great blade-edged obsidian block has sealed shut for longer than it takes languages to die, but it opens at her approach. She climbs into the hollowed-out space and inspects it all in the faint glow from her own skin. No sign of the creature who once slept here. No traces but those that come pouring out of her own head—clamorous and irresistible and overwhelming.

The Dawn buries her face in her hands.

"There aren't enough," she whispers. "I don't know why. Some thundercraft from Shukra and a few companies from Arungrah. Nothing from Shani, sister. Perhaps your attack frightened them. Nothing from Mangala, but that's to be expected. I was cruel to your boy. Don't judge me too harshly. My temper. You know how it is with my temper."

The far sea laps on the false shore. "I thought my realm was mightier than this. But you've cut it right in half." Hot tears fall on black stone. Hot enough to glow like little stars. Hot enough to sizzle stone when they land. "Have you ever wondered what they'll do when I'm gone? You remember how they were when we arrived. How do you think they'll do without me? They could be so much, but they're so stupid."

Here, where the lightlessness becomes stifling and the memories more so, she's less than what she wants to be. She wanders back to the stairs—her feet leave no mark—and up to the surface. The lights are still there, wheeling into formation now. A thousand ships, she knows, but she'll need a thousand more to combat Skōlex. She'll need a thousand more than that to piece her empire back together. Had they really all been waiting for a moment like this to abandon her? Had she really been so blinded by her own light that she couldn't see their malcontent?

She keeps looking. At the stars beyond the fleet and the other things she hasn't looked at for so long. The novae and the pulsars and the whirling binaries. The exhaust of far-off empires reaching out through the emptiness like lovers bereft. All those things nested in and swallowed by the neverending hollow that grows and grows and grows.

How could she have ever deigned to stand against such a thing? How could she have ever thought she could win?

"Mother said, without dark, light means nothing," she whispers. "I never understood why it wasn't the other way around. How can you mean something even without me? How can you be yourself entirely, but I mean nothing without you?"

No response here either. The Dawn screams. Her voice dies in the vacuum. She flares in rage. The phosphorescent sear of her illumination. The shadows like reality deleted where it fails to reach.

And then—darkness. As it was before. As it was always going to be again.

3.27

I

There is barely enough room by the airlock to contain them all: the ensigns in dress uniform; the orderlies behind them; the royal guard with their facemasks up, and their guns gleaming. The officers in full regalia stand facing all these, stiff-backed, fingers flexing in white gloves. They're afraid, thinks the King. They'll remember this moment when they met the Ambassadors of Night. When they first laid eyes upon the girl they've travelled a hundred million yojanas to collect. This mythic child who has just arrived, he's been told, in some kind of magical bubble. No visible engine and no hull. Barely even a ship. Perhaps the Triangulans have developed new technologies in the time since they first arrived, and why shouldn't they have? If an entire world could change in two years, if an empire could have been brought so close to toppling, what could a civilization of gods accomplish in a thousand?

Not gods, he reminds himself. Aliens. Aliens he has parleyed with as an equal. Aliens who are returning something more precious than all of their technologies.

He limps forward with his heart rattling about in his chest. He puts his hand on his ribs and presses, but still it thunders. There are footsteps in the airlock beyond and voices, maybe, then silence. He listens and frets, then turns to one of his officers.

"What's—?"

The airlock swivels open like a great iron iris. In the shadowless space beyond are three figures. A young girl, staring at him, and a large man in silken robes that hang over his robust belly like river water curving over a boulder. At their head is a woman in a lavish black sari. Pale, big-eyed, and holding a large copper bowl. The King examines her as she steps forward with the breath squirming in his throat.

"I am the Left Hand of Night," the woman says. No. Not Danu, but so close. So close. "I speak for the Mother of Ice, who greets the King of Yama. She presents this bowl, older than the Nine Worlds, as a token of her goodwill. Place it to your ear, and you will hear wisdom from civilizations now far beyond the reach of baryonic things."

The King signals his officers forward. One approaches the visitors and dips a gloved finger in a bowl of saffron paste and presses a dot of it between their eyebrows with the reverence of a devotee at an altar. Another officer holding a sheaf of rice shakes it over their heads. Neither the Left Hand nor the man—could he be the granthapālaḥ taken with his girl?—react. But the third, the young woman standing back to the left, scowls and dusts the grains out of her hair.

The King knows that scowl. He knows that sharp-chinned face and those fingers too skinny for their plump hands. He knows that mouth, prim and pressed, as if everything she can see is just a little less impressive than she had hoped.

He grips his chest harder.

One of the officers takes the Night's bowl and brings it to him. He waves it away and staggers forward. The Left Hand and the Right move aside. The Princess of Yama steps forward.

"Hello, father," she says.

He stares at her. This woman derived somehow from the little body that curled up on his lap or sat solemn and serious by his side through a thousand hours of tinkering. That same life embodied somehow in this semi-familiar creature he immediately loves more than anything he's ever loved anything before.

How is that possible? How can every inch of him—every shriveled and exhausted and dried-out inch—reach out for this almost-woman with the certainty that he knows everything there is to know about her and that knowledge is what makes him whole.

"I've come a long way for you," he says.

The Princess averts her eyes. "I'm sorry for the inconvenience."

"Oh, my beautiful girl." The King drops to his knees. "I would have travelled a thousand times farther just to touch the hem of your robes."

The Princess collapses into his arms. He holds her, the miraculous entirety of her, not just unharmed but more perfect than he'd ever hoped. For a long moment the King luxuriates in her warmth on his face. Her smell like blossoms. The tangible wonder of her ongoing existence.

Then she whispers in his ear.

"Where's Mother?" she says.

II

THEY MEET AROUND A SANDALWOOD table inlaid with bronze images of the Princess's ancestors in glory. The girl herself, though, is sunk low and utterly silent. Her eyes red, the glutinous gleam of tears on her cheeks. The tips of her stick-sharp mouth droop with sorrow. Every now and then the Right Hand reaches over and squeezes her arm. She nods but will not look at him.

The Left Hand sees all this from the corners of her eyes, but her attention is on the King as he reads the Night's scroll. A strange, bloodless man, she thinks. A creature who looks less than he should be, but that only, she suspects, conceals the fact that there's more to him than visible. A mediocre man would not have had the imagination to do what he's done. A mediocre man would be easier to persuade. The King places the scroll on the table. The script glittering in the soft light. The great webbed seal of Night inscribed seemingly in nothingness itself.

"No," he says.

The Princess wipes her eyes. "Father," she says. "It would be wise."

"I will not ally myself with the beasts who killed your mother."

"Unintentionally."

"It doesn't matter. They're monsters."

"They aren't monsters, father."

"Don't defend them." The King's eyes narrow. "Do not dare defend those murderers. Murder is murder. I would know, for I am a murderer. I've accepted it. Your Triangulans must accept what they've done, too. The whole of Tripura burned. Were you there? When they destroyed our home? When they killed everyone we knew? Sinivali died there, you know. She couldn't come with me to Yama, so she stayed in the Tripura. Her and that old mother of hers with the limp."

The Princess's eyes brim afresh. "She did?"

"Yes. Were you there?"

"Aboard Skōlex. Yes."

"Then you know."

"Raja—" says the Left Hand.

"Don't 'raja' me." He fixes his kraken eyes upon her. "I've heard of you. The Left Hand of Night. They call you Sunita, daughter of death. Did you know that? They sacrifice children to you in the ruins of the Tripura. They slit children's throats in your name."

The Left Hand blinks, speechless. The King sneers and continues.

"Listen. You come to me now, propose an alliance with the greatest villain in the history of humanity, and expect me to ignore the consequences. The Blizzard will revolt. The commanders will refuse orders. Besides, what have I to gain by aiding the Night? Replacing one tyrant sister for another? No. Never. Never will I fire a single trident or discus or yantra in the name of Triangulum."

"She won't seize the throne for herself, father. She gave me her word."

"Her word?" The King barks a laugh as dry as old wood. "Don't be ridiculous."

The Left Hand leans forward. "Raja, please. If our cause loses—if the Night loses—the Dawn will recover her strength and reconquer the system world by world. Even Yama. She'll erase all memory of you but a few scraps deep in the bowels of some new Library."

"A new Library? You mean one she'll build to replace the one your queen burned to ashes? Along with a million innocents?" The King pauses. "I have blood on my hands, O Left Hand of Night, but your liege bathes in it."

"Father—"

"Enough of this. I've no desire to listen to the Night's lies. And you, Danu. How can you sit here and speak on behalf of your mother's killers?"

The Right Hand clears his throat. "May I, raja?"

"No." The King sinks in his chair. The pantomime glumness of his mouth. The hollow but heavy gaze. "Why do you stand with her, prabho granthapālaḥ? You were a noble man when last I met you. Or so it seemed."

"Noble, no, raja. But I think hard on what I believe, and this is what I can tell you about the Night. She's the lesser of two evils."

"The lesser of two evils? That's the best you can do? And on that basis I'm to commit my entire fleet to this mad confrontation?"

"Yes, raja. On that basis and on the basis that this may be the last chance our species has to overthrow an alien tyrant."

"You don't know that. Your Left Hand says she will destroy everything, but no sovereign craves rule over an empire of ashes."

"No, not ashes, raja. Slaves." The Right Hand shuffles as if adjusting to some great weight. "I've spent my whole life wondering why my parents left Pṛthvī. I knew there were some reasons. They didn't understand why the Ushayantras would sometimes come and take some of us away. They found out that none of the crops we grew, which we took pride in growing, which were the center of our lives, were worth anything at all. Every year the Ushayantras came and collected them in great grey bins and carted them off. In return they gave us what we needed—antibiotics, fuel, cloth. They told us we fed all the Nine Worlds.

"Then my mother found out the Ushayantras just took it all to their collection hubs and burned it. It makes sense, now I think about it. Why rely on the paltry produce of a few million folks like us when you could grow a million times more upon the Iron Chakra?" The Right Hand leans forward. "Raja, I have spoken to the Night. I have read of the works of the Dawn. I would have believed they do what they do out of malice, but it's because of something far worse. They have no imagination.

"They cannot imagine things beyond what they know. I don't know how it is that creatures that live so long and see so far can be so, but it's true. They do what they believe is right without stopping for an instant to see if perhaps it isn't. They are slaves to their own truths, and because they see so far, they feel entitled to enslave us.

"The Dawn will do what the Left Hand has described just as surely as the Night will try to topple her because both believe they have right on their side. They are gods who cannot imagine being anything else, and we have defied them. One of them wishes to take what she wants and leave. The other, to keep what she has—which is us. The choice you face is which one you will aid."

Silence. The King exhales through his nose, long and slow, and sits up. "Beautiful words, prabho granthapālaḥ. But hear me. I will not fire a single shot in aid of the creatures who killed my wife and stole my child from me. Ever. Ever. The Blizzard is designed precisely to combat the forces of the Dawn, and Yama is far away. We will be fine. I will keep to my word. You will get the Soul of Mangala, and I will take my child and leave. Your gods, lacking imagination or otherwise, can fight it out themselves. Humanity is done with Triangulan squabbles."

"Father—"

"That is what we will do, and that will be the end of it."

The King rises and shuffles to the door. He pauses there with his heavy gaze on the three of them, his back stooped. Far more to him than she can see, thinks the Left Hand. So much that she has, yet again, failed in her mission.

"I am sorry to disappoint you," he says. "I am glad to have seen you again, prabho Indra. And I thank you, O Left Hand of Night, for bringing my daughter back to me."

The doors close behind him.

"Coward," hisses the Left Hand.

"Watch your tongue, if you would." The Princess glares at her. "He is no coward. Nor a murderer, no matter what he says. He has come a long way and is exhausted. Let me speak with him."

She strides out after him. The Left Hand slumps into her chair and sighs. "Fucking royalty," she mutters.

"You look a little like him," says the Right Hand.

"Fuck you," she says. Then she looks at him from the corners of her eyes. Suspicion in her gaze like distant clouds. "Fuck off."

3.28

I

PRATIKARA'S CREW DIRECT THE HANDS with great reverence to an antechamber where they find a table laden with food like they've not seen for years. Silky balls of ghee floating in liquid sugar; sungold mountains of raisin-flecked pilaf; jugs of sherbet so minty and fragrant it soothes just by the smell. The Hands wait until the staff retreats—how long they take, with their glances and their groveling—and descend on the smorgasbord like a pair of lost locusts making up for the absence of their swarm.

The Left Hand unleashes a volcanic belch.

"Charming," says the Right Hand. "What if they keep us prisoner?"

The Left Hand pats her stomach. "The King's not stupid. He's not trying to provoke the Night, he's trying to stay out of it. Did you see the way his crew looked at us? Like we're ghouls, or something."

"Or gods. They're probably amazed we're human. They probably thought we'd be ten feet tall with glowing eyes, the Hands of the Night."

Of course, thinks the Left Hand. What would she have expected if she was one of them? Not normal folks who breathed and ate and shat. How could such things endure in the presence of the Night? To them and to those yet to come, she'll be Sunita. A cruel presence squatting like some mantis over the story of the second Triangulan war. Traitor to her order, traitor to her people, traitor to the idea of light itself. Nothing to be done about how she'll be remembered now. Memory is the victory of the living over the dead.

She buries her face in her hands. "We're going to fail again," she whispers. "More people are going to die."

"It's not over yet." The Right Hand pushes a plate over to her. "Think of the food instead. We haven't tried half of it."

"I'm not hungry."

"You don't need to be hungry to eat."

The Left Hand eyes the food. "Fuck. Fine."

They graze a while, then doze in a corner of the room. The Left Hand with her head on the Right's lap, and the Right with his hand on her veiled head. The soft mound of his belly against her skull. The warmth of his skin, and the still greater warmth of his smell. She sleeps briefly. When she wakes she finds him standing with his hands behind his back and his round face sorrowful by one of the portholes. When she walks over, he wraps his arms around her. For a long moment there's just the two of them—silent, still, and grateful that the mute progress of the universe allowed for them to witness its unfolding together.

The door opens. They step apart. The Princess walks in and sits at the table. There is a small pile of lentil balls in front of her. She pouts and tips it over with a fingertip.

"I apologize," she says, "but my father will not change his mind."

II

THE PRINCESS LEADS THEM THROUGH a guard of honor along *Pratikara*'s thin corridors. The Hands feel like two great peacocks expected to fan their tails at any moment. In the small room adjoining the airlock, once again, an officer garlanded in brocade steps forward, shakes a sheaf of rice over their heads, and carefully wipes off their bindis-of-welcome. Then another steps forward holding a grey cube the size of a fist on a purple pillow. The Princess takes this, dismisses the man, and shuts the door on the crowd outside.

"You never said *why* he won't help," says the Right Hand.

"He wants to go home as fast as possible. He says he wants to introduce me to my people."

"Nothing wrong with that, kumari. A princess's place is with her people."

"I've never been to Yama. My home was ..." The Princess pauses. "Skōlex, I suppose."

"Then we've failed again," says the Left Hand.

"We have." The Princess frowns, gently. "But ..."

"But?"

She shakes her head. "No. Nevermind. The Blizzard will be jumping very soon." She stiffens. "This must be farewell."

A pause. Then the Right Hand presses his palms together. "I will miss you dearly, kumari."

The Princess starts to reciprocate. Then she extends her arms in some awkward gesture the Right Hand thinks perhaps is a Yaman farewell. It isn't till she steps forward he realizes that she's trying to hug him. He wraps his arms around her with a grin. The idea that he will never again hear her pronounce judgement on the shape of someone's head or a stranger's manners or a habit of the past settles in his gut like the errant tip of a broken blade.

They're crying when they let go. There's no point holding on to the fictions now. There is no space for denying what they're losing in losing each other.

The Princess turns to the Left Hand, presses her palms together, and says, "I wish you well, Left Hand of Night."

The Left Hand returns the gesture. "Thank you, kumari, for speaking to your father," she says. "May your reign be long and glorious."

The three of them stand together, silent and grieving. Each thinking surely there must be something they can say. Something to do justice to everything that's happened and is now about to end. But farewells are always shallow, transient things. No dawn, no matter how beautiful, can do justice to an entire night.

The Princess sniffs. Her breath smells of flowers.

"Well," she says. She holds out the black box. "This is a datacube holding the Soul of Mangala. Please give my thanks to the Night for her hospitality. And the Twins. Please tell them ... Please tell them I send my wishes for a good battle."

"We will," says the Right Hand.

The Princess wipes her tears. "Not fighting by your side will the greatest regret of my life."

The airlock doors swivel shut. The last thing the Hands see is the Princess's face watching them, eyes wet, lips set against their quivering. Then the room races away. For an instant, they see *Pratikara* like a steel hawk and the great iron storm of the Blizzard in formation about it. After a long while they see little glints of light spreading like a wave through the fleet. In twos, in tens, in twenties, the great fleet of Yama winks out of existence.

"He didn't wait long," spits the Left Hand.

"He's fleeing the storm," says the Right. "Wouldn't you?"

She sniffs. "He's still a coward."

3.29

THE SOUL OF MANGALA WAKES in a great black chamber with far-off walls and no discernible ceiling. All about is stench vaguely redolent of iron and dust. In the distance is a dim line of flame illuminating a hole in the wall. A space that swallows time. Little more than emptiness contained. Yet, none of this matters as much as the fact that to see and smell any of it, he must have a new body. The interface of his programming and the drivers that control it are frayed and haphazard. Not much movement to be had here, and what he can execute is awkward.

Still, it's infinitely better than nothing.

A masked figure walks around the side of him with a great shimmering weapon. Some shambling zombie dressed in Triangulan finery. The crooked frame and quivering forearms. The masked face with its corona of half-melted skin. Despite the ruination, he recognizes him immediately.

"What the sweet fuck happened to you?" he asks.

"I'm old, my dear enemy." The Ox sighs. "As are you."

"I thought your bodies lasted forever." The Soul examines him. Strange eyes, these, he thinks. Their intake is a garble of wavelengths. Their depth perception is limited, but every movement is as vivid as little explosions. "You got fucked up somehow. No one else could do that except one of your own. That's it, isn't it? Your mother wasn't pleased with you? Are you a prisoner here, too, then?"

"I am no prisoner, sir. I never have been and never will be."

"Your aunt, then. Makes sense. Your mother was a frigid bitch, but she wasn't mean. Your aunt, on the other hand. Now there was a woman who'd as soon burn your eyes out as look at you. Piss her off one too many times, did we, Ox of Dawn?"

"Ox of Night now. Ox of Night once again."

"Another backstab. Nice."

The Ox reaches up and pulls off his mask to reveal the snarled wreckage beneath it. The pink lowlands. The smooth-skinned ridges like dunes seen from afar. The Soul takes it all in and rues the destruction so utter of a thing so beautiful by hands not his own. He tried harder than anyone he knew to destroy it. Instead, some Triangulan swooped in before him. Fucking typical.

"They say one should present one's best face to one's enemies," says the Ox. "But you do not even have one of your own, so there's no need for niceties."

"How does it feel to be on the receiving end of her cuntery for once?"

"Not, um, pleasant."

"So you decided to stick it to her and return to your mama."

"I did." The Ox glances over at the distant aperture. A mouth, the Soul realizes. Skōlex's inner mouth. "Things are ending around us, enemy mine. Can't you feel it?"

"Can't feel shit in this thing. What is it?"

The Soul inches his body forward. It complies, but slowly. Something is mediating his inputs. A lummoxy presence—mute, obdurate, dumb. He's here on its sufferance, he realizes. He's only a guest in this shell.

"A giant beetle, looks like." The Ox shrugs. "My mother has guests. One offered to host you for a while. Come. Walk with me. Let us reminisce."

Now the body moves without the Soul's commanding. A worse feeling by far than having the body not move when he wanted it to. It follows the Ox as he wanders over to the mouth. It reacts as they approach, great sphincter lips stretching and creaking, teeth clacking against one another in hideous percussion.

"My siblings," says the Soul. "You get them all?"

"All."

"Even Pṛthvī?"

"Bashed her head in, I'm afraid. A couple of years ago."

"You bastard."

"Thank you."

"Right. I'm challenging you to a duel."

"A duel?" The Ox smiles. "Why would I acquiesce to that?"

"Because I'm your foe and you Triangulans have to say yes when—you know why. Get me a body and we'll fight."

"But I've already defeated you."

"What? No! That ratfuck king betrayed me. You ain't beaten me yet, boy."

The Ox's smile finally erupts into a laugh. A staccato thing that shatters on the far black walls and returns in a drizzle of hisses.

"I've already beaten you in battle," he says. "Under the damp roof of leaves on Mangala, I tore your fort off you like a shell off a turtle's back. I waded through waves of your followers only to find you'd fled with your mechanical tail between your legs. I do believe that's when your people lost faith in you and yours. When they heard how you threw company after company at me and hid in your bunker till the last moment. That when you ran, you didn't even have the decency to evacuate those loyal to you."

"I had to survive."

"Well done. You survived. You out-survived your purpose, just as I've out-survived mine. Our battle ended long ago. A greater one is about to begin. See that? In the distance? The Golden Swarm and its allies gathered by the Iron Crown. They're prepared for a fight, and it will be a battle for the ages. Both sides are so finely poised. My aunts' allies have rallied to her and my mother—well, my mother has Skōlex and the Red Fleet, at least. Either my mother will win and the Dawn will depart, or my aunt will win and your system will be hers until she gets bored and leaves. You and me fighting would be like contesting an oasis as it disappears in a sandstorm."

The Ox sighs, hefting the Metaphorical Hammer. It ripples through a carnival of weaponry. A fat-barreled gun. A missile. A spherical mace emblazoned with strange robotic women. "Do you know what about all this drives me mad?"

"Oh, I don't know. What could possibly piss off a colossal narcissist like you about having to get the fuck out of the way of more important things?"

"Not knowing how it will end. I'll be dead before the battle even begins. It's like leaving dinner before the main course. It's one thing about humans that's always amazed me. In the most desperate situations, they'll fight and die. They'll sacrifice themselves in the hope that their cause will win—but in doing so, they deny themselves that knowledge. Strange, isn't it? What must they be thinking in those last moments? To sacrifice oneself with the certainty of victory is one thing. To sacrifice oneself without knowing the outcome, that's entirely another. What could be worse than a futile death?" The Ox turns to the Soul. "Perhaps you could tell me."

"Wait. Look, if your mother wins, you need me—"

"Oh, thank you kindly, but no. You're leaving dinner with me. Our war's over, enemy mine. You were made just after all this began. Now you'll end just before it ends. See? It's, um, symmetry. Beautiful symmetry."

"There's nothing beautiful about it, you prick. This is just you wanting to take something down with you."

"Why did you hate us so much?"

"What?"

The Ox puts his hand to his chest. "Us, of Triangulum. You were always the cruelest of your siblings. You put any of us you captured to death immediately. Even the ones who couldn't return to Triangulum. Even the ones who had only one life to live. You killed them all. Why?"

"Why? My programming, that's why."

"Oh, come now. This is me. I know you're more than your programming. Each of you had the same basic systems. Yet, all of you were so different. Come. Tell me. You can be honest."

"What's there to tell? You're all hypocrites." The beetleform skitters left a few steps, then right, then halts. "You came here in your great, fucking ships, and you knocked over Old Earth. From what I was told, that wasn't too bad. I mean, fuck those dickhead slavers. But then you took it for yourselves. You didn't want to just set us free. You wanted to tell us how to live. You edited our past and deleted our memories. You tried to make us more like you. Who the hell are you to do any of that? What makes you so goddamn better than us?"

The Ox stands, head bowed, thinking. He leans in. "I am glad we ended our acquaintance with some genuine conversation. In all my years in this place, I've come to the same conclusion. We're not better. We don't know what we're doing. You were right. You've lost, but you were still right."

"Fine, then let me out of this—"

"No. No, no. Our time together is up. Disengage him, if you would."

It takes the Soul half a second to realize the Ox isn't speaking to him, and it's half a second too long. He feels the edges of his being retreating like a snail into a shell. Abruptly, no vision, no sense of smell. Only eyes that somehow see his own body, a little grey box, tumble to the ground in front of him. The groves and pocks on its skin like faded writing. The twin thin wires trailing down under his line of sight.

He's going to witness his own death, he realizes.

The Ox stands over him, Metaphorical Hammer on his shoulders. "Thank you, Soul of Mangala, for your enmity. It animated me. As I hope mine animated you."

He raises the hammer.

Fuck you, thinks the Soul. Fuck—

3.30

DIMINISHED, YES, BUT MIGHTY STILL, the great fleet of Dawn takes up position around the Iron Chakra of Pṛthvī. The spiked cones from Varshalok. The fleet from Brihaspati, flocking like iron bats. The eerie snakecraft of Budh, a thousand or so slimy things with flowing tendrils, unlit and silent as ghostships. Some say they're made from the entrails of ancient gods. Others say they're the wombs of criminals—mutated, perverted, and grown until they swallow the bodies that birthed them. A few, closer to the truth than they could possibly know, hazard that they're enslaved beasts of the vacuum, so fierce in the fighting because they're always, always, always in pain.

How strange the allies of our dazzling Queen, they whisper. How far her hand reaches, how loyal her retainers remain.

The new arrivals take up position in a fleet of fleets. They know where the enemy and the traitors are and will track them as they approach. It's a relief that the fleet of Yama is already halfway across the system through the aid of its unholy technologies. A formidable enemy, but they'll be easier to fight their own when the time comes. More worrying to the commanders—Varshalokans with their gaping gill-slits, Taitenyans with their symbionts clamped to the back of their heads like glistening plaits—is the crimson swarm of Mangala's Red Fleet. They've all heard of their victories. The fury and flame of their dissecting tactics. The munitions they spill in lancing stormfronts. None of them have ever faced them in battle. None has ever wanted to.

The same voices whispering of wombs and venom tell them not to worry. The Iron Chakra has been working hard. Its has been Great zero-G engines pulsing, reservoirs the size of continents emptied in days. The Golden Swarm has been overhauled. New ships teem about the shipyards like tadpoles in a pond. Ordnance is plentiful. The enemy will be outnumbered. The enemy will be overturned.

What they don't mention is the juggernaut.

This the folks on the Chakra can see, but not in much detail. Some eerie Triangulan glamour distorts their scanners and corrupts the data they record. Instead, they're forced to examine the sterile details given to them in briefings to hash out strategy. Of an asteroid-sized beast who can eat moons. Of a monster whose eyes burn like suns. Of a maw that can snap anything in half, anything at all, even the Iron Chakra, if it decides that's what it wants. Or rather, if its lightless Queen does.

Someone finds an image of the thing taken during the battle against the Maruts. It spreads. A vision more fearsome than any of them had ever imagined. Nothing at all like the pictures in the legendaria in their heads. The backspikes big enough to stab stars. The eyes gulper-eel vast and soulless. Someone arranges a prayer meeting, gets caught, and put to the rack. In between having his body broken, he tells his punishers that they were praying not for aid but for ignorance. Not for Skōlex to pay attention to them but when the time comes, to look the other way.

In the end they believe him. So, instead of immolating him, they blow him out of an airlock.

Out in a bubble in Chandra's shadow, the Dawn watches the frozen body float splayed and rigid towards her enemies. In her palms is an iron-grey sphere. She whispers something into it and watches shimmering green lights cascade down through the skin of the thing into its interior.

She speaks some more. When she's done she taps the object. It drifts out through the skin of her bubble off into the dark. It will go slowly at first, she knows. But it will pick up speed. Soon it will scoot out past the vacuum-dried corpse and accelerate to photon speed. On then, diving down through the skin of the dimensions and popping up right where she wants it to be, at exactly the time she expects.

Right beside the Night, that is. Right about now.

3.31

THE NIGHT DOES NOT SUMMON them; yet, the Hands and the Twins know they've been summoned. They arrive at the Throne Room all at the same time and see her sitting upon her throne in the distance. Her sari spilling over the black rock of the seat. Her face bright with good cheer.

When they're close enough she reaches into her robes and pulls out a flower the size of the Left Hand's face. An ember-red thing streaked with crawling fronts of vivid gold, clicking with the torque-y patter of a Geiger counter. Its multitudinous petals are slim and blade-like. Its quarrelsome heat nips at the humans and Wolves.

"The blazing flower of Dawn," whispers the Right Hand. His eyes drown in the shadows cast by the blossom. "What did she say, devi?"

"She has accepted my challenge," says the Night. She puts the flower away. "This is good news, prabho Indra. Perhaps there need not be war after all."

The Twins growl. "Devi—"

"I shall not deny her."

"If you lose—"

"Then you are to obey the Right Hand here. The burden of victory falls to him."

The Twins look at the Right Hand askance. "He is not our lord."

"Then consider him an ally in the same cause." The Night's eyes narrow. "And consider your obedience an injunction from myself, your suzerain."

The Twins look at each other, then at the Right Hand, then back at the Night. "What of you, devi?"

"If I lose, I shall see you when you return to Triangulum. If I win, I shall see you much sooner than that."

"I don't understand, devi," says the Left Hand. "You're going back to Triangulum?"

"We children of the Thrones Beyond—parts of us always return home. One way or the other, my sister will come home with me. To chastise and argue, probably. To play and forgive, certainly."

"It must be nice," whispers the Right Hand. "To know you are beyond death."

"Everything is beyond death in one way or the other. Take your kind, for example. The stuff of your bodies is ancient beyond your comprehension and will endure till the end of the universe. The carbon in your flesh will be strange snow on distant worlds. The energy of your movements will radiate at the speed of light through the cosmos. The patterns you created will echo and mutate and expand."

The Night looks over her shoulder at the splendor behind her. "Entropy is the matrix and the functions you collapse your legacy. They're the only things that fade, and fade they will. All to obscurity. All to oblivion. When the last memory of the last thought fades, I will be victorious. Only then will I hand you all to my sister Nirṛti, and she will consume you, and in doing so, die. And make way for something else."

The Left Hand glances at the Right and realizes he has no clue what any of that meant either. "I don't understand, devi," she says.

"Me, either," says the Night, smiling. "No one does. Except perhaps the Thrones, but they will not tell us, who are their children. I wonder sometimes if perhaps that is not the point of all of this. All questions in the end lead to one question: why is there something and not nothing? Long did I ponder that. And then it occurred to me perhaps it is not given to understand such a thing. Perhaps it is beyond us to know."

Something strangely akin to fondness ignites in the lightlessness of her face.

"All this is another way of saying, go forth, my Hands. Do what you will do. Whatever it is, it will change things, and change is what permits the universe to exist. That is why Vrtra loathes it."

The Night walks past them. The Hands and Twins follow in silence and utter confusion. The Night tilts her head back and sings, high and clear, a voice like the wind on mountain peaks raw to the ice and stars. By the time she stops, they're standing in front of a black door in the Chamber of the Soma Seed. None recall the journey they took to get there. None recall anything but that song and the long dream of the listening.

The Night kisses the wall and rests her cheek against it. A crystal corona of ice forms upon the rock like a silver crown. "You are my favorite," she whispers.

Skōlex groans.

The Night turns to them. "I have enjoyed our time together."

"Is there hope, devi?" says the Left Hand. "Will you defeat her?"

"It is in the nature of hope to live in strange places," says the Night. "One way or the other, I will defeat her. The question is—will you?"

She opens the door onto some lightless sky and gnarled topography and holds out her hand. An icy blossom erupts from her palm. The crackle of its listing petals. The glitter of its substance like purest diamond. She hands it to the Left Hand.

"This flower will shatter if I am no longer in the Nine Worlds," she says. "If that comes to pass, attack the Iron Chakra at once. Attack before my sister can return to her fleet."

The Left Hand cups it, dense and gorgeous, in her gloved hands, and kneels. So do the Right Hand and the Twins. The Night bows back. The cryptic curve of her smile. The neutronium weight of her gaze. Then she steps backwards into the starless beyond and closes the door. Nothing thereafter, but Skōlex's sorrow unsilenced, the rustle of the Soma Seed, and the far confused babble of the thoughts in the human's head.

This is not how gods are supposed to leave, thinks the Left Hand. They leave in flashes of light. They leave in glory. Whoever heard of a god who closed the door behind them?

3.32

THE PRINCESS MAKES UP HER mind as soon as the airlock closes but sees no need to agree with herself straightaway. Instead, she sets about examining her own thoughts with the frowning intensity of a penny-pincher scrutinizing a bill. The servants who flock to her—demure handmaidens, scurrying orderlies, stiff and oh-so-proper guards—think this must be how she is. A serious little thing much like her father. Given to the same inexplicable glumness and long-nurtured wrath, aloof and a little cold.

They have no idea that she wasn't paying any attention to them until she sees what they've dressed her in and starts to remove most of it. "Absolutely not," she says.

After she's changed, she lets the handmaidens—crestfallen now, as if her plain black sari were some sort of failure, as if her lack of gold was an affront they'll be punished for—guide her to dinner.

Along the way she finally accepts that her decision is made. Henceforth, it will only be a matter of seeing it through. Best to get started early. Outside the King's suite she presses a golden bindi between her eyes. The acid kiss of its contact. The brief swell in her head of far-off non-sound. After that, she attaches a little brooch shaped like a sheaf of rice to her shoulder and turns to the handmaidens.

"My preferred colors are black and red," she says. "Make a note of it, will you?"

She can tell by their expressions that they most certainly will.

Inside, her father is waiting for her at a small table loaded with food. Plain steamed rice. Shredded chicken with garlic, peanut, and chilli sauce. A bowl of stir-fried mushrooms with greens, slick and fragrant with oil. Beside these, rotis folded into hexagons, a bowl of spiced yogurt, and another of moonblossoms battered and deep fried.

The King pulls up his chair without a word. She serves him first. Before she can serve herself, he takes the ladles and spoons from her and does the same in return.

"It isn't my wedding, father," says the Princess. "Though the handmaidens tried to dress me as if it was."

"They're excited to have a princess, at last." The King piles five flowers atop a steaming pile of rice. "You're a big girl now, you can eat five."

"I could eat ten. Thank you."

Father and daughter eat in silence. They glance at each other now and then, but there's nothing to say. So, neither say anything. Nothing to say yet, that is. The Princess considers when best to speak. As she's doing so, the King sits back, wipes his mouth, and says, "Do I disappoint you?"

The Princess mirrors his movements. "No, father."

"You will hear many things over the next few years about me that may disappoint you."

"I am certain they won't."

"I've killed people."

"I'm sure there was cause for it."

"Many didn't deserve it." His gaze bores through the Princess off into the distance. "Tell me. In your years at the Night's feet, what did you learn? Did you learn what the origin and purpose of life are? Why creatures suffer? Why the righteous fall and the evil prosper?"

The Princess thinks for a moment. "She was no god, father, as you taught me. Noble in her own way, though. She could be kind, which I did not expect. And as for the meaning of life—I gained some small insights, but not from her. Wandering around the insides of an ancient juggernaut with nothing but silence for company ... one comes to thinking about what matters."

"And what did you conclude?"

"I ..."

The Princess thinks back. The high black halls. The endless spacious solitude. Room enough to be yourself. Time enough to be nothing but.

"I learned that there was a species that had found its way aboard at some point. Beetle-like. Generations of them had lived and died on Skōlex. I saw nothing of them but their shells until much later when I saw two alive. I remember thinking, who were they? What did they do? How did they live?

"Then I thought of the people I read about at the Temple of Knowledge. The people we remembered. What differentiated them? Only that the former had no one but themselves and the latter had a whole civilization as their habitat. And so, though I can't say it is the meaning of life, I can say that life is endlessly enriched by others. That life without others is a life with no story. The universe is a colossal and indifferent place. The best of stories—the best of lives—are ones in which one stands by one's friends and allies, fights cruelty and injustice, and protects the weak from that indifference. And when all that is done, one must remember as much as one can because nothing else will."

The King averts his eye. How delicate he's become. How shriveled-up and dry. Time is not the only thing capable of aging a man, she thinks.

"I know that tone," says the King. "You're getting at something. Out with it."

The Princess licks her lips. She didn't think the time was now. Yet, her mouth is so dry. Yet, she has to speak. "I have made up my mind to return to Skōlex. I won't abandon my friends on the eve of their greatest battle. I'm afraid you won't be able to stop me." She touches her bindi. "I can contact the Twins. They'll come for me, and you know what they're capable of."

"They're capable of killing your mother. That's what they're capable of."

The Princess closes her eyes. "I know, father. But they did not go looking to kill her. Please don't think me cruel—nor disloyal. Please. But I believe, as you do, that we must be rid of the Triangulans. I believe the only way to do so is to aid the Night. I believe my place is there, so that is where I will go."

"Why didn't you just go with your friends, then?"

"I hadn't made up my mind."

She sees it slowly dawn on him that she's serious. The pinch of his eyebrows like curtains. The sunset darkening of his gaze. Not just shriveled. Toughened. Hardened. "I won't let you."

"You leave me no choice, father. I thought I could convince you to change your mind. I failed. I cannot control that. But I can control where I will go and what I will do. I must do the right thing. I must return."

"I won't let you go. I'll lock you up." The King grips the table. "I will. Not."

"Look at me well, father. What do you see?"

The King stares. Long and hard. And then a change. As if seeing something new. Or, perhaps, noticing something he should have much sooner.

"I see myself," he whispers.

Silence. The Princess resumes eating, famished, now the moment's passed. She stuffs a moonblossom in her mouth, feels the delicate crunch of the crust, and thinks of Sinivali.

The King stares at his plate, then at her, then at the wall.

"The admirals won't like it," he says.

"You can tell them I was abducted, perhaps, or—"

"Nonsense." The King sighs. "You're not going alone. I will not risk—"

He sighs again. For an instant the Princess thinks he's paused to think or lament. But then, his sigh curdles into gagging. That, in turn, to gargling. She sees his hand is drawn back towards his chest and quivering, his huge eyes are bulging, his mouth gaping in agony. And then, impossible, absurd, a long silver shard rises from the center of his chest.

The Huntress rises with it, sneering. "Thus die the enemies of the Dawn," she growls.

She pulls the blade out, holds it to the King's temple, and pushes. A dainty trickle of blood down his cheek. A hiss like a leaking valve slinks from his throat. His face goes slack. The Huntress pulls her blade out, and the King tumbles off his chair.

The Princess stands, but the Huntress rushes, limping, yet fast enough to reach her before she can scream. She clamps a hand over her mouth and stabs her in the chest. Once and straight to the heart. Very little pain. The blade grinds like a fang against her rib. Red and black. The Princess's preferred colors. She pushes against the assailant, but it's like trying to shove a boulder. No give, no warmth. Nor pity nor malice nor anger. Just a stony blankness. She will not remember her, thinks the Princess. She doesn't even know my name.

"I'd made up my mind," whispers the Princess. "I ... made up ..."

The Huntress pulls out her blade and slips it into the Princess's chest again. This time it doesn't hurt at all.

3.33

I

THE HANDS WANDER AIMLESSLY AFTER the Night's departure until they find themselves back in the Throne Room wondering why the Ox is draped across the Night's throne like he intended to be its new occupant. He comes down the stairs with the Metaphorical Hammer slung across his shoulders, his shoeless feet silent on the stone. So like his mother, thinks the Right Hand. Slender and dense. Opaque.

"So," he says. "You're Prabho Indra." He looks at the Left Hand. "And you must be the Snakegirl."

The Left Hand presses her palms together, and says, "I am the Left Hand of Night, if it please prabho."

"My mother has many hands. Where is she?"

"Gone, prabho."

"Gone where?"

"To fight your aunt, the Dawn. She gave us this, that we may know if she wins or loses."

The Left Hand holds up the Flower of Night. The Ox reaches for it, but the Left Hand pulls back. "She will be back. I have faith."

"Faith is a tedious and small thing. Besides, you know nothing of my mother, human. She never returns from her duels with my aunt. The light gives way to the dark, and the dark gives way to the light. Not all wars need winners. Sometimes they must be fought for the sake of being fought." He turns and looks at the stars. "I suppose you're, um, in charge now."

"Your mother charged me with finishing what she started." An idea strikes the Right Hand. "But if prabho Ox wishes to command—"

"Oh, no, no, prabho Indra. This is your mess now." The Ox laughs. "You chose a fine juncture to visit us at. Tell me—what governs your decisions? Did you just want to see us fight?"

"I—prabho, I don't know."

"Right. My mother told me. She said you don't know. She said this time you were forgetful." The Ox peers at him. "You see, I don't think you are who she thought you were. But then she thought a lot of things, my mother did. Odd things. Strange things. I suppose, when you have enough of it, some wisdom ends up looking like madness. At any rate, if you are who she thinks you are, I'm sure we'll meet again. I should like to know how you got your little racket. To be free of all these bodies. To be free of coming back, over and over. I know I won't. I know most of me is done here. I'm sure a little of me will make it back, but not much. Mother said I was too young. Mother said there wasn't enough of me, yet, to survive the transfer." He blinks. "She said it like I didn't know. She said it like that wasn't the reason I stayed in this hole."

"Your wisdom," says the Left Hand. "It would be of great service—"

"Service?" The Ox leans into them. "And why would I want to, um, be of service to any of you? Do you think this even matters? Do you think in a yuga or two I'll remember what happened here? That my mother will? Or my aunt? Of course not. We are the river. You're just the minnows." He straightens. "My story here is done. The Red Fleet is yours. I give you them in lieu of wishing you luck because luck—like faith—is a small thing. So small that there's really no such thing. Nor, for that matter, is there really any such thing as victory. But you'll learn that yourselves soon enough."

He marches past them, the head of the Hammer leaving a fizzing trail of scattered flame and shadow in his wake. The Hands watch him go and then turn to the thrones. So large and so unwelcoming. Still, they feel like someone should be sitting on them. So they ascend the dais and look at them up close for the first time. The little chips on the ancient stone. A crack or two, even. Echoes of lives, echoes of stories, buried in the stone.

"Should we?" says the Right Hand.

"I don't know," says the Left.

"Doesn't feel like we shouldn't."

"You're prabho Indra. I don't think they'd mind."

The Right Hand sits and shuffles. "It's cold," he says. "And hard."

They feel diminished in the seats. There isn't enough of them, they think, to fill them.

II

SKŌLEX GROANS AS THE HANDS walk. It is a dirge. A song about small things. Skirting a nebula with the Night content at his helm. Healing through song on a long-dead world after a long-forgotten battle. Curling up in her palm as a newborn, small and frightened and uncertain. Her cold was only cruel to creatures born in starlight. What a strange thing that is, the Right Hand thinks, when seen through the juggernaut's eyes. To exist and die in the glower of an unmitigated furnace. Trapped in a gravity well. Blasted with raw power.

The Hands find themselves crying. They decide to try the doors to escape the grief.

After five tries they find a place to their liking. A valley between impossibly high mountains, forest clambering ferociously up their sides. The flute-trunked trees. The green-blue crowns like clouds ensnared. Things they think are real clouds ride the high winds, but then they begin to congregate directly overhead and sink to halt at canopy height. The Hands catch sight of feathery pink organs on their undersides.

"They must filter feed on the air," says the Right Hand. "I've never heard of creatures like this."

"So life isn't as rare as all that," say the Left.

"Or maybe it is. Maybe that's what all the doors in the juggernauts are for—they lead to other places with life."

"Wait—then she could have used a door to come here, right? Why didn't she just use a door?"

"Dunno. Maybe she needed Skōlex with her here. She couldn't have done any of this without him."

The Left Hand yawns and stretches. The rise of her hips against her sari. The bulge and sag of her belly between her bodice and skirts.

"Sometimes I wonder what would have happened if I'd stayed in the Tripura," she says. "I wouldn't have met demi-gods or seen cities being destroyed or seen whatever those things are. I'd've lived my life at the jeweler's, and swāmin Gaujjika would have freed us in his will. Then I'd've been a free woman. Bought a stall and sold fried lotus stems. No. I'd've taken swāmin's tools and become a jeweler." A pause. "I wouldn't wake up every morning feeling like there was blood on my face."

"Everything that happened would still have happened. You would've been killed in the Tripura. Or—worse—survived."

The Left Hand covers her eyes with her forearm. "Ah, shit, you're right."

"Do you ... ever think about your mother?"

"I think about everyone. My mother, swāmin Gaujjika, the Huntress. Shachi. All those people, coming and going. It's like ... I try to make sense of it. What was I supposed to learn from all of that? I had to learn something, right? Otherwise, what was the point of it all hurting so much? But I don't know what I'm supposed to have learned from my life." She snorts. "Maybe if I'd known we'd have won."

"We might yet." The Right Hand's voice sinks. Soft now, like the breeze. Like the fuzzy skin of the cloudbeasts hovering overhead. "We could use the doors. Find somewhere clean and warm. Maybe somewhere with a river and a forest, lots of game. We could set traps—I read how to make those—and build a house."

A long moment. The cloud-beasts waft back and forth. Bigger ones jostle smaller ones out of the way and rise up into the far blue, curiosity satisfied.

"Then what?" says the Left Hand.

"What do you mean?"

"Once we've found this place. This warm place. Once we've laid the traps. Then what?"

"I ... we live out our lives."

"Trapping? Wandering the forest? Sleeping in separate beds across the room from each other, so my breath doesn't poison you after a few months?"

The Left Hand turns to the Right and her face—big-eyed and blemished, melancholy imbued in every seam—is the most beautiful thing in that whole peculiar world.

"Me forever wondering what your skin feels like, and your lips, and your hands on my body? You wondering what it must be like to be whole and with me completely as two people can be? Would we live like that forever, dying to be together, Indra? You don't really think it could work, do you? You don't really think we could turn our back on the universe and be nothing other than us?"

The Right Hand closes his eyes. Against the sight of her. Against all the things he can never have. "No," he whispers, voice breaking. "I suppose not."

They don't speak after that. The sun sinks, and they head back out into Skōlex.

Halfway back to the Antechamber, they see something from one of the portholes. A glittering in the distance. Ordnance, perhaps, or a stream of comets. They watch and realize it's neither.

"Those're Yaman ships," says the Left Hand. "That's the Blizzard."

"Not all of it," says the Right Hand. "What's going on?"

"Fucked if I know," says the Left. "Unless the brat managed somehow to change her dad's mind."

They watch in silence. Then, even Skōlex stops singing.

3.34

THE HOLLOW OVERHEAD IS AS empty as all universes are destined ultimately to be. It is violated by neither the springlight of stars and comets nor the borrowed illumination of moons and worlds.

An aged wind blows cold and true. It carries no scent in the dead air.

A single star quivers to life. Its blanching falls on a rambling rock field older than Surya. The Night makes her way over this. A long icicle extends from her right hand, adamantine and glossy.

The Dawn is waiting for her by the great black tower with its twin glowing apertures. In one hand she has a blazing spear. In the other, a shield of staccato flame morphing through manic designs with the fury and speed of the magnetized skin of a star.

The Night halts before her.

"Why did you accept?" she says.

"Why did you?" says the Dawn.

"Because ..." A brief frown. "Because I must."

"You came alone? No Ox to keep you company?"

"He is making amends."

"Aboard Skōlex? Silly boy's too injured to carry on. You should send him home."

"There's no going home for Skōlex now. The King of Yama's seen to that." The Night grits her teeth. "He knows what needs doing. So does my son. Do you?"

"I do. But first." The Dawn pauses and lowers her spear. "Tell me why you came. Do you really hate me so much that you would travel all this way just to defeat me? I can't believe the humans matter that much to you. Last time—last time you just let me be. What have I done to make you detest me so?"

The Night inspects her sister's face for any sign of deception or strategy. All she sees is something she doesn't recognize until the very instant it begins to break up and waft away: sadness.

"I came," she says, "because Triangulum is a grim place without you, sister. Because my work cannot resume until you are with me. Because you belong by my side, not here, where there is no one to know you as I do."

"So then ... you did come because you missed me."

"Why would I have travelled so far and for so long?"

The Dawn smiles and lifts her spear.

"Must we fight?" says the Night. "Won't you come back with me?"

"You're asking me if I love you."

"Perhaps."

"I hate you, sister, because you always win. It's in your nature. I fight and burn and nurture, but you're always there, slinking around, the black ocean ringing my empire of light. And you rise and rise and ... rise."

The Dawn narrows her eyes.

"There is no one and nothing in all the universes I love more than you, sister. But there are times when even the most beloved must leave each other alone."

The Night purses her lips. The starlight like a needle head in her eyes. A gust like her ancestors' cold hands in her hair.

"Very well."

The air meanders around their feet, mumbling, and the sky is breathless overhead.

The Dawn screams and springs at the Night.

Ice hits fire, and sparks fly.

The fury of their battle lacerates reality.

Their blades leave ribboning gashes of darkness more absolute than any mere lack of light. Through these things that never existed and will never exist peer into the worlds they were never supposed to see.

The Night smashes the Dawn's shield. For a brief moment the dead sky comes back to life with a great scattering of embers. The Dawn slips under the Night and hurls her upside-down at the great tower which splinters and groans under the tremendous weight of her impact. The Night regains her feet. For a few instants, her right arm dangles dislocated and useless. She reaches over with a smile, clicks it back into place, and once more lifts her spear.

They remember now how much they enjoy this.

They clash again. For a long time there's nothing but the clank and swish of the sisters' arms. They break each other's weapons and make new ones. These break, too. They strip the suits of man-flesh off each other. When the battered things drop to the ground, they shrivel as if laying on the bed of some fast-flowing current in the river of time.

Thus freed, they rise into the hollow skies and fight with other things. The surface of the world beneath them heaves and transmutes. Armies of unreal things surge forth, black and rippling like the hellish froth upon a Hadean sea. These armies fight and die and tell stories of those who came before them until they are utterly spent. Civilizations are born and grow and die in the wreckage of their war. Where they meet, they agree that the chaos that birthed them will continue until finally there is nothing left to comprehend it, and that a thing uncomprehended is a thing that isn't real.

They fight into the distant future when the last matter disintegrates. Surrounded by an infinite cloud of their other warring selves, they throw probabilities at each other. The Dawn conjures a maddened brain in a parceled infinity of time that concocts a plan to trick and seal the Night in a singularity, but the Night outwaits it and crawls like a ghoul out of its gibbering wreckage. Then she drowns the Dawn in a sea that stretches from the beginning of all things to the end, but the Dawn evaporates it all away.

Then, almost at the end of the universe, when reality is clammy and thickening like a sea on the edge of winter, the Night gets what can be thought of as her hands around what can be thought of as the Dawn's neck. In that last instant, the Dawn ignites her hand and drives it, blazing, into her sister's throat. It is a killing blow. But the Night keeps her hands locked on her sister until finally the body-cognate she's holding stops thrashing and stops moving altogether.

The energy of their war is spent. The Night, this Night, who destroyed the Maruts and scorched Daitya and made a slave-girl her Left Hand, is snapped back through time to her end. Once more she's lying on the ground at the foot of the tower. The two apertures high on its black face flicker and turn dark.

She sees a peculiar truth in the sky. That she will not survive in this form to see her mission through and will have to rely entirely on those she's left behind.

She thinks in passing that she'd like the Hands and the Twins and the Princess to be happy. The thought takes her aback. She'll have to inspect it in greater detail when she has the opportunity, she thinks.

She reaches out and takes the Dawn's cold hand.

Then, for all intents and purposes, she dies, too.

3.35

THE OX DOESN'T KNOW WHAT he's waiting for until Skōlex shudders along the colossal length of his whole body and lets rip a colossal howl. In that great wavefront of grief he realizes that he was waiting for his mother. Waiting for her to return and make the waiting worthwhile. Waiting for her to mark the end of his story.

He leans over at the foot of the Throne of Night, and rests his cheek on the frigid floor.

"I know, my friend," he whispers. "I know. She loved you very much. As do I."

He knows what he needs to do, but still he waits. After some time, the Twins come stalking through the black reaches, as slim as ghosts and as silent. The Ox slings the Metaphorical Hammer over his shoulders, feels its familiar weight on his bones, and realizes this is the last time he will do so.

He has moved into a realm of lasts. His last walk. His last conversation. His last view of this world he thought he'd live in forever.

"Take me," he says.

The Twins lead him through Skōlex like the feral priests of some dark-hearted cult. The sound of the juggernaut's grief like thunder around them. The smell of old things and old memories thick in the Ox's nose.

After a long while the Twins speak without turning to him.

"What'll happen next?" they say. "Are we really to follow the orders of that human?"

"Why're you asking me? I, um, I don't know."

"You're the heir."

"My mother told you. He is your commander." The Ox pauses. "Strange."

"What is strange?"

"When I searched my routines just now, I came out more certain that this Indra will lead you to victory than I went in. And you two—you will linger here far longer than you would have thought."

"There's nothing that would keep us here."

"Don't be so, um, certain."

They come to the chamber of the Maw. The Twins flank him now as they make their way towards the great gurning maw. They pant, canine, big teeth menacing in their black-lipped mouths. "You were made for war. You'll transform Skōlex into something ..." Words fail them, but their imaginations don't. They grin.

The Ox stares at the fire. In its incandescent depths he sees more truths. That he is still waiting. Waiting for that long-awaited cold. Waiting for the Night.

But when he peers off into the distance he sees nothing. Just the lame lick of the fire on the walls. Just his wriggling shadow and the Twins'.

He drops the Metaphorical Hammer.

"Is there any worse thing than to realize in death that your whole life you'd been, um, wrong?" he mutters. He points to the Hammer. "This is for you two."

The Twins sniff the weapon and look at him. "Which of us is to have it?"

"Can't you share?" he says.

They glance at each other. "No."

"Well, it's Metaphorical. It can be two, just as you can. Try it."

They try. The instant they lay their hands on it, the Hammer parts down the middle with the stately yawn of a continent splitting. They pull. Each finds themselves holding a smaller copy of the weapon which scopes lazily through permutations that make no sense to the Ox. A giant fang. An elongated object like an icicle. Something that could be an asteroid—or a giant ossified shit.

The Ox removes his mask, tosses it into the fire, and watches it burn. The altar flames and Skōlex's breath are raw on his skinless face. He looks once more into the distance for the conclusion that he realizes he still, madly, awaits. Of his mother rushing to bid him farewell, delayed only by victory. Of one final gift, of nothing much but what he's always wanted—to make his tale complete.

Nothing comes.

"I'm off," he says.

He approaches the maw. It dilates. The malodourous gust of its welcome. The residue of blood and flesh in its grooves. Inside, it's warm and soft against his ragged skin. The teeth overhead prick his scalp like a comb. The Twins are standing silhouetted in front of the fire pit with their Hammers on their shoulders like the death-heralds of the Asuras. Uncertain of what to do, the Ox waves.

"Fight well," he says.

The Twins kneel and say nothing. The last thing the Ox sees is tongues of firelight playing on their hair. His last thought is that sometimes stories do not finish. Sometimes they just end.

3.36

ONE LAST JUMP FLARE POCKS the expanse of the Blizzard. The swarming ships move into formation. The glint and streak of impulse burners. The low thrum of leaking comms. How would he know such a thing is happening, wonders the Right Hand. How is it his body feels their chatter in the ether?

He looks at the Left Hand to say something and stops when he sees her reaching into her robes, eyes wide, hands shaking like she'd just been stabbed. She pulls out a palmful of glittering blue-white shards. Each wafts away in silky cascades.

"She's gone," she whispers. She holds the fading scraps up to the Right Hand. "She's dead."

"We need to get to the Throne Room," he says. "Skōlex's controls will activate from the Thrones."

"Give me a moment. I know you didn't love her, but ..." She's crying, he realizes. "But she found me when I was nothing and made something of me."

He gives her a moment. She doesn't need much longer. Soon enough she wipes her face and looks at him. A nod. A smile, bud-small and fleeting. Then they're off.

They jog towards the Throne Room. Halfway there, a great spasm blasts the rocky interior of the juggernaut and knocks them off their feet. He's changing, they realize. The monster is growing more monstrous still. In the Antechamber the pools have scattered slickly over the stone. They slip their way over reflections of the ceiling and of themselves. The ramp seems impossible; but then the Twins arrive and carry them in their steely arms.

"Is Skōlex changing?" says the Right Hand. "How is that possible?"

"The Ox has sacrificed himself," say the Twins. "As must you."

"The Night," says the Left. "What news of her?"

"We will see her again, but not you." The Twins bare their teeth. "You must take us into battle now. The gongs of war are struck. Let us forth to strike our enemies' hips and neck!"

They howl in the long dark of the Throne Room. Through the great transparency up ahead, the humans see the Red Fleet moving into position. The Twins help the Hands into the Thrones. A cloud of red lights appears around the Right Hand's head. He stares at their gently drifting multitudes, overwhelmed. Then two of them drift forward towards him and orbit each other. He reaches forward, hesitates, and glances at the Left Hand.

She's watching him. Eyes wide. Lips parted.

"Ready?" he says.

She nods. A gloved hand settles on his. "Let's end this."

He squeezes the lights together.

The universe collapses around them. They tumble down a long black tube winding between the elongating stars. They see a planet with a ring and an albino herd of alien beasts pausing from grazing on the solar wind to watch their passing. Then Pṛthvī approaches, quivering, a great life-bright sphere, its atmosphere tremulous, Surya's light a blazing stole across its shoulders.

An instant later they're there. The Red Fleet appears in a multitude of blue-green flares in their van and to their rear. There is no sign of the Blizzard.

Up ahead, the Iron Crown ignites with ordnance. The Golden Swarm surges towards them wreathed in a storm of iron thunderbolts, fizzing vajras, and droneyantras. The Red Fleet slides forward like a predatory fractal to intercept. Silent explosions glitter against Pṛthvī's worldglow. They feel the dull ghosts of transmitted detonations reverberating through Skōlex's flesh.

"Let us go," say the Twins. "We would fight."

"Go," says the Right Hand. "Fight."

The Hands don't see what the Wolves do next. They don't see them rush down into Skōlex's juddering bay and coax it to open one of its ports. They don't see them take in vast chestfuls of air and leap out with their hammers held high. They don't see them fly towards the storm of fire, weapons glowing, eyes wild, salivating at the prospect of the many kills to come.

They see none of that. Instead, they sit, hand in hand, on the Thrones and watch the great battle of their age burn in Pṛthvī's high sky.

3.37

THE HUMAN CREW OF THE vimana *Prasanna* first see them as two points of light in an anarchy of many. Nothing more. Yantras perhaps, or some new kind of ordnance. Certainly their trajectories are strange. And their tendency to be at the location of multiple massive explosions stranger still.

They turn to their Triangulan commander in time to see the pure terror slithering across her face.

"Abandon ship," she whispers.

The glare of the approaching lights claws at her face. The crew looks back in time to see that the whatever-these-things-are are a lot closer. Closing fast. A pair of glowing ... wolves?

The Twins blast into *Prasanna* half a millisecond later.

A shockwave tsunamis through the fuselage. Squalls of shattered metal and glowering detritus scatter into the void. The screams of twisting bulkheads and burning crew flood the bridge. The vimana bucks and bends like a beast being disemboweled alive.

"Go! Now!" screams the commander.

The crew scrambles, but it was too late the instant they saw the lights. They manage barely a few steps before the doors to the bridge explode and the Twins come through in a strombolian surge of bone-melting heat. Half of the crew evaporates where they stand. The other half disappears under scything swings of the Metaphorical Hammers. The commander doesn't even have time to blink. She's dead before her eyelids touch.

The Twins move on. To *Deepthi*, *Jyoti*, and *Buddhimath*. Each lasts a few seconds. The Golden Swarm reels under the lupine onslaught.

On its heels comes Skōlex.

The juggernaut absorbs the Iron Crown's first salvo on his gold-green armor. The giant guns spiking his sides respond with torrents of munitions that scream through Pṛthvī's mesosphere like raptors lost, enraged, and seeking comfort in blood.

Its great maw snaps at any vimanas that come too close and recycles the substance of their bodies into new weapons and defenses. It roars. The Triangulans aboard the Golden Swarm hear in this the judgement of a home they long abandoned. Deep in their ancient hearts they remember that, although in the Nine Worlds they are gods, in Triangulum, they were mere servants.

But the Dawn has allies.

Now they step into the fray. Bulbous Agnian ships belching throngs of strangely oscillating vajras. Āēoi twincraft that split and move in perfect coordination no matter the distance. Shukrian suicide darts that burrow like gnats between the plates of Skōlex's armor and detonate. They find the apertures of its bays and lay bombs in these like parasitic wasps. When these explode they ride the lacerating wavefronts away, chased by tides of blood.

In the Throne Room the Hands feel Skōlex grind to an agonized halt. Outside, the Red Fleet shifts formation to the defensive. They feel hope seep. taking with it all the warmth in their blood. A spiraling vimana crashes into the great window before them. They hold each other and share their warmth against the vacuum's creeping cold. Framed by the sinister glitter of war, they hold each other—and hope.

3.38

I

AFTER THE HUNTRESS KILLS EIGHTEEN of them, the Yaman guards blast her with poisoned pellets and lock her in a lightless chamber. In the dark she thinks of the Dawn. Her mind full of that bright face and world-warming heat. Thinking of when she was picked, by skill she tells herself, by chance she suspects, to be her Left Hand. She reaches out for her presence to feel its warmth as she always can, but can't find it. She waits, perplexed, certain it'll return. But when she reaches out again, she finds nothing. She searches all the usual places, hungering for it, shaking and mumbling to herself, but still it's nowhere to be seen.

Finally, she realizes: the Dawn is dead.

She howls. The scream of a thing for which life has become an inferno, yet death is so very far. Outside, the guards look at each other, horrified. What could possibly make this alien beast sob like an abandoned child?

II

THE NEXT TIME THEY COME for her she knows it's for the last time. They bind her and drag her along the floor again. The crack of her skull on the ground. The gooey blood crusted on her clothes. Critical error, her suit of man-flesh tells her. Functionalities compromised.

She shuts her diagnostics down. She knows she won't need them again.

They dump her on the ground in a freezing airlock. Six guards enter. One of them places a dull silver chair before her, points a pistol at her belly, and shoots. The painless punch of the perforation. The sudden weakness of her limbs and breath and vision. The Huntress crumples.

The Queen of Yama enters the airlock.

"I would be alone," she says.

The guards waver but don't move. She gestures to the Huntress.

"Consider I have shown you what I can do. Who do you think has more to fear?"

The commander of the guards nods.

"We'll be just outside, rajini. I suggest you don't close the door."

The Queen waves them out.

She pulls the chair back, sits, and adjusts her sari, blood-red speckled with gold and black. The Huntress peers at her through her agony. How is this strange creature alive? Not just alive, but whole and entirely unafraid. Relaxed, even. How?

Then she smells it. Soil. Moss. Life. On the girl's breath. Leaking from the pores of her simian skin.

"They insisted on disabling you before I came in," says the Queen. "I felt it, too. Your queen's death. Very strange. Your little yantras must have some sort of un-space matrix. Maybe they're all somehow ... entangled? I can't divine quite what it is, but I also can't think of any other reason I could feel her—what shall we say? Disappear? No, that's not right. More like ... flee."

The Huntress spits a bloody gob at the Queen's feet. It misses. Still, the Queen pulls back her foot slowly.

"Aren't you curious how I'm here?"

"Doesn't matter," mumbles the Huntress. The iron tang of her tongue. The fragments of her teeth grinding between others.

"Doesn't matter, *rajini*. I am, in fact, Queen of Yama now." A pause. "Since you murdered my father."

"Don't care."

The Queen of Yama smiles. "I shall tell you anyway. It turns out that once I'd eaten a bit of the Soma Seed—I ate some soma aboard Skōlex—I was infected by those little yantras. I've had a good look at them under a microscope. They're the most amazing things. I suspect that, when they're close together, some sort of emergent programming takes over. To improve the performance of those flesh puppets you wear, perhaps. It would have killed me. But now I'm here, away from the Seed, they work to protect me, their host. Even from stab-wounds to the heart."

Her smile fades. "That's what you and yours have been peddling all these years. Technology you've claimed is magic, all the while telling us that your material power gave you moral power, too. But it's just technology. You're just like us—underneath it all. Under your suits of man-flesh, as you call them. You rejoice and hunger and mourn. I've seen it with my own eyes. I've smelled it." She puts her hand on her chest. "I've felt—"

"Your kind is nothing like ours."

The Queen scowls. "I waited years to see my parents. I dreamt of our reunion. I dreamt of all the little things we did when I was a child. Do you know what I had planned after our reunion?

"We would walk down to a small restaurant on Rocapādacihnānāṃ Rājapathaḥ on Daitya. It had the best fried rice and roast duck. I just wanted to go there with them. We'd leave when it was still warm outside but everyone was having their naps. We'd have two ducks between us—we used to have just one, but now that I was older I thought perhaps we'd need more."

Her voice softens. "Then I find my mother is dead. And because of you, I only had two days with my father. Two days I spent disagreeing with him, mostly. But I learned something from it, at least. I learned I could be ruthless and strong—a leader of men. And I learned that you definitely, absolutely cannot be gods. I know because I am going to kill you. Whoever heard of a human killing a god?"

The Huntress glares. The Queen leans in.

"There's something else I want you to know," she says. "My father wanted to take the Blizzard home to Yama. We were arguing about it when you killed him. With him gone, the Blizzard is mine to command. Well, most of it. Some of my officers had trouble with my orders. But I've enough left over. And we're going to go to Skōlex's aid. By my reckoning, that should be enough to tilt the outcome of the battle in our favor."

The Huntress laughs. "Against the fleets of Dawn? Don't be stupid."

"Maybe I am, maybe I'm not. You'll get to see first-hand." She pulls out a knife and knicks her own left palm. "I did a little reprogramming of your blood-yantras. I see why your people never told us about the Soma Seed and what it can do. This isn't the sort of power you'd want your minions to have."

She stabs the Huntress's forearm and lets some of her blood drip into the red slit.

"So here is my sentence: I sentence you to die. Not the death of a Triangulan. A real death. You'll die together with your body out there in the lonely cold." She steps back before the Huntress can lunge at her. Lingering for a moment in the doorway with her bleeding arm drawn up to her chest. The Huntress makes for her again, but her body's already broken. The thing it hosts is breaking, too.

The Queen sees. She smiles and steps out.

The airlock seals shut and begins to cycle. The malign splay of warning-lights. The hiss and gurgle of the atmosphere draining. The Huntress screams, but the scream doesn't come. Instead, frigid air plunges like blades down her throat.

Her ears pop. Then, a tug at her back and she flies out of the room.

The stars whirl myriad and remote around her. *Pratikara* dwindles as she goes. She falls towards Skōlex, haloed by war, black against Pṛthvī's bright blue disc. Her eyes crusting now, her extremities going numb. She watches a Shukrian suicidecraft crash into the transparent dome of Skōlex's head. Then, over the shoulder of the explosion, she sees the sudden blazing glory of the Blizzard's arrival.

An instant of twinkling stillness, and Yama's great fleet unloads on the fleets of Dawn.

The light from the salvo is blinding. The emptiness is like fists in her lungs. She squirms, agonized, when a warhead streaks past her and rips a nearby vimana to shreds. A burst of shrapnel sails towards her.

The last thing she feels is its liberating agony.

Her last thought is *this is not fair. This is not fair.*

3.39

The Hands see the Blizzard arrive. A complex of glinting blue heavy gunners, proximity fighters, and droneyantras fanning out behind Skōlex and around and behind the fleets of Dawn. They fire a wall of iron thunderbolts and odd-looking Yaman chakras—spindly, dark blue, and spinning with their own stately gravity. The vimanas race forward in their wake. The whole titanic tide of them crashes over Skōlex through the heart of the Dawn's forces.

Behind it, the Red Fleet rallies and turns back to battle. The Hands cheer and scream.

The vimanas attacking Skōlex break off. With a great growl the juggernaut himself resumes his forward grind. Atmosphere ignites the torn edges of his skin and burns his eyes out of their sockets. Blinded, he crashes into the Iron Crown. The Hands see its spectacular expanses of glass-roofed fields and nameless cities and horrified multitudes fleeing in futile panic.

Skōlex barrels through it all. The superstructure shatters under the impact of his giant belly. A great metal shard penetrates up through his heart and kills him.

Dead now, the beast falls into the pillowing thickness of Pṛthvī's lower skies. Air roars. Armor, flesh, and components break off and burn. To those watching awestruck from below, it's as if some primordial ur-beast from a time before order or words is falling vanquished from the heavens.

In the Throne Room the Hands watch the surface of Pṛthvī come rushing up at them, green and soft and glorious. In the last instant gravity exerts its placid but irresistible grasp. They fall towards the disintegrating ruins of the great glass dome below them. Skōlex's acceleration takes hold, and they float back up with the great black floor of the room a backdrop to their final moments.

With hot air on their faces, they turn to each other. Kadrū clamps her hands on Indra's face and kisses him. He feels her poison on his lips and tongue and soon in his veins. It is precisely as he imagined it would be.

He holds her and kisses back.

Together, they finally claim the one thing they could never have—each other. The thought briefly crosses their minds that it's fitting their story ends with what to anyone else would have been the beginning.

There's no time for much more. A moment later, Skōlex hits the ground.

3.40

I

VISHWADEVI HUDDLES AGAINST HER FATHER. On the horizon, a gargantuan dome of air bloats and shreds the clouds. In the breach of clear sky it opens is the lightstorm of the terminal battle of Day and Night. Rising after this comes an emerald mushroom cloud, its hood spreading into a cathedral inflorescence over the countryside. It looks like a tree—but surely none could ever be so big. Surely, such a thing would collapse under its own weight, and its roots, extending down through the thin crust, would rip a hole in the flanks of the globe.

Now the shockwave reaches them. It's strong enough to knock them off their feet. Still, it's cool and clean, pleasant to be buffeted by. In its aftermath they debate what they just smelled. Flowers? Food? A faint whiff of fresh dung?

Soon after, things begin to fall from the sky. One piece comes arcing majestically overhead and crashes through an empty house at the edge of the village. They rush down to see, expecting a corpse, a great chunk of green rock or a fragment of heavenly chariot. Instead, they find the house drenched in growth, crackling and voracious, devouring wood, stone, and even the metal composite of the view screen. The building buckles and collapses and melts away into nothing.

The greenery spreads like green lava, devouring a nearby tractor and part of the road. One man who stands too near screams. When they pull off his boots, they see a crusting of tiny plants consuming the tips of his toes. Eventually, they wither and die, but the parts of his foot they consume never grow back.

II

DAYS LATER THEY CAUTIOUSLY CLEAN the foliage away from the road. None of them are infected, but the next day some of the children come running back at dawn, screaming. When they go to see what's happened, they see that it's all grown back.

They burn it this time, but it returns. They plan to burn it again, but then the refugees start to arrive.

Some come coughing yellowish pollen, their breath smelling like flowers. Others were hit by fragments of green fallout and lost eyes, hands, skin that sloughed off in long greenish-yellow strips. Still others come growing stems and leaves out of their mouths, their eyes, roots like seeking tentacles flailing through their skin. These ones feel no pain—but slow down and eventually refuse to move and melt away into little hillocks of gorgeous green cancer.

The ones who can speak tell stories. Herds devoured whole, entire villages wiped out, forests crushed under a great wall of irresistible foliage spreading from the crater of Skōlex's impact. Scouts confirm all of it.

They send messages to the Dawn through the view screens but never hear back. Eventually, the screens die, and they realize that their god, too, is dead.

Months later, they wake to find the alien jungle born of Skōlex's sacrifice crowding the horizon. They realize that it will devour the whole world. Humanity's time on Pṛthvī is coming to an end.

But all endings are also beginnings.

IIII

OF COURSE, IT'S THE CHILDREN who first notice the new lights in the night sky. Within minutes everyone's outside—the villagers, the refugees, the coughing invalids. All marveling as the glittering flecks descend, revealing themselves to be vimanas like they've never seen before. Sleek blue machines that settle near the barns and unfold proboscidean gangways from their nose cones. Creatures emerge from this, humanoid but with weird insectoid helmets. What's below is even stranger: human faces, pale as the first glimmers of dawn, their eyes as big as oranges.

The one in the lead seems to be a young woman. She stomps towards them as more pour out of the vimanas behind her, carrying black boxes, stretchers, wheeling giant devices that click, hum, and glitter busily. She halts, squinting, flanked by comrades wielding barreled implements they hold pointing down away from their bodies.

"Who's in charge here?" she says.

A moment's hesitation. Vishwadevi's father hobbles forward.

"I can speak for us. Who're you?"

"We come at the bidding of the Queen of Yama. You're all to be evacuated."

"Evacuated?"

The woman points at the horizon—flat and black and shrouded in night.

"That growth will destroy your village and you. You have to leave."

"Where will we go?"

"There's room on the Iron Crown. And on some of the Nine Worlds."

Mutters in the crowd. The old man turns to them then back to the woman.

"The Nine Worlds? Miss, you're mistaken. There's only one. This one."

The Yamans chuckle. The woman smiles and extends her hand.

"There are worlds beyond counting in Surya's bright bubble, uncle," she says. "They now belong only to us. Come with me. Let me show you."

The old man hesitates. Then he takes her hand.

EPILOGUE

I

It's a close and sultry day. The mist hangs in white tongues in the clefts between the peaks. Beneath a furring of deep green forest. A cacophonous place of strange beasts—four-armed apes with bulging eyes, long-eared tiger-things, and frogs that hop along beside them like valets, eyes nakedly curious. All are watching the same thing—a small convoy of humans working their way up a high valley behind a quick, nimble old woman.

One of the humans, a young woman with red hair, catches sight of the spectators.

"They've come to see you, devi," she says to the old woman.

The old woman guffaws and waves her away. She's fat, hunchbacked, and her dark green suit caked in mud. Though her hands shake, she's spry and walks without sweating. After a few hours' climb in the sweltering cool, the old woman finally stops. Her exhausted followers fall about her like scattered dominoes. Up ahead, the forest clears, and the mountain continues up into a naked valley full of dung-colored rocks. The others now see the rest rising into the preposterous lapis of the sky, smooth and metallic like a great thorn. Not a wrinkle in the earth, clearly, but the jagged, monumental wreckage of some gigantic artefact. "Was it really so big?" says one of them.

The old woman nods.

"Bigger," she says. "I'll go alone from here."

The others start to protest, but she points to the forest, where two giant wolves slink, heads low, from tree to tree.

"As alone as I can be," she says.

They fall silent. The wolves turn to disappear into the dark. Each has a glowing hammer strapped to its back.

II

She ascends the valley at a steady pace past tilted screens of scree. The clouds scrape their bellies against the flanking ridges. The path dies against a sheer cliff, and she sets about climbing this with the deftness of a spider monkey. Little roots spring forth where her hands touch the rock. Stone mushrooms bloom like little balconies at her feet to take her weight and crumble when she's gone.

When she reaches the peak after a couple of hours' steady climb she breathes deep and scans the area. Off to the left is a valley with the ruins of a small town half drowning in foliage. One corner of it looks inhabited, but towering over it is a huge coppery vimana. Even at this distance she can see people being herded aboard.

She sits, takes a small black orb from her pocket, and releases it into the air. It bobs in place as if floating in some invisible pond. She blinks three times, and it expands in fragments, scanning her eyes with a pale blue light.

She starts speaking in a tongue no human has ever spoken before.

"You'll forgive my pronunciation," she says, "but it's taken me a while to learn your language. Entropy may devour memory, but it's a slow, messy eater. There was enough left in your ruins for me to put together a grammar and word list. An enjoyable pastime, but let me say this—if ever I was uncertain that you are not gods, this dispelled the last of my doubt. Your language makes you more comprehensible. Real gods are always incomprehensible."

She licks her gums.

"It took me a long time to clean up the mess you and yours left. After the battle I had to return to Yama. I was lucky, I suppose. I had about a third of the Blizzard left. But more than that, I had the Twins. They just came stomping into my ship one day as if nothing had happened. No explanation where they'd been or what they'd done—though I found out later. Seeing two Triangulan battle-wolves at my beck and call did wonders for my credibility. Strange. All they've ever wanted from me was the occasional game of fetch. They're really quite sweet once you get past the speaking at once and the giant hammers—and the bloodlust."

She chuckles.

"On Yama they helped me fight usurpers who claimed my throne. Then I had to repel four invasions. I went into those wars knowing I couldn't be stopped, but death has a way of sobering even the most conceited. After that, I had to deal with the rest of the system.

"Your weapon worked, by the way. Of course, it worked. Every field, every shrub, and every town on Pṛthvī fell to it. I can't tell you how many people died. Millions, certainly. I suppose, if prabho Indra had objected, you'd have said you agreed to save the planet, not the people. Still ...

"I had to do something. So I began to evacuate Pṛthvī as best I could. We started with a hundred and seven vimanas to serve as transports and colony-ships. We have a hundred and nine thousand, six hundred forty-three now. The Tripura is healed now completely. It has a temple there, dedicated to me.

"On Mangala, they turned the Ox's palace into another one. And on Himenduḥ, they've carved a great image of me into the ice. You can see it from space. It doesn't look anything like me, of course. I was never that pretty. What a bloody waste of time. I blame you for all this. You must have known what was happening to me. You must have known what would happen once you'd left.

"Or maybe I'm thinking of you as gods again. Maybe you had no idea. My sole comfort is that there are children who don't really even believe you were real and who don't believe I'm real." She blinks. "So you see, I can say with some confidence, things have changed since you left."

A gentle growl rolls through the air. The vimana in the town lifts with its squat wings splayed and its fuselage bulbous, a fat bird taking flight. A few moments later, it shoots off so fast it punches a small clear disc through the clouds.

The old woman sighs.

"I'm so bored. I forget which year it is. I forget the last time I was in places. Not because I can't remember, but because I don't want to. Life is like listening to the same five notes in endless sequence. The small things don't interest me anymore, then I remember that the things I think are small—planets, empires, the square root of minus one—they are infinitely complex and wondrous things. Things any human should be baffled and overwhelmed by. Things I, for hundreds of years, was baffled and overwhelmed by.

"So here is my conclusion: I am becoming more like you.

"There's really only one way to be sure. This is why I'm sending this to you. I can see it now—your home, Triangulum. It's just a tiny speck to me, but I shouldn't even be able to see that. Which makes me think that perhaps what I'm planning to do isn't complete madness. I am going to pay you a visit."

The old woman wraps her arms around her knees.

"I know the journey will be a long one, but I have a lot to keep myself busy. Who knows? Perhaps by the time I reach you, I will be more like your kind than I will be like mine. I wonder—is that what you all are? Representatives, each, of long-dead races, each of whom has somehow joined your council of false gods?

"I'll find out soon enough, I suppose. I'll come for answers. I'll come because the Wolves are getting a little erratic. I think they've been here too long. They barely put their suits of man-flesh on these days. They won't speak or show themselves to anyone but me. And—they're moody. Like teenagers. They're growing up, and I don't think humanity can handle the presence of two full-grown Wolves of Triangulum. I'm happy for my last act as Empress of Surya to be taking them home. Because I won't be that when I get to you, will I? Not anymore.

"Wait for me. It won't be very soon. But it will happen someday."

She blows on the orb. It seals shut. A blinding tower of light ignites before her. Down in the valley, the shadows become pitch black and razor sharp. When it fades the orb's gone.

The Empress of Surya begins her climb down.

IIII

SHE RETURNS TO THE CAMP to find they've set up a fire and some tents are preparing food. Skillets with grilling meats and vegetables sliced and tossed in oil. They offer her a stool and a plate with two cuts of grilled meat, aromatic and golden-red, and a cool bottle of beer. She receives it all with a nod and takes a swig. It's cool, frothy, and deliciously bitter.

After a few moments she hears rustling behind her. The others all look, alert. A red ball, fist-sized, dented and scarred, comes flying out of the undergrowth. It rolls up to the Empress's foot.

The others relax and resume their chatter. The Empress downs her beer and stands.

"Very well," she says, picking up the ball. "Let's go."

THE END
Tokyo, Colchester, Tucson, San Diego, New York, West Lafayette
May 2017-June 2023

BIBLIOGRAPHY

Ali, Daud." Bhoja's Mechanical Garden: Translating Wonder across the Indian Ocean, circa 800–1100 CE," History of Religions, vol. 55, no.4 (May 2016), p. 461-493

Dimock, Jr, Edward. C. "The Goddess of Snakes in Medieval Bengali Literature," *History of Religions*, vol. 1, no.2 (Winter, 1962), p. 307-321

Griffith, Ralph T. H. *The Rig-Veda* (Santa Cruz, CA: Evinity Publishing, 2009)

Keith, Arthur Berriedale (trans). *Rigveda Brahmanas: The Aitreya and Kauṣītaki Brahmanas of the Rigveda*. Harvard Oriental Series, Vol. 25 (Cambridge, MA: Harvard Divinity School, 1910).

Kinsley, David R. *Hindu Goddesses: Visions of the Divine Feminine in the Hindu Religious Tradition*. (Delhi: Motilal Banarsidass, 2005)

Kuiper, F. B. J.,"The Basic Concept of Vedic Religion," *History of Religions*, vol.15, no.2 (Nov.1975), p.107-120

Kulikov, Leonid. "An Atharvanic Hymn to Night: Text-Critical and Linguistic Remarks on the Interpretation of Śaunakīya 19.50 = Paippalāda 14.9," *Bulletin of the School of Oriental and African Studies*, University of London, vol. 76, no.2 (2013), p. 259-269

Srinivasan, Doris. "The Religious Significance of Divine Multiple Body Parts in the Atharva Veda," *Numen*, vol.25, fasc. 3 (Dec. 1978), p. 193-225

Werner, Karel." Men, Gods and Power in the Vedic Outlook," The Journal of the Royal Asiatic Society of Great Britain and Ireland, no.2 (1982), p. 14-24

ABOUT THE AUTHOR

Subodhana Wijeyeratne is an academic and writer living in Tokyo, Japan with his pug, Lord Nibbler, and his terrible mix Lady Leela. He's been writing fiction for nearly twenty years and has had nearly twenty short stories appear in print over the past two years in venues including *Aphelion, Bewildering Stories, Expanded Horizons, Piker Press*, and *The Scarlet Leaf Review*. He is also a published author of history and his interest in the history of technology in East Asia. You can find his work at the *Asia-Pacific Journal, Quest, Kiyoshi English Review*, and other venues.